Praise for *The Octagonal Raven*

"*North by Northwest* meets *Logan's Run* in this SF novel, complete with intriguing philosophical passages . . ."
—*Publishers Weekly*

"There is enough of Modesitt's trademark philosophizing to make it worthwhile for his fans. The action fireworks and mystery elements make this a pretty fine SF thriller for everybody else."
—*Netsurfer Digest*

"This new adventure is one of his better efforts."
—*Science Fiction Chronicle*

"The pacing is excellent, and the sociopolitical expatiating on the plot proves integral to the story . . ."
—*Booklist*

"The author of the Recluce series demonstrates his talent for near future technothrillers in this standalone tale of intrigue and adventure. Modesitt's careful examination of his characters' motivations and perceptions creates a sense of immediacy that lends credibility to his story."
—*Library Journal*

TOR BOOKS BY L. E. MODESITT, JR.

THE COREAN CHRONICLES

THE SPELLSONG CYCLE

THE SAGA OF RECLUCE

THE ECOLITAN MATTER

THE GHOST BOOKS

*Forthcoming

THE
OCTAGONAL
RAVEN

L. E. Modesitt, Jr.

A TOM DOHERTY ASSOCIATES BOOK
NEW YORK

THE OCTAGONAL RAVEN

Edited by David G. Hartwell

A Tor Book
Published by Tom Doherty Associates, LLC
175 Fifth Avenue
New York, NY 10010

www.tor.com

Tor® is a registered trademark of Tom Doherty Associates, LLC.

ISBN-13: 978-0-8125-7008-3
ISBN-10: 0-8125-7008-1
Library of Congress Catalog Card Number: 00-048807

First Edition: February 2001
First Mass Market Edition: July 2002

Printed in the United States of America

0 9 8 7 6 5 4 3 2

To Catherine . . .

for her honesty in a culture of hypocrisy

DISCOVERING THE UNKINDNESS

Had the orbital watch alert satellite contained a human being, or even a sophisticated duoclone, that being might have scanned the data and reported something like, *Object classified as cometoid ... spherical-octagonal, diameter forty-three meters, density two point five, composition approximately eighty-two point four percent water ... carbides and carbonates approximately fifteen percent ... iron and sulfides, silicates and oxides below detection levels ... orbital ... trajectory at variance with origin in either Oort Cloud or Kuiper Belt ...*

Instead, the AI merely squirted its data analysis to the Long Watch Asteroid Collision Center satellite inhabiting the L5 point above the water planet below. In turn, the AI calculated orbital mechanics, trajectory, and mass composition and, after ensuring the object did not trigger any action parameters, stored the data for later retrieval.

In time, the comet-like object intersected the thin upper atmosphere on the planet's night side, creating a long and brilliant trail that flashed across the high latitudes and lasted but for a few long seconds before vanishing.

The thousands of particle-sized contaminants also eventually slowed and began to drift through the atmosphere toward the oceans and landmasses below.

The central AI in the Long Watch Asteroid Collision Center satellite received the report of the ice-meteorite's dissolution and added the data to the records of others of that class.

Eventually, a human methodizer reviewed the data, frowned at the octagonal dimensions, checked it again, and then shrugged.

Before stepping out of the foyer of my villa, I glanced at my reflection in the shimmerglass of the antique twenty-first century mirror. The dark blue singlesuit and powder blue formal short jacket still fit, even though they dated from when I'd left the Federal Service years before. I'd decided against wearing the gatekeeper's belt repeater. The last thing I wanted—or needed—was getting calls at a social event. Besides, I'd have to turn it off at the concert anyway. I nodded, and my reflected image did so as well.

I took the side steps from the foyer down to the hangar. My single vehicle rested on the gray permacrete that could easily have held three gliders, but I certainly didn't need that many, not as an unattached edart composer, although there had been times when the hangar had held two. Those times just hadn't lasted all that long. Then, all the equipment I used for maintaining the glider, and making unauthorized modifications, such as removing the ground clearance governors and replacing the limited flitter gyros with the unlimited ones used by orbital shuttles, took more than one bay anyway. Automatically, before stepping inside, I checked the systems of the glider, putting the ring finger of my right hand into the covered slot where the almost imperceptible flexconnection under the edge of the nail mated with the filament slot. I could have done it with remote sensors, but that took longer, and gave me a momentary headache. Besides, I always liked the certainty and backup of a direct link.

After a microsecond where data from the glider meshed with me, I lifted my finger. Everything was normal. Although the glider was technically more than half as old as I was, its internal works were not, and it retained its perfect function and shimmering silvered green finish. The canopy slid back, and I left it back after I opened the door and slid into the seat. I almost could have walked to Kharl's, but the walking would have upped my metabolism, and I'd have arrived sweating.

That thought brought a laugh as the hangar portal irised open. Seven thousand years since the first baths of Mohenjodaro, and we still worried about sweat and scent. I was still smiling as the portal irised shut behind me, and the glider whispered southward along the grass path that led to the upper hill. The scents of fallen leaves and damp grass filled the air of almost-evening.

To my left, out over the valley, the twilight sun was painting the Navaho sandstone bluffs to the east crimson. The contrast between the green of the cedars and the red sand and rock was never more striking than at the end of the day. I'd occasionally scanned twilight scenes, the more striking ones, sometimes with the thunderstorms rising up over the mountains, as backdrops for my edart pieces—where the scene fit.

I had to wonder why Kharl had invited me. His soiree was supposedly just a reception on behalf of the Arts Committee and the Warsha Symphony, and that meant I'd had to commit to attending the concert. I hadn't minded. He'd always been a friend, as well as a cousin, and, in some ways, closer in spirit than my brother Gerrat. Kharl and I both understood that there's nothing quite like a live performance, no matter what the technophiles say about VR and rec-reality. Maybe you have to have been a pilot or someone whose life depended on direct-feed interpreted reality to understand that. Gerrat certainly didn't seem to.

I shrugged. The concert would be good, especially since I hadn't heard a live performance of the symphonies they were doing—a performance of Uphyrd's *Gate of Conquest* paired with an ancient work—*The Planets* by an Anglian composer by the name of Holst. There wasn't a straight audio recording, let alone a VR performance, of the Holst piece anywhere in the net, or even in UniComm's restricted archives. From what Kharl had told me, Dhuma, the conductor of the Warsha, had required his musicians to learn the music from transcriptions taken from the ancient paper score.

After avoiding a teenager on a magscooter, I followed a cinnamon-shimmer glider, one with the canopy polarized, the last quarter klick to Kharl's hilltop villa. The profusion of gliders arrayed on the grass receiving pad to the south of the multilevel villa testified that I was far from the first to arrive.

The couple stepping from the cinnamon glider nodded politely, and I returned the nod and gestured for them to precede me. I didn't know them, and that was surprising. He was tall and angular, with a not-quite jutting jaw, and she was more my sister Elora's height, although the skin of the woman before me was a light olive shade, set off by black hair so dark and lustrous it shimmered blue. The faint scent of gardenias trailed her.

The front double doors to Kharl's villa were wide open, but I could sense faintly the repellent screen when I followed the couple through them.

My cousin Kharl was standing in the vaulted entry hall with a red-headed woman I didn't know, not with his wife Grete. He always seemed to be smiling, surprising to me for a doctor specializing in the more obscure aspects of nanitic medicine, and when I entered the foyer was no exception. He was talking to Rynold Tondrol and Tondrol's consort for the affair, since Rynold never seemed to show up anywhere with the same woman, not that he had to as the sole heir to and the chief operating officer of TD Reclamation. Reclamation was a nasty business, so nasty that the Federal Union allowed the use of monoclones for the dirtiest work. The licensing requirements were stiff, but I, and most people, had trouble with disposable synthetic people. If only the ancients hadn't buried so many toxics and radioactives.

I pulled my mind back to the reception to study the people once more. Ahead of Rynold was a norm couple, walking away and down toward the great room where dozens already mingled. Seglend Krindottir was the advocate general of Noram. I didn't know what her husband did, except that he was a mid-level manager in the Desret conglomerate. She was known for her practicality and legendary fairness, a norm as brilliant as any pre-select, but she had refused pre-selection for her daughters, or so it was said.

Rynold gave a last bow to Kharl, and my cousin turned his attentions to the couple before me. "N'garo . . . Aalua . . . I am so glad you both could come."

N'garo bowed. "Our apologies for being on the late side. There was some sort of rally—"

"A protest meeting," corrected Aalua. "Something about school testing."

"Foolish complaints about perceptual testing. Norms never understand," N'garo continued off-handedly. "People were all over the square, and we had to take the long way to get here."

"I'm glad you weren't delayed that much, and I know Dhuma will be glad to see you at the reception afterwards." Kharl focused on the olive-skinned woman. "Have you decided whether you can discover a lower effectiveness threshold for—"

"Kharl . . . no shop talk tonight." The woman laughed. "N'garo hears enough medical terms at home."

Kharl inclined his head, with a boyish grin. "Your wish . . ."

The two passed on, and I stepped forward.

"Daryn. I'm glad you could come." Kharl nodded to the red-haired woman by his side, who wore a deep but muted green gown. "This is Elysa. Elysa Mujaz-Kitab." He smiled more broadly, as if he were enjoying a joke. "Elysa . . . this is my cousin, Daryn Alwyn. *The* Daryn Alwyn." He added more to me, "Elysa had some doubts. She said that someone was using your name as a cover for a scap."

Someone using my name for a system-created artificial persona? I couldn't help raising my eyebrows.

Elysa's smile was warm. Even her brown eyes sparkled. "That is *not* what I said. I said I wanted to meet you."

Kharl smiled indulgently.

I returned Elysa's smile. "Me? Anything I say goes under the real persona, not an artificial scapegoat, and I'm not that much to meet. As you can see."

"I couldn't believe that an Alwyn . . ." She flushed.

Although the flush was doubtless artifice, if one my nanites couldn't read, the effect was charming. "Would you like an explanation?"

"If you wouldn't mind . . . and if you will forgive me for my boldness."

"You're already forgiven." I raised my eyebrows to Kharl. "I'm not sure about you, cousin." I offered my arm to Elysa.

"You never are. Enjoy yourselves." Kharl laughed and turned to the couple who had just walked into the entry hall. "Marcyla . . . Elfons . . ."

Elysa's fingers, cool and smooth, brushed the back of my wrist as she took my arm, holding it but lightly as we walked down the steps into the great room that overlooked Vallura. The light floral scent she wore was similar to roses, but not exactly the same. I had the feeling that everything about her was like that—almost familiar, but not.

On the inside wall behind the three-meter grand piano was a large painting—a nanite-scanned replica of an ancient Homer, showing a boat on a dark sea. I had no doubts that the scanning of the original probably cost Kharl as much as any of the most expensive works painted in the last three decades. But then, I supposed that was the point, in a way. The frame had probably been re-created in the same fashion.

The spaces along the glass expanses overlooking the valley were taken by couples and knots of people, and we found ourselves near the center of the room, standing beside an inlaid wooden table, one that held a chess board—an antique game nearly meaningless now that anyone who wanted to could instantly call upon the strategies and games of the past millennia.

"You really thought I didn't compose my own work? That I used a scap?"

"That's what I told Kharl," she replied. "He laughed."

"Scaps aren't good at creative work." I glanced toward the server who approached with a tray on which were two goblets of wine. "You didn't think that I might have some creative ability . . . there is a certain commsystem talent that runs in the family. . . ."

"Your sister certainly has it."

"Why do you think that? Because she had the nerve to work her way up to the top with a competitor?"

"She seems to have . . . a different . . . outlook."

"You know her?"

Elysa gave a minute headshake. "A friend of mine follows those things. I'm intrigued with . . . more artistic types."

"You just intimated that you couldn't believe an Alwyn could be creative." I laughed softly as she flushed.

She was rescued by a server, a young man who, after edging through the growing crowd, offered the two goblets of wine remaining on his tray, "Sir? Lady?"

Elysa took one goblet, and I accepted the second with a nod to the server. "Thank you."

"You're welcome." The server's smile was pleasant, professional, and that of someone brain-damped.

Idly, I wondered what the man had done, although he was a norm, since he appeared barely into his twenties.

My eyes passed by his shoulder as I recognized another semi-familiar face, that of Kymal Aastafa. I hadn't seen that much of Kymal since I'd left Blue Oak Academy to go to The College, and he'd departed for the Byjin Collegium. He lived somewhere in the Sinoplex, and I was surprised to see his face, but as we exchanged smiles, someone tapped his shoulder, and he turned.

"You know him?" asked Elysa.

"Kymal? We went to school together years ago."

"He's a noted chaos theoretician, isn't he?"

"More of an applied theoretician, if you believe the journals." I paused. How had she known him? Kymal had lived mainly in the Sinoplex for years, only occasionally returning to Calfya, and Elysa didn't appear to be even my age. I looked into her young-appearing face, although I would find no sign of age or youth, since most pre-selects had young-appearing faces until the decade or so before their deaths. "Mujaz-Kitab? That's an unusual name."

"Let's just say that it reflects the family heritage and history. That's as good a way as any of explaining it, and any other would become hopelessly confusing."

I could sense both the tension and the semi-accuracy of

her response, but I didn't press the issue. If she didn't want to say more, who was I to insist? Especially on a purely social occasion. I took a sip of the wine. It was good, and a vintage and vintner I hadn't tasted, scarcely an unusual occurrence, since Kharl always enjoyed surprising his guests with wines no one else had discovered, or so it seemed. Wines didn't replicate well, even with the best of scanners. My internal system let me know that it was a dolcetta, probably from the Snoma valley, a darkish red with a bouquet I couldn't begin to describe. I like good wines, but I'm far from a connoisseur in any way, even with nanites to help. "Good wine."

"Everything Kharl serves is the best. What would be the point otherwise?" Elysa replied.

We both laughed.

"Where did you meet him?" I asked.

"He's family, of sorts. I'm a distant cousin of Grete's . . . from Cedacy, at least recently."

"Not quite so . . . social?"

"Exactly." She raised her eyebrows.

"And from where before that?"

"One of the colonies you've never heard of. I lived in Hejaz for a time."

"I see. Not exactly well known." I'd never heard of the colony, and I should have, but she seemed to be totally truthful on that.

"No." She flushed slightly again. "It's not."

In the swirl of people, I saw another norm coming down the steps—Eldyn Nyhal—with his wife. The contrast was amazing. Eldyn wore a dark Prussian blue vest over a brilliant blue singlesuit, and with a shimmering silver-like medallion—roughly oval—that seemed to shoot lightbeams. She was tiny, probably not even a hundred and fifty centimeters, and dressed in dark gray. Nyhal had been a medical researcher—the one who had tamed the pre-select plague. That had been when I was in the Service so I hadn't been around—most fortunately. After that, he had gone into business for himself, and made a considerable fortune in developing some form of nanite processing based on the results of neglected and obscure research that he held closely. The bottom line was that he'd made nanite food processors both more effective, allowed greater directed variation in replication, and reduced their energy costs by close to twenty percent. In short, he had transformed himself from a doubtless undercompensated scientist into a very well paid food appliance magnate of sorts. His apparel was conventional enough in cut—just not in color—and several couples seemed to edge away from him.

"Do you do anything else?" asked Elysa. "Besides study people?" She hadn't even seemed to notice Eldyn.

I bowed for not paying her the attention she clearly deserved. "Besides writing sardonic commentaries for those dissatisfied with our ultraperfect way of life, you mean?"

Elysa blushed once more, again charmingly.

"I'm a methodizer, currently under contract, for now anyway, to OneCys and to some smaller clients. That pays for my modest dwelling." I smiled pleasantly as Kharl and Grete stepped down into the great room and slipped toward us—through the people who seemed to part without even being aware of their movement.

"Not that modest," suggested Kharl with a laugh. "He lives on the lower Hill. On the top."

"You live on the upper Hill," I riposted. "On the very top."

"Why not? It's only family creds." He grinned. "I save my own earnings for supporting the arts."

"Kharl likes to distance himself from the family," offered Grete.

"I couldn't say much to that," I pointed out.

"That's why you're always welcome," he replied. "We need to stick together, we family outlaws."

"I'm the one who needs us to stick together," I suggested. "You're doing quite well on your own. Your own research and medcenter, scholarly articles, research breakthroughs . . ." I shrugged. "I'm just a barely known edart composer, and a contract methodizer to ensure I don't have to ask Father for support."

"You'd die first before you asked for family support," suggested Grete with a gentle laugh. "So would Kharl."

"They both sound stubborn," offered Elysa, inclining her head to Grete, as if inquiring.

"Are Gates distant? Are nanites small?" Grete arched her eyebrows.

Rather than comment on any of those, I looked at the wineglass, then took another sip.

Kharl smiled as I drank. "Good, isn't it?"

"Anything you have in your cellar is good."

"Not always . . . but it's unique. That I can promise." He smiled once more. "We'll have to leave for the concert before too long."

"A half hour?"

He nodded. "I'm glad you both could come." With a last smile, he bowed, and then he and Grete slipped toward a group of five to our right, one that included Majora Hyriss, a truly nice woman I sometimes wished I'd pursued when I'd had the chance.

"What do you do?" I asked the redhead, whose straight mahogany hair was swept back with a pair of jade and silver combs.

"Me? I'm an medical researcher who's lately become an adaptor in the field. Very junior . . . very poor." Elysa smiled wryly. "I don't move in these circles normally, but . . . Kharl and Grete are very understanding." She stepped back, then glanced toward the doors to the outer terrace, empty, unlike the great room.

"Do you work for a medcenter?"

"A series of contract assignments for professionals and for research centers. This one is for . . . well . . . I can't say, but you would know the name if I could."

I was intrigued and puzzled by the redhead. First, there were very few redheads left in our world, because the gene-links weren't optimal. Second, while my readings of her indicated that her statements were generally true, the underlying anxiety level was higher than it should have been. Social concerns? Or something else?

As I took another sip of the dolcetta, Elysa eased another step or two toward the French doors and touched her forehead with the back of her left hand.

"Are you warm?" The press of people had warmed up the great room, not uncomfortably, but noticeably, and I was getting warm myself, notwithstanding my nanitic infrastructure's efforts to balance matters.

"If you wouldn't mind . . . could we . . . go outside for a moment?" she asked.

"Fine." We stepped around a group of five, discussing something about why Holst had to be less accomplished than Uphyrd, and through the double French doors—phase-polarized armaglass set in real, if enhanced lignin oak—out onto the terrace. When I closed the door behind Elysa, the terrace was dark, not a photon of light escaping the phased armaglass, not that it mattered.

The light breeze was welcome, though it held a hint of molding leaves.

Below the terrace, the hillside sloped gently down to the stone wall that guarded the steeper bluff. Vallura lay below, and the lines of the dwellings and the paths and few hard-surfaced roads appeared clearly in my sight, even though the only lights visible in the valley were those from the south side of the city and from the scattered neighborhoods of supplemented housing.

"It's beautiful here," Elysa murmured from close beside me.

"It is. It's also quieter. Does the noise bother you?"

"Sometimes . . ."

We walked to the edge of the terrace, out from beneath the balcony, and for several minutes, just stood in the fall breeze that was stronger away from the house.

"I suppose we should head back inside, or we'll be late to the concert," I finally said.

"You're probably right. But it does smell so good."

For a moment, the fragrances of summer wafted around me, dispelling the previous scents of autumn—even though the chill of a fall night held Vallura. I took a deep breath, almost involuntarily.

Nearly instantly, I could feel my system going into shock, a feeling compounded by the warning jolt of the nanites . . . the massive histamine jolts delivered by the nanospray concealed momentarily by fragrance weren't exactly subtle. . . .

I turned toward Elysa . . . except she wasn't there, or rather, her figure wavered, and she seemed to be stepping away from me.

The dozen or so steps I took toward the terrace were the longest and slowest I'd ever taken, but I did manage to turn the door handle and take a step into the great room before my knees buckled and star-flashing darkness rolled up around me.

Chapter 3
Fledgling: Yunvil, 414 N.E.

It was sixth period, and I was thinking about Ertis. I'd asked her to go to Henya because I knew she wanted to see an exhibition at one of the galleries, and I'd even made a reservation for dinner at the best uniquery there. The only problem was that I hadn't checked my free cred balance. Father insisted that we pay the distance tolls if we took the gliders anywhere, and I wasn't sure I had enough to cover everything, and I wouldn't get my stipend for my systems programming work at UniComm until the end of the next week. The tolls were automatic, and I'd probably lose all use of the glider for the next month if I couldn't pay Father immediately—and that meant I couldn't take Ertis anywhere because we weren't that close to the induction tube.

"Since marks appear to be the principal, if not the sole motivating force in determining your scholarly applications . . ."

I tried not to sigh. I'd heard old Rosenn give the same lecture the term before, and when Tomaz had sighed, he'd gotten a real lecture on the arrogance of sighing.

Still . . . Master Mertyn Rosenn paused. He was one of the strictest instructors at the Academy, and he looked even stricter when that long narrow face frowned, and he was frowning at me. "Mister Alwyn, I dislike supercilious expressions of boredom almost as much as I detest sighs."

There were muffled snorts and snickers from behind me.

Old Rosenn turned and gestured at Brytt. "And I dislike expressions of mirth at the expense of others even more, Mister Ehler. So much so that any further expressions of either mirth or boredom will lower the grade I assign for classroom participation. One full grade this marking period. Is that clear?"

That left the room silent. You could sometimes challenge a mark on a test with a master, but classroom participation could be weighed up to thirty percent, and it wasn't challenged—not at Blue Oak Academy, anyway, and a failure in class participation meant a conference between the master, the student, and the parent. The last thing I wanted was my father getting together with Master Rosenn.

So I sat and waited for old Rosenn to hand me the test. He also didn't put his tests on the system. No one saw them until he handed them out—on paper. Very old-fashioned. I didn't see why he just couldn't implement decent system security.

"As I was saying . . . since none of you seems to have an innate desire to learn, marks will have to substitute for that desire. I do not wish a mere regurgitation of facts. I do not wish high-sounding generalities without support. . . ."

I listened, even though I'd heard what he'd said too many times before. He was one of the few who insisted on a hand-composed essay test. The consoles in his classroom were strictly processing units, without a dictionary, thesaurus, or any memory. You couldn't upload or download. If you didn't know it, you were dead.

As soon as he handed me the single sheet, I could see it would be tough. Just two questions, and that meant trouble. I read the first question.

Discuss the following quotation with reference to the Noram collapse and the Diversist movement. Provide specific incidences and dates to support your contentions.

"Life is never perfect. Even a good society is not perfect, and perfection is the enemy of all that is good. Those who seek perfection will destroy an imperfect good."

Perfection again. So he was a history instructor. I couldn't see why he was so concerned about perfection and collapses. No civilization lasted forever. Greece collapsed. Rome collapsed. So did the Russian Communalists. And so did the Noram Commonacracy. People made mistakes, and everything fell down. That was history, but he acted as though it were something special.

I looked at the second question. It wasn't any better.

It has been asserted throughout history that improvements in science and technology have been responsible for creating societies with increasing levels of personal freedom. Attempt to prove that this is not an accurate statement of the case.

Attempt to prove?

Great! An hour of writing answers to trick questions, and I still didn't know what I was going to do about Ertis.

Chapter 4
Raven: Vallura, 458 N.E.

I woke in an unfamiliar bed. My eyes were gummy, my vision still blurry, and my fingers were the size of tennis balls, and whatever they rested on was gritty. In addition to all that, the sense of place was wrong—and there was no response from my internal nanitic monitors. None. "Mmmm . . ." When I tried to talk, I discovered that there were tubes down my throat, tubes that smelled of chemicals and acridity.

"Don't try to talk, Daryn. You'll be fine." Someone blotted my face and eyes, and I could see that the someone was Grete, but her voice reverberated in my ears so much that I hadn't recognized it. "I'll get Kharl."

Within moments, Kharl was standing there. Or maybe I had dozed off, and it had been longer. I couldn't tell. My nanites and internal systems were still not working—or not reporting to me.

For one of the few times I could remember, he wasn't smiling. He spoiled the serious effect immediately. "You missed a very good concert, and you caused me to miss it."

I swallowed, wondering if I could talk, but the tubes were gone. So I had to have slept or rested longer than I had realized.

"I guess I'll do anything for family ties," I finally mumbled. The words didn't come out quite right, but he nodded.

"You've been under my care for nearly two weeks," Kharl went on. "The first days were pretty bad, but none of the damage was permanent."

I hoped he was right. All an edartist has is his mind—and his perceptions. For that matter, that was all I had as a methodizer, either.

"The diagnostics confirm that. We had to keep you in an artificial coma to control the tendency of your brain to swell." He shook his head. "Never seen an anaphylactic reaction like that before. Not personally. Not one that augnites couldn't handle."

"I suddenly . . . developed an allergenic reaction to something new?" Halfway through the words, I found myself coughing. My lungs burned.

Kharl waited until I stopped before replying. "It does happen, even now. Cases are more rare, but usually more severe."

Although I didn't believe a word, I merely nodded. After a moment, I added, "Those of us who stray too far from the family develop ultra-severe allergies to life. Is that it?"

"Allergies do happen, and they're more likely in modern life." A faint smile crossed his lips. "You know that. Besides, your father certainly wouldn't want anything to happen to you."

Even in my exhausted condition, I did know that. Father would want me to survive to see the error of my ways, even if it took years. "What happened to Elysa?"

Kharl's face blanked.

"Don't tell me . . . she wasn't Grete's cousin."

"She told you that? She told me that she was a cousin of Rhedya."

"I know . . . all Rhedya's family—Gerrat suggested . . . politely . . . I should know his wife's relations. . . . bet there's no Elysa."

Kharl nodded. "I know. There's no Elysa Mujaz-Kitab in the system. She's not even in the family's system. And no variations . . . even distant ones. I had Gerrat check."

"Great . . ."

"In fact . . . no one like her exists," Kharl said.

"She wasn't . . . VR projection. You're not saying . . . she's a duoclone?"

He smiled slowly. "You're still interested after what she did to you?"

"Have to admit it wasn't boring." I tried to laugh and ended up coughing. The coughs hurt, more than a bad Gate translation, a lot more. "Do I . . . have . . . any lungs . . . left?"

"They're fine, or they will be, if a little sore and stressed."

"What about Elysa, if that's even her name?"

"She didn't behave like a full-imprint clone, either mono or duo, and I would have known if she were. I'd bet she's genetically human. She's just not in the system. She's probably someone who wanted to get to meet you."

"So . . . you're betting she's a multiclone, raised from exo-birth to adulthood?"

"Hardly that. While she could have been gene-switched, and backaltered, the simpler explanation is just that she's from off-planet where the databases aren't as complete."

I frowned. The resources required for either genetic option were not inconsiderable. Nor the time in a full-sized exo-womb, if she'd opted for backaltering. I couldn't have afforded it, even if I'd dipped into my inherited holdings. And interstellar travel, by individuals not on Federal Service contract, was almost as expensive. But she had said she was from a colony planet, and she could have been traveling under the Federal Service.

"You aren't that unpopular, Daryn."

"I suppose you're right. My royalties aren't high enough for that." I kept my voice low, not whispering, just low.

"You don't know what this sort of thing can do. Remember that. It could be some sort of off-shoot from the treatment of the pre-select plague. You weren't here, but you had to have gotten the treatment when you returned. Some people ended up with allergies similar to this. There were some odd side effects."

"So I get blindsided years later?"

"It happens. At least we're all alive. Not that the Dynae and some of that ilk seem to approve in the techniques that made it possible."

I gave the smallest of headshakes. Even in my more strident edart commentaries, I hadn't even bothered with the semisecret society and its members' strident opposition to pre-selection and nanitic augmentation. They belonged to the long and honorable human tradition that had spawned the Luddites, the flat-earthers, various bible-thumping faithies, the scientographers, and the back-earthies, not to mention all the other forms of the true believers that had parasitized human society over the millennia.

"How anyone . . ." I murmured.

"The human mind remains a fractal," Kharl observed. "Even down to the leptonic level, and to the levels of the sub-leptonic strings below."

"The mind is not the brain," I reminded him. "And . . . that's a good image. Irrelevant . . . but good."

"That's my point. Nothing's relevant. What happened to you shouldn't have."

"Do you have any idea what triggered this . . . attack . . . seizure?"

"In general terms . . ."

I waited.

"You reacted to something, perhaps someone's altered floral fragrance . . . or something . . . who knows? Your system created a galvanic allergic reaction—the equivalent of thousands of bee stings or insect bites."

"What . . . ?"

"I don't know. Whatever it was created such havoc that all that's left are assorted nanites and nanite fragments and carbon compounds. We've got nanites everywhere these days. It could be anything. Once you're more stable, we'll set up a nanitic system that will protect you from anything like this happening again."

Even without my internal nanites, I could tell Kharl wasn't telling the whole truth, again, but I let it pass, especially since I was in no shape to contest him, and there was no sense in starting an argument, one way or another. And he was probably right, if only medically speaking, and in terms of direct causes. I was already thinking beyond that. Kharl was trying too hard to convince me it was an allergic reaction. While it *could* have been, it also could be the beginning of something else.

I'd smelled something—like an unfamiliar flower—and then I'd gone into massive shock. The problem was—if Kharl were wrong about the medical side and it hadn't been an allergy—I hadn't the faintest idea why anyone would want to give me such a reaction.

Even the possibility of something like that made me more than a trace nervous. I wasn't sure I wanted someone that sophisticated out to neutralize or eliminate me, especially since I didn't even know why.

"How long will I be here in your private ward?"

"You should be able to go home tomorrow. You probably could today, but I want to give you some more protection. There's no sense in taking chances. I've boosted your augmentation, and tomorrow, we'll be adding some special nanites."

"I appreciate the care." I paused, then nodded. After a moment, I let my eyes close—almost.

After a time, he left, and I did sleep, if uneasily.

Supposedly, there was a cold August fog across the Bay. You sure couldn't have felt it on the hilltop tennis court a hundred klicks to the north. My relatively new internal nanite sensors told me that the temperature around my knees was over thirty degrees, and the sweat oozed down the back of my neck.

The court was old-style clay, except it was harder than those used by the ancients old Rosenn exalted and condemned. I waited while Gerrat went through his serve routine. He always showed off when he tossed up the ball. His serve was fast, maybe two hundred and fifty klicks per hour. He'd even told Ertis how fast it was, giving her his dung-eating smile the whole time.

My racquet was moving before the ball even crossed the net.

"Got that one!" I called as my return angled toward the tape on his backhand side, nearly as swiftly as the serve.

Gerrat stopped dead, then reversed three steps. He even got set enough for a solid stroke.

I saw it coming, but couldn't quite reach it. It should have been out, but there was no flash from the line sensors. Somehow, he managed to nick the tape—a lucky shot if I'd ever seen one.

I nodded and walked to a point behind the baseline on the left side of the court and waited for Gerrat's next serve. It was another laser, but I got my racquet on the ball. Sweet drop shot, too, right on his backhand.

He'd been charging the net. He was there before the ball dropped, and his return sliced along the tape on my backhand side again. I went after it, but skidded on the sand enough that I didn't get there fast enough. He'd have been dead if I'd hit a lob, but he'd guessed lucky again.

Most of the match went like that. If I hit a good shot, his return was better. Sometimes, it was skill, but he was lucky more than a few times, and I wasn't sure that all the line sensors were working, either.

Then . . . our matches usually were like that. At times, I wondered why I bothered, except that there was no point in playing someone who wouldn't challenge me, and in all of Syerra Calfya the only one who could was my own older brother. He was pretty good, but not nearly as good as he thought.

Then, while I didn't like being beaten, I didn't like to concede, and Gerrat would have to prove he could beat me— each and every time. And, once in a while, he couldn't, even with all his luck, and when he wasn't lucky . . . he usually lost.

At the end, I smiled. "You played well."

"I had to." He returned my smile with one that flashed both warmth and understanding. "I'm not sure you've ever played better."

"Not often, anyway." I slid the racquet into its case, then blotted my forehead. "But as I get better, so do you. And you are lucky, you know."

"That's life." He grinned. "I'll take the luck any day."

We walked off the court and down the magnolia-shaded walk of the Contra Tennis Club. Father never believed in private luxuries like tennis courts. The only exceptions were our house and the pool behind it, and Father justified both on the grounds that so many family members enjoyed them that neither was really a totally private luxury.

As we continued down the path to the glider-park, I had to blot my forehead again. Gerrat didn't. For all his words, he hadn't worked as hard, and he didn't sweat as much. Maybe people who are blond don't, or maybe his pre-select profile included less active sweat glands.

We were almost at the end of the walkway, where the ramp turned into steps leading onto the flat thick grass of the glide-park, when someone on the other side of the hedge spoke—in a low voice, not meant for us.

"There go the modern gods." The words were whispered, and tinged with bitterness.

I let my head turn, and my eyes swept over the two youths. Then I realized that they were norms who had been watching the match. They were probably within a year or two of my age, although they could have been even older, even if neither stood much higher than my shoulder, let alone to Gerrat's. Gerrat stood nearly two meters; I was a good three centimeters shorter, and fractionally stockier.

I let my head keep moving, not to embarrass them, and followed Gerrat down the low steps.

". . . the best genetics and nanites creds can buy . . ."

"They're people."

"No . . . they're not. They can bend iron bars bare-handed. Could you have raised your racket before one of their serves went by you?"

The murmur that was almost silence was answer enough.

I couldn't conceal a frown. Better genetics didn't mean that much. Not in a world where brawn had limited usefulness. Besides, the Federal Union genetic selection program operated by Genetic Services was open to anyone who wanted to pay for it. I knew that from all the times Father had drummed into us—too often, for me—how deferred payments were available even for the poorest couples.

"You guide," Gerrat said, settling into the passenger side of the glider and leaning back under the canopy.

"This time. Next time it'll be you." I grinned.

"Maybe." He just spread his hands before adding, "You're the one who's always fiddling with it."

"That's because I don't like not knowing how things work." I checked the systems before easing the glider around.

The loser always controlled the glider on the way back to the dwelling, not that the trip was that long, only about two klicks. I would have just as soon used a magscooter, but Father wouldn't have them in his household. So we'd walked to the tennis club until Gerrat was old enough to use a glider, even if he didn't understand how it worked, and later, until he could set it up so I would drive him.

My lungs still burned if I took too deep a breath, and I kept smelling, intermittently, an acridity that made everything taste a shade bitter, but I was back in my own dwelling, back in my own study, looking out over the valley, past the empty bird feeder that I needed to refill, and toward the red Navaho sandstone ramparts of the East Mountains—and too far behind in my contract work for OneCys. I sat down behind the flat surface that served as desk, console, snack table, and whatever, and called up the comm plan I'd been working on. I still had a week, and I could *probably* make the deadline.

OneCys had decided to invest the resources in a comp analysis of all the profit centers of UniComm—from the porndraggies to high opera VRs, from double-bluff chat salons to Gate-dropping interstellar space combat simmies— not that the Federal Union had ever had any space combat or had run across anything but the comparative handful of artifacts found beyond Pavo 31.

I smiled, briefly, recalling my own first encounter with a forerunner Gate. We still weren't sure if it had been a Gate, no matter what I or any scientist claimed, but the similarities were there, and the location argued for it being a Gate—and there had been some odd occurrences.

Reminiscing wasn't going to pay the tariffs, and I began to go over the work I'd already done on the comp analysis, beginning with the VR high music dramas. I liked them, but I had to wonder about their appeal. Still, UniComm was scooping in creds, especially on some of the revivals, camp stuff like *Socrates in Corinth*. The orchestration was lush. I could tell that the UniComm contractor, probably Vebyr, had used a real orchestra—maybe even the Warsha. Competing with that would be expensive for OneCys, but not competing would cost even more, especially if UniComm managed to reclaim market share it had been losing before revitalizing the VR high music stuff. Of course, the ancient philosopher hadn't ever gone to Corinth, not so far as I knew, anyway, but that didn't seem to matter in getting netshare, especially in entertainment.

My providing analysis to OneCys—the netsystem trying to take back market share from UniComm, the family firm run by Father and Gerrat—was more than a little ironic, but while Father occasionally gave hints of appreciating my abilities, Gerrat never had, and Gerrat was the one half-running the operation and being groomed to succeed Father.

When I finished running through the analyses and comp recs I'd already completed, I put through the screen to Myrto. I just toggled the two-way holo, rather than using the headset for a complete VR interaction.

Immediately, an image appeared in the middle of the study, that of a man of average height for the pre-selected, not quite two meters tall, with short black hair, deep blue eyes, and a winning smile. "As you can see, I'm really not here, but I'd like to hear your message, and I'll get back to you when I can."

Myrto was honest with his sims. He didn't program them to lead you on or pretend that they were him with various routines. According to Gerrat, some of the UniComm execs had sims so elaborate that outsiders couldn't tell for certain whether they were dealing with a hurried and harried real person or an elaborate VR. Gerrat did, too, but he'd been careful to instruct his gatekeeper not to use it with me.

"Myrto . . . Daryn here. I'd like a few minutes. When you can."

I leaned back in the chair, gingerly, looking blankly toward the red stone bluffs across the valley to the east.

Elysa—the face that probably didn't even exist any more—drifted into my vision, and the way that she'd blushed, so charmingly . . . and effectively. I snorted. Had there been the equivalent of a nanite aphrodisiac in that spray that had triggered every histaminic reaction in my system? Kharl's explanation notwithstanding, I still thought it was that fragrance, and the odds were that it had been deliberate, and that the fragrance had held more than mere altered scent. Did my wondering about Elysa mean that I was a sucker for a woman—or construct—who had nearly killed me?

I didn't think so. Elysa was a risk, and I was definitely risk-averse. That might be why I was still unattached. Besides, I was in no shape to go looking for her. A quick read of my nanite monitors confirmed that.

That thought didn't help. I still found myself slipping on the headset. Scanners had implants. So did at least half the methodizers I knew, and so did Gerrat, but I'd avoided another set—having a pilot's set was enough, and those weren't keyed to any of the popnets. I could have had them re-keyed, but I'd never done that, probably on some unacknowledged principle, or just to be contrary.

I *hated* dropping into the net. Most former pilots did. After the clean systems of a ship, after the ice whispers of space, the mists of faint hydrogen, the best human nets were filled with noise and scum. When I could, I just used a holo projection, but the net was where I had to start. First, I wasn't in shape enough to travel physically, and second, the net was the easiest way to eliminate possibilities quickly. The screen was too slow for that kind of a search.

For a moment, I felt myself standing in a green-shaded darkness. It could have been red, or a marble entry hall. I'd chosen darkness as my standard entry to minimize the sensory shock, since everything's slightly *off*. Even with a full palette, and millions of shades, the colors are too harsh, and they scream past you. And the sounds. . . . There are clicks, and hisses, and low freqs that climb up your virtual back like dull knives scraping stone. Some netfans have scent in their systems. I'd avoided that. The last thing I wanted was off-scent roses, and lilacs with the hint of oil and metal.

Gerrat once told me that it was all in my mind. He was right. I couldn't trick my mind into believing electronically re-created reality was the same thing as physically experienced and perceived reality. So . . . don't tell me that netting and VR beat full-body reality. Unless you're a dep or down—or a latent masochist—they don't.

Finally, I took two virtual steps forward, through the curtain of darkness and into a long hallway, plain metal gray, with roughly a dozen doors on each side of the corridor. Again, I could have had one virtual door, with the name changing each time I blinked. But I didn't.

For a moment, I stood there, thinking. Despite what Kharl had said, anyone who had the capability to create an Elysa, and instant anaphylactic shock, had to have left a trace somewhere. And a good methodizer ought to be able to find it. The place to start, obviously, since I had the keys, was with the UniComm net.

I walked down the VR hall to the third door. Having it third was my own affectation, as was having it of brass, trimmed with silver. I'd always imagined Father would have had his door of gold, trimmed with silver, and perhaps an understated eight-paneled mahogany or cherry door. No matter. My door into UniComm was brass, trimmed with silver.

After mentally extending the first key, the one any subscriber has, I watched the door vanish, leaving me standing in a yet another VR hallway, this one like the holos of Karnak. The sunlight poured down around me and the pillars. Yet the sunlight had no warmth. Nothing on the net does— all light and no warmth.

I couldn't help frowning, since I'd coded in images of a dusty room filled with wooden filing cabinets, not a re-created ancient temple. The frown dropped as a silver cloud appeared, then disappeared, leaving the smiling figure of the director general and chairman of UniComm. Father looked almost as imposing as a VR figure as he did in person.

"Slumming, Daryn?"

"I thought I'd check out the family treasures, sir."

A flat smile crossed his face. "She's not here. Neither is whoever created her." He extended a symbolic file, brass-bound.

I had to grin at the brass edging of the file, but waited for him to continue.

"Right after I heard about your allergy attack, I had my own team do a search. I don't believe in coincidence, especially when your companion is unknown."

"You talked to Kharl?"

"Of course. He claims he doesn't know her, and I think he's telling the truth there." Father paused. "There's not much on the net. That file has what's there . . . and the keys you don't have in case you think we missed something."

"Thank you, sir." I always disliked Father's superiority . . . but then, unfortunately, in many areas he was unquestionably superior.

"I wish you well. Gerrat or I will let you know if we discover anything you might find of interest."

I nodded. I wasn't so sure I'd hear from Gerrat.

Then the restored VR temple of Karnak was vacant, and the sunlight without warmth fell on my shoulders again. Almost immediately, the temple vanished, and I stood in a room with dusty antique wooden filing cabinets.

Not that I didn't trust Father, but the first search was for Elysa Mujaz-Kitab. There wasn't one person on Earth or in Federal Service with that name—or on the out-of-date data from a half-dozen outsystems. I tried Elysa, but there were over two thousand people with that name as part of their registered identity. I couldn't sweep for redheads. That was privacy-protected. And a sweep of medical adjustors netted exactly ten Elysas, from what I could tell, none of them anywhere close to the woman I'd met.

So . . . I went to a sweep of the multis who acknowledged biological expertise, and who had more than nanite template capability . . . then ran that against a resource capability macro and a personnel macro and then against a product output macro.

While those were running, I set up another series of screens, a junk screen that took in wealthy individuals, private foundations and action groups, and netmedia figures, running those against the same resource and talent macros. That took longer, a great deal longer.

Once I had that personalized search-and-winnow engine running, I began to set up the parameters that would describe exactly what kind of technical ability was necessary to create advanced nanites of the type that had presumably been targeted at me.

I hadn't quite finished putting together that search when the bright green flash from the half-open wooden door—and the gentle bell—informed me that someone wanted to appear.

I checked the gatekeeper, and slipped out of the net and let my vision readjust to the real light of my study, watching as Myrto's image appeared. He looked less perfect in realtime than his sim, with the black hair longer, slightly on end. "You wanted to talk?"

"I don't know if you heard," I said quietly, stifling the urge to cough—I knew coughing would hurt—"but I got iced with some sort of stiff allergenic reaction. Put me out for nearly two weeks. I'd gotten a lot done before it happened, and it looks like I'll still be on schedule." I shrugged apologetically and scanned the OneCys head compositor's face closely, watching for any reactions.

"Heard something along those lines. Your brother. I wasn't certain if he let me know for fairness or to gloat."

"Both, probably." I laughed, *very* gently. "We're not immune to sibling rivalry."

"How is it—the plan?" Myrto asked cautiously, feeling me out as to whether I'd done anything at all.

"It looks good, especially the high-culture offerings. How are things going with everything else?"

"Smooth . . . we've really got something here, and the rest of the team's humming. . . . The option possibilities are almost done."

Meaning that I was behind a bit, and that they'd be waiting. Also meaning that nothing else was off schedule. I'd figured that, but needed to know.

Myrto smiled. "You can have another couple of days if you need them."

"I don't think I will. If I do, I'll let you know."

"Do that." With a practiced and warm smile, he, or his realtime sim, vanished, and I was once again looking eastward, over the valley, at the clouds that would probably climb into thunderstorms later in the afternoon.

I slipped back down into the net and checked the results of the first reduction. Among the multis were five possible candidates, just five, although my target could as likely be an individual as a multi team. More likely, in all probability, because teams left more traces.

Then I went back to structuring the third search. One of my side searches showed that there was no name Mujaz-Kitab, or any translated or transliterated variations, but that Mujaz and Kitab were both transliterated versions of ancient Arabic and both were key words in the titles of tomes by an ancient Arab physician, a man whose names took up two entire lines. All that elaboration of a subterfuge bothered me, but I didn't know why.

The sun had vanished behind the growing October clouds by the time I stepped out of the last VR hallway, and slowly stood and stretched in my study. Father had been correct. There was certainly nothing definite in the UniComm net, nor in those parts of the pubNet, or the OneCys net to which I had access.

And all I had was a listing of two thousand women whose first or second names were Elysa and those who *might* have the capability to create an Elysa or the massive histamine-producing nanospray used on me. And those institutions or multilaterals with the possible resources to fund and support such an effort. There were eight multis and three foundations, and three private individuals, one of whom was, not surprisingly, Father. There were nine scientific/medical types with the theoretical background to tackle what I'd specified. There well might be more, given the pre-select tendency to avoid reporting all but the absolutely required.

I closed my eyes, thinking.

Father was worried. He wouldn't have had all the keys waiting. He also had as much as told me that whoever was after me wasn't, at least to his knowledge, within UniComm, or even known to UniComm. And if he and his staff didn't know . . .

Then . . . there was Myrto. His reactions had been predictable, and while it was far from sure, I'd gotten the impression that nothing had happened to anyone else on his team. He needed a good methodizer, but I wasn't irreplaceable. Myrto could find another methodizer, nearly as good, perhaps better.

So . . . it seemed unlikely that my work with OneCys was the cause of Elysa's appearance . . . not totally definitive, but a good indication. Still . . . I couldn't believe that someone had gone to all that effort to stop my edart compositions. There were other composers who were more radical than I, and far more popular.

I hoped that I hadn't overlooked something, and worried that my mental faculties weren't as sharp as I thought they were.

As I massaged the back of my neck with my left hand, I tried to ignore the burning in my lungs, and to forget that a strikingly beautiful woman had tried to kill me for a reason I couldn't even guess at.

Chapter 7

. . . The perceptual integrative ability test [PIAT] was first developed by Fitzgerald Rachlin [JMSEU, V.1, 242 N.E.] and later refined by Dyris and Janes [JMSEU, V.3, 287 N.E.]. The PIAT consists of a series of pseudo-experiences and an artificial dataset and is administered in a controlled state of sensory deprivation through both a degenerating nanospray and a VR tap.

The test measures the subject's ability to integrate diverse perceptual inputs, along a belief axis encompassing artificial norms ranging from verifiable historical environments to artificial cultural constructs . . . care is necessary because in a suggestible state, belief axes can not only be assessed, but inadvertently modified . . .

Dyris's objections to the potentially confrontational nature of the original constructs led to the revisions and

refinements of the later versions of the PIAT, embodied
in the changes adopted by TanUy, which have been designed to ensure that the constructs embody no overtly
aggressive challenges to the underlying belief system of
the subject. Use of the refined system requires baseline
reality assessment and psychochemical discernment
testing.

. . . principal advantage of the revised PIAT is its improved accuracy in determining "raw" perceptual integrative ability . . . the test has limited applicability,
however, because its accuracy is directly based on the
precision of the baseline testing, and such testing is an
exhaustive and lengthy process, even in the best of medical facilities . . .

> *Diagnostic Aids*
> WideComm, Vancov
> 411 N.E.

Chapter 8
Raven: Vallura, 458 N.E.

After three days of work, I'd finally finished the review and
comp analysis for Myrto and sent it off. I needed to get to
Klevyl's engineering assignment, since the specs had arrived
while I was in the middle of finishing the analysis for Myrto,
but I was taking a brief break because I couldn't face another
grind-it-out methodizer project immediately. I wasn't sure
how I ended up with such a range of assignments, except
that I'd made a practice of taking anything I thought I could
do.

I was staring out the window, sipping verdyn, enjoying
green cinnamint tang, forcing myself to take a dose of
InstaNews—the OneCys immediate reporting net. The holo

image before me was that of a fuzzy off-white toroidal octagon set in against vaguely familiar stars.

... the high commissioner for Interstellar Transport announced early this morning in Geneva that a second forerunner Gate has been discovered ... near Gamma Recluci ... apparently identical to the first discovered more than twenty years ago. ...

I nodded. That was bound to happen. The image shifted to a reddish building set before verdant trees, trees I didn't recognize.

... students at the academy level schools in Ankorplex and in Kievplex have filed petitions with the secretary director of the Federal Union ... claiming that the proposal to use perceptual integrative ability tests—the so-called PIAT—effectively grants an advantage to students who have undergone genetic pre-selection ... petitions also state that the use of the PIAT smooths the orbit for other subjective criteria. ...

That was no surprise. Students who had greater perceptual integrating abilities had an advantage, but it didn't matter how they got the advantage. Some norms scored high on the PIAT. The image flicked again.

... delegate Diem offered the Union council a proposal to increase the distance penalty on privately owned gliders ... claiming that the present tax-charge and ownership requirements are merely designed to prohibit private use of gliders for all but the wealthiest. "The charges mean nothing to the wealthy. Do you see them on the induction tubes?"

With a headshake, I broke the news link and let the holo images fade. The charges certainly weren't "nothing" to me. Probably twenty percent of what I made went to fees for the glider, and I did my own maintenance, and was careful when I used it.

I didn't even finish the thought because the commplate lit, and the gatekeeper informed me that I had a message. Myrto was the one I half-expected, but the image that appeared in mid-air, cutting off the sweep of the sun-splashed red stone of the East Mountains, was that of a smiling Kharl, wearing a dark gray singlesuit.

"I know you've got a lot of work to catch up on. So I'm just sending this to you so that you can see and hear it when you can. It might even give you another idea for an edart composition. And no, I still haven't heard from Elysa. I don't expect either of us will. When you have a minute, let me know, and I'll fill you in on what I know about what caused your reaction." With those words, Kharl's image vanished.

The databloc he'd sent was a VR—of the Warsha Symphony concert that Elysa had been so successful in keeping me from attending.

I needed a break from the routine of heavy-duty methodizing, anyway. So I blocked any incoming inquiries with direct routing to gatekeeper storage, pulled on the headset once more, let myself drop into the VR concert hall, a VR recreation of the large hall in Vallura, and began to listen.

I hadn't intended to listen all the way through. After all, I'd heard the Uphyrd before. But I found myself listening first to *Gate of Conquest*, and then to the re-creation of *The Planets*. When the VR ended, I just sat behind my flat desk for several minutes, looking blankly in the direction of the window, but I didn't really see the valley below. Even though it had been a VR, and not a live concert with all the overtones and electricity created by a real orchestra, one thing was brilliantly clear—Uphyrd was an amateur compared to Holst.

I'd never heard of Holst until Kharl brought his name to mind, and despite the directness and the brass—I'd always preferred strings over brass—I had no doubts about my reaction. The ancient work left Uphyrd's *Gate of Conquest* looking pallid by comparison.

That brought up another question. Why would that be so?

Without an easy answer, I began to think, and one thought led to another until I had the rough outline of another edart piece. Once I had the outline in mind, I began to speak and to throw in ideas and rough visuals to accompany my words.

> Over the past month, all across Noram, the Warsha Symphony has been presenting two symphonies—one almost one thousand years old, and one less than two hundred. . . .
> . . . You might think that modern is better—I did before I heard the older work, and most of us would. But is it?

I searched for the clip of the "Mars" section, then fed it in after my next words.

> This is Holst, his music describing Mars. . . .

The screen filled with a rough and reddish pink image of Mars.

> And here is Uphyrd . . . with his departure from the inner system. . . .

After a moment, I keyed in Uphyrd, banal after the Holst, but I let it run a good minute, too long by VR standards, but I could get away with it once.

> Let us hear Holst on Jupiter. . . .

I used a stock net image of the gas giant. I could refine or replace the images later.

> And now Uphyrd . . .

Then I followed with the "Finding the Gate" section of *Conquest* . . . and a clip of a SysCon Gate—the supra-ecliptic one, I suspected, from the stellar background.

*   *   *

We could follow a dozen passages from each composition, but the comparative effect would be similar. . . .
    . . . *Conquest* is simple . . . just like the idea ex-
pressed by the word. And so are the melodies.

I stripped the Uphyrd down to eight simple notes, repeat-
ing twice.

. . . You can hear how much more Holst expresses in
The Planets. . . .
    It's not that I am a lover of antique music, or an
antiquarian. In fact, *Conquest* was always one of my
favorites . . . until I heard *The Planets*. . . .

Then I let the concluding section of Holst's work run,
accompanied by an image of the solar system spinning
against the spangled darkness of space. When the music
ended, I left the solar system spinning silently for a long
moment.

So . . . from this edart composer . . . the thought for the
day is that modern may not always be better . . . in fact,
modern may not even sound as modern as something
written long ago. Modern may not be as advanced as
the ancient. Remember, we still don't know how the
forerunner Gates operate . . . and they were built a *long*
time before we even broke the orbit of our own home
planet. . . .

The piece needed work, a lot of work, and I'd need to
figure out the exact net-royalties I'd owe for using the clips,
but I liked the idea. I'd let it sit for a day or so, then go
back and check it over before it went up on the UniComm
net.
    During the time I'd roughed out the edart piece, nothing
new had showed up from either Myrto or from Klevyl. So I
pulsed an inquiry across the net to Kharl.
    Surprisingly, he was in and appeared, if wearing an off-
green singlesuit that was either for lab work or for some

other medical effort. He stood before a set of French windows that framed a northern section of the East Mountains. "You caught up on all your work?"

"Not really, but I wanted to thank you again. I've got a little time before I get the input I need from the clients, and I did want to know what you've been able to find out."

"Not very much. There were some strange nanites in your system . . . or maybe they were pathogens—the structural differences are getting smaller."

"Could it be a version of the pre-select plague? You'd suggested an allergenic off-shoot, but what about some form of the plague itself?"

"Someone might have used those pathogens as a base, but the symptoms were even more rapid, too rapid in my screen, and they didn't have any defense against what I dumped into your bloodstream. Pre-select plague strains probably would have shown some defensive reaction."

"What *did* you use?"

"SADs." Kharl's voice was matter-of-fact.

"Search and Destroy nanites?"

"I figured I could rebuild your augmentation later—and I did—but SADs were the quickest solution. From your systemic reaction, if I hadn't . . ." He shrugged. "Well . . . we wouldn't be discussing it."

"So . . . there were invader nanites?"

Kharl looked embarrassed. "That's my best guess now. At the time, I was just trying to keep you alive, and treating symptoms as much as anything. Your symptoms were violently reactive—just like an acute allergenic reaction."

"You're telling me that they were strange. How strange?"

"They don't have any antibody defenses. None at all."

"Then why did they almost kill me?"

"They're programmed to act against augnites—and only against augnites. And they release a lot of heat in the process."

"You mean, if I were a norm . . ."

"You wouldn't have felt a thing. You probably would have been a carrier for some other unsuspecting pre-select."

"Elysa didn't act like a norm."

"I don't think she was. She might not even have been the carrier."

I pursed my lips. "I don't like that." Whether she'd used a spray or just been there, it meant that she'd been immunized by someone or something, and that someone had definitely gone after me.

"Neither do I." Kharl wasn't smiling.

I nodded slowly. "Is there anything else?"

"I'm still working on some angles. I'll let you know if I find out anything. You probably ought to stop by the med-center tomorrow for a screen . . . and a system boost."

"Any more thoughts on Elysa?"

He shook his head, not as convincingly as I would have liked to see.

"Did you monitor the gathering? Is there a VR reproduction that shows her?"

"I've looked at it. There's nothing there that I haven't tried to track. I'll send you a copy. You can see for yourself."

"I'd appreciate it."

"You'll have it." He paused, then added, "I need to go. I'll see you tomorrow, at the medcenter."

"I'll be there." It wasn't as though I had a real choice. Not with Elysa and her friends still lurking somewhere out beyond Vallura.

But she had been charming. I wondered if the VR would show that as well.

Chapter 9
Fledgling: Yunvil, 416 N.E.

I took a long hot shower in the fresher, the kind that made Father frown. Then I dressed for dinner, in a dark blue semi-formal singlesuit with a cream half-jacket, the one both Ame-lya and Ertis had liked. I kept thinking about the comments made by the youngsters at the Tennis Club, except they had really been our age, even if Gerrat and I were nearly a third of a meter taller.

I left my room and started down from the third level, almost catching Gerrat at the bottom of that flight.

"Still worried about losing?" Gerrat wore a dark green singlesuit, with a pale green jacket. Somehow it went with his white-blond hair. He could wear anything, do anything, say anything, with élan. There were times, especially around the girls, that I wished I had half that much flair and charm. But then, Gerrat would never know how anything *really* worked.

We were standing in the upper hallway. That was right by the Meraal sculpture of a young woman star-surfing star clusters in the block of darkness that rose from the pedestal. Father had already declared that the sculpture would someday go in the UniComm Art Museum.

That was fine with me. I had my eye on the more traditional Hui-Lui painting in the salon, the one of a dark-haired woman standing by an open sunlit gate.

"That match is done. I'll get you the next time," I answered. "And if you want to think about taking a real beating, just wait till the next time we go to the islands. I'll make you swim all the way to the point—in rough water."

"It's not about the tennis." Gerrat shook his head. "You still have that thoughtful look."

He was right, as usual. He could read people, but he was always analyzing things when he should have been acting. "Do you think pre-selecting genes is that good an idea? What if we select wrong?" I mused.

"You've been listening to Mertyn again."

To Gerrat, now that he was working at UniComm, old Master Rosenn was Mertyn. Sometimes, Gerrat acted like Father. I ignored the superior mannerisms. "What if I have? It's still a good question."

"If we select wrong, then that selection doesn't get to the next generation. We all see to that. All we're doing is speeding up evolution," answered Gerrat. "We know the parameters. That's why we don't have three meter giants or dwarves . . . or huge braincases." He stopped short of the archway to the family dining room, since the room was empty.

We stood, waiting for our parents.

"Why us?"

Gerrat laughed in his irritating, older-brother way. "Because we value pre-selection and because we can afford to pay for it and for augmentation." He gave me that too-perfect smile. "You don't like being considered a modern god? That's a compliment. They just wished they could be that good."

"They can't. They never will be," I pointed out.

"Look . . . younger brother . . . they've got baseline nanitic protection that ancient emperors would have killed for. They can invest in their own children's selection. And if we stopped genetic upgrading this moment, and returned to totally natural breeding, nothing would really change that much, except that the rate of human evolution would slow down. Elites have existed in every human society, and always will. Our elites are based on ability, not on inherited position." He laughed again. "And if we do inherit, we have to have the ability to keep it."

I couldn't deny that. No one could.

"Do you see rampant poverty anywhere—except perhaps by choice among the netless or the faithies? Do we have starving children anywhere in the Union?"

"Starving children?" came a stern voice from behind my shoulder. "Don't tell me that one of your instructors is dragging out that moldy lemon?"

Gerrat smothered a smile as we turned to face Father.

"No, sir," I replied. "That was Gerrat's phrase. He just said that starving children are something of the past."

"You wouldn't think so the way some of the edartists attack UniComm." Father snorted. "Or the way the naturists whine about pre-selection."

"What a surprise." Mother's bright tones filled the hallway. "All my gentlemen waiting for me. That hasn't happened . . . in . . ." She smiled at the three of us. With her slender figure and youthful face, she almost could have passed for our older sister.

"Since last night," I suggested.

My father's eyebrows furrowed, and he no longer looked like an older brother, at least not his eyes.

I half-bowed to my mother.

"That's all right, Daryn. I appreciate the humor. Your father's just hoping you maintain a certain decorum once you head off to The College."

"Longer than that, dear," confirmed my father, the most honorable Henson Gerrat Alwyn. "Much longer than that. Young fellow has the family to think of."

"They won't think much of us," my mother said with a gentle laugh, "if he doesn't have a sense of humor."

We stepped through the golden wooden archway from the upper hallway into the family dining room. The table was set for four, since Elora had already taken the suborbital shuttle from the Bay and was on her way back to Mancha. She never stayed long.

Father had never been totally pleased when she had decided against taking a position with UniComm. She'd told him she'd never work in the family business until she proved she could operate someone else's operations—better than anyone else he had. She was an ops-manager for NEN—NordEstNet, and from what Gerrat had gathered and passed on in his first year with UniComm, she was actually taking accounts from UniComm.

"What's for dinner?" asked Gerrat.

"Coq-au-vin."

"Straight from the replicator?" I asked.

"No. The uncooked bird was, but it's a new recipe for Naria," Mother replied.

That made sense. The replicator could only replicate. Original prepared food was always different, and Father and Mother prided themselves on always serving something original at their dinners, sort of like a uniquery, if more private. We, of course, tasted them first, and until they were perfected.

Gerrat eased out mother's chair, and then we all sat down. Naria carried in the platter with the pheasant, and Father prepared to carve in the dignified old-fashioned style that was making a resurgence.

Dinner would be good. It always was.

I sat in my study, before the holo scene that cloaked the cast end of the room. Then I pulled on the headset, and put my fingers on the small oblong keyboard that controlled the vyrtor, my wrists on the flat table.

For a moment, I watched the net scene—a golden eagle swooping down on a raven as both crossed a canyon—green junipers clinging to steep walls of red Navaho sandstone. Usually, I just watched the East Mountains, but it had been raining all day, and so, before I got back to work, I called up a scene of sunshine, except, of course, just like on the net itself, the holo sunshine was without warmth—largely because of the energy costs for most people, especially norms. I suppose I could have programmed in directional heating units, but what was the point of adding one simulation on top of another?

Some methodizers direct their vyrtors verbally, some with visualization, but I found I was more precise with the keyboard or the pointer. When he wanted to needle me, my brother Gerrat claimed that was because I was a throwback. Compared to him, I probably was.

The sorting and re-sorting of lists, and the additional searches, had yielded little beyond the first rough cut of the week before, and no real pointers as to which or if any of the multis might have actually been involved. The name search hadn't done much better, since the permutations of names based on the two lines of the Arabic physician's name had turned up more than ten thousand possibilities. At some point, I'd have to rethink that—in my copious spare time.

All that wasn't progress, but at least my lungs didn't burn with every breath. Every really deep breath, there was a touch of a stinging sensation, but even those had gotten milder, and my sense of smell and taste had returned, and I could again access the nanite monitors of my health.

After looking blankly at the eagle's pass at the raven, and the single black feather that remained, slowly twisting downward toward the Virge River that lay below the bottom of the image that seemed to hang before me, I banished the holo scene. Some day, if I ever had time, I wanted to reprogram the scene so that the raven won. Ravens were smarter than eagles, but everyone except me, it seemed, found ravens unattractive. I'd always preferred the intelligence and the way of the raven.

Lions roamed in prides; geese clustered in gaggles; but ravens? Ravens together merited the term "unkindness of ravens." While I liked the intelligence of ravens, most cultures in human history had identified with eagles. Because of the eagle's raw power? Because intelligence unchecked is always suspect? Or because humans were still hardwired from a million years of hardscrabble existence to respect strength?

I took off the headset to readjust it, then looked to my right, out through the window into the late rainy afternoon, and the featureless gray clouds that hung barely above the lower hill on which perched my modest villa. The clouds had brought mostly a light drizzle, and swirling winds, but little real moisture to either the lower Hill, or to the valley below.

Klevyl should have zapped me the revised environmental specs package to go with the first cut that I'd already received, but when I touched the comm plate, the only message that tingled in my head was: *You have no new messages.* I'd already left fullface messages everywhere Klevyl might access, and there wasn't much else I could do on his project without the latest parameters. I wasn't about to guess and then have to redo everything, especially since I'd taken on his work freelance, and in addition to the OneCys contract.

My lips quirked into a smile as I eased on the headset and my fingers called up the latest edart piece, the unfinished one I'd started after the Holst piece. I hadn't posted the Holst piece, either. I'd made more revisions, but it still didn't feel right.

So I listened to my newest set of words as they scrolled down one side of the projected holo, with the images of hungry and wide-eyed children burning their way across the foreground of the display area.

When the ancients developed the entire basis of nano-technology, few if any of them envisioned the world they created. They were too preoccupied with eliminating the evils of the world that surrounded them.

I nodded at the re-created image of the hollow-eyed children scrabbling toward the smiling woman extending some form of ration packs—a woman flanked by uniformed soldiers in the antiquated mottled green and brown camouflage fatigues with rifles leveled. Then came the scenes of the bombed out cities, and the broken bridges, and then the smoldering ruins of Hylanta.

To us, those days seem all too raw—barbaric, if you will. People being shot on the streets with projectile weapons . . . others starving because there was no way to transport food or convert the raw organic material into foodstocks. . . .

I froze the image, and the words. How could I make the transition? After a moment of indecision, I moved ahead to the next section, letting those words roll past me as the holo image depicted an aerial view of a pleasant town, not Vallura or Cedacy, although it could almost have been either.

. . . today . . . we think of starvation, of wars that pitted nation against nation, or sometimes family against family within the same nation, as something from the remote past, as something before the millennium of chaos, as almost inconceivable. . . . Yet . . . has our mindset changed all that much from that terrible past? Or have we merely adopted a different and less obvious set of distinctions which still pit individual against individual?

The next image set depicted a tall and lithe couple, intelligence radiating from their eyes, poise from their movements as they walked down a set of steps outside the municipal building at Porlan. Then that image shrank into the left half of the projected viewing area, and a second couple appeared, set against the same backdrop. While they were also well-dressed, they were nearly a head shorter, and their movements appeared hesitant by comparison, their eyes duller, their carriage subdued.

This is Daryn Alwyn . . . offering observations from the hill.

I frowned. The idea was good, but it wasn't even close to being ready, and I wasn't sure I had the insights yet to finish it. Then, I hadn't finished the Holst piece, either. Was it because I worried about Elysa . . . or what she represented? Or the fact that I couldn't figure out why someone wanted me dead?

There was also the cost aspect. Commercial posting cost creds, and posting something incomplete or not up to my standards would be costly in more ways than one.

So I called up the VR that showed Elysa. What Kharl had sent showed her walking in his front entry, talking to him and waiting. She looked like a natural redhead, just like the silver and jade combs in her hair appeared natural, and the deep muted green gown accentuated her color. The image swirled on transitions, but nothing seemed to have been edited as the system marked my entry. When we had walked into the great room, the view switched to a panorama of the entire room. I switched the focus to Elysa and to me, and the resolution got fuzzier, but what happened was exactly as I recalled it—except that the VR switched once more when we had stepped onto the terrace. I watched that closely again. I couldn't see Elysa do anything except talk to me, no hidden hands, no tube, no nothing. I staggered, and tottered toward the door. Elysa watched. Once I collapsed in the great room, she turned and walked quickly away from the house, into the darkness, her image fading away as she left the scanning field.

What was surprising to me was that there was essentially nothing that I had not already remembered—nothing at all. I turned off the VR and let my eyes rest on the East Mountains as I thought.

I suppose Kharl and I could have gone to the Civil Authorities, but what good would that have done? We couldn't even prove anything for the CAs, not from what I knew. I'd had a supra-allergenic reaction after stepping onto a terrace with a strange and beautiful woman who claimed to be a distant relative. There was no physical or visual evidence that showed she had done anything. That was attempted murder? Kharl had only been able to find a few strange nanites, and they didn't even cause harm to norms.

I shook my head.

For a short time I sat, then called up the accounting on the edart pieces—for some sort of inspiration. The most popular one had been a fluff piece on the struggle between the established Snoma vineyards for credit as the oldest . . . with my own sardonic outtakes about why no one seemed to be able to prove who was the oldest or the best. Then there was the one on the terraforming of Venus—the three hundred year project that was already entering its seven hundredth year.

My favorite of the older pieces had been the one I had done on the forerunner Gate, only about two years before. I'd hesitated to touch on that until the newsies and other commentators had, although I'd known about it as soon as anyone had, and that had been years earlier, back when I'd been in Federal Service.

Calling up the forerunner piece, I watched and listened, hoping I could capture the feel of what had made it so popular.

The first image was that of darkness. Then points of light appeared—stars—bright, but with just hints of color, the way they really looked in deep space, not with the false color enhancement that remained so popular. The music was from Jetecayst's *Deep Space Suite*, low and lonely, with a single oboe just slightly louder than the rest of the orchestra, not quite plaintive, nor complaining . . . but suggesting a separateness.

. . . deep space . . . lonely space . . . Even millennia before the development of the Gates that are opening the Galaxy to us, men and women looked into the night skies and wondered if we were alone . . . statisticians and astronomers cited numbers and the size of the universe as proof that we could not be alone. . . .

The image shifted to show a Gate—a human Gate—and a ship passing through it at the moment of incandescence that preceded translation.

. . . We traveled our system, and then found a way to reach others. Finally . . . we discovered another kind of proof—an ancient artifact similar to our own Gates in shape and size.

The stars jumped, and another star-field appeared, and in the foreground loomed a dull octagonal shape, re-created as well as I could recall.

Is it a Gate? Was it once? We do not know. Who made it? We do not know that, either, nor from what star they came. We have an object, a few scattered suggestions from that artifact that whoever built it was not much larger nor much smaller than are we, and that they required an atmosphere, probably similar to what we breathe. . . .

Next came a close-up of an exterior black octagonal airlock door, and with the octagon-within-octagon lock control panel.

. . . the only clear and convincing conclusion that leaps from this artifact is that its builders based everything on octagons. While this ancient Gate-like artifact looks like ours from a distance, it is not a torus, but an octagon, with an octagonal cross-section . . . even the octagonal doors are operated by octagonal panels . . . octagons everywhere. We build with arcs, rectangles, circles, cubes . . . but seldom if ever with octagons. . . .

Every forerunner entry and every exit is guarded and controlled through octagons. . . . One might almost imagine that these forerunners had octagonal shapes, or octagonal cells . . . but imagine is all we can do . . . for now. . . . We can ask, we do ask, "Who were these fore-runners with their octagons?"

The image shifted back to the star-field.

We can ask. We continue to ask, but neither stars nor ancient Gates provide answers to our questions. . . .

I flicked off the image, my thoughts back on the present and incomplete edart composition about differences, trying to focus on what it was about differences that seemed to draw humans into conflict.

What about some phrases on skin color . . . or background tests? I cleared my throat and began to speak.

Once, human beings categorized the worth of others, selling them as chattels if their skin colors were not of an accepted shade. Other cultures defined superiority in the ability to master arcane symbolic languages. Later, still others tried using written symbolic tests as a measure of superiority. . . . Scientific studies later suggested that virtually all of these were being used as mere pretexts . . . and when there was a scientific basis, actual usage and education tended to emphasize the cultural background of those in power and disparage sheer ability in favor of artificial credentials. . . .

Today, it is said that we have come far from those bad old times. Have we? Or is genetic pre-selection merely the current test of superiority being adopted by a race that seems to need magical means to ascertain who is fitted to control society?

I paused. The transitions weren't right, and some logic was missing. But I saved what I had and released the VR images before my eyes went back to the window again. The clouds had darkened and dropped lower over the valley. I still didn't have a finished edart piece or the specs I needed from Klevyl—or the feedback from Myrto. Either way, my income would suffer if I didn't finish one or the other soon . . . and the time I'd lost to Elysa's nanites had scarcely helped.

It wasn't so much the creds, but the pride. I'd been able to survive, even prosper, without touching the funds from my inherited interests in UniComm. Part of that was from my early retirement from Federal Service, but the pension was far from enough to cover my expenses. I didn't want to touch the UniComm assets, but unless I got the specs soon, or could put another edart piece on the nets, I was going to be severely tempted. Although the number of viewers and the royalties from their viewing were growing, I needed the continuing methodizer contracts. The royalties from sysnet subscribers from all my past presentations still amounted to less than a third of my annual income, and they tended to sag if I didn't keep producing.

I looked from the valley to just outside the study window. There, below the shimmering tube that was the bird feeder, a handful of juncos scrabbled across the stone looking for the few seeds that the feeder dispersed nearly randomly. The old verse that had once crystallized a part of who I was came to mind as I watched.

When ravens reigned, eagles dipped their wings,
and juncos foraged cold winters and colder springs. . . .

I don't know who said it—it was one of those fragments that came out of the Noram collapse—but I'd always liked it, and now, when the juncos returned to their winter feeding spots almost before fall had arrived, it boded ill for all who flew.

Then . . . I certainly had never thought of myself as an eagle. Gerrat—with his adaptation of sensoria to vyrtor projections and his machinations to try to merge the subnets of Afrique, Mercosur, and Etunie—was certainly aiming to be the highest flying in the family—except for Father, of course. I paused. Elora wasn't that far behind, for all of her modesty.

Like the juncos, or the ravens, I was definitely a ground-feeder. That's why Elysa's effort to murder me made little sense.

The commplate glowed, and the bell sounded. I just hoped I was getting Klevyl's specs.

Chapter 11
Fledgling: Willston, 418 N.E.

The College was one of those institutions that predated the Federal Unity Act, even the chaos years and the Mandate, and dated back almost into the days of the ancient Anglish hegemony over NorAm. It had survived the collapse of the North American Union, almost untouched. It even had a building that had been built as a chapel, although it had been turned into a recital hall and classrooms. Still, the few faithies who attended The College used Thompson on sevenday for their rituals. That was their business, but I preferred to sleep.

That twoday afternoon I was attending the three hundred level major class in methodizing. I was seated halfway down the table on the Professor Trebman's right. He always tossed the hard questions at those on the left side and those at the very end of the table.

Professor Trebman glanced down the table. "Ms. D'Ahoud, would you explain Kessel's objections to the validity of the Rochford SocioTech Norming requirements?"

Ibaran D'Ahoud smiled. She had the whitest teeth, and the smoothest latte complexion, and she talked like a professor. "For all his objections, Kessel never really refuted Rochford's empirical observations and theoretical construct that a minimum number of intelligent entities is required to support a given technology and an elite or that a mature society with multigenerational survival must adopt in function a pyramidal power structure, assuming, of course, something along the lines of a P(3) definition of power."

"You claim Kessel did not refute Rochford. Please be more specific." Professor Trebman's mild voice carried to the end of the seminar table.

I smiled. Ibaran would have an answer. Like my brother Gerrat, she always did.

"The essence of Kessel's rebuttal centers on two factors," she answered immediately. "First, he contended that intelligence is a subjective assessment on the part of the elite, and defined to maximize and legitimize their control of the instruments of power, much as the ancient Anglish forced the Gaels into illiteracy and then used literacy as a measure of intellectual ability or that—"

"You can skip the rest of the examples," Trebman said wryly. "Your last essay showed you knew them all. So does most of the class."

"Second," continued the dark-haired student, "Kessel argued that the pyramidal distribution of power documented by Rochford, and thus the entire structure of social hierarchy, was related to purely physical dynamics, rather than socioeconomics. Because that distribution was based on physical limits, he contended that nanotechnology and advanced materials technology effectively removed such limits." Ibaran paused and nodded to Trebman. "He explicitly assumed that technological capability had no environmental or economic limits—or rather that those which existed at that time would cease to be limits within a century." She paused briefly again, moistened her lips, and continued. "On the first issue, Kessel totally ignored the work of Raon and TanUy in establishing accurate quantifications of the various discrete kategoria of intelligence. This earlier work has been further confirmed by additional studies by Ng and Gonsalves. . . ."

Trebman nodded. "You can skip the details there, unless anyone in the seminar wants to contest you."

"What about the work of contrarians like Shatnich?" queried Wil Jimson—one of the few norms in the seminar. Then, only 10 percent of any class was norm. As my father always said, genius can come from anywhere—it's just rarer among norms.

"Shatnich's basic contention was that human intelligence is integrative, and that while its components are measurable, no testing protocol can measure the sum of those components because the interaction approximates a log scale. Gonsalves's study does confirm that total integrative intelligence does not amount to the sum of the parts, but that the distribution from the theoretical curve apex follows an inverse bell curve, that is, those with the greatest variation in component scores—either on the high end or the low end—show correspondingly greater variation."

Professor Trebman sighed. "In short, Ms. D'Ahoud, while the ancient Anglish may have used the skill of literacy to oppress the Gaels, as did the priests of Egypt and the mandarins of China, intelligence can be measured and assessed relatively objectively, as shown by centuries of studies, and the talented do show greater integrative intelligence and the untalented show less." He paused and added, "In general."

"Yes, sir."

"Does that answer your question, Mr. Jimson?"

Wil nodded.

"You did not address the question of whether intelligence, even if it can be measured and assessed accurately, is merely a rationale for control by the elite. Mr. Hamelfar?"

"It is, sir, but the rationale is based on experience, practicality, and history. In the last years of the North American Union, the legislators who controlled the government failed to use their intelligence. They enacted laws and rules that the less informed majority desired. That was so that they could maintain power, even when such rules were wrong economically, socially, and environmentally."

"So?" asked Trebman. "What's your point?"

Hamelfar swallowed. "They couldn't maintain control because they subordinated their brains in order to keep the power that they got through media-generated identity politics."

"And if you wished to retain power in that culture, what would you have done, Mr. Hamelfar?"

Hamelfar flushed, belatedly understanding the professor's point.

Trebman waved his hand across the end of the table in a vague gesture. "Power is—in its simplest form—the ability to get other people to do what you want. In a neolithic culture, no one cared directly if you had greater intelligence— not unless it was coupled with a modicum of physical force. The use of intelligence to mobilize force is a construct of a post-industrial society. All of you at this table could probably dominate a neolithic culture, but that's because technology has been employed to enhance your health and physical ability. Because you're what the late industrial and pre-collapse cultures would have called 'beautiful people,' most of you probably could have easily mastered the personality cults of business and politics necessary to gain power. Today, where even the lowest norm has better health and education than ninety-five percent of the teeming millions of that time, power comes from the successful integration of intelligence, knowledge, and education. . . ."

I forced myself to listen as Trebman went on and on, and I had to work to keep my eyes off Ibaran. Then, she wasn't likely to look my direction because she was sitting beside Alou Darcia. But I could look.

I eased the glider off the automated guide-road and onto the dark way winding between the massive redwoods that towered nearly a hundred meters above the mulched dark bark of the path, a twisting access lane barely wide enough for two gliders if they had to pass side-by-side, and irregular enough in width that it would have been hard for a casual passerby to realize a private guideway lay beneath.

While I could have accessed the private control guides, I preferred to take the glider through the trees on manual. Once I was well under the trees I flicked off the ground limiters, with one of the manual switches I'd installed, bypassing about a half-dozen manufacturer's safety systems, and eased the glider upward until we were running a good twenty meters above the hidden guideway.

After about two klicks, I eased back down and restored the limiters, wondering about the inductors' response and whether I'd have to rebuild them. But then, I'd practically rebuilt the entire glider at one time or another, and that included the installation of full orbital maglifter gyros. All that wasn't bad for a methodizer and edartist, or even for a former pilot who hadn't been trained as an engineer.

The UniComm headquarters complex lay another three klicks through the forest and over one ridge. I hadn't wanted to seek help there, but all my net searches had come up blank, and, besides, intrigue had never been my sport. So, much as I disliked the idea, I had called my brother Gerrat, and made an appointment.

He'd been most gracious, as always. "Any time for you . . . any time." His smile was as warm and friendly as ever, tinged with concern, as it should have been.

My mind dropped back to the effort of navigating the bark

throughway, and I slipped the glider around a Gate-like grove, maintaining speed and concentrating on the physical challenge involved. Neither Gerrat nor Father, nor my grandfather, had wanted the direct physical surface access to UniComm easy. I could have taken the induction tube, with its private station for the UniComm area, but there were guards and scanners everywhere that way, and I always tried to avoid the tubes on the few times I visited Father and Gerrat at UniComm. There were scanners hidden among the darkness and the cool of the redwoods, as well, but far less obtrusive, and I could enjoy the illusion—and the scents of the redwoods and the forest—except when my internal system informed me of yet another scan. Still, the glider had an access chip, which meant I'd only have to pass one personal scan—when I entered the building on the upper garden level.

Although the glider's surface shimmered when observed closely, even in the deep shade beneath the redwoods, it looked dull from any distance, a green-tinted silver dullness, created by the thousands of flexible solar panels coated with the polarized polymer. If I had eased it into the underbrush between some of the redwoods, it would have almost vanished in the shadows.

In time, the glider slipped out from the trees, then over the last ridge, where the lane ended in a tree-shaded glider park. The park held all of eight gliders under the shade of the redwoods and the lower firs that filled the lower part of the hill into which the UniComm spaces were built. There were three magscooters locked to loop-poles—transportation for young norms who lived west where the tube line did not extend, in all probability.

The glider resealed itself after I exited and headed toward the northeast side of the hill, the net repeater at my belt routing the signal to my internal systems, confirming the glider's security. I walked through a light breeze a good five degrees warmer than the air had been among the trees. At the end of the stone way from the glider park, polished gray granite steps led up to the three meter high stone archway, an arch of glistening black marble. Beyond the archway was a formal garden, sunken into the hillside, but open to the sky, and the polished gray stone led to a second smaller archway, without doors. Through the second arch was an entry foyer and black stone podium desk, behind which sat a guard who wore the green-trimmed gray singlesuit of UniComm security.

I smiled and announced, "Daryn Alwyn . . . to see Gerrat."

"Yes, ser. Is your profile on the system?" Her voice bore the slight dullness often heard from the brain-damped. Some of the lower-level security types were—but they were totally honest.

"I do hope so." I grinned.

"Yes, ser." She nodded to the scanner before the inner door. "If you would step through, ser? The door will open if you are cleared. Would you like me to call Director Alwyn's office?"

"Only if the door doesn't open."

She nodded seriously, and I stepped through the scanner. The door did open, and I took the right-hand corridor, and then the inclined ramp past the orchid gardens, up to Gerrat's office, second in size only to Father's.

I'd read some of the old literature which had insisted that larger organizations would do without people gathered together, that virtual offices would be the rage, and, for a time, many had tried them, and gone back to putting people together, if in smaller numbers than before the collapse. Part of the reason had been social. People are still herd or clan animals. Part had been economic. Energy transmission costs rose with the volume of data, as did the costs of external infrastructure. And part had been security. Even in Uni-Comm there were systems totally isolated physically from the worldnets.

There was a complete scanning unit set before the door to Gerrat's office. It hadn't been there the last time I'd visited my dear sibling, but, then, that had been several years before. There was also a muscular young man standing by the scanner unit. He was probably a pre-select himself, except he'd been pre-selected for physical attributes and reactions. While Gerrat and I might have bested him on a good day, the day and week before had been far less than optimal for me.

"Daryn Alwyn. I'm here to see Gerrat."

"Yes, ser. He is expecting you, ser. If you would, ser . . ." He gestured to the scanner.

I stepped through, sensing from my own nanite feedback a far more than casual scanning, one that seemed to last several minutes before the guard opened the door to Gerrat's sanctum sanctorum.

Unlike Father, whose desk was handmade of real cherry, Gerrat affected a desk fabricated as an expanse of transparent armaglass, polarized just enough that it neither reflected nor totally absorbed light. It looked like an ephemeral object made out of mist, even though it would have taken all my strength to move it.

"Still sitting amid the mist," I offered. I didn't mention that mist didn't smell as sterile and lifeless as Gerrat's office. The only scent was the cologne that he liked. I couldn't remember the name, probably because it reminded me vaguely of the interior of an interstellar ship.

"Of course." Gerrat stood and beamed, then glanced down almost apologetically. "The effect is relaxing, and that's useful." He gestured to the loveseat to the left of the mist-desk.

I eased into, or onto, the green leather, turning slightly on the firm cushion to face him directly.

"Father said you might want to talk." Gerrat had reseated himself and leaned back in the swivel that molded to his large but muscular figure. His blond hair picked up the light from somewhere. He might have had nanite-guided low-intensity lensors directed on him. The effect would be heightened if he were in a VR conference, and would give him an appearance that the ancient sun gods—Re, Aton, Apollo, Helios, all of them—would have been pressed to create.

"He told you?"

"What affects one of us affects all of UniComm."

"I doubt that I affect UniComm much." I paused. "Assuming that the attack wasn't specifically personal, who would have gained by it . . . in your opinion?"

"No one." He smiled. "Who *thinks* they would have gained is something else entirely. I can see the Dynae deluding themselves along that line, and certainly the NeoLudds. Even possibly some mid-level types at OneCys or AsyaNet, although they're not that big. NEN wouldn't stoop to that. Elora would destroy anyone who did."

I grinned at his reference to our older sister, who'd rejected Father in her own special way. "The mid-level types probably wouldn't have access to the specialization required, not without leaving a track."

"You're right, and there wasn't any track," Gerrat confirmed.

"And somehow . . . can't see the NeoLudds embracing all that they decry to use specialized nanites."

"Fanatics have been known to do stranger things," he pointed out. "They might find the irony delightful."

"I'm sure they would. But they probably wouldn't know a bacterium from a nanite."

"Not that there's much difference."

I ignored Gerrat's quip. "What do you know about the Dynae?"

Gerrat smiled and gestured idly toward the fist-sized black case on the corner of the mistingly transparent armaglass table that served as his desk. "I'd already thought about that. Everything that can be put in data form is there."

"What about the information that can't?"

"There isn't much. Not even from our sources. They're either more successfully secretive than we are, or they have no secrets." He shrugged. "I doubt that you're their preferred target. If anyone is."

"It seems unlikely someone would go to the trouble of tailoring nanites for a prank or a blind target."

"No . . . they wouldn't. But . . . what if you weren't the target? You know, I had Kharl check you most carefully."

"Meaning you are? Or the more important members of the family?"

"Kharl says that they were self-replicating. That's why you were scanned before you came in today and why I had Kharl check you over thoroughly."

"You think they wanted me to convey all those odd nanites to you?"

He frowned. "I wouldn't have done it that way, but I can't

see any other rationale. You're not important enough to spend that much effort on killing."

"I do so appreciate your judgments, Gerrat."

He smiled. "Surely, you're not going to object to my objective analysis. You're a good methodizer. According to some people, you're one of the best, if not one of the top five. You're also a watched edartist, and one with a growing following. But you don't control or influence anything directly. You haven't upset any women—or men—and everyone likes you personally. Because of that, you can and do go everywhere. Kharl's of the opinion, and I tend to agree, that someone miscalculated. This mysterious woman overdoscd you."

"Why didn't they just go for you? Or Father?"

"How?"

Gerrat had a point—in a way. Getting through Uni-Comm's security and his and Father's personal systems would have been difficult—but not impossible. I could have, and I wasn't an expert in it.

"Plus," he added, "if we were attacked directly, the CAs would have to show an interest. If you had died from an anaphylactic reaction . . . there would have been sorrow . . . a little mystery perhaps . . . and it would all have been forgotten by now. You have neither spouse nor partner, nor position in UniComm." He grinned ironically. "You can imagine the CA reaction. 'So sorry your brother died, Director Alwyn. He showed real promise as an edartist.' "

With that, he had a better point. Much better, unfortunately. "And you can't think of anyone else who might want me dead?"

"Neither Father nor I can, and that worries us both."

I nodded slowly as I stood. There wasn't much point in staying. I reached forward and took the small black case. "You'll let me know?"

"Just as you will."

I was afraid of that, but I smiled. "As soon as I find something . . . if I do."

"Daryn . . . do be careful."

"I will. I don't want to be a rate-hit on your instant

AllNews show." I could certainly assure Gerrat of that.

He actually looked worried as I left, and some of it was real. What worried me most was that he hadn't even questioned that what had happened to me had been an attack of some sort, and that meant more was happening than met anyone's eyes, and that neither Gerrat nor Father knew much more than they had already said.

Chapter 13
Fledgling: Yunvil, 421 N.E.

Father's study was on the third level of the dwelling at the rear. There, in cooler weather, the armaglass doors and windows could be slid open to allow the breeze unfettered access. He preferred natural air to the conditioned variety.

I sat in the green leather chair across the replica of a pre-Collapse businessman's desk from Father. Besides the desk and the concealed vyrtor that he seldom used at home, the study held little except three leather chairs and a real cherry bookcase that stood nearly as tall as I did. Father hated window hangings, relying instead on polarization of the wide sweep of armaglass that overlooked the rear veranda and pool, and the long grassy slope behind.

As usual, I listened as he leaned forward to emphasize each word.

"Federal Service is an obligation of worth, Daryn, and one I cannot gainsay, especially in your case, but that does not mean you need to take it to extremes." Father's eyebrows furrowed, narrowing the gap between their bushy edges, the way they always did when he was angry, and didn't wish to show it.

"I have to get through pilot training first," I pointed out.

"If you want to, you will."

That was fine for him to say, but I had more to say, and I could use his own words. "You always told me that if I had to do something, it was stupid to do a poor job. Being a pilot is a good job, not something like managing a supply center on Mars or serving as the logistics officer on a cargo boat that shuttles between Earth and gamma whatever."

"Being a pilot is a dead-end position," he countered, straightening in the high-backed antique-looking swivel chair. "There's no market for interstellar pilots except in the FS. The whole interstellar travel operation is totally uneconomic. It only makes sense for the survival of the species and the gathering of knowledge, and neither pays off quickly, nor well. The times of big payoffs from science ended with the Collapse. That means that actually working with a logistics system would give you an understanding and a feel for what is required in any kind of business. Those are honorable positions, Daryn, and ones in which you can learn much."

"I can learn more of what I need as a pilot." I could feel my jaw stiffening, and triggered the mental keys to let the augmentation system relax me. "You always said I needed to learn things the hard way."

"The minimum obligation is ten years, son, ten years personal objective time. That could be close to fifteen years or more system objective time, even with the Gates." He paused for effect.

Much of the effect was lost on me because I knew he was exaggerating the time dilation factors. Once they had been that large, but not in recent years.

His eyes focused even more narrowly on me. "Nothing I can do will change that. Ten years is ten years and then some."

"I understand." I already knew that.

Father smiled, shaking his head. "You probably do need those ten years, at least in your own way. Just promise me that it won't be all or nothing. If the pilot training doesn't work out, and they offer you something else worthy, you ought to consider it."

I nodded. "I will."

That meant I couldn't afford not to succeed in becoming an interstellar pilot. The last thing I wanted was to end up as Gerrat's implementer and errand boy. If I didn't make it through pilot training, that's where I'd be, because I didn't love running people and their lives the way Father and Gerrat did. I wanted to know how things worked far more than making sure that others worked for me.

Chapter 14
Raven: Vallura, 458 N.E.

Although the hangar on the lowest level of my dwelling was cool and dim, outside the open hangar door, the sun shone out of a deep blue late fall sky, and the hint of chill and dusty grass slipped into the hangar on a brief gust of wind. With a smile, I stepped into the glider, on my way to Yunvil to see Mertyn. He'd been my history instructor at Blue Oak Academy before I'd gone east to The College, and we'd kept in touch over the years, as he'd gone in my mind from "old Rosenn" to "ser" and then to "Mertyn." His insights and advice were usually keen—and applicable, and I needed keen and applicable. And Mertyn refused to talk more than pleasantries on the net. So I needed to visit him.

Every avenue open to me to track down Elysa or whoever had backed her had come up blank. Gerrat's information on the Society of Dynae had been interesting, and I'd certainly be looking farther in that direction, but the Dynae were strictly philosophical in their opposition to the nets and the VR worlds and those who controlled them. Never had an action of any sort ever been traced to the organization's members.

Once out of the hangar, its doors irising closed behind me, I turned the glider uphill, and it straightened and began to slide above the grass, only the faintest of humming indicating that the magfield inducers were working. I'd left the canopy back, enjoying the crisp and cool air, and the hint of dampness from the night's rain.

Blue glare flared over me—glare and heat.

I could sense my personal field nanites ablating as I ducked down in the glider, even though I had to do that by feel since, with the laseflash, I'd gone blind—at least momentarily, while the nanites floating on the moisture of my eyes opaqued faster than I could have blinked. That would help save my vision.

The fingers of my left hand toggled the canopy switch, and I could sense the darkening around me as the canopy slid forward. I also grounded the glider, since I couldn't see to guide it, and wasn't about to trust the automatics under the circumstances, not until I had a sense of what was going on.

As the glider settled onto the grass, I could also smell the same scent of flowers and the fragrance I had not been able to identify when Elysa had used the first spray, and that scent filled the enclosed glider. My nose began to run, almost immediately, and my throat was scratchy . . . but that was all for the allergenic symptoms. My lips quirked. So far Kharl's special nanites were doing their job.

My fingers brushed the controls . . . feeling for the stud that would summon the CAs, much as I disliked the whole idea.

Nothing happened after I sent the signal, and I waited. The sensor alarms weren't showing anyone approaching the glider, and I was beginning to get flashes of vision back. So I touched the "house return" stud and let the glider cart me back inside the hangar.

By the time the hangar door had closed, I was getting back even longer flashes of blurry vision, but I sat in the glider until I could see and feel enough to link with the house security systems. No one was there, and no one was anywhere on the grounds—if I could trust the systems. But they didn't feel cooked. So after several minutes, I flicked the stud to open the glider canopy.

Then I made my way back up to the study to wait for the CAs.

As I sat behind my flat table desk, blinking, and feeling as though I'd been badly sunburned, I considered what had happened. Someone wanted me dead . . . and this time, it wasn't someone trying to use me as a way to get to Gerrat or Father.

Worst of all, I still hadn't the faintest idea who or why. The heavy-duty nanite personal protection system Father had insisted on when I returned from Federal Service had suddenly become worth the inordinate investment, at least from my perspective. Otherwise I would have been waiting for eye clones to regrow the blistered tissue, and suffering under an artificial epidermis and more.

The ground alarm system noted the approach of two gliders, and then verified the Civil Authority transponders. The CAs had arrived. I stood slowly, then walked from the study out to the front entry. I was still seeing stars, and there were vacant spaces that crossed my field of vision when I opened the door.

Two CAs stood there, a short and slender man and a taller but more blocky blonde woman, both in their off-white and gray singlesuits, both with the streamlined equipment belts and the impact helmets, but with the visors up. Two gliders rested on the grass outside the hangar door, and a third blockier glider hovered next to the stone wall nearly three hundred meters along the side of the hill, the wall that separated my grounds from those of Rokley Barres.

"Ser . . ." That was the woman.

"I'm Daryn Alwyn, as you probably know from the call. Someone used what seemed to be a laseflash on me as I was leaving the glider hangar a little while ago." I paused.

"Yes, ser," she replied. "We checked the skytors on the way." Her voice and the emotions beneath revealed a certain disgust/dislike.

Why? Because I lived on the lower Hill? Because I was a pre-select?

"Why don't you come on in?" I motioned for them to enter, and then walked into the front sitting room, where I sat in the straight chair.

The two followed me, the second closing the door. After a moment, they sat in the matching armchairs opposite me, but they sat on the forward edges.

"What did you discover?" I asked.

"There was a single-burst laser set up on the top of your neighbor's wall. It was set in a plastic. The plastic was the same shade as the stone. According to the skytors, the burst was for four hundred microseconds," the woman CA replied.

I winced.

"You're augmented, aren't you, ser?"

Theoretically, that was none of the CA's business, but it didn't matter, and I really didn't want to give her more reasons to dislike me. "Yes."

She nodded somberly. "If you weren't augmented, under that much intensity, you'd be blind and in the medcenter right now."

But not dead, not from the laseflash.

"I assume it melted down."

"Mostly, ser."

"What about past records? When was it placed?" I asked.

The two exchanged glances. The shorter male CA finally answered. "We don't know. The skytors' records are on a three week loop. We had the whole loop downloaded and scanned once the energy spiked. It set off the skytors' alarm. The duty tech thought it might be a fire at first."

"So no one came near that part of the wall in the past three weeks?"

"No, ser. Except for the gardeners, and they didn't get that close," answered the man.

"And there were no remote signals to the unit?"

"It could have been set off locally . . . but the tech says it looks like it was coded to recognize you and your glider, and to discharge." He paused before adding, "There was no high-power signal, and there were only three people within a klick, and all of them were . . . modified."

Norms hated the term brain-damped, but if the skytors, with their resolutions and scans, had only been able to pick up three people, and all were brain-damped, or modified, those three hadn't been the ones. The CA wasn't lying. He was a norm, and my systems could read him well enough to be sure of that.

I blinked. My eyes still watered. "Thank you very much."

"Do you have any idea who might have done this, ser?" asked the female CA.

"I have no idea. No idea at all." That was certainly the truth.

"Have you done anything . . . that might have upset people?" she pursued.

"I'm an edartist . . . that's always possible, but I haven't received any messages or anything to indicate that might be the reason." That was also true, so far as it went.

"No one has sent you any strange VRs or other . . . communications?"

"Not anything out of the ordinary," I admitted.

The questioning seemed to last for hours, but my system told me it was closer to thirty minutes before they both stood and bowed ever so slightly.

I followed them to the door.

"We'll let you know if we find out more. Ser . . . if you find out anything we should know . . . you will inform us, will you not?" asked the woman. Underlying her even tone of voice were hints of contempt and dislike.

"I certainly will." I could promise that, especially given the way she'd phrased the request. I could ignore the contempt.

I closed the door and walked slowly back to the kitchen where I poured a long drink of cold water—just water—and drank it. I decided against netting Gerrat or Father. They'd find out soon enough, since UniComm had monitors of all the CA freqs.

Someone had set the laseflash well before Elysa had attempted her nanospray, or they had sophisticated enough equipment to bypass the scans of the skytors. I didn't care much for the implications of either possibility. And either way, I should have noticed the changes to the glider.

I shook my head. Anyone could have gotten to the glider in the time I'd been in the medcenter recovering. Anyone with the right equipment to bypass the security systems, and early enough, and they wouldn't be on the skytors either. But that meant someone with a great deal of expertise and credits.

The way things had gone didn't make a great deal of sense, not from what I'd seen, but that meant that I wasn't seeing enough. After refilling the glass of water, I headed out to the study.

The gatekeeper offered a gentle ring, and a light on the commplate. I looked at the ID—Gerrat—and accepted.

"Are you all right?"

I gave him points for asking about me, first. "I'll recover. My internal system says so, even without heading back to the medcenter." I wasn't about to mention the second nanospray attempt.

"That's good."

"Very good."

"You really like trouble, don't you?"

"It wasn't my idea. How did you find out?"

"Our monitors. The energy spike came across the skytors system, and it triggered our alerts. Someone tried to hit you with an FS-type laseflash. It's a good thing Father insisted on a full protection system for us. For you, anyway."

"Has anyone ever tried something like that on you?"

Gerrat shook his head.

"So . . . does the whole world know?"

"Of course." My brother's tone turned cheerfully cynical. "Noted edartist Daryn Alwyn—attacked with a laser as he left his home this afternoon. Alwyn was burned, but is expected to recover. The perpetrators and their motivation are both unknown at this time. The Civil Authorities have withheld comment."

I nodded, trying to ignore the continued blurs and holes in my vision and focus on the holo image of Gerrat that blocked my view of the late afternoon sun falling on the East Mountains. I could have gone VR, but for short conversations, I usually didn't.

"Real news like this doesn't happen that often," Gerrat offered apologetically. "I didn't put it on . . . my team had it there almost at the time I found out."

"And if they hadn't, OneCys would have had it within a few more minutes on InstaNews," I pointed out.

"An hour . . . but those viewcreds add up."

"I'm certain they do."

"You still ought to have Kharl or someone check you out," Gerrat suggested.

"I will." He was right about that. "Do you have any better ideas about who's behind this?"

Gerrat's smile vanished. "Like you, brother, I can speculate, but I don't even have a good guess. They could be testing your personal systems in preparation for an attack on us, but that doesn't make sense, because whoever it is can't be sure they're the same. Personal systems are personal systems."

That meant he was more worried than he was saying, and that didn't help my mood much either as his image vanished.

I looked at the East Mountains until my eyes began to blur. It didn't help. Neither did another round of searches through the various netsystems.

Chapter 15
Fledgling: Kuritim, 422 N.E.

The walk from the long and low one-story quarters building was hot, despite the early morning breeze off the lagoon. Centuries back, the SysCon engineers had enlisted the environmental specialists from HMudd University to develop a hardier coral. They'd rebuilt and reshaped the atoll to meet Union needs because of its near-equatorial location, and it had become one of the principal SysCon Lift Centers. As a result of the storms during the chaos years, it also had the advantage of having few neighbors who might interfere or complain.

I turned from the sunlit blue waters of the lagoon and glanced at the brunette who walked beside and slightly ahead of me. "I didn't see you last night. . . ."

A slightly shy smile was her first response as she turned her head. That shyness that didn't seem contrived or coy. "I came in earlier, on the afternoon lifter . . . from Mancha. I slept through dinner." She was almost as tall as I was, perhaps the tallest of the women I'd seen in and around the quarters who had not been wearing FS uniforms.

"Long day?" I asked gently.

"Very."

I nodded. She was merely being polite. "I'm Daryn. Best of luck."

Surprisingly, she smiled. "I'm Wyendra Shann. Good luck to you."

"Thank you." I returned the smile. "I've read all the briefing materials they sent. Do you have any insights beyond that?"

"I've heard that the first physical training isn't quite impossible, and that the integrative abilities the FS requires make advanced study oral exams seem extraordinarily simpleminded." A shrug accompanied her open smile.

"What was . . . is your field?" I asked.

"Astrophysics, specialties in applied string dynamics and tensorial undertime flux determination."

"That's how you determine Gate placement, right?"

"One of the factors." She grinned, showing a wide mouth with white even teeth. "Transit and energy economics are the most important, though, I discovered. What about you?"

"Me? Spendthrift younger son . . . I did manage a blue in methodizing, and I'm passable on the tennis court and in swimming long distances at moderate speed."

"Then . . . you must be *the* Daryn Alwyn. I read your study on cross-optimization of multimedia inputs. The analysis was elegant, and very well written. Too well written for a methodizer."

"I thought you were an astrophysicist."

"I am, but it was fun to search the nets and come up with the most likely candidates for pilot training."

"Fun?"

"The data's all there, and it only took me an hour or so to come up with the search routines. They did the work."

I shook my head. Had my father been right—that I would be better off as a rear echelon supply officer putting in time and applying my methodizing training to the workmanlike business of logistics?

"You'll do fine—if you want to," observed Wyendra as we turned down the walkway toward the low dome.

I grinned. "Are you sure you didn't study some aspect of mental dynamics as well?"

"Practical applications. My mother."

The presence of a pair of uniformed FS rankers beside the open doors damped the conversation as we entered the small theater-like auditorium or large seminar room with slightly cushioned chairs in rows that sloped down to an open floor area. There were perhaps fifty seats, and only a handful of would-be pilots had arrived before we did.

Being contrary, I sat in the front row. Without speaking, Wyendra sat on my left.

"Do you think classes were larger?" I ventured.

"They use it for meetings of the staff," she replied.

"Have you been here before?"

"For my field work . . . but I was never in this building."

I nodded, as if I knew what her field efforts really were.

By just before eight o'clock came—zero eight hundred, I reminded myself—there were twenty-five of us in the room. Most were dark-haired, like Wyendra and me, with complexions ranging from pale white to very dark latte, although there were a few blonds. Fourteen were women, eleven were men. Most of the men were within five centimeters of my height, and all but one of the women were around one hundred eighty-five centimeters. The exception was a small blonde. She couldn't have been more than one hundred sixty-five centimeters.

"That's Cyerla Arisel," Wyendra said from where she sat beside me.

The name meant nothing to me, and I didn't bother trying to link into the net to find out why she was important. From what I'd heard, once we officially started training, the FS severed all personal netlinks anyway.

"Diplomate in three physical sciences, and that's just the beginning. . . ." Wyendra let her words trail off as, exactly at zero eight hundred, an officer stepped into the flat and circular open floor before the seats.

"Greetings." The woman in the black and silversheen Federal Service uniform smiled politely and surveyed the twenty-five of us before continuing. "You have all volunteered for training as FS interstellar pilots. As I'm sure you all know, this is an extremely difficult program. You could have screened what I am telling you, but, as you all also know, a direct verbal presentation carries more emotional validity for human beings.

"So . . . let me be absolutely clear. For each one of you here, approximately one hundred fifty others applied and were found less qualified. Based on past experience, somewhere between three and seven of you will successfully complete the course and be certified as pilots. Another two to four of you will be offered FS commissions in related work because of your particular skills and determination. In short, more than half of you will fail, and for all of you, this training will be the first significant experience in your life where you will face such a large chance of failure." She paused. "Your direct access to the netlinks will be blocked, and you will turn in all repeaters and other such devices. Once you're aboard a deep space vessel, you are limited to the ship's system, and if there's trouble, you may not even have that."

I tried not to frown. From what I had read, the chance of a ship's net failing was almost nil, unless the ship itself failed. Then, survival in any form was an extremely shortterm proposition.

No one else raised that question, either.

"A few other notes. If you wish to be a pilot, you *will* complete a military indoctrination course. Several of you will fail, not because you lack ability, but because you will find yourselves unable to accept discipline and the orders of others. You are all used to automatic superiority over others. Just remember that every line officer above you comes from the same superior background. And they all have the benefit of training and experience that you do not have, and will not have for years to come. . . .

"You signed a privacy waiver release as part of your

agreement . . . every move you make is observed—any-where. We don't care who sleeps with whom. We don't even care if you don't want to sleep. But everything you do is weighed into the determination of whether you'll be a good pilot and FS officer. . . ."

In a transparent world, and the world was transparent, that should have been obvious, and I wondered why the officer emphasized that particular point.

"You may be good pilot material, and not good officer material. We'll send you home. If you're good officer material, and not good pilot material, FS *might* offer you a commission elsewhere, but that depends on what we need. . . ."

I kept concentrating, even if what the FS officer said seemed to be obvious.

"Also, I understand it has become the fashion, once more, to refer to men as 'sir' and women as 'ma'am' or 'lady' or whatever your local linguistic equivalent may have been. I will remind you that in the FS, all superior officers are 'ser.' Period. No discussion." The professional smile reappeared, but only for a moment.

I waited for the twist, because that's the way all organizations operate. First, the ground rules, and then something to make you think, reconsider, or just feel doubtful or inadequate. I imagined that ancient samurai apprentices had faced the equivalent.

"You all are waiting for the trick or the gimmick. Every group does. There isn't one," the FS officer concluded. "We don't need one. Just meet in the adjoining building to draw your gear."

Wyendra nodded, to herself, not to me.

We stood with all the others. My hands were sticky with sweat and salt air, and I rubbed them on the legs of my singlesuit. I felt very much like a raven among eagles.

Another two days passed before I attempted to go to Mertyn's again, because after the laseflash incident, I'd pretty much taken the glider apart, or where I hadn't, at least inspected it piece by piece to make sure that there weren't any more surprises waiting for me. I didn't need anything else like the nanospray, but I didn't find a thing that shouldn't have been there.

The late afternoon trip was thankfully uneventful, late afternoon because Mertyn was still teaching, at least part time, uneventful because I'd left the belt repeater in standby, so that all incomings would be taken by my sim at the house.

The glider park next to the path to Mertyn's, if one could call the overgrown space that, was barely big enough for two gliders side by side, and marked by a weathered wooden sign, into which was carved the single name: ROSENN.

To get to what Mertyn called his cottage, I had to walk nearly a half kick from the sign along a winding path through half forest, half garden. Wild raspberries—their leaves tattered and brown-edged in late November—grew on the bottom part of the low hills whose higher levels were filled with ancient blue oaks. The wild nasturtiums filled the shaded spots below the oaks, and the air was somehow both musty, yet damper than in the lower sections of Vallura.

The path straightened and passed between two trimmed junipers. Beyond the junipers was a short stretch of grass. A two-story gray stone dwelling rose in the middle of the clearing, a dwelling with white wooden pillars that certainly had no roots in Westam. On the wide stone porch under the pillars, to the right of the white framed oak doors, were two chairs. A figure sat in one and raised his hand, motioning for me to join him.

Mertyn sat on the open front veranda that appeared unchanged from when I had visited him a year earlier—and it had remained unchanged for more than twenty years before that. The structure looked nearly two millennia old . . . with wood-framed windows, aged armaglass—rather than true antique and brittle glass—and the two wicker rocking chairs that flanked the white wicker table. All had to be reproductions, just as Mertyn was, in a way, a reproduction of an ancient pseudolib.

"You're not quite so well as the last time we met," Mertyn observed as I stepped onto the veranda.

"A little older, a little laser-burned . . . that's all."

He gestured to the other rocking chair. "A rocking chair does wonders. The pitcher is verdyn. I would have poured it, except I wasn't sure how long you'd take to walk from your glider. You used to dawdle when you were a student."

"I probably did." I settled into the rocking chair, my fingers touching the age-smoothed wood as I readjusted my weight.

"Laser-burns? Those aren't good for your health, Daryn." Mertyn looked the same, with the long narrow face, the fine dark brown hair, neatly trimmed, except for the forelock that always eased down across his forehead toward his left eyebrow, and the pointed almost-elfin jaw. "Then, you were always a little careless about that."

"It's hard to maintain one's health when people seem interested in ensuring the opposite." I poured some of the green-tinted amber verdyn into the beaker, then took a sip before setting the beaker back on the table and leaning back in the rocking chair, looking out at the late afternoon shadows that almost totally covered the short expanse of grass between the veranda and the junipers and blue oaks to the south.

"You're sure that someone is after you, and that it wasn't a mistake?"

"Once might be a coincidence. Twice is not."

"The casts just mentioned—"

"That was the second time." I took another sip of the verdyn before continuing. "I can't find any traces of who might be after me. Neither can Father or Gerrat. Nor can the CAs, but then, nobody has much to work on. It still seems rather odd in a world where almost every square millimeter is monitored one way or another."

"The only thing that might be odd is that someone exists who is motivated enough, and bright enough to carry out something like that. Oh . . . and patient enough. True motivation and patience are rare these days."

With the patience, Mertyn definitely had a point.

"I must confess I did see one of the casts. You couldn't see much but a flare of energy shrouding your glider, and the skytors' resolution left something to be desired."

"Well . . . Gerrat's people do monitor the CA net," I pointed out.

"Your brother's operation has access to everything that can be monitored."

"And he says he can't find anything."

"That's not surprising. A gardener arrives near your house a month ago and works on something. A repairman delivers something else. Or a power assessor checks a malfunctioning system. The systems monitor what people appear to do, not what they really do."

"That implies both organization and conspiracy."

"Most unsolved crimes fall into that niche. Spontaneous violent crimes show up on some monitor, and most people can't hide erratic behavior for long when they know they could always be watched. It takes organization and supreme confidence, but these days, if someone isn't discovered immediately, they seldom are." Mertyn smiled ironically before he took a sip of the pale ale he had always brewed—to me it tasted like soapy water. "And, as I said, it takes a certain motivation."

"So who's after me? The Dynae? The naturists? They have motivation."

The fine dark eyebrows lifted. "I doubt that your parentage alone, or your mildly skeptical observations on society, would raise the wrath of either the Dynae or their followers or of the naturists. You're more likely to be a target of the norm students who think all pre-selects are evil."

"That's absurd. . . ."

"Or of some radical norm organization," he continued.

I shook my head at the idea.

"What people believe, Daryn, is what they wish to believe, and that includes you."

I tried not to wince.

"As for the Dynae and the naturists, in fact, there have been favorable references to you." He laughed. "Yet you're such a creature of the establishment that you think of them first."

"So whom should I suspect? My few business acquaintances? My family? Or some students or norms who don't even know I exist?"

"Not your immediate family. Their honor—particularly your father's—would not let him even consider that. And if he had something like that in mind . . . well, he is very effective."

"You're saying that I'd already be dead."

Mertyn nodded. "Also, there's no point for Gerrat to remove you, and, unlike your father, I doubt he has the expertise or the contacts."

"I seem to have raised someone's wrath, and neither of the attempts was inexpensive." I took a sip of the verdyn.

"Perhaps you're being groomed to be a martyr. That's a good destiny for a younger son who hasn't established himself in the power structure."

"Me? I'm not a good martyr candidate, Mertyn. I'm too cynical, and I'm certainly not associated with any great causes."

"That could always come after you're safely dead." A twisted smile appeared on his thin lips. "I'm not suggesting your family is martyring you. If . . . *if* that is the motivation, it would be someone else in UniComm or the communications field who would use your death to show your father's inability to protect his own family. Or his organization."

"A power grab . . ." I mused. "Someone high within UniComm . . ."

"Or a competitor."

"Someone who knows power," I added.

"That's only one possibility," he pointed out. "There are always revolutionaries, and you make a less protected target, and you can be depicted as a playboy, dilettante edartist living off your name and the fat of the land."

"But . . . I'm working hard as a methodizer. . . ."

"Daryn . . . what you do is immaterial to how you can be depicted."

Mertyn was right about that, and it was so obvious I wondered why I hadn't considered it.

"You hadn't considered it," he added, as he often had, as though he had read my thoughts, rather than my face, "because you want to reject the image of your family. You think you're different."

Mertyn's voice said that I wasn't that different, and maybe he was right. "Who are the revolutionaries, and why would we have any?" I gestured toward the south. "People have never lived so well—even the poorest. They have a good life."

"Life is never perfect. Even a good society is not perfect, and perfection is the enemy of all that is good. Those who seek perfection will destroy an imperfect good."

"I seem to recall a lecture along those lines—and a test," I said, reaching for the beaker once more.

"Kyciro used to lecture on that. That's one of the few statements I've chosen to remember. When one can recall anything, one must be careful what one chooses to recall."

"You've said that for years." I laughed.

"It becomes more important each year," he countered. "People forget. The old pre-Collapse Noram culture had the best and most fair society in the history of the world to that point. That didn't stop it from collapsing into anarchy and civil war. The diversists insisted that the system was destroying their individual heritages. And it was. It was showing their pettiness, the lack of accomplishment, and their failures to meet the material needs of most of the members of those precursor societies. The diversists couldn't counter that argument. So . . . they focused on two things that couldn't be countered. One was that spiritual values were more important than material ones, and the second was that the dominant culture still oppressed women. Since you can't measure a spiritual value, the materialists were lost there. And since women were in an inferior social and power position, the materialists' argument that women were better off there than in any place and in any time in history before came off as mere apologism." Mertyn shrugged. "You should know the rest. Human technology may have changed, but not human nature, or not that much. Now . . . we have people protesting once more that the system isn't fair." He snorted. "Of course it's not. No system is fair. It's only a question of being as fair as possible, given the physical limits of the world and the various limits of the population. But people don't think that way."

That was history, and Mertyn had certainly beaten it into me those years before. "You're telling me that the Dynae aren't the revolutionaries. Maybe you should offer some insights into the Dynae."

"I'm never been that extreme, Daryn."

"I didn't say you were. I was talking about insights."

"You always did have fixations." He sighed. "The easiest way through this one is to disabuse you quickly."

"Please do."

"You know, Daryn . . . sometimes you're still an arrogant prig."

I winced inside. "I'm sorry."

"I don't know why I bother, except you're the best of the lot, and because I'm an old optimist." He took a long swallow of the amber brew I couldn't stand. "It goes like this. The Dynae believe in evolution, natural evolution. They oppose what they see as the misuse of genetics, particularly nonocloning. They don't believe that pre-selection is evolutionary, mainly because most parents pre-select to maximize the characteristics which allow success in the present culture. Those tend to be a combination of physical characteristics that optimize strength, reactions, and longevity and the ability to handle abstracts and spacial reasoning. Nanite augmentation is particularly helpful in further enhancing those abilities. In our current society, those are the most valuable traits. Will they always be so? The Dynae don't believe so.

They also believe that the negative long term impacts of such selection could be considerable—and greatly delayed. You aren't vociferously championing this basis of society, and you've even expressed mild concerns. You haven't gone after the Dynae or the naturists. For that matter, neither have your brother or your father. So why would the Dynae want you disabled or dead?"

"They don't, you're saying." I grinned. "Then maybe your contacts there could look into who might. I'm not having much success."

"I can ask . . . very indirectly."

"That's all I can hope for."

"It's a great deal more than you should be able to hope for, you scoundrel." Mertyn lifted his glass. "But I still have hopes for you. I might yet make you into a radical."

"What good would that do?"

"At least I'd have the satisfaction of corrupting the son of the most powerful man on the planet—and the brother of the next most powerful." He laughed.

"You haven't done that in more than twenty years."

"I'm not done. Besides, you might end up in communications yet. In a way, you are already with your edartistry."

"More than that would take both miracles and catastrophes, and I'd just as soon avoid both."

He laughed. "Such a nonconformist you are, for all of your fine words about the problems with our society."

"I don't see that radical restructuring of society or natural disasters ever improved matters much. Look at the chaos after the Collapse. . . ."

"You're quoting my own words at me, Daryn, and I do believe I know them." He grinned disarmingly.

I grinned back. "All right." Then I poured more of the verdyn. "What have I overlooked?"

"Most of the possibilities. What about wealthy women you've spurned? Or rival edartists who can't match your connections? That doesn't take into account invisible aliens, mad scientists, or disturbed eccentrics. Or distant relatives who want a larger share of the family fortune . . ." Mertyn laughed.

I shook my head. "I haven't even met any wealthy women to spurn."

"You see?" Mertyn counterfeited a mournful expression. "How's your sister?"

"You know as much as I do. She's effectively running NEN, and giving both Gerrat and Father fits. It's now the number three net system, and gaining on OneCys, and maybe even UniComm."

"Good for her! Do you hear from her often?"

"We talk once or twice a month, but it's all gossip. I know about her garden; she knows about my edartist ideas. She prefers it that way." I shook my head.

Mertyn stood. "I'm going in for another brew. I'll be right back."

So I sat in the twilight, knowing Mertyn had said and promised what he would.

And I still didn't have a solid clue. Or any thoughts about a more focused approach to find one.

Chapter 17
Fledgling: Kuritim, 422 N.E.

My strokes were long and clean as I swam out toward the channel edge of the reef, an edge marked with the black coral that the HMudd bioneers had created over five hundred years earlier. I swam at about eighty percent of my capability, according to my internals. That was the best trade-off between speed and the energy I'd have left after the swim back for the long run to the west end of the liftway.

Stroke, stroke, breathe . . . stroke, stroke, breathe . . . easy strokes, long strokes . . . I kept the rhythm constant.

When I'd finished the first klick, with another three hundred meters to the black coral, no one was within a hundred meters. The closest was Wyendra, and she was pushing harder than I was—but for the same reasons. We both would need all the lead we could get for running through the fine sand.

Stroke, stroke, breathe . . . I touched the monitor plate on the extension from the reef and turned, careful not to push off from the coral. Most of it was worn, but there were patches that were newer, and knife sharp, and running through the salty sand with a cut foot would be about the last thing I needed. While I could damp the pain, it would still affect my whole body . . . and my overall performance and time.

Stroke, stroke, breathe . . . the rhythm was so automatic that my fingers almost brushed the sands of the shallows beneath before I realized it was time to stand and start running.

The only rule about the running was that you couldn't hinder anyone else, and you had to run on dry sand. Each step on the wet sand after the first three steps out of the water added a second to your time.

It was hard to stick to my plans, but running was faster than swimming, and that meant I needed as much speed as I could spare in the first half-klick, then to settle into an even pace for the remaining two and a half klicks.

For the first two klicks along the soft white sand, I was well ahead . . . but I could sense the gap narrowing. Another three hundred meters, and there was the sound of footsteps and even breathing on the threshold of audibility.

With the course end less than two hundred meters away, I could hear clear steps in the sand behind me, not immediately behind me, but closing. I knew the steps—I'd heard them all too often in previous runs. They were those of Cyerla Arisel, and she'd always managed to catch me just at the end. My preselection profile hadn't been for long-distance running. I had the wind, but not the right kind of legs. Few among the other candidates were faster in sprints, but three klicks was a long, long way for a sprinter/swimmer.

But I'd managed to grind out another ten seconds or more in the swimming leg, and if . . . if . . . somehow I pushed it. . . .

Cyerla's steps were louder, but I eased out my stride, listening to my internal monitors, trying to balance the anaerobics with the need for speed, trying not to tighten up. But those steps kept getting closer and closer.

With a little less than a hundred meters to go to the finish monitor, I ignored my internal monitors and pulled out everything. I knew I'd pay later, but I was tired of getting nipped at the finish. It seemed insane, but I decided to try to sprint.

Cyerla didn't catch me, not this time, but only barely did I break the light beam before her, and my legs gave out a step or so past the monitors, and the two officers who watched impassively.

I had to sit on the hot sand for what seemed several minutes before I could stand, but it was really only about twenty seconds.

Wyendra had panted up third, right after I'd dropped onto the sand, and just ahead of four others.

Glancing back eastward along the expanse of sugary white sand, sand that had also resulted from the efforts of the long-ago bioneers, I watched the last ten runners struggling toward the finish.

"Daryn . . ." Cyerla was both panting and laughing as she eased her slight runner's frame toward me. "You sneak . . . all week . . . you held . . . back . . . on the swimming. . . ."

". . . You're too fast on the sand . . ." I gasped.

"Stop congratulating each other," Wyendra said. She spoiled the growling effect with a smile.

Major Ngara broke up the conversation by motioning to me. "Alwyn."

I forced my legs to carry me the few meters to where he stood. "Yes . . . ser?" The gasps I couldn't help.

Ngara's clean latte features were impassive as he studied me, probably gauging everything from respiratory rate to lactate overload. After a minute, he spoke. "Candidate Alwyn . . . you had that paced all the way from the first stroke, didn't you?"

"Ser . . . as much as I could, ser."

"You're the closest thing to a professional distance swimmer that exists, aren't you?"

"I've always liked distance swimming, ser. I've practiced a lot."

"You sprinted the last hundred meters on the sand."

"I tried to, ser."

"Good." He paused. "Try to remember that your body is not just a machine regulated by your mind and your nanites."

"Yes, ser."

He nodded brusquely and turned. "Candidate Garcya?"

"What was that all about?" asked Wyendra quietly.

"I think I got the modified lecture about not being too mechanical." I had to take another series of deep breaths.

"You didn't look that mechanical to me." She grinned. "You just couldn't stand the thought of her beating you again."

I nodded, managing a wry grin. Even after standing there for several minutes, I was still heaving deep breaths.

"Candidates!" Ngara's voice overrode all the murmured conversations. "You've got forty minutes to get back to quarters, clean up, and cool down before you're due in class. Dismissed!"

"Ser!" came the chorused response.

I turned slowly to the walkway that was hard on aching legs, but easier than lifting feet through the sugary and clinging sand.

"See you two in a bit." Cyerla smiled politely as she jogged past us back toward the quarters building.

Aaslyn strode by us right after Cyerla.

Wyendra took a deep breath. "You aren't even breathing that hard."

"Now . . ." I admitted. "My legs hurt. I'm not a runner, not really."

"You could have fooled me—or Cyerla."

"I'm not a long distance runner, then."

"You could sprint by them now. You've recovered." She grinned. "Do it one of these days."

"Too much work," I replied, smiling back at her. "Besides, I'd rather walk and talk to you."

"Don't you think that the observers will see through your façade?" She brushed her short dark hair off her forehead as we walked—quickly, but not at a jog, onto the second walkway, the one that led toward the quarters building.

In the distance, above the rustling of the palms, from somewhere out over the Pacific, came the dull boom of the mid-morning orbital lifter climbing through the atmosphere to Orbit one.

"I'm sure they do," I admitted. "That was what Major Ngara was hinting at. They can monitor my physiological reactions and get an idea of what I feel. They do that all the time. I could behave like the modern equivalent of a male gorilla beating my chest the loudest. But what would be the point? Except to prove that I can? And dissout most of the class. Also, that sort of behavior isn't exactly useful in the confines of a spacecraft. The machismo military hero went out before the Collapse."

"You're more machismo than you'll ever admit." She laughed. That was a sound I enjoyed.

All I could do was grin sheepishly.

All too soon, that walk ended, and we were both in separate quarters, scrambling into the pale gray summer singlesuit uniforms, and then on our way to class—the second day of classes, since we'd had nearly a month of physical conditioning before we started learning the knowledge basics.

This class was held in one of the rooms off the hall where we had first gathered. Wyendra and I sat in the second row. Everyone stood when the FS major walked into the classroom.

"At ease. Take your seats." The dark-haired man in the black and silver singlesuit of the Federal Service nodded brusquely. He surveyed the class "I am Major Cheng, and I will be your instructor for engineering. . . . Before we get into the engineering basics, Commander Almyra has requested that I address one of the practical aspects of your training." Cheng paused. "Why don't we put you in space with a ship and keep you there until you learn? Because piloting doesn't work that way. Neither do your bodies, and that's another kind of engineering.

"First, we don't have antigravity, and it takes gravity to keep people in top shape. Acceleration or deceleration at one gee is a fair substitute, but that's only good for insystem travel. Once you reach orbit, you're dealing with weightlessness again. Trying to spin ships or stations doesn't work either. It plays havoc with designs and maintenance, especially with the mass requirements. It is extraordinarily expensive. Since the interstellar space program is a net resource drain, we design to optimize energy and resource usage.

"So the simplest solution is to train you under the same circumstances you'll pilot and travel under. That means time on Earth getting in top shape, followed by a short period in weightlessness, followed by constant gee acceleration to a destination and then weightless. Then, in some form or another, you repeat the pattern." He smiled. "Now that we've covered that for the major, we'll get down to the engineering basics of why you're here." He looked out over the class. "Why do we have a basic engineering class at all? The guts of an LDD are very simple in theory, and impossibly complex in practice. That's just the drive, and that doesn't take into account the magscoops and fusactor conversion system that creates the reverse spin fields. Except for the three of you who are physicists and engineers . . . we'd have to take every hour of every day of your training period, and it still wouldn't be enough. So . . . why?"

I had a good idea, and a better idea that it wouldn't be the best thing to attempt an answer.

Apparently, everyone else thought the same way, because the classroom was silent.

Cheng grinned, not exactly pleasantly. "I expect answers. This isn't status game-playing where withheld information gets you points and where enthusiasm is considered gauche."

Several people nodded and offered hands, not raised enthusiastically. Mine was one of them, unfortunately.

"Candidate Alwyn, your answer?"

"Because we need a working knowledge of the power we control, ser?"

"Not just a working knowledge, but a practical and emotional understanding of exactly what an interstellar ship and Gate system are. You are expected to learn all that, and you'll be tested on it, and not in just the conventional spit-

back-the-knowledge ways, either. I don't mind telling you
why because those of you who won't appreciate it never will,
and those who do can pat yourselves on the back for the next
three seconds." Cheng paused theatrically. "The reason pilot
training is so tough has nothing to do with mechanics. Mechanically, mentally, and physically, every single one of you
has already been qualified as having the talent to be a pilot.
That's just the beginning. As I noted before, a space vehicle
represents an enormous resource commitment that we cannot
afford to lose except under the most dire of circumstances.
Second, a space vehicle capable of going to the stars is potentially the most destructive weapon ever developed in human history. We don't want just any brilliant young officer
sitting at those controls. We want someone who fully understands that, and yet who can still make nanosecond decisions—the right decisions. . . ."

As Cheng continued, I began to understand. At least I
thought I did, but that was also something I decided to keep
to myself.

Chapter 18
Raven: Vallura, 458 N.E.

I didn't sleep well the night after talking to Mertyn, and I'd already been up early the next morning reworking some of the
package for Klevyl, even though I didn't have any feedback.
When a methodizer doesn't get feedback, there are usually
only two reasons. Either you did a good enough job, and the
client doesn't want to pay for more work on that project, or it's
beyond them—unexpectedly good or even more awful. Being
too good can be worse, sometimes, than being awful, because
no one wants to admit that someone outside the organization
came up with something that good. They'd prefer a modest
improvement with which everyone is comfortable, and about

which everyone can delude themselves that, if given time or budget, they could have done as well.

As I sat before my flat desk, headset on the wood before me, fingers tapping on the smooth surface, eyes looking at the East Mountains, my mind drifted back to Elysa of the clean profile and the charming blush. She hadn't seemed like a killer. But I'd never known anyone who could have been said to be a killer, unless you counted the family . . . and that was different. Gerrat and Father made and killed parts of society, not people. Not directly, anyway.

Did Elysa belong to another family like mine? How could she and there not be any record of her existence? Or maybe that was proof in itself.

I tried to be more methodical in looking at the situation.

Item: Whoever created/modified/found Elysa had access to sophisticated nanite equipment, as least as sophisticated as Kharl's and probably more so.

Item: Elysa was intelligent, intelligent enough to have passed an informal scrutiny by both Kharl and me, and, more important, from Grete, who would have noted instantly whether we were merely looking at physical features.

Item: Expertise with genetic modification was also probably involved, one way or another, and that meant enormous financial reserves.

Item: Someone also had compiled enough of a dossier on the family to know that (1) I preferred intelligent women, and (2) where and how to catch me in a less-guarded state, one where I thought Kharl was watching who the guests were, and where I took Elysa's presence at face value.

Item: There were more than a handful of plausible reasons for the attempt: (1) dislike of my edart compositions; (2) an attempt to strike at the family or at UniComm; (3) an effort to make me an involuntary martyr; (4) an interest in harming either Klevyl's engineering firm or OneCys by slowing down their key projects; (5) a personal vendetta of which I was unaware; or (6) semi-random violence against a moderately well-known pre-select.

Item: There were probably other reasons I didn't know about.

I looked out toward the east, squinting because the sun was barely above the East Mountains, then looked away.

In one sense Father had been right. There wasn't a trace of anything . . . but what if I attacked it from the other side? Looking for what should have been there . . . and wasn't. Could I build a picture of who was after me from what was missing—an old-fashioned negative, which, when completed, could be inverted to depict my attackers? Or reveal something about them?

First, there were no obvious trails. Second, while sophisticated techniques and resources were required, there were no public spending patterns that could be traced, even by UniComm. Third, nothing was last-minute. Fourth, no one had tried to contact me—except Elysa. Fifth, Elysa didn't exist. Sixth, whatever motive existed . . .

I shook my head. The motive was power. I didn't know what kind, and I didn't know how an attack on me fit in, but someone wanted to use me as a way to power—or to destroy power. And that meant someone who already had power, and had it closely gathered, one way or another.

Elysa was the only known key. Everything else had led to the shore—it was like looking out at the ocean, where every minute was different, and no landmark stayed the same. There were the remains of the laser—every part stock, and all melted down. There were nanitic remains—very few, unique, and related to no known or registered enterprise or research institute. Even the nanite spray dispenser in my glider—I'd had it examined by a nanitic fabricating engineer I'd worked with a year earlier on a Gyster project—and he'd informed me that it was standard medical issue.

So I called up the VR of Elysa and me at Kharl's, opaque-

ing the study windows, pulling on the headset, and setting
the image for maximum contrast. Even in VR, she remained
special, and I couldn't see why. She had a clean profile, a
strong but not overpowering nose, a determined chin, and
very intent brown eyes. Trim, but not thin. Muscular, but not
overly so.

I tried looking at her more analytically. She'd worn little
adornment—silver-worked jade combs in her hair, small
matching silver ear clips with jade stones, and a jade choker.
No rings on her fingers, and a wide silver bracelet set with
spherical-looking jade stones. All her jewelry matched. Not
hugely expensive, if real, but certainly not apparently synthetic, and the style was too tasteful to be popular—and that
argued that the pieces were real, and custom-made.

Could I set up a net routine to find who might make such
a set?

It might come up null, but everything else had—or come
up so broad and inclusive as to be just as useless. I readjusted
the headset, and dropped into the net once more, this time
hopefully for a more targeted foray through the various systems. I walked down my VR corridor and opened the second
door—the searching garden with the boxwood hedge maze.
I'd liked that symbolism.

Then I got to work. The first attempt was a disaster—as
restrictively as I thought I had set the parameters, there were
more than a thousand possibilities. I tried another approach,
with cost and real stones as the principal determinants. That
wasn't much better.

In the end, I set up four different routines, each winnowing
through each other, and left them, slipping out of the boxwood maze and easing off the headset.

I looked out into the noonday light. That was one of the
problems with netting—it was all too easy to lose track of
time. My stomach growled, not surprisingly, since I'd last
eaten nearly six hours earlier, and most of my muscles felt
stiff and tired.

Standing, I stretched gently, then more vigorously, then
walked to the kitchen. I needed a break—and something
to eat.

My eyes flicked outside, to the vacant expanse around the house, and I ran a systems and security check.

Nothing, as usual.

Nothing—except two attempts to injure or murder me.

Chapter 19
Fledgling: Kuritim, 422 N.E.

Five of us stood in the coolness of the arched underground chamber, a chamber walled in a gray-tinged stone and a good hundred meters across and fifty high, an open space that would not have been possible a millennium earlier, before the development of sophisticated bioneering. The smooth white-gray walls blurred into indistinctness when I stared at them. Although we stood at near-attention, I could sense my eyes, and the eyes of the other four, looking up at the five capsule-like devices mounted on curved pedestals and gimbaled to move in any direction. I wondered why they were designed to move, when you could get the same visual effect through VR, but, like the others, said nothing as we waited for Major L'Martine to speak.

The major was small for a pre-select, no more than a hundred-eighty centimeters in height, brown-haired, broad-shouldered, and almost blocky. He studied each of the five of us in turn, starting with Sylvie Garcya and ending with me.

After another long silence, he finally addressed us. "I can see what you're all thinking. Why is FS using capsules that move when you can replicate the effect with VR? First . . . you can't replicate all the effects, as you are about to discover. And second, the visual inputs are only a part of the data you will have to process. What you will sense in the simulator is only a fraction of the intensity of both input and signals that you will experience if you reach actual deep-space training on a real ship. According to your physical evaluations, you all possess the basic neurological ability to sense the signals. Only working with the simulator will tell whether you have the mental and neurological agility to actually interpret and act upon those senses. For the purposes of the simulator, and to save resources and grief for those of you who will not make it, you will use complete headsets for the first stages of training. Those of you who make it to in-space training will be required to have implants when the time comes."

I had the very definite feeling that some of us would vanish after the simulator runs. I hoped I wasn't one of those who disappeared. Somehow . . . I had to make it.

"The simulators are actually the same as those used for training orbital lift pilots, and those of you who make it through training will hold certification as second pilots for orbital lifters. This first session is merely a familiarization. Some of you will make the mistake of regarding a mag-lifter as merely a bigger version of a ground glider, because they use the same power source. Don't. The gyro system of a glider protects you. These will allow you to destroy yourselves." His eyes raked over us again.

"Even if you're careful, the odds are that you will all crash. The question is merely how long you can maintain control and how you do it. You'll each get at least three attempts. Now . . . why are we throwing you inside a control capsule right now? Because it saves time and credits."

Major L'Martine sounded like Father, and I wanted to nod, but didn't. I also wondered how Wyendra had done. Probably better than I would.

"We've discovered that, if you understand how disoriented you can get, and how much you have to juggle, all of you who are serious study harder and learn more quickly. That's less wasteful for all of us." He smiled. "I do hope that you've all studied the checklists and the procedures." He gestured toward the arched step platforms that led to each of the simulators. "Take the one closest to you, and go and strap in."

Since I was on the left end, I walked toward the left-most capsule, and then up the curved synthetic steps that arched from the smooth stone floor up to the simulator capsule. I didn't look down from the top of the gantry-like platform, but ducked and stepped quickly inside the small space.

Once I had slid onto the replica couch, the hatch eased shut with a very definite and dull *click*. I took a moment to study the capsule—except that, since it wasn't powered up, all I saw was the dull expanse of gray before the control couch, with only a single red-lit stud. I hooked the harness leads to the headset, eased the headset on, adjusting it so that it fit snugly, and then strapped myself onto the control couch.

My fingers finally rested once more on the single lit stud in the capsule. I pressed it.

The gray expanse filled with color and all sorts of virtual readouts, most of which didn't resemble anything I'd seen in the training VR sessions, not at first. I tried to sort them out, and began to recognize the more obvious ones—like altitude readouts and speed. Above the manual data representations was a view of the liftway at Kuritim. That, I could recognize without struggling. I forced my eyes back to study each of the manual readouts, for the several moments before the system came online and buried me under streams of data. Rather they were more like comm lasers in different colors and frequencies, each conveying data in a different language or set of symbols.

As the procedures manual had indicated, I went through the abbreviated checklist, then lifted my eyes once more to the VR view of the liftway at Kuritim, the one at which we always finished those grueling runs—each and every day.

"Have you finished your checklist, Shuttle Alpha two?"

I winced.

"Shuttle Alpha two, ready to lift," I said—and added the phrase mentally.

"Cleared to begin lift-off roll, Shuttle Alpha two."

"Understand cleared. Beginning lift-out roll." Using the headset as I might have my own vyrtor, I mentally torqued the Rochford delimiters, monitoring the magfield constriction to ensure a smooth acceleration through the initial ground effect along the liftway.

Abruptly the information surged through me . . . so much that the liftway image blurred before my eyes . . . I didn't so

much hear the words or the signals as feel them . . . and my
mental translation was running far behind the inputs and my
reactions.

. . . *acceleration one point three . . . one point four . . .*
delta vee one nine zero . . . liftway remaining . . . eight thou-
sand . . . seventy-seven . . . delimiters at point nine-nine . . .
acceleration two point eight . . . attitude plus three red . . .

I eased the orbiter's nose forward—just slightly, I thought.

. . . *attitude minus two . . .*

I tried to edge the nose up just slightly.

. . . *attitude minus one . . . liftway remaining sixty-six . . .*
acceleration three point one . . .

The lifter screamed-staggered—that was the way it felt—
off the lift-way.

. . . *yaw at twenty degrees . . . increasing . . .*

The nose pitched up—why, I didn't know, and I tried to
correct. Then the left side of the lifter rose . . .

. . . *attitude plus four . . . DELTA VEE WARNING . . . DEL-*
TA VEE WARNING . . .

At the near-electric-neural shock of the warning, I mentally wrestled the nose down.

. . . *magfield imbalance . . . IMBALANCE . . . **IMBAL-***
ANCE! . . .

I cut back on the left delimiter. The nose centered.

. . . *yaw at ten degrees . . . centering . . . attitude minus*
two . . .

Before me, the screen showed the water beyond the break-
water reef screaming toward me, and I pulled the nose up . . .

. . . *delta vee warning . . . DELTA VEE WARNING . . .*

This time I was too late in readjusting the nose, and the
shuttle stall-spiralled into the blue waters of the VR Pacific.

A strobe-like flash of darkness and light, and pain
slammed through my skull before I found myself lying on
the couch looking at the same blank-featured console wall
as I had after first strapping in.

"Shuttle Alpha two, please commence checklist in preparation for lift-off."

"Commencing checklist," I answered.

The second attempt was even worse. I tried to keep the

nose centered, ran out of ground effect and skidded along the liftway, then pin-wheeled sideways into the water. The electric shock and the darkness were almost a relief.

My third attempt at lift-off was not the disaster of the second, but somehow I missed the transition to the upper mag belts, and ended up plummeting into the ocean. So I was hanging upside down, strapped to the couch waiting for the simulator to recenter itself.

"That's enough, Candidate Alwyn. When the capsule rights itself, you can unstrap and come on down." The Major's voice was laconic, matter-of-fact.

The headset went dead, and the capsule rolled upright. I was drenched in sweat when I fumbled my way out of the straps. Three of the other candidates were already standing on the smooth gray stone floor of the chamber when I reached the bottom of the steps. Sheryla Heyne was the last to join us, and she looked greener than I'd felt.

We stood there, waiting, for a good five minutes before Major L'Martine rejoined us.

He offered a perfunctory smile and then spoke. "Congratulations. You've all just discovered the basic differences between your gliders and orbital maglifters. Orbital craft have a number of advantages over various chemical-based lifters. First, they don't require nearly as much onboard power, and therefore, their empty weight to payload ratio is higher. That means they're cheaper to operate. Second, so long as no one pilots them the way you five just did, the wear and tear on the equipment is far less and they last longer. Third, they have far greater range and reliability. Around Earth, that is." L'Martine smiled. "As you all have discovered, they also have some definite downsides. They require constant monitoring, and so far, at least, even nanite-based processors are inadequate for all circumstances. Now . . . we play a dirty trick on all candidates. On a regular orbiter, there are stabilizing systems . . . but they have to be monitored constantly by the pilot, because they can't handle all field fluctuations. The reason why those systems are turned off here is so that you can learn to handle an orbiter without a stabilizer. All orbiter pilots do. Another part of that reason is that a number of the outsystem planets have nastier magfields than Earth, believe it or not. And the fields around Jupiter can be as bad as any atmospheric field. Add to that the fact that you don't have the back-up stabilizing effect of planetary gravity in space. One attitude *feels* almost the same as another. You think this was difficult? Before you're through you will be doing loops in the simulators, and it's not for stunt training, but because you could get thrown into some strange attitudes, and we want you to be able to recover from anything." Another perfunctory smile followed. "Actually, you five weren't as bad as some I've seen. But don't get any ideas . . . you have a lot of surprises coming."

Just how much worse could those surprises be than three crashes out of three attempts?

Chapter 20
Raven: Helnya, 458 N.E.

On fourday morning, I was wearing a gray singlesuit, with a dark green vest, rather than a jacket, looking over the results of my net search queries. They were quite clear. There was only one place Elysa could have gotten the jewelry. Or put another way, the search routines had found one establishment, and only one, where such jewelry was designed and sold. Again . . . that didn't mean she'd gotten it there, but it did mean that the people there might have some insights that I didn't.

The place was in Helnya—less than one hundred klicks up the coast. That fit. Why, I couldn't say, but it did. Since it wasn't exactly next door, and since I had the feeling that I needed to go there in person, I VRed.

A young man appeared on the other side of my flat table desk, just a small circular holo image—inexpensive equipment. "RennZee's," he announced.

"I just wanted to make sure someone was there before I came out."

"We only do custom work, ser," he said politely.

"My name is Daryn Alwyn. I have some questions about custom work."

Sometimes, the name is worth something. His eyes widened, slightly.

"Those Alwyns, yes," I said. "Will someone be there in two hours?"

"Yes, ser."

"Thank you." I stood and walked down to the lower level hangar.

I had already decided against taking the induction tube from Vallura to Helnya, although it would have been far quicker—and far less expensive, given the distance tax on using a glider for any travel more than five klicks. Probably I was deceiving myself, but I wanted at least the illusion of being alone, and I'd certainly get that if I took the inland ridge trail, rather than the scenic coastal path.

Once in the hangar, I slid into the seat in the glider, not without a certain amount of trepidation, although I'd already checked the glider before I went to Mertyn's, and then scanned it again after I'd returned. If someone wanted, they could still track me by tapping the public monitors of the skytors, or by calling me and letting the signal come through my belt repeater, but both taps and VR calls were monitored, and there would be a trail of sorts. Or they could have placed an inert burst locator somewhere on the glider, one that would only signal after the glider stopped and was silent for a while.

I didn't feel even half-relaxed until I was on the mid-ridge trail north. Only then did I slide the canopy half-back, and let the cool air, half-screened, flow around me under a clear blue fall sky. Some might have called the open canopy foolish, but it wasn't. No one could have known where I was headed, or how, until earlier in the day, and it would have been impossible to have mounted a laser unit that quickly without detection. When I got to Helnya, I would have to be more circumspect.

In the meantime, I enjoyed the trip. The air held the scents of oak and wine. The trail was fully instrumented, although an ancient would never have guessed how much was hidden beneath the grassy way, nor would they have guessed how many years and how much effort it had taken to create the grass itself.

As the glider gradually climbed along the route that had once been a far wider thoroughfare, say, in the time before the Collapse, I looked out to the east, out over the valley and the mixture of trees and vineyards, and isolated dwellings. I couldn't help smiling at the serenity and the beauty. Calfya was truly a beautiful place to live, despite the occasional tremors.

On the trip north there weren't more than a handful of gliders that passed me going south, and all bore couples enjoying the scenery, and the scent of the winemaking that permeated the whole region from early to late fall.

By the time I reached the outskirts of Helnya, though, there were more gliders on the byways. I closed the canopy, switched to full manual, and eased the glider along the wide and grassy ways in a general westward direction toward the bluff overlooking the ocean, passing a pair of teenagers on a magscooter, the girl seated behind the young man. The dashplot had the route to RennZee's outlined. I tried to be alert while still taking in the charm of the artists' colony.

I hadn't been in Helnya in years, not since my school days, and that had only been because Ertis had wanted to see some painter's work in one of the galleries there. Since I'd been enchanted with Ertis, and she'd wanted to go, and since I'd been low on funds, we'd taken the tube, and seen the paintings, and then I'd taken her to dinner at a uniquery—I'd had to choose between dinner or the glider, as I recalled. I didn't remember the name of the place, but most of the eating places remaining in Noram—or elsewhere, I supposed—fell into a handful of categories, those providing standard replicator fare for travelers and others away from home, those designed really as meeting places, and the small handful of uniqueries, where every element of a meal was hand-prepared and guaranteed unique. Uniqueries were expensive, needless to say.

Still . . . while I didn't remember either the paintings or the uniquery, I did remember Ertis being pleased. I smiled. She'd been very pleased—even if I hadn't been able to get the glider. I could still remember checking my credit balance, and deciding I didn't dare anger Father.

Glancing around as I followed the directions on the dash-plot toward the center of the place, I tried to recall and identify what I'd seen years before. The center of the town was almost lost among the trees, and the gardens, in which were set houses that looked frozen in time—a low hacienda from nearly two millennia before set less than three hundred meters from a pre-Collapse media house, and that was adjacent to what might have been an Anglish cottage.

Then there was a square, and something I did recognize—the tube station. Past the low gray stone and green tile roofed building that was the upper level of the tube station, there was a clustering of artisan shops, and three art galleries—right in a row ahead on my left.

I eased the glider past another magscooter, this one bearing a white-haired norm woman with large sack strapped in the second seat.

The first gallery's sign was simple—"Gallery West." Beyond the third gallery was a stone retaining wall, dating back centuries to when people actually cut into hills and thought their work would last. Above the wall seemed to be a park of some sort. I looked more intently. It was an old, old cemetery.

Off to the side of the glider path on the right, on the same side as the galleries, but after the last gallery, the one Ertis and I had visited so many years before, there was a larger squarish glider, a delivery type, with a side panel open. Two men were bent over, inspecting something inside.

I nodded sympathetically. Even the best equipment sometimes had problems. I'd seen that often enough in Federal Service.

"Oh!"

At the sound of the high yell that sounded girlish, my head

flicked back to the retaining wall. A small figure hung from the top coping stone of the vine-covered wall, her body swinging a good three meters above the stone walk below.

"Help!" came a second call.

I pushed the glider ahead, past the men working on the delivery vehicle, seemingly oblivious to the girl, then jerked it to a stop at the edge of the gliderway. I half-climbed, half-vaulted from the glider, automatically linklocking it, as I sprinted toward the child whose fingers seemed to be slipping, loosening so that she started to swing across the front of one of the huge gray blocks of stone.

She wore a pale blue singlesuit, and her eyes were wide.

My fingers reached up to help the child down . . . and touched nothing—brushing the stone, despite the realistic image.

Supraholo image! I glanced back toward the glider, but the canopy was still locked shut.

Craaacckkk . . .

I looked up to see the entire stone wall seemingly toppling down on me—slowly, with stones that suddenly seemed as large as small gliders arching toward me. Slow as they seemed, I moved even more slowly. I still thought I might get clear when the ground underfoot gave way.

Again . . . as the very real antique stones and the darkness crashed over me, I had the feeling that I'd been more than a little slow—and very stupid.

Chapter 21
Fledgling: Supra-Ecliptic Space, Sol System, 423 N.E.

"Deceleration halting. Deceleration halting. Commencing weightlessness. Commencing weightlessness. Fifteen minutes before maneuvers commence. Fifteen minutes before maneuvers commence." The voice was that of Sylvie Garcya, Pilot

Candidate Garcya, as she completed her stint at the controls of the *FSS Prasad*.

With my body suddenly lightening in the harness, I glanced sideways from the student couch where I waited toward the candidate strapped in to my right.

"That was a little rough," murmured Aaslyn Muriami.

"Aren't we all?" I murmured back with a rueful smile.

Aaslyn rolled his eyes.

I glanced up at the overhead. Everything in the *Prasad* seemed to be some color shaded with gray. The overhead was a grayish cream. The deck was a darker gray, although, in half the time the *Prasad* wasn't accelerating or decelerating, it was impossible to feel which was which. That was probably the reason for the colors, some form of reminder as to what was where when the ship was under power, except that even half that time what was "up" was really down, or the other way around, except on long decels.

In a way, the ship also smelled "gray," with the odor of oil, people, metals, and composites of all temperatures, and food all swirled together.

Major L'Martine had been clear enough about some of that when he'd said that there was no way to build a ship cost-effectively that would allow every exposed surface to serve effectively as overhead, deck, or bulkhead. So the Federal Service didn't. The deck was down for acceleration, and—on long runs—for deceleration. For training maneuvers, everyone was just strapped in, and if your harness weren't snug, you ended up with a lot of bruises.

As I waited, I took a slow deep breath, knowing what was coming.

"Candidate Alwyn. You're up next." Major Imoro's voice was pleasant enough, but she had a reputation of being tough on candidates. The increasing raggedness of Sylvie Garcya's handling of the *Prasad* confirmed that—at least to me.

"Yes, ser." After releasing the harness and sliding out, careful to keep a boot toe locked under the couch coaming, I relocked the harness, then hand-over-handed my way along the narrow passage between the couches in the candidate waiting area to the control center.

My stomach had finally adjusted to weightlessness, and I pulled myself down toward the couch where Sylvie had just unstrapped. Her back to the major, who remained strapped in the left couch, Sylvie floated beside the student control station, her face composed. Her face was always composed. "Good luck," she murmured.

"Thank you." I offered a grateful smile. I knew I could use the luck, and more than that.

I readjusted the harness, then slid into the couch, where I connected the control line to my own helmet, testing the links to make sure I had complete bandwidth control. Then I had to tighten the harness, struggling to ensure that the straps were tight, since using leverage in weightlessness wasn't automatic to me. Next came the personal testing routine, and the start-up checklist.

Major Imoro's head turned slightly.

Sylvie had slipped back to her student couch behind the bulkhead beside Nikko Patel.

I mentally checked the time since Sylvie's announcement. "It's six minutes to go."

"You're cleared to make any announcements." The major's voice was low, but it carried.

I waited another thirty seconds, and then keyed the ship's system. "Resume acceleration stations. Maneuvers will commence in five minutes. Maneuvers will commence in five minutes."

Major Imoro touched the console, and I was flooded with inputs from the entire ship.

... sixty degrees absolute ... stern sensors ... fusactors at ten percent ... absolute speed less than point five NL relative Sol ... magscoops in shield mode ... no EDI traces within one thousand LS ... converters at twenty ...

The ship felt red against the black cold of semideep space, where the molecular density was less than dozens per cubic meter. Nearer the center of the ecliptic, the sensitivity of the sensors had to be adjusted, because, otherwise, they gave a pilot the impression of guiding the ship through a fog. But the greater sensitivity was necessary farther out because a pilot needed to be able to monitor the loads on the system, particularly the stress on the magscoop fields.

I moistened my lips and began the second checklist—the one for all ship systems, the important one. My mind still felt as though it were moving through a gluey fog as I ran the comparisons against the optimal level.

Abruptly, I frowned. "Scoop sensor three . . . no reading."

"Good," pulsed Imoro. Just as suddenly the sensor registered on the system.

"System review complete and green," I announced when I finished.

"You have the con, Candidate. Proceed to accelerate to point one ell, then execute a Kirwan turn, and commence a standard approach to gamma three." Major Imoro's tone made it clear that something would go wrong on the approach to the beacon that served as the reference point.

"Maneuvers commencing in one minute. Maneuvers commencing in one minute." My voice sounded harsh over the net and the ship's speakers.

I scanned the motion detectors and harness locks to make sure all the ship's personnel were in their couches before pulsing the major. "All personnel are restrained, ser."

"You are cleared for full power-up and scoop extension."

"Understand cleared this time. Commencing power-up and acceleration." I eased up the power flow from the fusactors, watching as they climbed past twenty percent, then twenty-five, where the scoop fields began to extend. Initial acceleration was barely noticeable, just the slightest of pressures, because the gathering efficiency of the magscoops was a function of power and velocity, and without the input from the scoops, the LDD that created the photonjets was only operating at a fraction of potential output. While the ejv was near max, the photon stream volume wasn't.

Even though the *Prasad* seemed to be moving slowly at first, that velocity built within seconds to speeds that would have ripped an atmosphere apart with the ship's passage. The acceleration increased almost as quickly, pressing me back into the couch.

. . . acceleration at point four gees . . . point eight . . . one point one . . . two point three . . .

I could feel the sweat oozing from under the soft helmet, even as I continued to try to check everything, wondering what and how the major would ensure went wrong.

The sensors showed the beacon dwindling behind us, and I automatically switched scales on the relative plot.

"You can begin the Kirwan turn any time, Candidate."

I'd already programmed the turn, and brought the macro online, monitoring the system as the scoopfields altered their configuration, and as the ejection field nozzles redirected the photon flow.

Just as I'd let out a long slow breath against the still increasing gee force, the left half of the magscoop net vanished, and the ship slewed, its acceleration decreasing precipitously, and the attitude dropping seventy red. Demand draw on the fusactor skyrocketed, climbing toward the red of overdraw. The ship's heading immediately began to revolve to starboard, into what would become an ever-tighter spiral down into the ecliptic and probably the Kuiper Belt and all the garbage that would shred the now-unprotected port side of the *Prasad*.

... *scoop imbalance* ... *IMBALANCE* ...

The left half—that meant the left converter had gone. I dropped power to half on the right net output nozzles, then reconfigured the net phasing so that the entire net was handled by the right converter.

My stomach lurched as the acceleration dropped from nearly three gees to near-nothing, and I swallowed.

The magscoop shimmered back into a unified and balanced energy net—if one invisible except to the ship's sensors—but its area was more like forty percent of what it had been moments before, and the acceleration climbed back to around point five gee, then edged up.

Major Imoro said nothing.

I corrected the heading and attitude to "climb" back toward the beacon that served as a representation of either a Gate or an orbit station. Needless to say, no one was going to let any of us near the ecliptic or a real Gate or station—nor in a ship with passengers or real cargo—not with the power of a magscoop, photonjet ship—until they were quite assured of our capability.

Then I had to replot the entire turn and approach to take into account the lower acceleration and the power requirements. The time seemed to drag, but it was less than two minutes before I had a stable profile for the lower gee approach.

The magscoop vanished entirely. So did acceleration— leaving my stomach lurching in sudden weightlessness—or, more properly, without the artificial gravity provided by acceleration.

. . . Shields at minimal . . . shield reserves at thirty, declining . . . twenty . . .

My mind felt as if I were slogging through heavy syrup as I flashed through the diagnostics before I discovered that an interrupter had taken the power conduit from the fusactor to the right convertor off-line. I patched the conduit from the left convertor through the standbys, and then reduced the overall power load, reconfiguring the magscoops to twenty-five percent of full span, hoping my calculations were correct.

Once again, the acceleration built, leveling out at around point seven gee.

"Do you know why you lost the scoops?" asked the major.

"Because the power load creates more heat when it's asymmetrical?" I was trying to recall the exact language.

"Close enough. In another two minutes, the conduit will be cool enough to put back online. I'll give full scoops then. Otherwise we'll be out here for another three hours for a single approach. And that won't set well with the other trainees, and it certainly wouldn't set well with the captain or the passengers on a real run."

"Yes, ser."

The conduit did cool, and I got full magscoop capability back and I didn't incinerate the beacon on decel the way Aaslyn had. And I *thought* I'd actually brought the *Prasad* to an absolute halt relative to Sol.

I just waited for the major's orders after that.

Her words followed a silence of about a minute. "Announce a thirty-minute stand-down, and then a constant acceleration return to base," Imoro ordered. "We'll start with your debrief once we're under way back to Earth Orbit Three. Get something to drink. Your system monitors say you're dehydrated, and you won't understand half of what I tell you."

"Yes, ser. You have the con."

"I have it. Be back in twenty."

"Yes, ser." I eased out of the harness, and disconnected the leads, pulling myself back to the small officers' galley. I swallowed back a touch of nausea.

Sylvie Garcya offered a smile as I passed the candidates' couches. I returned it with a smile of my own and a shrug.

We both knew that the "bad" part of the trip was just beginning—a day plus of constant one gee acceleration/deceleration to take us back down to Earth Orbit Three. After several hours of intensive debriefing for each of us, there would be a period of two hours in the couch with one of the instructors, being taken through ship system after ship system, quizzed, grilled, and thoroughly worked over. There were five instructors—all majors—and all *very* thorough.

Chapter 22
Raven: Kewood, 458 N.E.

I dreamed for a long time, and most of the dreams were nightmares of various sorts, ranging from being a raven pursued by eagles, and falling walls, to being swallowed by octagonal Gates in deep, deep space. I felt hot and cold by turns, sometimes shivering in ice, other times feeling as though I were being turned on a spit over a fire.

When I woke for the first period of real awareness, Kharl and Gerrat were both by my bedside, except it was a medcradle and not a bed, and every part of my body itched. My arms and hands were restrained, of course.

"You're going to be all right," Gerrat said.

"But it's going to take more time," Kharl added.

"A lot more." I tried to speak, but the words came out mumbled.

"You need to know you'll heal," Kharl said.

"When you're better, we'll need to talk about why you were climbing on shaky walls," Gerrat said.

I tried to shake my head, but it was also restrained.

"You'll be better than new," Kharl promised. "You're stronger than anyone thought." He laughed, softly, and even pain-drugged as I was, I could sense a certain irony and bitterness there.

But the last of his words blurred, and I dozed off.

When I woke later, lying cradled in the medweb, nanites scurrying to rebuild me, I wondered how I'd gotten to the point where people were trying to kill me—a not-quite-obscure edart composer, from a far less than obscure family. And I still didn't understand why they weren't after Father— or Gerrat.

Whoever it happened to be knew me well . . . far too well, yet paradoxically not well enough . . . or so it seemed. They knew my likes, knew I would be intrigued by Elysa, knew I often guided a glider with the canopy open. They knew my fondness for children, and my impulsiveness.

But pushing a wall over on me? That wasn't anything that could be identified as a murder, not really, and neither was an anaphylactic reaction. Only the laser attack fit that definition. What bothered me was the means—or the combination of means, really. If I were a threat to vested interests in society—those with the means to get me murdered—the anaphylactic attack and the wall were perfect, because I would have died from seminatural causes, with no great publicity, and the like, associated with my death.

Contrary to popular wisdom, death itself does not automatically create well-known martyrs. The death must be highly visible, and martyrs have usually been created by the living to further various ends of those still alive. I had no desire either to die unknown or to find what I espoused being twisted for other purposes—say by the Dynae, who could use me as a martyr by claiming that the pre-selects had tried to eliminate me because I was beginning to espouse their cause, or by the naturists, who would be even more extreme . . . or conceivably by my own family, who, while mourning my demise, would have little difficulty in using me or my death to bolster UniComm and their way of life.

Yet I knew Gerrat well enough to know that he didn't have the guts or the coldness to mastermind my death. He'd be happy to use it, if it suited his purpose, but not create it.

Was the laser attack meant to fail, unlike the other two? Was it a warning? And if it happened to be, why? And by whom had it been set up?

How had I gotten into such a mess? What in my life had led to all this?

That question reverberated through my mind as I slipped back into darkness. . . .

Chapter 23
Fledgling: Kuritim, 425 N.E.

The black and silver uniform looked good in the quarters' mirror, especially with the short dress jacket, and I did spend a moment looking at my image. After more than three calendar years, and two years personal objective time, I was actually going to get my wings.

I laughed softly. The symbol of wings remained, even though wings were of no use beyond an atmosphere, although I had already received, the afternoon before, just left in my lockerbox, a small certificate with the Federal Union logo which proclaimed that I was a licensed orbital shuttle operator [second], and a licensed commercial flitter pilot [unrestricted]. There had also been two certs added to my quals on the Federal Union roster.

I straightened and adjusted the black beret, permacotton soft to the touch, then stepped out onto the walkway outside the door of my quarters. The breeze off the lagoon was just enough to keep the heat from being overpowering. For the moment, the rooms beside mine were quiet, since the candidate trainees in the group behind ours were off-planet. I caught a glimpse of brown hair and another new FS uniform singlesuit ahead of me, and walked quickly to catch up with Wyendra.

"Congratulations," I offered with a smile.

She stopped and smiled back, somewhat shyly. "Thank you."

"It's been a long time since the first day we walked here."

"In some ways," she agreed.

We turned and walked toward the same hall where we had begun three years earlier, almost lagging, as if . . . I wasn't quite sure why.

"Life will change, Daryn. More for you than anyone."

"You think I'm that different from when I came?"

Her fine eyebrows lifted. "What do you think?"

I shrugged. "It's hard to tell. I haven't seen anyone that's not in the Federal Service for what . . . a good year now, since our last holiday leave."

"And how was that leave?"

I nodded, then grinned. "You're right. Again." I paused. "What about yours?"

"Better than yours, I would guess." Her generous mouth offered a smile. "My family sees it as an honor."

"My parents are proud. Mother even VRed this morning— or last night, really."

"Proud . . . but your wanting to do it bewilders them."

I shrugged. "I think everything I do has bewildered them."

"Good!" Wyendra laughed.

So did I, even as I wondered why, but for the moment her smile and laughter and the coming ceremony were more than enough.

We turned down the walkway to the hall, followed by Sylvie Garcya and Lara Cliena. Cyerla Arisel was already waiting at the back of the dimmed dome, talking quietly with Takeo Kurami.

The sunshine boys—Mikhail Petrus and Ibrahim Halevi—strolled up shortly—all smiles.

"Lieutenants . . ." The quiet voice came from Major Ngara. "If you would fall into ranks . . ."

I held back a smile. It was the first time I could recall that the major had made a request, rather than given a order. We all lined up. Then a tall commander in the black and silver singlesuit and a formal jacket with a lot of silver on the sleeves stepped forward at the front of the hall. My eyes raked the seats. There were perhaps two dozen people there, most of them FS officers who had trained us in one way or another. The scene was being relayed via the net to our families, but it was clearly a Federal Service ceremony.

We marched forward, then redeployed into a line abreast. I was at the far left, Cyerla at the far right, with Wyendra roughly in the middle. We stood there in silence for a moment.

"In a modern technological society, ceremonies might appear anachronistic," began the slender commander. "They are not. Ceremonies at their best should mark outstanding effort and achievement. They should signify passages of import and commemorate the outstanding. These become more important in a world where anyone can achieve some measure of notoriety through mere persistence and outrageousness.

"Only the very best apply to become FS pilots, and only one in a thousand of those applicants, on average, completes the training successfully. That is a notable achievement. A most notable achievement based on ability, education, dedication, and skill." The commander's lips quirked into a rueful smile. "Having said that, I must also caution you that much of your real learning and achievement lies ahead, and that, again on average, only one in ten of you will ever command a starship. Part of that is because some of you will choose career paths that lead elsewhere, but even so, the journey ahead is not only brilliant with starlight, but difficult. . . ."

She nodded briskly. "As your name is called, please step forward."

I didn't have to know the first name. It was mine. As Wyendra had predicted, Cyerla was first in the class; Wyendra was fourth, and I was eighth—and last . . . and happy to have survived.

The commander waited for me to approach and halt.

"Lieutenant Alwyn, you and this group have perhaps the most unique distinction in many years. This class is the largest class ever to make it through training. As a matter of fact, the curricula and the training were reevaluated several times because of your efforts. We wished to ensure that standards were being maintained." She looked beyond me. "Every one of you here might well have been first or second, certainly no lower than third, in any other group of candidate officers over the past decade. It is a distinction to recall with pride." Her eyes went back to me as she slipped the wings into the holder on the black formal jacket, and her voice lowered into almost a murmur, one clearly not designed to be picked up by the VR system. "Your determination, Lieutenant, was particularly noteworthy."

"Thank you, ser." I managed to keep the smile off my face, but probably not out of my eyes.

"And I imagine the personal pressure was greater than anything FS could have applied. Just keep up that effort. It doesn't stop with the wings."

"Yes, ser." Her last sentence wasn't quite a jolt, but it was a sobering reminder that the FS would always be looking over my shoulder more than the shoulders of others, because the Federal Union and its administrators prided themselves on the Union's objectivity.

She nodded, and I turned.

"Lieutenant Garcya."

I was glad Sylvie had made it. She'd worked harder than anyone.

"Lieutenant Halevi . . ."

"Lieutenant Shann . . ."

I did smile when the commander slipped the wings on Wyendra.

Then, after the commander finished winging us all, and we stood in line, she said. "Now . . . repeat after me. . . . 'I . . . do affirm with all my spirit and ability that I will support and defend the peoples of all the Earth and the Federal Union which represents them, that I will never abuse the powers and authority that may be granted me, and that I will respect and obey the laws of the lands of the Federal Union. . . . ' "

There was a moment of silence after the affirmation.

The commander looked at each of us in turn. "Your postings are awaiting you, and you each have two months home leave. Congratulations, Lieutenants."

She nodded once, and the short "Fanfare for Mortals" rang through the domed hall.

At that, I turned and grinned at Sylvie. "You did it."

She smiled back. "So did you."

Wyendra joined us, and for a long moment we just exchanged glances under the raised dome of the hall.

"It seems so strange," Sylvie murmured.

"You'll get over it," offered a new voice, that of Major Ngara. "After about three hours as junior pilot on a long run to Gamma Gate." He laughed. "But enjoy it now. Congratulations to all of you." He looked at me. "Just keep remembering that you do have a body, Lieutenant."

"Yes, ser."

He was gone, and Wyendra raised her eyebrows.

"Remember the first time I finished the run before Cyerla?"

She frowned, then shook her head.

"He does. He said something like that then."

"Daryn . . ." Sylvie said gently.

I turned.

"Everyone will always remember what you do." Her words weren't particularly loud or forceful, but I knew I would remember them. "Always."

Half-encased in regrowth and back-cloning/replacement apparatus, and not feeling terribly creative, there wasn't much I could do except watch the nets and listen to whoever came into my room. Mostly, that was Kharl, although Mother used the VR nearly every day, as well as visiting several times, and so did Father and Gerrat. Kharl stopped by at least once a day, but he kept things to the medical side, even when I baited him, saying that we'd "talk about it later."

Then, finally, he came in with a serious expression on his face, and I knew he was sure I was fully back to normal, at least mentally.

"I've been thinking, Daryn."

"So have I." I gestured around at the equipment. "That's one thing all this doesn't limit. And you've decided we can finally talk?"

He nodded. "How did you manage to have a wall topple onto you?" Kharl tilted his head slightly and quizzically. "And why in Helnya?"

"Well . . ." I dragged out the word. "It's like this. My cousin the doctor introduced me to this lovely woman. I immediately get a violent allergenic reaction and almost die. I start trying to find this woman, and someone else tries to fry me with a laser. When I discover another lead on her, someone else lures me out to rescue an illusory child and drops a wall on me." I smiled brightly at Kharl. "And my cousin the doctor wants to tell me what? That my allergenic reaction was an accident, that a laser beam aimed at my glider was a malfunctioning comm laser, and that I just imagined that there were rocks falling on me?"

"The report was that you were climbing a cemetery wall."

"I was. There was a little girl about to fall." I shook my

head. "Of course, she was a holo image, but by the time I realized that, it was a little late."

"Have you told the CAs?" he asked.

I laughed, but only for a moment, because it hurt my ribs. "I'm not exactly in shape to run down there, and what would I say? I was chasing a holo illusion, and the illusion dumped rocks on me? I'm going to VR them from a medcenter and say that?"

"They've been calling to see when you could talk to them. I finally said yes when they called a while ago. Someone will be here to talk to you shortly."

"Kharl . . . just what do you think? You tried awfully hard to get me to think I was just suffering from an allergenic reaction. Why? What's going on?"

"I don't know." Kharl shrugged. "I really don't. I don't know who Elysa is, but I couldn't and I can't believe she meant you harm." He paused, almost as if to let me sort out his reaction.

That bothered me, because my nanites and every feeling I had said he was telling the truth.

"I didn't know anything about the laser or this accident until after each happened."

He was telling the truth about both of those as well, and I began to get really concerned, because I'd been thinking he had something to do with it. But he looked as worried as I felt, and generally, I could read Kharl pretty well.

"I just think you'd better be very careful," he added.

I'd already figured that out. I'd also realized that being careful might not help me get to the bottom of things, either.

"What else should I know?" I asked.

"I wish I knew." He smiled sadly.

That was all I really got out of him, and after he left, I decided to study the short message that Mertyn had left for me sometime while I'd been unconscious. As much as anything, I wanted to see it again to get my mind off the itching and the sweet-acrid odors of regrowth solutions that permeated the medcenter room.

I called it up again, and got his image, half-cut off by the equipment surrounding me. But it was Mertyn—fine dark hair, elfin jaw, and the slightly ironic delivery.

... whoever it may be that wishes you less than the best of health, I can assure you that those involved are not the ones you mentioned as first suspects. Those you mentioned would much prefer you and your sister enjoy a long and healthy life. . . .

That brought a frown, especially the mention of Elora, but I kept watching and listening.

... my suggestion is that you watch for less obvious sources, and consider that perceptive elites try to avoid discontent by whatever means possible. This is particularly true of those members of the elite whose positions are most vulnerable to change. Look at societal discontent, and then analyze who benefits from change and who will suffer.
... I'm headed for a wilderness hike for the next few weeks . . . we should get together when you're feeling better. . . .

Mertyn had more to say, but he wasn't about to say it except in person. He never had, and I couldn't say I was surprised.

I had barely blanked the image when the Civil Authority officer in his off-white and gray uniform appeared at the doorway to my room. He was tall and lanky, especially for a norm, and very young looking. He had big hazel eyes, and an apologetic manner, even before he spoke.

"Daryn Alwyn?"

"That's me, or what's left of me."

"The office asked me to talk to you."

"Yes . . . about the . . . accident?" I certainly wasn't about to call it attempted murder, even though that was what it had been, because I was sure there would be no hard evidence, as I'd already told Kharl.

He nodded as he pulled out a small VR recorder. "Would

you mind if I VRed this? That way, no one will have to bother you again."

"VRed? Ah . . ." I didn't know quite what to say. Was I in trouble? For getting hit with a wall? Yet my own internal nanites showed no tension in the CA, and usually someone about to give bad news showed tension.

"There's been talk about restitution from the Helnya Town Authority for neglect of the cemetery wall that collapsed on you, but that requires a CA report."

"Oh." The way he talked made me very wary. I wasn't wary about him. Even in my impaired state, I could tell he was telling what he thought was the truth, and that he was truly innocent and trying to do his duty. That worried me more than if he hadn't been. I looked down at the tubing and pressure slings around my legs. "And you'd like my story."

"Yes, ser."

"You can tell that a lot of stones fell on me," I inclined my head toward the consoles to the left of the bed. "I was headed westward toward the ocean, when I thought I heard someone crying for help, and I stopped the glider. I got out and hurried over to look—and then there were stones everywhere." All that was the truth, not all of it, but certainly an accurate physical description of what had happened.

"Did you ever see anyone, ser?"

"I couldn't be sure," I said. "Then, I didn't have time." I looked at the young CA and asked, "Didn't the skytors pick up anything?"

"Yes, ser. They showed just what you said."

"I thought there were some men with a glider-van somewhat farther back toward the center of town. Perhaps they saw it, too."

He spread his hands helplessly. "If they were there, they were too far away. The monitor frames for the area around the old cemetery just show you and your glider."

I frowned. "I thought they were closer, but then, I might just have remembered them as closer than they were."

"That could be. The doctor said you were very fortunate to have survived."

In short, the young CA felt I was confused by my near-death experience. "What about the wall? Was it . . . I mean, how did it happen?"

He shook his head. "It could have happened to anyone. The drainage system had a leak, and it had softened the ground under the wall, and loosened most of the old mortar, but the front of the wall had been sealed years ago, so there was nothing visible. And there was a sinkhole right under the front of the wall, that collapsed under your weight and all the stones. Probably, when you touched the wall, that was just enough."

Except that my fingers had barely brushed the wall stones. I still recalled the shock from when they had gone through the supraholo image. "Whatever . . . it certainly was a shock." I paused. "Now what happens?"

He smiled shyly. "I don't know everything, sir. The super, he just said that they needed a report from you, and they'd send it with everything to the local FU Claims Authority. This is the first one of these I've done. He said to tell you that you'd get a copy, and that probably your compensation would be based on what your personal medical doesn't cover and your annual earnings for the past two years."

"I see." I shook my head. "I'm glad someone is on this. I'm certainly in no shape to handle it."

"Thank you, ser." He snapped off the VR recorder and slipped it back into the small case attached to his belt. "I'm sorry to bother you, ser."

"I'm not doing much else, officer, and I appreciate your coming by." I did, if not exactly for the reasons he might have thought.

After he left the room, I wanted to shiver. There was no record, even in the skytors banks, of the two men and the glider-van. All the records showed was my reaching for the top of the wall, as if to yank out a stone, and then the entire wall just cascading down around and on top of me. And the "sinkhole" explained even more. I'd have bet that someone had used nanitic excavators to remove that dirt.

Had I just been imagining the men and the child? I shook my head. The girl's image had been projected VR, and at the right angle, wouldn't have been picked up by a satellite scanner, even with high resolution. But I hadn't been imagining the men. That, I was sure about, and that bothered me. A great deal. It was theoretically possible to project an image—had the two men projected an image that just showed their section of the road as empty? That kind of equipment, while not horribly expensive, showed both resources and all too much forethought for me to be a casual or incidental target, as did most of what had happened to me recently.

First, a woman who didn't exist tried to kill me. Then, a device planted in a way that no one could detect tried again, and finally, two men who didn't even show up in the FS skytors monitor banks dropped a wall on me, and there was no record of anything except the wall falling. The town of Helnya was very sorry and would probably compensate me.

All that meant that someone had known where I was going, and possibly why. They'd either tapped my system or the jeweler's. Probably the latter would have been easier, but that meant they knew who I was looking for. Any way I looked at it, the possibilities were unappealing.

And then Mertyn had sent a message suggesting that people who might have been friends were my most likely enemies, and those I'd considered possible enemies were friends.

And I still didn't know who or why.

Chapter 25
Fledgling: Yunvil, 425 N.E.

Wearing a uniform as dress for dinner wasn't forbidden, merely in bad taste. So, when I arrived home on predeparture leave, I wore my uniform down to dinner—the silversheen and black dress version, and the double bars of a full lieutenant and the silver wings with the star and ship.

As always, I was the first one to arrive in the upper hallway, and I nodded to the star-surfing young woman, murmuring, "We do have a few things in common, young lady."

I had seen, of course, that the star clusters and the darkness looked nothing like the way that Meraal had sculpted them, but that only gave me yet another rational reason to prefer the traditional Hui-Lui painting of the woman and the open sunlit gate.

"Daryn!"

I turned to see Gerrat coming from the front of the upper level, accompanied by two attractive women, one black-haired, one red-haired, the first redhead I'd seen in years.

"Daryn . . . this is Rhedya." Gerrat nodded to the dark-haired woman.

"Enchanted to meet you." I bowed my head to the beauty who was about to become Gerrat's spouse.

In his tailored deep blue singlesuit, Gerrat offered his winning smile before turning to the younger woman to his left. "And this is Emelle. My younger brother Daryn. He's just finished deep space pilot training and is on leave before his first assignment."

"I see you younger folk have already beaten us." My father's voice filled the corridor, and his eyes went to my FS uniform. His lips formed a pleasant smile, the smile reserved for the times when he was less than perfectly pleased with me. I'd grown up learning that smile. "You look most official, Daryn."

"I'm certain I do, sir." I bowed, knowing that refusing to explain, and merely agreeing with him, would be far more useful.

"He looks good in it, dear," added my mother slipping up beside Father. "And he's certainly earned it . . . and the wings. So he ought to be able to show them off." She smiled brightly. There had been just the faintest emphasis on the words "show them off."

"You are most effective, Mother." I grinned.

"Thank you, dear. One learns."

At least there was a smile in her eyes.

"Shall we?" asked Father, although it wasn't a question.

We all followed him into the dining room and seated ourselves, with Emelle to my left, next to Father on our side, across from Rhedya.

The spring greens and alerca melon strips on the plates set before us were crisp, perfect, but, then, even salads had to be perfect.

The young redhead offered me a warm smile. "How was the training? People say it's difficult."

"Very difficult," Father answered for me, "even with all Daryn's background and advantages."

"Very hard," I said with a smile. "Long . . . and I'm glad to be done."

Emelle nodded.

"It's quite an accomplishment even to be selected," my father said. "They select the very best, and the attrition is between seventy and eighty percent."

"I'm glad to be here." I smiled politely, and waited for Emelle to take a spoonful of the alerca melon before I followed her example.

"What do you do now?" she asked.

"I have two months home leave. After that, I'm posted to the *DeGaul*."

Emelle frowned, and I could sense that she was accessing the net to see what there was on the ship or anything related. She had to have an implanted link, and I wondered at that. I hadn't gotten one that sophisticated until the FS had given me one as part of the mods for the last stage of pilot training, and I tried not to use it in company, perhaps because my parents had suggested that doing so was impolite.

I took another bite of the melon and smiled at Rhedya, knowing that we'd be exchanging smiles for a long time. Her smile was vaguely sympathetic, but there was a cool mind shielded behind the trained smile.

"He was a pre-Collapse leader, wasn't he? The one they named the ship after?" asked Emelle.

"I didn't look it up," I replied. "I probably will before I report. What else did you find out?"

"Gaul was the name of a part of East Euro in ancient times, and a Roman politician once wrote a book about how he conquered it." Emelle offered the smallest of shrugs.

"Nothing new there," commented Gerrat. "Every piece of the globe has been conquered at least a handful of times."

"And the conquerors promptly forgot that they stole it from someone else so that they could claim some sort of moral right to the land when someone else tried to take it away from them," I suggested.

"But . . . of course." Gerrat beamed his utterly charming smile. "And you are going to become one of those conquerors in a few weeks, I dare say."

I hadn't thought about Federal Service in quite those terms. While FS ships carried nothing that was expressly a weapon, the magscoop fields were shields, and the ship certainly had capabilities for wreaking destruction on hostile objects. But the only thing that had seemed to menace humanity since the collapse had been humanity itself—and one or two rogue asteroids that had been redirected.

"That's rather unlikely," I pointed out mildly. "You have to have some form of intelligent life to be a conqueror, and we certainly haven't found that—a few planets with primitive ecologies that we can colonize, a few others that might once have held life . . . and not a single sign of another intelligent species."

"They're out there . . . somewhere. With trillions upon trillions of stars . . ." Gerrat grinned. "I'd just rather not waste a finite life traveling and searching the infinite."

Even Emelle winced.

"I can see that. I'd rather not waste my life figuring out yet another way to get people to pay me to provide gossip and information most people already know or don't need and never will."

Mother's glance—first at me, and then at Gerrat—was almost a match for a laser in intensity.

I grinned. "But difference is what makes life interesting, isn't it?"

"How did you find the melon, Daryn?" asked Mother sweetly. "Interesting?"

"Very tasty." I turned to Emelle. "Did you enjoy it?"

"It was quite good." Her voice was almost as syrupy as Mother's.

Two months might be a very long time, I decided.

In the end, it took Kharl and the medcenter nearly another two months to put me back together enough so that I was ready to leave under my own strength—or rather under my own newly-regrown legs. The last month or so, I'd been able to do some work, and I'd actually finished up two edart pieces, including the one on Holst and the Warsha Symphony, but I was ready to get back to my own place and start working up to full capacity.

I'd tried to reach Mertyn, but he was either still hiking through some wilderness or not answering his gatekeeper—probably the former, since I'd left messages and gotten no response. It seemed odd, but he'd been known to spend months out of touch, and there wasn't too much I could do immediately, anyway.

As I was packing my gear for the short trip back to Vallura, waiting for Kharl to appear and give me his final words or whatever before I left, I was still thinking, wondering why I'd remembered some incidents more clearly than others while I'd been half-dreaming, half-remembering in the medcradle. There were so many incidents that I had passed over. Because my subconscious said they weren't that important? Or not related to why someone was trying to murder me?

As I reached for one of the small pen scanners, the belt net gatekeeper chimed. I tabbed it, looking up as the small image appeared right beside the medcenter bed I hoped I wouldn't be needing again, or at least not for a very long time. The VR image was that of a man not quite two meters tall, with short black hair, deep blue eyes, and a winning smile.

Myrto, the head compositor, and Compositor Director of

OneCys, glanced at me. "Daryn. I see you're finally out of confinement."

"Almost."

"That's good." Myrto cleared his throat. "There's something we need to discuss."

"You should have everything you need for the last project."

"I do, and it was good work. You always do good work, Daryn." He flashed another professionally warm smile. "You're one of the very best."

Even if I didn't know why, I could sense what was coming, but I decided to make Myrto work for it. "You and OneCys have gotten my best work."

"We've certainly had no problem with the quality of your work, Daryn," Myrto offered.

I refused to bite. "You shouldn't. You'd be hard-pressed to find better."

"The senior directors are worried about the timing. They think that could be a problem."

"A problem? I was late once, when I was in the medcenter, and that doesn't happen to anyone very often."

"But you were close with two other projects, and that's three times this year." Myrto shrugged apologetically. "It's not my decision. I can't give you anything that's time-sensitive."

In short, he couldn't give me anything, because I'd never gotten anything from OneCys that hadn't been time-critical. If it weren't, someone in his organization would have been tasked with it.

"Who made this decision? Can you tell me that?"

"I made it."

"Myrto . . . please don't lie to me. If you had a problem, you would have let me know before this. So . . . someone ordered you to drop me. Who . . . and why?"

"I'm sorry, Daryn. But that's the way it is. I didn't tell you earlier, because I wanted to make sure you were in good shape." Myrto offered a last smile before his image vanished.

After almost ten years of perfect methodizing for OneCys, I'd been dropped. For no real reason, and by a very nervous compositor director who didn't want me to know why or who had ordered it. And like the attempts on my life, I still didn't know the reason why, except I was getting the feeling that they were connected. I just wished I knew what everyone thought I did that made me so dangerous.

The thing was that no one else seemed to know anything. There was no record, even in the skytors' monitoring banks, of the two men and the glider-van or of anyone installing a laseflash on the wall beyond my house. Even Gerrat and Father couldn't find out anything, and with them I knew they were telling the truth—and that might have been the most disturbing bit of all.

All I could do was think and keep packing, and I had finished checking the two small bags that held the remote relay equipment that had let me work from the medcenter when Kharl walked in.

"Already hard at work," Kharl said as he stepped into my room.

"I've been hard at work for weeks, mentally, anyway. I'll need to get back into shape physically."

"Do it gradually," my cousin the doctor suggested. "Solid exercise, but don't overdo it, and listen to your systemic nanites." He paused, then added, "You don't want to undo a miracle."

My eyebrows lifted.

"By all rights, you shouldn't have lived," Kharl said slowly.

"With a modern medcenter?"

"Oh . . . once we had you here, that wasn't the question. It might have taken a lot longer, but we could have put you back together."

"The accident was set up to make sure I was crushed and died on the spot?"

"I'd have to say so . . . now." Kharl nodded.

"Why didn't I? And why do you think so?"

"Apparently, those strange nanites have other functions. I couldn't get rid of all of them, and they must have multiplied in your system. You had a very high concentration. They protected your brain . . . mostly . . . I'm not quite sure how."

"You left them . . . this time?" I asked.

"I wasn't successful in getting rid of them last time, and your system is adjusted to them, and they saved you. I'm not about to damage something that works and cause you more harm in the process. We'll want to watch them, though. And you should let me know if your internal systemics show anything strange."

"So I'm a lab animal now?" My voice was dry.

"You're a very live lab animal," he pointed out equally dryly.

We both laughed.

"Why did you change your mind?"

"The same reason you did," he pointed out. "Once might be an allergenic reaction . . . but two more times isn't coincidence or allergies or accidents."

What he said was true, but I had the feeling there was more. "What else?"

"I've told you all that I know."

Again, that was *mostly* true, but he wasn't about to say more, and I'd have felt strange really pushing my only really close friend who'd saved my life twice.

"I want to see you in a week, immediately if you feel the slightest bit strange or out of sorts," Kharl said.

"I will."

"Promise?"

"I promise. After all this, I'd be stupid not to," I admitted.

"You would." He smiled again. "Have to see to a few others. Take care, Daryn, and don't climb any more old rock walls."

"I'll promise that, too."

He was gone, and I bent down to finish packing the two small bags. It would be good to get home, although I was beginning to get worried about having to roust up more business from other clients.

Past conditioning and physical strength notwithstanding, my lungs and chest were beginning to ache as I lay pushed into the form-fitting bridge couch by the *DeGaul*'s three gees of constant acceleration. The cream gray of the overhead blurred if I tried to look at it directly, and most of the time I kept my eyes closed, using the direct links to monitor the ship's systems and all the scanners.

The *DeGaul* was angling out of the solar system, angling because getting away from the dust envelope was harder leaving Earth than with any of the colony systems. Our home system was one of the few where the orbital ecliptic plane was nearly at right angles to the galactic plane. So, it wasn't that leaving the system's ecliptic wasn't any harder, but getting out of the system ecliptic *and* to where the Gates were placed was, and that meant a longer acceleration.

Then the whole business of Gates was another matter. The theory had been around for a long time, back in the days of the Noram Commonacracy, although they didn't call it that. There had been two problems—generating and focusing enough power to create the wormhole and making sure the exit was where it was supposed to be. In the end, both were resolved by the scientific equivalent of the larger blunt object wielded with greater force.

Creating a Gate system required lots of power, because you had to get the second two-way Gate set where you wanted it, well away from a system's dust corona. Even finding a system required enough power to hold open the wormhole long enough to see if where you'd sent the exploratory probe-Gate was the system you wanted.

In the end, for each final Gate placed, the Federal Union had sprayed about one hundred disposable gates across space

and time before translating a permanent Gate. After that, a
survey and tech ship went through to tow and position the
Gate, and then months went by while they tuned and cali-
brated everything. The same process was going on all the
time, slowly. It took almost ten years—and the expenditure
of a frightening amount of power—to set up each new system Gate. And more than two-thirds ended up on standby.
All of which was why my father had been right when he'd
said that interstellar commerce was a dead-end and why pilots and crew spent most of their time getting to and from
Gates.

"What's the density?" asked Major Schlerin through the
direct link, using that rather than trying to talk against the
gee force, even though his couch was less than two meters
from mine.

Since he was on-system, he could have done the scan, and
that meant I was probably missing something.

"Still at minus five red."

"Keep watching."

I kept watching, and after another ten minutes, the density
began to rise, although I could sense nothing in the scanners
to account for the increase. The gas and dust density was
just rising, although the area before the *DeGaul*, where the
magscoops were collecting all the diffuse matter, would have
qualified as a vacuum just about anywhere.

"It's up to minus three red. How did you know, ser?"

"Measurement anomaly belt." The laugh was only on the
link between us. "It's there, and all the pilots who've made
a number of transits know it, but since the scientists can't
explain it, and since all the transits since the development of
the photon drive have still only resulted in measurements of
a fraction of supra-ecliptic space, they just claim it's a construct of scanner anomalies."

"Give us enough time, and we'll reduce all the dust," I
suggested.

"Oh . . . we might create a dust-free corridor . . . in say a
million years."

I offered a net-nod. That was the major's idea of a joke.

"Drop back to one gee, Alwyn," Major Schlerin said. "Announce a thirty minute constant at one gee. Then you can take ten, and come back and relieve me."

"Yes, ser." I reconfigured the *DeGaul*'s magscoop intakes so that most of the matter they gathered—largely hydrogen—was either being diverted or stored, and eased back the volume coming from the photon nozzles. It took a minute or so before I had the acceleration stable.

Then, I clicked into the *DeGaul*'s main comm and speakers. "All hands. All hands. There will be a thirty minute stand-down at one gee. I say again, a thirty minute stand-down at one gee, commencing immediately."

Then I pulsed the major. "You have the con."

"I have it."

Once the major's links greened, and mine went amber, I loosened the harness straps and stretched, then I unfastened the harness and then the control links before I stood. Neither legs nor arms ached—not yet. I'd only been on for two hours.

The standard ship routine for pilots was four standard hours on the bridge, four for a meal and for handling auxiliary duties, four on, and then eight off. Neither the library records nor the data banks had any information on the source of that rotation pattern.

And that twenty-hour pattern was for a standard one gee departure. No one really got meals or aux duties done at multiple gee acceleration. They just lay in their couches. Some of the techs claimed that they could sleep under multiple gees. I hadn't been able to, but I'd only made one other near-continuous high gee transit in the three months I'd been on the *DeGaul*.

"All rotations ever tried by any military outfit in history share one thing. They never work quite right." That had been Major Schlerin's observation when Senior Lieutenant Baldau had questioned him, and on that I definitely agreed with the Major.

Unlike the other officers, I only had ten minutes of the thirty in normal gee. So I had to hurry to relieve myself, and then scurry to the mess to grab one of the high-cal, high-pro food bars. Several other officers were in the mess by the time

I got there, including Captain Belsever. He was talking to the ops officer, Subcommander deRieux. DeRieux was a thin-faced woman with very short hair and a square jaw, and she was gulping down one of the supplement bars as she listened.

"... some Gate drift that's not explained ... that's why they want full measurements as we near Gamma two...."

"... have the scanners on max sensitivity, and we're recording everything ... another planet?"

Captain Belsever shrugged his bony shoulders, and the wings on his singlesuit bobbed up and down. The captain of a ship had to be a qualified pilot, and current. So did the executive officer. "They're not saying, ops."

"Yes, ser."

I realized I was running out of time, and grabbed a sustain bar, then a cup of the liquid, alternately chewing and swallowing, chewing and swallowing, before finishing both and slipping back to the bridge.

Once there, I strapped back in and on-linked. "I'm online, ser."

"Eleven minutes." A net-chuckle followed. "Not bad." After a moment, the major added, "You have the con, Lieutenant."

"I have it, ser."

"Just watch the density. There's probably nothing else out here, but if there is, just reinforce the scoops and shields first. Then, start tracking, and call me. In that order."

"Yes, ser."

There wasn't anything out beyond the *DeGaul*, nothing but hydrogen and a few other scattered molecules per cubic meter. Even before Major Schlerin returned, the density had dropped back to red minus six, another indication we were clearing the system residuals, and I'd had to re-expand the magscoops to maintain even flow for the converters.

I even had time to wonder about why a Gate was drifting.

Once I was back home, I summoned up and inspected every software subsystem in the dwelling, then I went through the hardware. I wasn't surprised to find that everything had been checked, and that there were dumps and snoops hidden away in more than a few places. For the moment, I left them all, except three that I disabled in ways that would seem accidental enough, unless someone looked really closely, and enough to let me keep an info search and the data from being read—I hoped. Then I took a deep breath, sat down, and leaned back in the chair in the study, thinking.

I didn't know how much time I had before something else went wrong, but I was going to have to get into better shape, physically. That was for certain, and I'd have to buy more time, preferably by appearing to do nothing, while planning everything for the moment when I could act. I also needed to be in better shape to re-inspect the glider before I took it anywhere. Gerrat had had it brought home from Helyna, but I hated to think what might be lurking in it.

One of the first things I did after checking out the house and comm systems was call up the VR of the night that had started the whole mess, except this time I attacked it as a methodizer. I isolated every person in Kharl's great room, and then analyzed each one's behavior and reactions. I didn't stop at whether they looked in my direction, but at physical reactions and every cue I could develop. Then I went into the psychology references and dug up some more.

The results were, as with everything, both surprising and not so surprising.

Rynold Tondrol had been clearly oblivious to anyone but his consort of the evening, and she to him. Kharl frowned, out of nowhere, one minute before I had been sprayed on the terrace, and was actually moving toward the door the moment it opened, even before I was fully visible. Grete's mouth dropped open, and she let out an involuntary murmur of some sort.

The Advocate General of West Noram—Seglend Krindottir—looked totally stunned, even more so than Grete, as I fell, but immediately left the room, and apparently Kharl's dwelling, because she never showed up again. Nor did her husband.

My old friend Kymal Aastafa had been late to react, but the worry lines around his face indicated concern, and he'd gone to Grete—not Kharl—and apparently inquired and offered something, since Grete had nodded in agreement to whatever he had said, then shaken her head.

N'garo and Aalua had been the couple who had entered before me. Kharl had indicated she was a doctor, and that seemed to be borne out, because she'd hurried over and bent down over me when I'd fallen into the great room, and she and Kharl were clearly working on me. Her husband had looked half-stunned, half-puzzled.

Majora Hyriss had also gone to Grete, after Kymal, and remained talking to Grete for more than a few minutes. Like Kymal, she had appeared surprised and worried, very worried.

The other discrepancy involved Eldyn Nyhal, who had stood out with his brilliant single suit, and the glittering oval medallion. For all his flamboyant appearance, the oddity was that he hadn't reacted. With most of the people in the great room turning to see what had happened, including his wife, he had continued talking to a man I didn't know, and that man had politely slipped away to ask the woman next to him about something, presumably me, from the gestures. Nyhal had motioned to his wife after that, clearly into himself, looking as if he had been personally affronted that I had collapsed. Still . . . he hadn't reacted at all.

I scanned and studied all the faces, but if anyone else behaved unusually, I couldn't see it. Of course, that could only mean that any guilty party had been well briefed or prepared.

After all the studying, I still had the same question. Why would anyone be out after me? I had no role in running UniComm. Gerrat and Father controlled UniComm. My inherited interests were . . . what, five percent of the voting stock—the same as Elora's, I assumed. And, because I was stubborn, my legal testament directed my shares to Elora.

My edart pieces got ratings of just over a hundred—usually for the week or two after they were posted, but that meant on average, there were a hundred more frequented edartists. And my methodizing . . . well, I was so indispensable that my biggest client had just trashed me.

The gatekeeper clinged, and I noted the incoming—Majora Hyriss—and accepted.

"I just wanted to see how you were, Daryn." The tall woman looked the same as she had four months—or fourteen years—before. Dark brown eyes dominated a thin face. Her generous mouth and the eyes expressed concern, clear even through VR. We'd remained friends, but no more, over the years, perhaps because . . . I wasn't sure exactly. I liked Majora, but perhaps it was because I felt that nothing with her could be anything less than total commitment, and she was the sort of person I couldn't, and wouldn't, try to deceive.

"Are you all right?" she asked as I just looked at her image for a moment.

"Oh . . . I'm fine. You're kind to check on me. Kharl finally let me come home."

"I know. I've been checking with the hospital. How do you feel?"

"All right, all things considered." I wasn't about to say I felt weaker than I would have liked, not with more snoops and dumps that I'd probably even found. "I do appreciate your call."

"I wasn't sure . . . you looked awfully taken with the redhead . . . I wasn't certain, but I did call Kharl."

I shook my head ruefully. "She turned out to be a mistake, a very costly one." Except I still kept thinking about Elysa, but certainly not romantically.

"Kharl hinted at that. Do you want to talk about it?"

"No."

"It still hurts?"

"When someone tries to kill you, it hurts in more ways than one." That was certainly true.

"I'm here, and you know where to find me." She smiled that warm generous smile, and I wondered why I'd never pursued her.

"I know, and I appreciate it more than you know." I meant that.

She paused, then asked, as if recalling something, "You know Eldyn Nyhal, don't you?"

"We went to school together years ago, before I went off to The College. Why?"

"His wife died—suddenly. It's all over the news, but I think it was on InstaNews first."

I winced. "That has to be hard. You lose someone, and the nets are right there. But I guess he's famous. He's a norm and as wealthy and powerful as any pre-select—and probably brighter than most."

"You're lucky you're not that famous. Everyone trails your brother."

"I chose not to follow that orbit, remember?"

She laughed. "Then you were smart as well as lucky."

When she broke off, suggesting I get some rest, I agreed. But I wanted to check the news before I stretched out. So I tried InstaNews—that was the OneCys counter to Uni-Comm's AllNews. I had to wait almost ten minutes, but Majora had been right.

The first image was that of a Sino-style villa on a hillside above snow-dusted pines.

This is the palatial retreat of the ultra-wealthy food magnate Eldyn Nyhal. Reports from the Civil Authorities indicate that his wife . . .

The screen cut to a warm and smiling image of the small vivacious woman I had seen but once, showing her on horseback, then dropping back to a more distant view of her riding dressage in an arena somewhere. I blinked. Someone had used a graduated light effect, very subtle, but increasing the light around her, almost like an unseen halo.

. . . Merhga Pietra died suddenly of undisclosed causes. Ms. Pietra was a noted equestrienne, and beloved all throughout the Sinoplex for her devotion to childhood education. There were no reports of marital discord, but her husband Eldyn Nyhal has been unavailable for comment. . . .

I winced. What had Eldyn done to upset OneCys?

. . . the food magnate has recently been charged with preferential licensing violations and with the misuse of technology developed with Federal Union funds as the basis for his highly popular "Varietal" food replicator. . . .

The shot of Nyhal showed a tired-looking, small, and beady-eyed figure glaring at the viewer, followed by a view of a glimmering silver-finished replicator. He was in darker blue, not bright blue, and wore another ovalish medallion, except it was almost black.

. . . also charges by Delegate Dybna of Ankorplex that Nyhal had abused his position as coordinator of the medical team dealing with the so-called pre-select plague and diverted resources unnecessarily from early childhood syndromes—the largest cause of ill health and criminality among norms. . . .

InstaNews wasn't doing a slash-job; it was more like a public execution.

. . . arrangements for Merhga Pietra's funeral and benediction have not been set, and may not be for several days, pending ongoing investigations . . . Farewell . . . Merhga Pietra . . . a great lady and benefactor of chil-

dren everywhere . . . Now . . . to the Academic complex
in Byjin . . .

The image was that of students in a spacious classroom.

Here in Byjin, students study comfortably, their classes
based on their abilities and interests . . . but that may
change in years to come . . . depending on the policies
being reviewed by the Federal Union's High Commissioner for Education. . . . Sources close to the commissioner say that a groundswell of popular opinion is
rising against the use of tests such as the PIAT. Com-
bined with scattered protests around the larger
plexes . . .

With a yawn, I cut off the news holo images and sank
back into the chair. I thought about calling Klevyl, but dismissed that immediately. First, I was snooped, and, second,
if I did, it would show more than I wanted.

The involuntary yawns, and the blurriness around my eyes
told me that Majora had been right. I did need some rest.
Then, I needed to think, because I wasn't, not well.

Chapter 29
Fledgling: Sol Gate Gamma One, 431 N.E.

As I discovered in my three plus years aboard the *DeGaul*,
junior pilots stood a lot of watches on the periods between
orbit departures and Gate insertions, but the Gate insertions
were handled by the more experienced pilots, usually those
majors within a few years of being promoted to subcommander and transferred to another ship as operations officer,
and occasionally senior lieutenants with a major watching
them closely.

The other thing I discovered was that once junior pilots

proved themselves to be capable and ready to handle a ship under all other conditions except Gate insertions, they were immediately transferred to another ship. It made sense, but that was how I found myself on the *Newton*, initially as the most junior senior pilot, although that only lasted six months.

After I'd been onboard for about two years, I was headed for the officers' mess when I heard my name.

"Senior Lieutenant Alwyn to the bridge. Lieutenant Alwyn to the bridge."

Wondering what I'd done or was needed to do, I made my way up the ladders against the constant one gee deceleration until I was standing just inside the control section of the bridge. Major Tuawa was fastening himself into the right seat, rechecking the connections. He motioned for me to take the command seat. I must have looked dubious at the idea of holding the command couch while a senior major was in the junior pilot's couch because the second gesture was a command.

I strapped in and linked onsystem.

"You're ready, and you're going to do the Gate translation, Lieutenant. You have the con."

"Yes, ser. I have the con, ser." It wasn't as though I hadn't been through dozens of translations, but I still tightened up slightly at the thought that I'd be the one setting up and carrying out the insertion, even if the major were ready to take over if I botched something.

I didn't want to think about that. So I didn't. Instead, I ran through the complete onsystem checklist, and then through the Gate approach checklist.

Gates weren't all that large . . . less than four hundred meters in circumference, but then, the *Newton* had a cross-section of two hundred meters, and it was going to be my job to insert the ship through the Gate within two hundred fifty microseconds of activation, from close to a dead stop in deep space. It would have taken a lot less time if we could have simply hit the Gate at full acceleration coming out of the system, but it doesn't work that way, since the Gate has to be set up precisely for each ship, its mass and velocity, and its departure and destination Gates.

"Pre-Gate checklist complete, ser," I finally announced.

"Tell the captain, Lieutenant. You have the con."

"Captain, this is the senior pilot. We are approaching Gate Gamma One for insertion and translation to Beta Consuli. Request permission for insertion and translation."

"Systems are all go, Lieutenant Alwyn. You are clear to complete deceleration and to begin the approach for insertion at your discretion." The captain's advisory was clear in my mind, digitization and direct-feed having removed most of the edges that would have been in her spoken voice.

I scanned the systems once more and checked the readouts. "Estimate completion of deceleration in eighteen minutes."

"Proceed and keep me advised, Lieutenant."

"Yes, ser."

Then I rechecked the comm settings before making the next transmission, still conscious that Major Tuawa continued to monitor all that I did. "Gate Control, Gamma One, this is Federal Service Ship *Newton*. Approaching for insertion. Estimate arrival in approximately two zero standard minutes. Request configuration for Beta Consuli. Authorization and data follow." As I finished the transmission, I also squirted the FSS authorization and the data on the *Newton* that was necessary for the Gate techs to set the parameters necessary to send us to the Gate at Beta Consuli, and not somewhere else in the galaxy.

At close to one point five emkay, there was almost a twenty second delay before I got the response from the Gate. "*Newton*, this is Gate Control, Gamma One, standing by for approach and insertion. Understand arrival at Gate in approximately two zero minutes."

I rechecked the deceleration and the EDI bounce to verify decel and distance, but the system showed seventeen minutes, as it should have. I'd added the extra two minutes because most pilots did, to give themselves a little maneuvering time at the end. Reflecting briefly, I wondered if I should have added more.

After another five minutes or so of cross-checking I made the first announcement. "Deceleration will stop in ten minutes. Deceleration will stop in ten minutes. Prepare the ship for weightlessness. Prepare the ship for weightlessness."

The deceleration continued, as the distance between the Gate beacon and the *Newton* steadily decreased, if at a slower and slower rate. I kept the magscoops at seventy percent, just in case.

We seemed to be crawling toward the Gate when I made the next-to-last announcement. "Deceleration will cease in less than two minutes. All hands strap in and prepare for weightlessness and Gate insertion."

The *Newton* came to rest, or near rest, less than a klick from the Gate.

"Weightlessness commencing at this time. Do not unstrap. The ship will be commencing Gate insertion shortly. The ship will be commencing Gate insertion shortly."

Even while I was making the announcement, I had to use the side ionjets to reverse the ship and align it with the off-white torus that was the Gate and the sole sharp object against the spangled pinlights of stars that lit the darkness. At least, that was the way I sensed it through the ship's scanners. Then I checked the *Newton*'s position relative to the Gate, and used the ionjets once more to stabilize the distance between the ship and the off-white torus.

I linked to the captain. "Ship is stable and ready for insertion and translation, ser."

"You may commence insertion, Lieutenant."

"Yes, ser." I went to the outside comm. "Gamma One, this is *Newton*. Standing by. Ready for insertion."

"*Newton*, understand ready for insertion. Stand by to synchronize at the signal."

"Standing by to synchronize at the signal." As I pulsed the transmission to Gate control, I checked once more to make sure that all the magfields were closed down, and that all stray radiation was damped, that the ship was as energy-neutral as possible outside the hull. Then came the last checks of the ionjets, used only for orbit break and maneuvering close to other objects—or for acceleration prior to a Gate insertion and translation.

Then, I clicked in the macro that would use the Gate signal

as the basis for triggering the *Newton*'s acceleration toward, into, and through the Gate.

A green wave seemed to flash over the ship, accompanied by a single high trill, and I watched the ionjets and the fusactor feeds. With the direct links to the ship, at that point, as always, everything around me on the bridge dropped into slow motion, and the *Newton* began to creep toward the Gate. Acceleration was mild, not really even perceptible except through the shiplinks, because that close to the net, we were limited to the ionjets. Even a narrow and focused use of photonic drive would have distorted the Gate field—if not ripped it totally and left us in some unknown and uncharted section of the galaxy—if not in the darkness between galaxies or even in another galaxy. In the early stages of Gate development, the Federal Union had lost a number of unpiloted vehicles definitively proving that point.

The *Newton*'s nose slipped toward the whitened edge of the Gate's torus, and just as the ship seemed to reach that star-filled darkness encircled by the toroidal Gate, two things happened. I cut off all the external sensors. Although the sensors showed nothing, I knew that the center of the Gate was filled with blinding whiteness, a whiteness that seemed to create a tunnel of immeasurable distance. Inside the *Newton*, all images went to black and white, instantly reversing themselves, so that the cream gray overhead became a dark gray, and the dark gray deck became off-white.

The internal sensors, those just inside the outer hull, fed me the field strengths, and I could sense the power created by the Gate—momentarily the equivalent of a small black hole—and barely enough to stabilize a directed Hawking wormhole for the time it took for the mass of the *Newton* to translate from Gate to Gate.

When the field faded, I unblanked the sensors to experience a new set of stars and energy fields, a good thousand light years farther along the Orion Arm. Besides the *Newton*, there were only two high energy level sources—the G3 sun that was Beta Consuli and the second toroidal Gate through which the *Newton* had just passed.

"Consoli Gate, this is *Newton*, reporting Gate translation."

I felt I might have been slow in making the report transmission, but I kept the words evenly spaced.

"*Newton*, Consuli Gate, interrogative status."

As the transmission winked into the shipnet, I finished the quick check of all systems before replying. "Consuli Gate, this is *Newton*. Status is green this time. Thank you."

"Understand green. Give our best to Beta orbit control."

"Will do." After checking all the systems a second time, I let out my breath slowly.

"Very smooth, Lieutenant. Very smooth." Major Tuawa had been so unobtrusive that I had actually half-forgotten that he had been observing me. "You may transition to one gee insystem. Once we're stable, I'll have Lieutenant Resor take my couch, and you can finish the watch as senior pilot. Let Resor handle it all."

"Yes, ser."

"Gate translation complete," I announced over the ship system. "Commencing low gee acceleration. All hands remain in restraints."

Only then did I get a link from the captain.

"Smooth translation, Lieutenant."

That was all, but at least both she and the major had agreed, and the handful of passengers wouldn't be remarking on a rough transition.

Although we were accelerating away from the Gate on ionjets, the acceleration was less than point one gee, and I'd have to wait until we had greater separation before I began feeding power to the magscoops, and we could switch to photonjet drive.

Somehow, in a way, my first Gate translation had been a letdown. The stars were different beyond the *Newton*. The EDI tracks were different, even the dust and system fields, but I'd thought I would have felt more elated, rather than relieved . . . and mildly satisfied.

Over the next few days, I started to exercise, pushing my body exactly as far as my internal systems said was safe, but stopping just on the edge of that. I *had* to get back in shape, and since I'd always been known for exercising, the snoops didn't show anything that anyone wouldn't have already known. There would come a time when I would destroy them all, but not until I was ready. No sense in giving warning and giving someone time enough to reinstall everything in locales even more difficult to discover and remove. Or letting them know I was on to them and precipitating action I was in no shape to handle.

I also began to make a few more modifications to the glider and its security systems. Of course, I couldn't do much about netsystem monitors, or the skytors, or any number of other surveillance systems of which I knew nothing. So the best technique, as my unseen foes had already shown me, was to do something that appeared to be something else.

One thing I could do to sow confusion was catching up with family, something I'd neglected more than I should have before walls started falling on me. If anyone happened to be monitoring me, then they'd have to listen to a lot of gossip, and try to figure out if any of it might be important.

Another was to do a little cold-calling in search of methodizer consulting. After knowing I'd been dropped by OneCys, how could anyone not expect me to parade my expertise in search of projects? And, of course, I had to research the folks I was calling.

One of the ones I finally reached was NetStrait, a small netsystem that catered to people who comprised the fringe just short of the faithies and the netless. After we had exchanged messages several times, the image of Fylin Ngaio appeared in my study.

Ngaio was big, over two meters, muscular, and dark-skinned. His voice was deep and well-modulated as he spoke. "You have an impressive record, both personally and professionally. Why do you think you could help NetStrait?"

"Because I'm a very good and analytical methodizer who's worked in all aspects of commnet operations, and because I'm enough of an outsider to be objective," I offered candidly.

"One might question objectivity from one of the heirs to UniComm."

"One might," I admitted, "if they didn't look at my record."

His lips quirked slightly. "How does your record prove objectivity?"

"I've managed to make a good living for almost fifteen years, and I've never done any work for UniComm. That says that either my work is good or a large number of systems directors have very poor judgment."

"If you're good, why haven't you latched on with one of them?"

"First, I've never asked or suggested that I'm available. Second, one of my values is outside objectivity, and I lose that the moment I go to work for and am totally dependent on one net."

"Have you thought about reconsidering that?" asked Ngaio.

"You mean, with the OneCys run at UniComm? Or something else?"

"It's not just OneCys, as I'm certain you know. There's a feeling that UniComm represents, shall we say, a viewpoint that is less than responsive to the times. Now might be a . . . less rewarding time to be independent."

"That's possible, but doesn't some netsys senior director decide that times are changing about every decade?" I grinned. "Is now any different?"

"Maybe not. Maybe not." Ngaio grinned back. "Still . . . with your sister effectively running NEN and your family still in charge of UniComm, who's likely to believe your objectivity?"

"You are," I suggested, "because you can see that I don't have any interest in running anyone's net, and because you're smart enough to use a good tool that everyone else worries about. And," I added, "because you could tell immediately if I didn't deliver an objective product."

Fylin Ngaio laughed, almost a deep belly laugh, and then shook his head. "I hadn't even thought about hiring you. I just wanted to learn more about you—and your family. And I've got the feeling I'd be stupid not to at least give you something . . . just to see."

"I do small projects," I said. "And controversial ones to provide insulation."

"I will think about it."

"Fair enough." I paused, but not enough to let him get away. "And since you'll think about it, what did you want to learn?"

"If your independence is real or an elaborate Trojan façade . . . and what role you play."

"The independence is real. I never talk business to the family, except about my edart work, and that's no conflict. You seem to think that this is a very unsettled time. Why?" I smiled. "I probably should know, but it will take me a few more days to get back up to full speed."

Ngaio raised his eyebrows.

He had to have known, I would have thought, but it didn't hurt to explain. "I was in an accident. A stone wall fell on me." At his puzzled look, I added. "I'm serious. A very freak accident, but it did happen. I was casting around for clients, because I have time. One decided that he didn't want to wait for me to recover."

"I suppose that was what Myrto told you, but he's always had to fight to use you."

"So . . . that was why you responded."

"One reason."

I shrugged. "And the other?"

"I need objectivity, especially now."

"What would you like me to do?"

"A small project. Just a reasoned analysis and recommendations. As soon as you can do it, if you're interested."

"I'm interested."

"I thought you might be." Ngaio nodded slowly. "You'll have the specs and background tomorrow. Your fee schedule the same?" His head turned, and I had the feeling that someone had entered his home or office. He shook his head and looked at me.

"It hasn't changed."

"Good. Let me know if you don't have the package by tomorrow night." And then he was gone.

I wasn't so smart. Ngaio had wanted me from the start, and I hadn't seen it. He'd even known about Myrto. I looked over the desk out across Vallura toward the redstone slopes to the east, fingering my chin, and trying not to frown. Should I let Gerrat know about the intensified attack on UniComm?

I decided against it. If Ngaio knew already, then Gerrat did, with all the sophisticated intelligence and contacts he and Father had. In fact, they'd probably known about the OneCys move for months.

I wished I knew more. Did all this have anything to do with those who had tried to kill me? Or were the two coincidence? I distrusted the lady named coincidence even more than lady luck, but on balance, I also didn't want to feel paranoid, and that everything was somehow directed at me.

Myrto's actions unfortunately made perfect sense. He could replace me, and get his superiors off his back. That was my tough luck, but there was always the chance, once whatever was in the works actually happened, and time passed, I still might get work. If not, I had another potential client.

I straightened, then stood, and walked slowly to the kitchen, where I used the replicator to create an instant cup of Grey tea. Each cup tasted and smelled the same—exquisite, but exquisite with exactly the same nuances. Then, that might have been because I didn't have one of Nyhal's upscale and random-taste variable replicators.

After mentally noting the time—another half hour until

my next exercise session—I walked back to my study.

Barely into my chair, before I could sip the tea or check
the searches I'd set up earlier, the gatekeeper clinged once
more.

The blond-maned Klevyl—or his sim—appeared before
the desk and glanced at me. "You look fine. The last stuff
you did for me—when you were in the medcenter—was as
good as ever, maybe better. Why did OneCys drop you?"

"Do all the system directors in the Federal Union know?"

"Only those with intelligence, and there aren't as many of
them as directors with brains in enviro management. Now
. . . did Myrto tell you why?"

"No." That was certainly true. I had some ideas, but no
proof. "Have you heard anything?"

Klevyl shook his head, and his leonine mop of hair flopped
with the gesture. "Could be you're too good for him. He
used your accident as an excuse. You made his staff look
bad."

"I can't do anything about that." I shrugged and waited.

"Could be you're an Alwyn."

"More netsys wars?"

"OneCys is getting squeezed by NEN and UniComm. And
that's in spite of all the creds they put into this new push."

"My sister is number three at one, and my father and
brother direct the other. And I don't even talk to any of them
about netops."

"I know that. So does Myrto—but his bosses don't, and
they won't listen to the compositor director about that."
Klevyl laughed. "I've got another project on line . . . be about
two weeks. You be ready?"

"I will." I looked quizzical. "How did you know about
Myrto and OneCys? Engineering firms . . . or are you building structures for them?"

"We bid. We didn't get it. Any of them. But someone
asked about you, because we had to list our outside consultants. Struck me as strange. I made some calls." Klevyl
grinned. "I knew you were one of the Alwyns. It doesn't
matter in what I do, and I just figured you were some cousin.
My engineering contact at OneCys—she told me who you

really were. Got to say, Daryn, guts you got."

"Why? Because I wanted to live my own life?"

"Most people don't. Anyway . . . if you need anything I can provide, I'm here, and, like I said, probably a week or two on the next job."

"I'm here."

"Get some rest." Those were Klevyl's parting words.

But I didn't get either rest or exercise, because the gatekeeper clinged once more. I blinked. Apparently, I actually was getting a response from Elen Jerdyn from NetSpin—another small system, but one that positioned itself to deal with those who enjoyed the art world.

The image that appeared before me was of a woman of indeterminate age, with short and straight brown hair, in a conservative brown singlesuit trimmed with white, and with a short off-white jacket. Her eyes were large and gray, even as presented by the VR.

"Daryn . . . Elen Jerdyn from NetSpin. I almost sent the thank-you-your-work-is-great-but-not-exactly-for-us sim back. But I remembered I'd really liked the edart piece you did on the Warsha Symphony a couple of weeks back. So I checked out some of your other work."

"I'm glad you liked the Holst piece," I answered, coming up with a smile I hoped wasn't too forced.

"You do good work. Not just the feel, but the technical side." Jerdyn paused. "Word is that you got bounced by OneCys. Care to explain?"

I shrugged. "I think someone was looking for an excuse. I missed only one deadline in ten years, and that was because a wall fell on me."

"A wall fell on you?" Her eyes widened.

"The cemetery wall in Helnya," I said dryly. "I was trying to be a good citizen. I thought I heard a little girl calling for help. I went to look, and several tonnes of stone toppled on me. I finished my work for Myrto while I was still in the medcenter with my legs in regrowth. I was maybe ten days behind."

"The big outfits are like that." She grinned wryly. "Ten years don't matter."

"You hear that, but you always think you'll be different."
I laughed. "Then, you never know what's going on behind
the sim-smiles."

"OneCys is making a big push to unseat UniComm. Ru-
mor has it that one of their investor interest groups—
StakeHold Group—thinks OneCys should have a bigger
market share."

"I know about the push. I did some of the analytical work
on it."

Jerdyn shook her head. "It happens. Tell you what. We're
small, but we're not doing badly. You know our niche. I'd
like to send you a small assignment—analyze an interest-
time-combo slot we've had trouble with. I'll send a copy of
the format we like, and the parameters. Ten to twenty of your
billables, and we'll see if we fit."

I didn't have to force the smile. "I'd like that. It'll be fun
to work for someone who knows what they want, as opposed
to an outfit that tries to be all things to all people."

"The stuff's on its way. Two weeks?"

"Two weeks." I would have promised sooner, but that was
dangerous.

"Good. And I did like the Holst piece—and the one on
the forerunner Gate."

"Thank you."

The slightest cling in my thoughts, and Jerdyn's sim image
was gone, and I was looking out at the redstone cliffs to the
east.

StakeHold—I'd never heard of it, but it shouldn't take too
much to find it.

I set up the routines, and then stripped down for my ex-
ercises.

By the time I finished sweating and panting, and taking a
quick shower, the search results were waiting.

There were almost a hundred different outfits named
StakeHold, and from the capsule descriptions, they could be
almost anything, and that meant refining the search more—
difficult when I wasn't sure exactly what I was seeking and
if the information meant anything at all. Still, I set up another
round of searches on the names and organizations, and then

checked the system for incomings. Sure enough, the material from Jerdyn had arrived.

That meant I had to get to work, since I still wasn't ready, either in terms of physical condition or information, to follow up on trying to find out why people wanted to kill me, and who they might be. And whether there was a connection to OneCys . . . or whether that had just been an excuse triggered by my would-be killers.

Chapter 31
Fledgling: Supra-Ecliptic Space, Pavo 31, 435 N.E.

Lieutenant Alixan was fresh out of Kuritim, and I'd just made major, and we had a new captain, when the unexpected happened.

Alixan hadn't had the con for four minutes, less than ten minutes into our acceleration insystem from the Beta Gate "above" Pavo 31, when he was on the link again. "Major . . . there's an echo image from the Gate, but it's in the wrong place."

I was on-system immediately. Everyone talked about echo images, but they didn't happen often. In fact, I'd never seen one or records of one in the nearly ten years I'd been a pilot.

In scanning everything, I didn't take long to find the image—except it wasn't an image. It was the reverse of one, and that was probably what Alixan had meant. There was a lack of background dust and radiation that formed an image—almost toroidal.

"I have the con, Lieutenant."

"Yes, ser. You have the con." Puzzlement came over the net.

I ignored it, pulsing a direct link to the captain. "Ser . . . probable artifact ahead. Request permission for . . . three gee deceleration after notice."

"Artifact, Major?"

"Yes, ser. Forty-three point four, eighteen green."

There was a silence while the captain followed the coordinates himself. I hadn't expected anything less.

"Permission granted, Major. Maintain full scoop shields and initial ten emkay stand-off."

"Yes, ser." I went wide net. "All hands strap in. All hands strap in. Three gee deceleration commencing in two minutes. Three gee deceleration commencing in two minutes."

More than a few inadvertent comments drifted onto the shipnet.

". . . frigging FS . . ."

". . . another essing drill . . ."

". . . no more sleep . . ."

I checked the reverse energy image once more, but it remained stable.

"Deceleration in one minute. Deceleration in one minute."

Even at three gees decel just out of the Pavo Beta Gate, I still overshot the object—whatever it was, and while the rest of the ship was scrambling to deal with the aftermath of an unexpected three gee decel followed by weightlessness, I was using all the ship systems. But there was nothing there. Whatever the artifact or object was, it neither radiated nor absorbed energy—not from the direction of 31 Pavo.

"It's like it disappeared, ser," Alixan observed.

I ignored the comment and continued to scan for what wasn't there, and as I suspected, in the microwave range, there was a patch where there wasn't any universal background. I pegged the coordinates, and reoriented the ship with the side ionjets.

"All hands remain in restraints for maneuvering. All hands remain in restraints for maneuvering."

". . . not routine . . ."

". . . got to be something out there . . ."

"This is the captain. Keep the net clean!" His voice and persona came across the net like full photonwash, scouring everything.

I eased the *Newton* forward, then at an angle, trying to get some form of parallax to gauge the distance.

"Appears to be fifteen emkay," I pulsed the captain. "No EDI tracks. Energy dead."

"Approach to ten, Major."

I eased the ship to ten emkay, but outside of the lack of microwave radiation, there was still no way to discern the object. "Recommend circling."

"Approved."

I could tell that Alixan still remained puzzled.

"We'll get a better resolution with it backdropped against Pavo," I explained.

"Someone didn't want it to be found," the lieutenant suggested.

I'd already thought of that, and all the magshields were set full. But nothing happened, except the somehow not quite toroidal shape became slightly clearer once it was between the *Newton* and 31 Pavo. We sat and probed as we could, but nothing we had revealed anything.

"Request permission to approach to one thousand klicks."

"Granted, with full screens, and photonjets ready for full acceleration."

"All hands remained strapped in stations. Emergency acceleration is possible without warning. Emergency acceleration is possible without warning."

Even as close as a thousand klicks, with scanners at full sensitivity, the only way of detecting the object was by its comparative blocking of various background energies.

"Request permission to send scanner torp, Captain."

"Permission granted."

I eased one of the remote scanner torps away, and then we waited some more. Initially, the signals showed even less than did the *Newton*'s. Not until the torp was within five klicks was there anything but a faint haze on the screen that showed the image relayed from the torp scanner.

The captain and I both waited. I could also sense the ops officer on the private link, for all that subcommander Matteus had offered nothing.

Abruptly, an image appeared—a greenish white donut or torus, somehow off-centered. I blinked as I studied it, even though the image was mental, direct-fed from the scanner relay.

The object or artifact was massive. . . . and old. . . . It reeked age as it seemed to slide through the darkness of extraplanetary space, through the scattered molecules that the *Newton*'s sensors registered as hundreds per cubic meter, but which I felt through the sensors as a cold mist . . . colder than mere snow or sleet.

"It's big . . . bigger than we are, ser," link-whispered Alixan.

The data inputs confirmed that the object—and it had to be something like a massive ship or artificial satellite with the damped visual, EDI, and radar return, the albedo, and the shape—did indeed dwarf us. Secondary inputs suggested that the structure was of some form of composite with a metallic skeletal structure. It was roughly a klick in diameter. And it was cold and dead, its surface barely above the ambient of the deep space around it.

Something about the object felt familiar . . . in a different way . . . almost like a Gate station, and it was similar, if not exactly, to the toroidal structure of a Gate. It was certainly set far enough out from the planets and above the ecliptic. But it wasn't meant to be seen, especially from inside the system.

Letting the sensors gather the data, letting Captain Andruhka pour over it as well, I studied and waited.

I could feel the captain rummaging through the shipnet in his heavy-minded way, and I finally offered my own calculations to him. "There's no way to determine its mass or much of anything without sending a probe almost to its surface, ser."

"It could be antimatter, even . . ." whispered Lieutenant Alixan.

"Not possible," I said aloud into the stillness of the control capsule. "We're in real space, and there's gas around us . . . be an energy trail if it were . . . and there are no fields for shielding."

"You may send a probe, Major." There was a laugh. "No

one would ever believe us without some data, and space is too big to chance trying to find it again."

He was right about that. Luck and Alixan's alertness were all that had allowed us to discover it this time. While second-guessers might say we should have marked the locale and sent for the scientists . . . how many other ships had passed nearby and not found it? And what if we left and no one else could? Or took months or years to do so?

Readying the probe and ensuring the programming was accurate for what we wanted took nearly thirty minutes. Then I/the *Newton* eased the probe toward the massive artifact . . . and waited.

There were no energy bursts, nothing, as the probe glided toward the surface of the object and began a mapping survey of the surface from roughly four hundred meters away.

The mapping was almost complete when the captain touched my link.

"Bring the ship to one hundred klicks," ordered the captain.

"Yes, ser." With a light touch on the photonjets, and the magfields still up, I eased the *Newton* toward the enigmatic object.

Once stabilized that close, where the ship's sensors could actually pick up its image, if fuzzily, the ops team, the captain, and I studied the images and data coming back from the probe. All I could do was observe through the probe's sensors, with the captain's heavy mind panting across the shipnet.

"There are what appear to be exterior locks at regular intervals," offered Subcommander Matteus.

"Might as well look at one," suggested the captain. "Aren't any other surface details. Send the probe."

"Yes, ser," replied Matteus.

So the probe made for one of the apparent locks, a dark gray or black octagon roughly two meters on each side and set against the off-white featureless surface of the artifact. The probe's remote samplers had already indicated that the surface was some form of inert composite, a material beyond the remote analysis capabilities of the probe.

The remote scanners showed a bronzelike flat octagon, set in the white composite at one vertex of the far larger black octagon we thought might be an airlock to the interior of the octagonal toroidal structure.

"We're recording all this, ops?" asked the captain.

"Yes, ser."

"Send a message torp to the Gate station with a copy of what we have now, and with the location of the artifact."

"Yes, ser," answered Matteus.

We probably should have done that sooner, but when confronted with what seemed to be the first sign of alien life ever, I could understand the oversight. In fact, I hadn't even thought about sending off a message torp.

Matteus had a torp off even before the probe had finished its analysis of the octagonal lock door.

"The smaller octagon looks like it might turn," offered the ops officer.

"This is where we stop." The captain laughed, a harsh sound even over the net. "We wait for the experts, and make sure they can find our artifact."

That made a sort of sense. We weren't equipped to deal with alien exploration.

"Major Alwyn." The captain came through the net to me on a private link.

"Yes, ser?"

"Put the images on the passenger net, and announce something about the uniqueness of the situation."

"Yes, ser." I understood that, immediately. We were going to be weightless and hanging in the middle of supra-ecliptic space for quite a while.

That was as exciting as it got for a long time, because all we did was wait and orbit the alien artifact. There were no signals from the alien station, and all I could do was watch the featureless exterior. So I tried to compute the parameters for the alien station's position. Not surprisingly, at least to me, its position was in one of the least gravitationally conflicted positions out of the system ecliptic, or the least conflicted possible, assuming it was something like a Gate, because that was certainly what it felt like to me. I did wonder why, if it were a Gate, no artifacts had been found in-system in the past two hundred years of habitation . . . unless the Gate was indeed old in geological terms and such artifacts were well below the planetary surfaces.

But I was the first pilot on duty when the *Newton* found the forerunner Gate.

The *Newton* only spent three weeks floating off the forerunner Gate, because that was exactly how long it took for the Federal Union to send another ship loaded with experts and gear to relieve us.

Then we headed in-system. There we floated off the Orbit control station of Pavo 4, otherwise known as Newage, where we floated for another week while we were inspected from afar, and then from very close, to ensure that nothing alien had returned with us.

All that inspection found nothing, but I would have been surprised if they had, because the station was old—anywhere from ten thousand to ten million years, according to what we could figure, and the engineering types were marveling over the composite used in the outer walls. After all that time, it was still smooth. A standard laser wouldn't cut it, nor would any standard equipment we had. I suppose it could have been destroyed by a focused photonjet, but there wasn't much point in that kind of destructive testing, not after all the years of wondering whether we were alone in the galaxy.

And after all that, we went back to carting high-tech freight, equipment, and personnel between Earth and the various out-systems. Just as if we'd never even found the forerunner Gate—except that we were strongly encouraged not to talk about it.

After all the sysnet and data searches I'd run, the second round results were generally pretty dismal, not all that much better than the first. I was beginning to have greater appreciation for the news staffs on any of the networks. Data and names meant nothing out of context. I knew that with environmental specs, or quantity/quality program comparison, or all the other methodizer work I'd done—but the client had provided the context. In my own case, I had no context.

Fine . . . there was an organization or group called Stake-Hold. Actually, of the hundred I'd found the first time, the second search had dropped the numbers to a few more than a dozen in various parts of Earth, and even on Luna and in the Belt. Only one fit, and there was nothing on it, not directly, except a netsite and a charter, and the charter was as vague as vague could be: ". . . dedicated to the proposition that good organizational management shall reflect maximization of productive assets, the active support and promotion of excellence in services provided, products, and organizational policies, and impartial adherence to justice . . ."

From the short description, it seemed to be a loose federation of interests and individuals designed primarily to pool voting interests and clout to put greater pressure on managements of public-held outfits—mainly to force management improvements. At least, that was the avowed goal.

Buried through about a dozen links, and more than a few stories in obscure journals, I managed to track down at least some of the members—the PST Trust—another name I'd never heard of—NetVest, Private Citizen, and a double handful of individuals, presumably wealthy from the public information available on each. The only names I recognized were Cari Seldyn, Grant Escher, and Mutumbe Dymke, not that I knew any of them personally. So I set up more routines and let them loose.

The other result was a single piece of financial analysis, and it seemed to confirm what I'd gathered in my freelance-work-and-personal-information search—that several major sysnets were revamping everything from their financial structures to their operations and program contents—and that UniComm was not. The anonymous analyst suggested that the senior directors had decided that a shakeout was inevitable, and that the loser(s) would be relegated to being niche players, much like NetStrait and NetSpin. While that made sense of sorts, what I knew didn't track much to me, except to support the rationale for Myrto's decision not to contract with me. So I kept searching, intermittently, and not finding, and exercising, and working on and completing the small projects for Ngaio and Jerdyn—and waiting for Klevyl's package.

As spare time built up, despite more than a few hours spent on the glider, and as my free credit balance slowly dwindled, I also kept searching for signs of Elysa . . . and finding none.

So, it was inevitable that I'd have to go back to Helnya.

This time, I didn't VR ahead and announce my intention, and I turned off my belt repeater totally—reducing another signal that might be traced. I also wore a namite body screen, almost invisible, except for the blurring effect it created, and hotter than I would have liked, even in March, but the silversmith, or whatever he was, happened to be the only link—and that bothered me. He was clearly a trap, yet one I had to pass through to get anywhere.

The glider carried me only so far as the induction tube station in Vallura, and then I took the tube train to Helyna and a glidertaxi to the shop. We did pass the cemetery, and the wall had been repaired so well that it appeared nothing had happened there. If I hadn't felt the impact so strongly, I might have even doubted it had occurred.

The stonesmith's place of business was a long and rambling adobe structure, more like dwellings connected by covered porticos. The name on the sign outside the west end—

the one overlooking the harbor—was simple. RennZee, Stone-and-Silversmith.

I walked in, nanite screen heating me up and personal scanners searching everything, and finding less than normal background energy systems. The front display room was simple, just two armaglass cases set on polished hardwood cabinets. The walls were rough plaster, painted white, as was the ceiling. There were no chairs, just a stool behind the left-hand case.

"Hello, ser." A young man stood and greeted me, the same dark-haired one I'd VRed months before, but he didn't seem to recognize me, not surprisingly, since he'd seen a small holo image for all of three minutes.

I ignored the greeting, letting my systems check over the place before I nodded in return. "Are you Renn?"

"Oh, no, ser. I'm Achille. He's my uncle—really my mother's uncle."

"I hope he's around."

The young man lifted his eyebrows.

"I'm Daryn Alwyn. I was caught in an accident on my way here several months ago. I just recently was discharged from the medcenter."

He frowned.

"As I told you when I called—those Alwyns."

His face cleared. "Ah . . . I see."

"Is Renn around?"

"Ah . . ."

"If he doesn't want to see me, that's fine. But at least ask him. Oh . . . and tell him I wanted to ask about some pieces he did before."

"Yes, ser . . . if you would excuse me?"

I waited there for five minutes, sweating behind the body screen field, walking back and forth, scanning, checking, hoping I wasn't being set up once more.

Then, the rear door irised opened, and Achille returned, followed by another figure. Despite his obvious age and being a norm, RennZee was trim, muscular, and weathered, with a face like smooth old leather, and pale gray eyes that seemed to miss nothing as he studied me. "You don't look like that kind."

"I'm not. I'm a freelance methodizer and edartist, and I retired after a career as a Federal Service interstellar pilot."

"The eyes . . ." He nodded. "Good. You know, I once refused to do a ring for your grandfather, it was, I think. He wanted me to duplicate someone else's bad work."

I laughed, softly. "That sounds like Grandfather."

"What do you want?"

"Right now, I want your expertise as a jeweler and craftsman, and I'll pay for it at whatever rate you think is fair. I think . . . I know you're the only one, possibly in the world, or perhaps the whole Federal Union, who can help."

RennZee laughed, a generous belly laugh. Then he glanced sideways at the young man. "With a compliment like that, Achille, best you trust the man or run like hell."

"I hope you'll trust me."

"With you wearing a body screen?" The jeweler's eyes ran over me. "I recognize the energy fields."

"The last time I tried to get here, someone dropped a wall on me." Might as well be direct, I figured.

"And you want a jeweler, and not a bodyguard?"

I lifted the mini and projected the close-up of one of the combs. "This looks like your work. If it's not, I hope you can tell me whose work it is."

The older man smiled. "You have a good eye. I did that. There were two. Part of a set. Right after I set up my studio here. Say . . . fifty years ago."

"Fifty years ago?"

He nodded.

Achille's eyes darted between me and his uncle.

"Could someone have copied those?"

"Anything's possible . . ." Renn laughed.

"But . . . it's obviously unlikely for reasons I don't understand." I offered a helpless smile, which wasn't too far from the way I felt.

"Look at the stone."

"It looks like jade to me."

"It is . . . except it's not earth jade. It's a jadeite, but

cleaner in color and harder on the Mohs scale . . . something
to do with the alignment of the inosilicate chains . . . fellow
who brought it to me didn't know what he had. To him the
value was because it was from outsystem . . . said he got it
from a core drill somewhere. Wouldn't tell me where." Renn
looked at me. "You might know."

"I was a pilot, not an off-planet geologist."

He waited.

"You did earclips, combs, and a jade choker?"

The stonesmith nodded.

"I'm trying to locate someone who wore them. I thought
you might be able to help."

He shook his head. "Don't bother keeping records that far
back, but it wouldn't do much good, would it . . . not after
fifty years?"

"The woman who wore them is probably a daughter or
granddaughter," I suggested.

"He took them back to Hezira with him. Even sent me a
spacegram—arrived three years later. Said his wife really
liked them."

"Do you recall his name?" I had to ask, although I certainly couldn't go to Hezira.

"Amad something. Didn't look like an Amad . . . tall fellow, pale-skinned, black-haired. I still remember. Never got
another jadeite like that."

"He didn't mention her name, did he?" After fifty years,
I was casting in the dark, and then some.

Renn laughed. "Really are interested, aren't you, young
ser?"

I couldn't imagine being considered young, but in comparison to the older jeweler, I suppose I was. "More puzzled
than anything."

"Matter of fact, I do remember her name."

Behind him, his great-nephew raised his eyebrows.

"Strange name, that's why. Elysa. Pronounced it sort of
like Ell-iss-ya."

I managed not to swallow. "Strange enough that you remembered it for fifty years."

"Strange name and a strange jadeite—what else would it take for a good stonesmith?"

I nodded. "You wouldn't recall anything else, would you?"

RennZee shook his head. "I was happy with the work."

"I can see why."

"Did you see them?"

"Yes. A woman wore them to a reception my cousin held. I was very interested. She—and the jewelry—vanished."

"I would buy them back," he said.

"If I ever find them," I smiled, "I don't know that I'd let you. They're exquisite."

He shrugged, but his eyes twinkled.

"I said I'd pay for your time," I offered.

He shook his head. "Commission a piece for Achille, here, to do."

The young man suddenly became far more attentive, bending forward ever so slightly.

I thought for a moment. "A pin, suitable for me, of a raven. Simple, but tasteful. Not too large."

"That's it?" asked Achille.

"That's it," I replied. "You two are the jewelers and stonesmiths."

RennZee laughed. "That's the best way. Achille will understand . . . if not now, later."

"I'll leave a deposit."

"No need," replied the older stonesmith.

I nodded. We both understood. A good piece would always sell, and RennZee wouldn't let the young man offer something that wasn't good.

"Thank you very much." I bowed. "I do appreciate the information."

"I do also," the weathered stonesmith replied. "It's good to know that work remains valued."

After another bow, I turned and stepped out into the breeze. The wind helped some in cooling me, although some of the effect was blocked by the body screen. I thought about turning it off, but decided against it. After glancing around, and seeing only a couple strolling toward the point overlooking the ocean, I began to walk the two klicks toward the center of town and the tube station. That was one more net-locator I might not alert.

Although forcing myself to scan in all directions, I none-theless enjoyed the walk, and the stretching of legs and other muscles, and before long I was nearing the center of Helnya, and the older dwellings and the ancient blue oaks that sur-rounded them. I walked a trace slower, studying not only the path, but the dwelling on my left, a hacienda-like structure. Ahead, the oak limbs arched over the path, creating a shade welcome to me. The area beneath was clear, with only low beds of nasturtiums that were still recovering from the mild Calfya winter.

My head jerked forward at the sound of feet crushing the nasturtiums, and I froze, if but for a moment, as a vacant-faced man in a dull brown singlesuit lunged at me, a shim-mering blade in his right hand.

Even as my ingrained defense modules reacted, the vacant expression on the man's face bothered me.

He seemed to move so slowly, as I slid left, letting his lunge carry him past my body. Then one hand took his wrist, and a snap-kick staggered him. My strength wasn't what it should have been, and he spun toward me, trying to free the hand with the shimmering filament knife, against which the body shield was useless.

I managed to hold the knife arm long enough—just long enough—that a knee-elbow combination—and a last kick—left him on his back in the nasturtiums, convulsing.

I looked at him, as if I were again frozen, before my sen-sors told me his body heat was rising. The vacant face reg-istered fully, and I turned, and sprinted away, as fast as my legs could carry me.

The explosion was enough to give me a shove, but not much more, and I slowed to a rapid walk, ignoring the doors that opened a block behind me.

The attack and explosion had occurred under a heavy oak cover, for very good reasons, but enough energy had been released that the CAs would be there shortly, and I didn't want to be around when they were.

I was starting down the steps to the tube station when the CA gliders whined toward the oaks and the hacienda. Ignoring them, I kept moving.

I'd seen enough. My attacker had been a monoclone, programmed to seek me, to kill me, one way or another. The nanite suit barred something like a laser or a hand-held projectile weapon, but not a filament knife—or a large explosion close to me.

Someone was still trying to eliminate me—in ways that couldn't be traced. How could anyone track a clone that self-destructed, probably leaving little but a standard cellular pattern, and probably the most common one—the one used for the monoclones dealing with radioactive waste?

Sweat was dripping from every pore when I swung onto the train, and I wanted to turn off the protective fields of the bodysuit. I didn't dare. Instead, I sweated all the way back to my own villa.

Once home, I checked on all the systems, then purged everything, all the oddities, snoops, and dumps. Only then did I shower and clean up . . . and think.

Cup after cup of Grey tea helped, in a way.

Whoever was after me not only had resources, but access to clone production and full genetic mod facilities.

That started me on another search, and the results were quick—a list with nineteen names on it. Most of them I didn't know, except for Eldyn Nyhal, but several had become familiar, like Cari Seldyn, Grant Escher, Imayl Deng, Darwyn TanUy, and Mutumbe Dymke. All that they had in common was wealth, and connections to universities, research institutions, or hospitals with full genetics facilities.

Some, like Seldyn, I was pretty sure I could eliminate, since she was basically a rich woman who'd inherited the credits and used them widely and philanthropically, and didn't have personal expertise in the field. That didn't mean she didn't have intent, but it did mean she would have needed accomplices, perhaps a large number, and that would have left some sort of track—I thought.

The next search was a different sort, one to see if I could find a common factor that any shared. Several were on ad-

visory boards, and the like, of charitable organizations, but
no more than two on any one organizational board—except
for the PST Trust. Escher, Dymke, St. Cyril, Costilla, Deng,
and TanUy all were affiliated with the PST Trust. Eldyn, on
the other hand, was associated with none of them, but I still
remembered his lack of reaction at Kharl's, and knew he had
to be involved. But like the others, I didn't know how, or
how to obtain anything resembling proof.

After that, things got slow, because nothing else at all
turned up, and I finally went to bed. I didn't sleep well,
knowing that in all likelihood, the CAs would be at least
inquiring about an odd occurrence, and wondering how I
could handle that.

Chapter 33
Fledgling: Orbit Station, New Austin, 437 N.E.

The *Newton* was hanging in space, a good klick from the
only orbit station around New Austin. The planet was about
point nine Tee, with a marginal atmosphere that looked pink-
ish from above, and the Federal Union had been working to
increase atmospheric density for close to two centuries. The
single operable cargo shuttle was sliding through the night-
side space, back to the station, and probably would be occupied for several hours, as it offloaded the last shipment of
the four sets of biotemplates we'd carried out from Earth and
through three other systems and Gates first. Once the tem-
plates were transferred, the shuttle would have to offload
some other specialized and nanite-based planoforming technology. Then, after we offloaded, we'd load back up the
cases that held data and biosamples, and the FS personnel
being rotated back to earth or elsewhere, any passengers, and
head back to Earth. With the cross-system travel, we'd have
been gone from Earth almost seven months, and I was getting

a little ship-crazy, despite the planetside reconditioning along the way.

I cornered Commander Matteus outside the mess. We were both hanging above the deck, because photonjet interstellar ships aren't built to spin.

"Would you mind if I took the cargo shuttle to the station, ser?"

"You know someone there, Major?"

"No." I shrugged. "I might, but not that I know. I just felt restless, ser. If it's a problem . . . ?"

The exec looked back at me, then smiled. "Actually, you could do me a favor of sorts, Major. If you'd follow me . . ."

What sort of favor she had in mind I wasn't certain, because she'd never been forward personally or in any other way. I followed, hand over hand, wondering, until she reached her quarters.

The small cabin was as neat as she was, without a hint of anything out of place. As I watched, she touched one of the plates on the safe, then keyed in something. The safe opened, and she took out a small case that she extended to me. "Routine future authorization codes for the station for the next year. I was going to have Lieutenant Tang carry this, but he's behind on his training reports anyway. It goes to the station commander. If you take it, someone will turn white—or green."

"Meaning that when majors carry the dispatches, there's trouble?" I frowned, wondering why we carried the codes when other ships could have reached New Austin sooner.

"The ones we carry aren't that time sensitive," she answered. "You may recall Captain Flahrty," she half-asked.

"*The* Captain Flahrty?"

"I see you do. Just tell him that you're delivering the case with my compliments." Matteus grinned, almost evilly. "He'll probably find something for me next trip, if he's still here in two years, because it will probably be that long before we're rotated out here." A wider smile crossed her lips. "And if you could look stern or worried . . . I would appreciate it."

We both smiled.

I was smiling as I left her cabin, heading for the main personnel lock, where I donned an outside suit. Then I made my way aft to the cargo lock where I waited until I got the signal from the supercargo and pulled myself along the tether to the shuttle's hatch. It took a minute to get hooked into the air system, and it was stale, like that of most orbit transfer shuttles.

"Major," asked the shuttle jockey after I was strapped in and linked into thc simple commsystem, "ready for push-away?"

"Ready," I confirmed.

His touch on the ionjets was deft and easy, and in moments he had the shuttle headed back toward the cargo lock of the orbit station.

"Major . . ." he asked after a time of silence, "were you with the *Newton* when . . . ?"

"When we found the forerunner artifact?" I paused. "Yes."

"What was . . . what's it like?"

"It looked like an off-center Gate, sort of whitish, hard-to-see, and old. Very old."

"Did you ever go into it?"

"None of us did. We just scanned it with probes."

"Good thing you didn't."

"Oh?" His comment seemed a little strange.

"You haven't heard?"

"Heard what?" I asked.

"About the alien curse? Or virus? Or whatever?"

"We've been out six months. Tell me," I suggested dryly.

"They say that half the scientists who were on the *Darwin* were laid up with something. Two of 'em died."

"That seems far-fetched to me," I pointed out. "First, that artifact was so old that it didn't have any atmosphere left. For even a virus to survive that long near absolute zero would be almost impossible. Then, for it to be compatible with our physiology?" I found myself shaking my head. "Besides, they decontaminated the *Darwin* with a photon-plasma wash, and with nanetic medicine, there'd be no way a leftover virus from some other life form could survive. And that was over two years ago. If something like that had survived, there would have been talk sooner than this."

He shrugged. "I only know what they've been saying."

"Are there any hard reports? Anything like that?"

"Not that I've seen, ser. But the last two ships, they were saying the same thing, they were."

"Could be. I just don't know."

"I just know what I heard." The jockey sounded put out that either I didn't believe him or that I had nothing new to add. So that was that for the rest of the short hop to the orbit station.

Once there, I stripped myself of the suit and racked it in one of the transient lockers, and pocketed the microkey. Then, carrying my case, I put on a stern expression and made my way to upper level and the commander's section. Since all orbit stations were designed the same, that wasn't a problem.

A fresh-faced lieutenant wearing a logistics insignia on his singlesuit immediately addressed me. "Might I help you, Major?"

"I have a case for Captain Flahrty."

The senior lieutenant looked at me. "Ah . . . I could take it, ser."

"I was ordered to deliver it to Captain Flahrty personally, Lieutenant. I brought it over from the *Newton.*"

"Ah . . . yes, ser." He went rigid for a moment, apparently linking with Captain Flahrty. Then he gestured toward the hatch behind him and to his left. "The captain will see you, ser."

I inclined my head. "Thank you."

The hatch opened to my touch, and I eased/floated inside. Captain Flahrty was loosely strapped before a manual console in an office that was barely three meters square and not quite that from deck to overhead. He looked more like an ancient gladiator than a Federal Service senior captain.

"Yes, Major?" Captain Flahrty growled, as everyone had said he did.

"This is from Commander Matteus, Captain, with her compliments." I extended the case, then managed a slight formal bow, despite the weightlessness.

Captain Flahrty raised his eyebrows, but he took the case. "Thank you, Major. Is there anything else?"

"No, ser. Unless you have anything that needs to go back to Earth."

"If I do, Major, I'll send it over on the shuttle."

"Yes, ser. Thank you, ser."

With another bow, I propelled myself out of the smallish office. After nodding to the young lieutenant, I made my way back down to the main deck, where I stopped by the mess and tried some of their pastries. They weren't any better than those on the *Newton*, and no one on the station seemed especially friendly. So I went to suit up again and to find the cargo shuttle.

The shuttle had a new pilot, and she didn't mention the alien Gate, and neither did I, although I did wonder about what the other pilot had told me. But all I could wonder was how anything could have survived the time and temperatures for so long. And I still felt restless.

Chapter 34
Raven: Vallura—Helyna, 459 N.E.

I woke up groggy from not sleeping well. My home was probably safe—for a time—and the latest modifications to the glider were designed so that it would have been easier to blow it up with an antique tactical nuclear device—were there any left on Earth—than to tamper with it in a way that wouldn't register on my personal link system.

But something was happening, more than a simple attempt to murder me. I could take matters two ways—that someone was out to kill me or that I'd been given a serious warning. Stay home and out of whatever it was, or get killed. I'd never liked that kind of game. I suppose it was why I still occasionally played tennis against Gerrat, even if he won most of the time.

If I had to, I supposed that I could dip into my inheritance and go trotting all over the world to try to dig out more on the PST connection. Or I could go visit Eldyn—I certainly didn't want to talk substance to him on the net—and he'd probably talk to me, even if he told me nothing. But there was no certainty that I'd find anything. And there was no one else I could hire that could probably do much better. I knew nets, and systems, and I knew the people and the kind of people who ran them. If the kind of information I needed didn't happen to be accessible on someone's net, then it was either firewalled where breaking in would end someone on the Mars penal project, or it wasn't on any system. In a very careful way, I'd already been set up, set up so that almost any effective way to discover exactly who was after me or why would be illegal and dangerous, or both.

I did have some information to track down Elysa—but I didn't want to use any system I had . . . and if I went to UniComm . . . well, then, I could get further involved in the sysnet wars . . . if indeed they were part of the problem. Besides, something about going into UniComm *felt* wrong.

As I sipped yet another cup of Grey tea and looked at the early-morning shadowed shapes of the East Mountains, I had one thought. Probably a bad one, but I needed a friendly face as well as more information.

So I headed to get cleaned up and dressed.

I had gotten as far as getting dressed. In fact, I was standing in my office wondering what I'd need to implement my questionable idea when the gatekeeper chimed. The identification was about what I'd worried about—or feared—the Civil Authorities.

The image that appeared was that of a tired-eyed but young CA in a slightly wrinkled off-white and gray single-suit. "Ser, I'm officer Whitsenn, with the Helnya regional office of the Civil Authorities." He paused, I suspect, to see what I would volunteer.

"Yes?" I was wary, but I decided that I needed to get through the call. "What can I do for you, officer?"

"There's been an incident of sorts here, and we've been going through the skytors and tube records, and it appears

that you might have been in Helnya yesterday when it occurred."

"I was in Helnya yesterday," I admitted. "I was visiting a
jeweler, but I don't see what . . . " I frowned, then shook my
head, and offered a puzzled smile. I hoped it was a puzzled
smile. "How can I help you?"

"I'd like your permission to record this, if I might, ser?"

"That's fine," I agreed. There was no reason not to agree.
He was being polite, or putting me on notice, or both, since
he certainly didn't need my permission.

"Thank you, ser." After a moment, he continued, "You
took the two fifteen induction tube from Helnya to Vallura,
and a man of your approximate description was seen hurrying to the tube train station at about five past two." He
waited again.

I smiled and shrugged. "I'm sure that was me. I didn't
want to wait for another tube." I decided to be very coop-
erative. "What else do you need to know?"

"You seemed to be coming from the northwest."

"I'd guess so. I was just following the walkway. There
were oaks there. I was just walking, and then I realized if I
didn't hurry I might miss the tube."

"Did you see anything unusual?"

I frowned. "Where? There was a pair of youngsters on the
train, you know the type, with the wide-legged red leather
single suits with the white vests that strobe . . . "

"Actually, ser, we were interested in anything you might
have seen just before you got to the station."

I squinted, trying to remember just how the monoclone
had looked. "I only saw one person before I reached the
station . . . I mean just before. I didn't think it was that unusual. Maybe a little . . . There was a man in a sort of brown
singlesuit—a cheap one, and it struck me as a little odd for
Helnya at first, but he was standing in the nasturtiums, and
then I realized he was a gardener or something."

"Why did you think he was a gardener, ser?"

"Well . . . because he had knife in his hand and was doing
something to the tree. It looked like he was pruning some-

thing . . . so I thought he was a gardener." I looked at the CA's image. "Wasn't he a gardener?"

The CA politely ignored my question. "Could you describe this man?"

I shrugged again. "I didn't look too closely. I remember the brown, because it was cheap-looking, and he had brown hair . . . I think. I would have noticed if he'd been a redhead or a blond. I don't think it was black. Maybe medium-sized, not as tall as I am." I tried to look helpful. "That's the only person I can remember seeing. Does that help?"

"Yes, ser, it does." He gave me a professional smile. "Is there anything else you can remember?"

I tilted my head, trying to remember any other detail, but I couldn't, except for the clone's vacant face and the filament knife, and I wasn't about to mention those. Finally, I shook my head. "I really can't. I suppose I dismissed him once I realized he was a gardener." I paused. "Except he wasn't, was he?"

"No, ser."

"Can you tell me what this is all about?" I tried to be insistently polite.

"I really can't, ser. You've been most helpful. All I can say is that we're investigating." He paused, then asked, "Did you see anyone else who might have passed this man? Say, someone going the other way? From the station toward him?"

"No." I shook my head. "It wasn't that far from the trees where he was to the station. I suppose someone coming off the tube might have walked that way, but I didn't see anyone." In fact, I hadn't seen anyone except the monoclone until I'd gotten into the station.

"No one at all, ser?"

"No one. Not until I was in the station." And that was definitely true.

He kept at it for a time, asking about details, and rephrasing questions, but I struck to what I'd seen, and everything I told him was true—except for the little detail about the clone using his knife to prune the tree. I just didn't tell him everything.

Finally, he—or his image—looked at me. "You've been very patient, ser, and I thank you. If we run across anything else, might we contact you?"

"Of course."

After his image vanished, I went upstairs and had another cup of Grey tea. I'd need to wait a bit before I put my bad idea into practice, since the last thing I wanted to do was to go screaming out of the house right after a call from the CAs.

Chapter 35
Fledgling: Earth Orbit Station Three, 442 N.E.

Somehow, everything was less eventful, less mysterious, after the discovery of the forerunner Gate. I kept looking for stories about it, in the scientific netpubs, the journals, the pop news . . . but there was little outside of a few short articles on the basic inscrutability of the alien science, and one series of stories about how there had been a single huge energy spike from the Gate, but no sign of anything except what appeared to be a puff of gas that dispersed into deep space almost instantly. The stories went on, but no one had figured out how it had happened or triggered or why, and eventually those disappeared as well. Someone had begun to unravel the mystery of the composite hull and was hopeful that the material could be duplicated commercially within the decade.

As Gerrat and Father had said, if there's nothing new, it's not news, and there wasn't anything new, and the pop news went back to the VR entertainment hoaxes, and the scaps that were and weren't, the latest epidemic to come out of Southeast Eurasia, blamed on the uncovering of pre-Collapse biowar stockpiles in Chung Kuo but curtailed by rapid deployment of specialized nanites.

Along the way, I became and remained the senior pilot on

the *Newton*, until I decided to put in my papers on our way back from Delta Felini. Ten years was the minimum to fill the FS obligation for a pilot, and I'd put in sixteen, almost seventeen years, thinking I might go for retirement, before I decided that I couldn't see myself bucking for command and playing all the political games. Being senior pilot had shown me enough about that.

We were in the last few hours of decel coming into Earth, and I was scheduled to go on duty in an hour. I was looking around my cabin wondering if I should start to pack when the link chimed.

"Major?" The voice was that of Captain Matteus. She had finally succeeded Andruhka as the commander of the *Newton*, and she was personally the opposite of Andruhka—slighter, physically deft, soft-spoken, and with an understated sense of humor. She also never forgot a favor or a slight.

"Yes, ser?"

"I'm in my office. I'd appreciate it if you could stop by."

"Yes, ser. I'll be right there."

"Thank you."

What did she want? To wish me well? Change my mind? Tell me I was making a mistake? I didn't know, and wasn't about to guess, since Matteus had been the toughest officer to read of any I had served with or for. Unless she wanted you to know, you didn't. It was that simple. She had summoned me personally, rather than just talking over a private netlink, and that was unusual, to say the least.

I closed the locker I had been studying prior to packing and made my way out of the small cabin and along the passageway to her office. There I knocked on the door. "Major Alwyn, ser."

"Come in, Major."

I stepped inside and closed the door.

She gestured to one of the chairs, fastened firmly to the deck, like everything in a Federal Service ship.

I sat and waited.

"You're one of the best pilots in Federal Service, you know," she said quietly. "If you decide to change your mind, I'd take you back and offer you ops."

That was an automatic promotion to subcommander. "I didn't know we needed an ops officer."

"Subcommander Vehrens is being transferred when we reach Orbit Three."

I nodded.

"You don't seem surprised, Major."

"No, ser." It was better that I not say I'd been totally unimpressed with Vehrens, particularly since some of his duties had been delegated to me, and since it had been obvious that the captain and the exec had been covering for his lack of ability.

"He's eligible for early retirement. He was once a very good pilot." The captain smiled sadly. After a moment, she spoke again. "Before you make up your mind, there is one thing you should know. All transfers to and from orbit station have been frozen. No one who's been augmented or preselected can go Earthside until they've been medically screened." She gave a rueful smile. "And the equipment's Earthside and likely to stay there for a while. Then they'll have to sterilize Kuritim. . . ."

"Ser?"

"It came in about an hour ago. There's another plague or virus. It started in the Sinoplex . . . and a few other locales on the Pacific Rim. This one only attacks pre-selects who are augmented. All FS officers are both, and many of the senior techs as well."

I shook my head. I couldn't even leave the FS without difficulty. "Does anyone know how it started? Or why?"

"I'm sure someone does, but they haven't seen fit to tell me, or anyone on Orbit Three. I talked on the longlink with Marshal Hylui. He said they had matters under control, but since the orbit stations are effectively already quarantined, if they leave them isolated, then they can concentrate all resources on the affected areas and people."

I sighed. "I take it that if no one's coming up, then I wouldn't be going down."

"No . . . you could wait on Orbit Three. . . ." Her tone conveyed I would be waiting a long time.

"Do you still want me back?" I grinned at the captain. "Even as a pilot?"

With a rueful smile, she shook her head. "If you'll extend for six months, you can have ops, and the promotion. There's no one else close to you that's available right now."

And she wanted Subcommander Vehrens off the ship. That was quite clear.

"The quarantine?"

"That . . . and the rotation schedules. Sometimes, it happens."

"I'll extend."

Her smile was broader. "If you make it two years, you can take early retirement and the higher rank."

Thinking about Father and Gerrat, especially, there were suddenly reasons for taking her offer, reasons that looked very good. For that I could take the political games, for another year and a half beyond the six months. But only for another year and a half, and only under Matteus.

"Let's go for two."

Captain Matteus smiled and handed me a folder. "No one has seen your papers. No one will."

I raised my eyebrows. "Could I ask why?"

"Yes . . . but I won't tell you until you leave Federal Service." She reached into one of the drawers in her desk and pulled out the gold starburst insignia of a subcommander. "Here. You can have these as a loan, and you can start wearing them tomorrow."

"Thank you." I couldn't help smiling. "What would you have done if there hadn't been a quarantine?"

"I'd like to have thought I could have come up with something, Subcommander. That's something captains are supposed to do." Her eyes twinkled, and I realized, perhaps for the first time, that besides being enormously competent, behind that cool exterior, Matteus was a very warm soul, almost too warm for the FS.

"I think you would have, ser." I tried not to keep grinning. "I think you would."

She only raised her eyebrows. "I believe you're on duty in twenty minutes. Since it will be your last as senior pilot,

Subcommander, I wouldn't want you to be late."

"No, ser." I bowed slightly. "Thank you, ser."

"Thank you, Subcommander."

After I left her office, I was smiling—at least until I began to wonder about the epidemic . . . and worry. While my parents and family had the best of medical care, I didn't like the idea of an epidemic virus, and I resolved to send a tight-beam message once we reached orbit. Quarantines wouldn't affect that.

From the news reports, it seemed like there had been more and more strange viruses in recent years, despite advances in medicine and a far lower population than in the centuries immediately preceding the Collapse.

Again . . . I hadn't recalled reading or seeing anything in the secondhand beamed VRs that we got on the *Newton*, not along those lines.

But there wasn't anything else I could do . . . and I had to get ready to take the duty.

I hoped I could stand two more years.

Chapter 36
Raven: Vallura—Helyna, 459 N.E.

After the interview with the CAs, even after the next cups of Grey tea, I found myself pacing back and forth.

So, after what I hoped was a decent interval, I found myself in my glider, the canopy locked firmly closed, repeater turned off, gliding northward toward Helnya, and Majora Hyriss, who had been one of the few non-family members to inquire about me, and for whom I'd always had a fondness. As I guided the glider northward, I was already worrying about the distance taxes I was beginning to pile up. Yet I was far less vulnerable in the glider, if only because the energy expenditure required to hurt me there would be more easily detected and traced.

It was still early morning when I eased the glider into the oak-shaded and stone paved spot clearly reserved for gliders visiting Majora. After making sure the glider was secured, I walked along the stone path that followed a small stream uphill, past a cultivated or at least ordered, natural wetland garden. After several hundred meters, the path ended at a short grassy expanse sloping upward and westward, beyond which was a cottage-like dwelling set in a grove of young redwoods—by young, a mere two or three hundred years old.

I walked up the steps, hoping she was home. Although I knew that in recent years she'd done more and more work there, that was no guarantee. But I hadn't wanted to VR or leave a message.

After a moment of hesitation, I knocked. I could sense the exterior scanner, or maybe I just imagined I sensed the scanner.

The door opened, and Majora stood there in loose-fitting gray exercise clothes, her hair casually bound back and tied. "You certainly don't arrive when I'm looking my best." She studied me. "Are you all right?"

I had to trust someone. "No. Not really. Can you take a walk?" While anything anywhere could be recorded, all the skytors would show was us walking, and I could hope that no one had had time to set up outside directionals.

She nodded and stepped outside. The locks clicked behind her. "They won't do that much good against an expert, but we'll know if someone does open them."

I must have looked quizzical as we walked down the steps.

"You're the most self-sufficient individual I know, Daryn. If you're here in the middle of the day without a warning, and without flowers, or the equivalent, I'm out of my depth right now."

"That just proves you're not." I offered a gentle laugh.

She shook her head. "We might as well go to the lower garden. I wanted to check the basil anyway."

I walked beside her, noting how quietly and gracefully she moved along the stone path, and then through the narrower passages in the hedges of the upper garden, where the flowers were barely beginning to spread, and the lower garden, which seemed without flowers at all. The smell was mainly of turned earth, and the underlying perfumes of something I didn't recognize.

"It's my herb garden. Herbs don't replicate, not well," she explained as she bent down over the green leaves. "The scanners don't pick up the subtleties." She frowned as she studied a plant, but didn't explain. Then she moved to another plant with thin round tendrils, rather than leaves.

Chives, I thought.

"Good . . ." she murmured. Abruptly, she stood, and I realized, again, that she was nearly my height.

"Now . . . why did you bring yourself and your glider all the way here from Vallura?"

We stood in the circle of sunlight, with the faint rush of water over the rocks from the pond in the background.

"I need a friend, and I need your help."

"I'm flattered that you'd turn to me." Her smile was off-center. "And worried. Why me?"

"Because I trust you, and it's getting rather clear that I can't trust very many people."

"You're just discovering that?" Her thick eyebrows arched.

"No. Let's say I'm discovering that I'm into something that has to stay out of the family, and . . ." I shrugged.

"You mean that the mighty Alwyns . . ." She broke off. "That's petty and unfair, and I'd rather not stoop to that. . . ." She laughed, warmly. "Not any more than I already have, anyway."

Her laugh was infectious, and I smiled ruefully. "I probably deserve that."

"What can I do?" Majora asked.

"I'd like to run a search routine off your equipment. Mine's been snooped, and then some."

"You mean you want me to run it?"

"That would be better."

"And what are you, or we looking for?"

"A woman."

"I'm not helping you find a wife, am I?"

I tried to defuse that. "This is the woman who tried to kill me once. She doesn't exist—officially. Gerrat couldn't find her. Neither could Kharl. But there's one track . . . and some-one else sent a destruct-clone after me when I was tracking down the one lead."

"The one lead?"

"She wore some unique jewelry . . . only one person makes it. It was made more than fifty years ago . . . for some-one of the same name, but I'm hoping there's a connection." I shrugged. "It seems to be the only one I have. It's enough that people have tried to kill me twice following it."

"Twice?"

"That was where I was headed—the stonesmith's—when that wall fell on me."

"Why haven't you called in the CAs?" she asked.

"I have. They haven't found any trace of anything in the one case that was definitely an attack, and the investigation of the third time just showed that somehow the wall had eroded, and just happened to fall when I walked by. I didn't report the fourth time, although . . . well . . . there didn't seem to be much point."

Majora frowned. "Why don't you start at the beginning?"

So I did, and told her everything from the suspected nano-spray at Kharl's to the clone with the filament knife, and the latest conversation with the tired-eyed CA. I didn't tell her much about the possible UniComm tie-in, except that I'd been released by OneCys. ". . . and after that . . . well . . . that's why I'm here."

"There might have been residues from the knife," she pointed out.

"Unidentified hydrocarbons and silicates and other com-mon chemicals, plus the few cells of a standard mono-clone . . ." I shook my head. "They couldn't even track a laser caught on the skytors and melted down on a wall by my house. Their scanners were either intercepted or repro-grammed to eliminate the men in the glider-van, and not even Kharl's equipment could trace the nanospray used on me in the first attempt. I somehow don't think the CAs are going to be much help."

"I'll only ask once." Majora moistened her lips. "Are you sure all this happened this way?"

"There's not much question about the first two. You can ask Kharl about the first one, and the second. There's also a CA record about the third. We both know that a wall fell on me, and I guess it is just my recollection about the holo projection and the men in the glider-van. There might be something somewhere on a burned patch in the middle of Helyna—besides my recollections and the VR from the CAs." I spread my hands. "I've told you what I know."

"It might be worth checking to see if anyone reported the latest incident, or whether they're trying to keep it quiet." Majora said. "I could scan the local news."

"I don't think they'd suppress that."

"Because the suppression would leave more trails—or could?"

"They aren't leaving many trails, one way or another."

"Why would anyone go to such great lengths?" she asked.

"If I could figure that out, I might have a much better idea who's behind it. I'm no one, comparatively. I'm not in Uni-Comm; I'm not *that* well-known an edartist. I don't know any secrets."

"Let's head back to the house. I need something to eat, and we might as well get on with your search. I still have a report due by four this afternoon."

"I'm sorry. This can wait." And I was sorry. I'd dropped in on her without even asking if she had the time to help.

"If what you've said is true, then it can't wait. You're not like Gerrat, who's always subtly exaggerating his importance."

We walked quickly back toward the cottage, as peaceful-looking and solid as ever, and I had to wonder if I'd just been dreaming about all the attacks. I shook my head.

"Anything wrong?"

"No. At times, I just have to wonder." I gestured toward the stone stoop and the solid oak door that opened to her touch. "Everything here seems so peaceful and solid."

"I'd like to think so. I've tried to make it that way." She motioned for me to enter, and I did, coming into a foyer with white plaster walls. Beyond was a small version of a great room, with a stretch of mullioned windows overlooking yet another garden, this one of flowers, including golden daffodils. "Just sit down at the table there."

Her voice brooked no argument, and I sat, watching as a green-winged hummingbird darted from blossom to blossom.

"I love to watch them, too." Majora set a plate before me on which rested an enormous scone. "The preserves and clotted cream are there." Then came a large mug of Grey tea.

I was far hungrier than I'd thought. I ate two of the scones.

"You were starved."

"You ate two, also." I took a last sip of the tea.

"While you were destroying that last scone, I checked on local events." The left corner of Majora's mouth lifted. "There is a little item. Small fire near the center of Helnya, less than half a klick from the tube station . . . possibly an incendiary explosive device, according to the CAs, but the location under the heavy oaks rules out any direct correlation with skytors records. The CAs are checking with people known to have been in the area." After a moment, she added as she took out a small vyrtor keyboard, "Anyone would think that your brother would be the one people were after. He's not exactly beloved in the networld."

"No . . . but he's probably feared and respected. I'm not."

"Your father is the one who's feared." Her words were matter-of-fact. She gestured to the keyboard and headset she had placed on the corner of the table. "All right. It's set up for a search under my ID."

I eased my chair around the end of the table. After setting up the search routines I wanted to use, I slipped in the first inquiry—the historical one to see if I could find a record of an Ahmad who had taken passage to Hezira between forty-five and fifty-five years previously.

Majora watched. "That's neat," she said. "I could use that approach."

"I could explain."

"No need. I've got it. I even recorded it while you were doing it."

I'd known she was quick, but we'd never talked shop or

techniques before. I wasn't quite sure why—probably because Mother had thrown Majora at me when I hadn't wanted anyone thrust at me.

We both waited, but the answers were there almost immediately—three names with dates, and the ship involved. Instead of saving or printing them, I committed them to augmented memory and moved to the next inquiry.

"You are worried," she said.

"After something like four attempts on my life . . . wouldn't you be?"

The next inquiry showed five possible matches, with addresses.

"I'd bet on the Sinoplex address," Majora said.

"Why?" I asked, also memorizing and erasing the queries, and entering another, about the total volume of interstellar cargos, totally unrelated to the earlier questions, except in vaguely general subject to the first.

"I don't know." Her smile was more apologetic than generous.

"Are you telling me something? Or trying to?"

"No . . ." She smiled. "Even if I were, you wouldn't listen. You have to work things out yourself. I'll bet you were really hard to tutor for the PIAT."

"Tutor for the PIAT? It can't be tutored for."

Majora snorted. "Of course it can. Any test can be tutored for. Didn't your parents take you to different places . . . or tell you stories about imaginary places, and situations, and then ask you what you should do?"

I frowned. "Don't all parents?"

"And I'll bet they sent you off to sailing camps and survival camps, and places like that."

"Didn't your parents?" I countered.

"Absolutely." She smiled impishly, an odd expression on a woman so handsome and tall, and one that warmed me, even if I didn't know why. "Did you find what you needed?"

"I don't know." I shrugged. "I'll have to see."

"By net or in person?" Majora laughed ruefully. "Oh . . . why don't we see? You haven't ever been here, and after

today, someone might know you have been. Let's just see."
She bent forward.

I could sense she was linking, and before I could stop her,
there was a faint chime of a distant gatekeeper. She'd clearly
memorized the address coordinates as well.

"Please leave a message." The sim figure was that of a
woman possibly Elysa's age, but her hair was a dark brown
that was almost black, her coloring a faint latte. The image
turned slightly, and I caught the hint of the clean profile—
and the combs in her hair—not the same combs, but combs
worn in the same style. "I may or may not return it."

Majora broke the connection, almost before the words
were finished. "Are you all right?" she asked.

"She . . . it . . . they're . . . the facial structure's the same,
but the coloration is so different . . . it can't be cosmetic."

"Daryn . . . that was a sim. It doesn't even have to be her."

I managed a grin. "I know that. But . . . if she doesn't want
to be found . . . why any similarity?"

"Maybe it's close enough for her friends to recognize and
think she's just having fun . . . but enough to throw outsiders
off. How did you find the name, anyway?" Majora asked as
she handed me the mug of Grey tea that she had refilled.

"The name she gave Kharl was Elysa Mujaz-Kitab.
There's no one by that name anywhere on Earth. But . . . well
. . . the name had to mean something. I'd found earlier that
the key words were from ancient Arabic medical treatises.
So I programmed in all the combinations of the physician's
name—"

"All the combinations?"

"His name ran two complete lines of text," I pointed out
dryly. "That didn't quite work. It came up with thousands of
names, but I later found a different spelling of his most popular shorter names, and then I just guessed at some modifications."

"An interesting way to attract a methodizer . . . give him a
puzzle that's difficult but not unsolvable, and one that
wouldn't even seem like a puzzle to anyone else. The question is why," Majora mused.

"Because someone wants me to find her, and someone else

doesn't, and I haven't the faintest idea who is which or why."

"She wants to leave a trail, but not an easy one. Are you sure you're not just being lured?"

"That could be, too," I admitted. "But why would anyone go to such lengths?"

"I must admit," she said quietly, "that I believe you, and that is very disturbing."

"Why?" I forced a note of mischief into my voice.

"You're a rather stolid rebel, Daryn. You wouldn't be a rebel at all in any other family. You can appreciate the fantastic, and you can analyze and understand it, but it wouldn't occur to you to create it."

"That's not exactly a compliment."

"That's my curse," she said, "always saying what I see, and acting sooner than I often should."

I held in the wince, then reflected. I wouldn't have immediately guessed and tried an address, the way Majora had, but her reasoning was sound. "You're right, though," I returned musingly.

"What are you going to do?"

"I need to think, and make a living, and so do you." I stood. "Thank you. I haven't had that good a brunch or whatever in years, or such good company. And I do appreciate your listening."

"I listen well. I don't always speak wisely."

I took her hand and squeezed it, gently. "I meant it. Thank you. I'll let you know before I do anything."

"You don't—"

"I'd like to . . . and I won't show up . . . again . . . unannounced."

"You're welcome announced or unannounced . . . but I'm likely to be far more presentable if you warn me."

"You're very presentable." And she was. I hadn't even thought about it before my own words had blurted out.

As I stepped out onto the stone porch to walk to the glider, I was still worried, more worried than ever about the comparative ease of tracking down the woman who had been— or was still—Elysa.

I frowned as I approached the glider. Elysa had only men-

tioned the oblique medical reference to me, and without that
key . . . I never would have been able to narrow the search.

Why would someone who wanted to kill me leave such a
clue . . . unless she wasn't trying to kill me? But then, if she
weren't, who was? And why?

Chapter 37
Fledgling: Orbit Station Beta, Epsilon Borealis, 444 N.E.

Four of us sat around the mess table on the midlevel of the
orbit station, sitting being a loose term for being half-belted
into a chair lockpinned into the plastex floor. I was there
because the captain had asked me to spend some time on the
station listening. And listening to new voices in the orbit
station officers' mess beat waiting on the *Newton* while car-
goes and passengers were transferred. Also, the orbit station
didn't smell quite so "worn" and "gray" as did the Newton,
or maybe it just smelled different.

"What do you think about this revolt?" Major Tsao asked
me. We'd crossed orbits over the years. She'd been a year
or two behind me at Kuritim, I understood, although I'd
never met her there.

"The one here on Boreal?"

"Is there any other?" asked Major Tsao.

"Not that I know of." I shrugged. "But we don't exactly
get the latest news."

"You're stalling." Tsao laughed.

"I only know what I've heard or read, all of it greatly
delayed," I temporized, despite the fact that much of the
Newton's cargo had been specialized nanite manufacturing
equipment, designed to build everything from armed flitters
to treaded and armored tanks for the FS contingent and the
inhabitants of the smaller but older northern continent. "They
didn't like the planetary government that the Federal Union
set up. That's really all I know."

"The Ardees are norm throwbacks. They want to turn back time to pre-Collapse days. That's the guts of it," suggested Lieutenant Conyr. "Back to when a stronger arm and more weapons determined who ran things."

"As opposed to now, when a faster brain and greater integrative intelligence does?" asked Tsao dryly. "You mean you want a system where your particular abilities are the ones rewarded?"

Conyr flushed slightly.

"So do I," said Tsao with a laugh, "but let's not kid ourselves. Integrative intelligence is merely a superior weapon, and that's why the Ardees are already losing."

I almost shook my head. It wasn't quite that simple. The Ardees were losing because they didn't have the resources to fight the entire Federal Union. But even if they'd had equal resources, they probably still would have lost because they'd rejected a social structure that rewarded those most able to handle a modern nanotech society. Since nanotechnology offered the most effective way mankind had discovered to create and deploy everything from production equipment to weapons, they would have lost eventually—except the result would have been more like the Great Collapse.

Someone in the Ardee leadership had gambled that the Federal Union wouldn't care if a single continent on a planet barely out of the colony stage wanted a different form of government, especially when it was one of the most distant colonies. They'd gambled—and lost—because the FU wasn't about to allow that sort of separatist example, not with the dismal human history of separatism. The results of separatism, if looked at historically, almost always followed the same pattern.

The separatists left or revolted, after claiming persecution at the hands of the majority culture. If they succeeded in establishing their own culture, they invariably ended up persecuting those who didn't conform to their standards, thereby creating either strict repression and eventually another revolution or another separatist culture somewhere else to repeat the pattern. And if the separatists didn't succeed in their revolt, the majority crushed them to hold together the existing society. Either way, at every step, people died.

"You look thoughtful, Subcommander," said Tsao. "Would you like to share those thoughts?"

"I was just thinking that, in the end, separatism is a dead end where an awful lot of people die."

"Would it be," asked the other lieutenant—Merdyk, "if Gate and stellar travel were cheaper?"

"Maybe not," I replied, "but we'd have a lot more Ardees and even more people dying."

"But they could choose their own way of living," suggested Conyr.

"The people who ended up in control could," Merdyk countered.

"That's not much different from the Federal Union," observed Tsao.

"You're saying that we're no different from the Ardees?" asked Conyr.

"In basic terms, is any system?" asked Tsao. "Someone has to be in control—enough to set the rules, anyway. The only questions are who, how many, and how they obtain and hold power."

"There's a great deal of difference between an empire ruled by an emperor and the Federal Union," I pointed out, "but they both meet your basic definition. I don't think I'd want to live in an empire."

"Even if you were the emperor?" asked Tsao with a smile.

"I wouldn't want to be looking over my shoulder all the time, wondering who wanted to kill me and take over."

"That's true in any position of power. . . ." began Merdyk, abruptly breaking off as her eyes went to the mess door, where another major entered.

"You hear the latest?" asked the newcomer, looking at Tsao.

Tsao shook her head.

"The Ardees managed to duplicate the ancient nukes . . . dropped one from a flitter on the orbital liftway and the other on the FU admin building in Kayport. Sent a message saying that they had more, and demanding that the FU leave Boreal."

I winced. We all did.

"They're dead meat," murmured Conyr under his breath.

None of us disagreed, but no one felt much like talking after that, and I eventually caught one of the cargo shuttles back to the *Newton*.

Chapter 38
Raven: Vallura, 459 N.E.

I took my glider home, thinking more on the way. That didn't help much; so when I got back to my dwelling, I checked all my incomings, except there weren't any, or rather none that made any sense. There were two that came through blank, as if they had been cut off right at the address protocol. I frowned. It looked like a censorship program— the crude kind used to keep children from sending replies to certain addresses. Then, maybe some youngster had just mistransferred a popular address—or he or she had wanted to send a comment on one of my edart pieces, and edartists weren't on the family approved list. Then, perhaps someone was blocking, or trying to block communications to me.

That led me into another systems check, but I couldn't find anything within my own equipment and routines. That meant the cutoff was at the sender's level.

Whatever it had been . . . there wasn't much that I could do.

I was beginning to feel that way about too many matters. There was nothing definite anywhere, except the attempts on me and the strange details about Elysa. Someone had tried to kill me, and the thing was, she could have and hadn't. There was no record of her existence. She could have killed me on Kharl's veranda—with a filament knife or something more lethal. I hadn't been paying attention that way.

She hadn't killed me. And the laseflash hadn't been designed to kill me. But the wall and the monoclone had been. The key was the scent . . . and Elysa. I'd smelled the same odor twice—with Elysa and just after the laseflash. She'd left the hint of a trail . . . not much of one, but a hint. And as soon as I picked up on it, someone had tried to kill me.

Was that it? Or coincidence? Two groups of people trying to hurt or remove me simultaneously? Because of the OneCys-UniComm conflict? I'd looked into that, and found even less than about Elysa—just that a group of wealthy and influential individuals belonged to an organization that wanted management improvements and held stock in OneCys—and that some of them had resources enough to arrange my permanent departure. But none of that was proof, or even added up to motive. All I had was Elysa.

Did I really want to try again? Did I just want to wait for the next attempt?

Without a good feeling about either choice, I spent some time on work that would do something besides deplete my credit reserves. I'd actually finished Elen Jerdyn's project for NetSpin. Her combo slot wasn't the problem, from what I could tell. The programming was. There's a difference between catering to popular taste—for whatever niche market—and caricaturing it.

Explaining why the programming was a caricature was another thing, but I'd managed without being too blunt. Then, I'd gone back to work on the package from Fylin Ngaio and NetStrait. His problem was almost the opposite. The last thing he wanted to do was talk down to an audience that prided itself on being above the masses. The program was a drama, and the dialogue was fine. So were the plots of the five episodes he'd sent. But the backgrounds, the sets, alternated between rococo brothel and sand-dirt cheap. While it wasn't obvious, the ratings were pretty clean . . . after one or two viewings, people didn't come back. There wasn't much fluctuation during the actual episode, which argued that once people were drawn in, they stayed . . . but something was operating on them after the fact . . . and I bet—indeed I was betting that the settings were the problem.

Klevyl's specs hadn't arrived, but that wasn't surprising, since he was always late in getting material to me.

The gatekeeper clinged—the double cling that indicated something was on the news in one of the profiles I'd programmed earlier.

I debated ignoring it, but, then, I was almost finished with the NetStrait piece, and I wasn't getting anywhere with my thinking.

The holo image that appeared across the study desk from me was that of a twisted mass of metal and shimmering synthetic . . . next to a induction tube station platform. The image shifted from a car that was undamaged to a car that was twisted and blistered with extreme heat, to a third car— apparently untouched.

. . . here in Mancha, authorities are refusing comment about both the methodology and apparently targeted approach that turned one tube car into an explosive fiery inferno. . . .

I swallowed, watching, fearing the worst.

. . . early indications are that the Senior Director of NEN, Pieter von Bresleuw, and the Senior Managing Director of NEN, Elora Alwyn, were among those instantly killed in the induction tube incident here in Mancha. . . . Also aboard were the noted barrister Karamchand Nehru and . . .

. . . called one of the greatest transport disasters in the past century . . . Federal Union High Transport Commissioner Hyl has already commenced a thorough investigation. . . .

I looked away from the image, not that I was seeing it very well. Elora and I hadn't been that close growing up, but that had been age and distance and Father, not anything else, and I'd enjoyed the infrequent VR talks we'd had . . . and wished that there had been more. Especially now, I wished there had been more.

The high commissioner's investigation was itself an admission that no one was going to be found. And even if anyone were . . . I suspected selective nanites would have already erased any memories that they had.

I just stood there for a long time, knowing I should do something. But what was another question. My actions to date hadn't been exactly the most effective at anything except getting myself into the medcenter.

Finally, I put through a VR to Father at UniComm, and it wasn't intercepted by a gatekeeper or anything else.

"I just found out . . . about Elora. . . ." Those were the only words that came to mind.

"So did I." Even his eyes were slightly red. At least, I thought they were.

"I'm sorry." I didn't know what else to say. After a moment, I asked, "Should I call Mother?"

"She knows, but she'd like to hear from you."

We looked at each other—or our VR images did.

"If there's anything . . ." I said.

"I'll let you know, Daryn . . . and thank you." His image blanked.

I dreaded the next VR, but I placed it as well.

"Hello, Daryn. I thought that might be you." Mother was not red-eyed, but then, she was even more controlled than Father. There was a darkness in her eyes, though.

"I just found out about Elora," I said slowly.

"Gerrat told me a little while ago."

That didn't surprise me, either. "I'm sorry. I found out on the news."

"He was probably talking to me."

"Is there anything I can do?"

"Not now." She shook her head. "I do appreciate your calling, but there's nothing any of us can do right now."

No sooner had I stopped talking to Mother than the gatekeeper chimed. I checked the identifier—Grey Anne Bergamo, Solicitor. I didn't recognize the caller, but something said I should take it.

The VR of a thin-faced older woman appeared opposite my study desk. "Daryn Alwyn?"

"That's me." I managed not to choke on the words.

"Pardon me if I ask a few questions first, and they may sound silly, but please bear with me. What was your favorite work of art of those held by your father—or what was it when you left for Federal Service?"

The question chilled me, but I answered. "The Hui-Lui painting of the woman and the gate."

"Who was the Bergdorf?"

"She was . . . Elora. . . ."

"And what did she send you before you went to The College?"

"A miniature silver bolt-cutter."

A faint smile appeared on the stern face, then faded as she nodded. "I am . . . was . . . your sister's solicitor. She left explicit instructions for me to contact you immediately in the event of her death. I trust I am not the one breaking this to you. . . ."

"Close . . . but no. I just found out."

The solicitor nodded. "I am sorry. Most sorry, but Elora told me that I was not to waste time on condolences." The woman swallowed, then continued. "She was most explicit."

"She could be."

"She said that it was important you know the disposition of her assets before anyone else. First, all of her shares in UniComm are bound over to you. That includes those she inherited, and also another set of holdings. You have immediate voting power of all those. They amount in total to eighteen percent of the outstanding common stock in UniComm."

It was my turn to swallow. With my own shares, according to the annual reports, I was suddenly the largest single shareholder in UniComm. Father held twenty percent, and Gerrat had about nine.

"Second, there is a coded transmission, the contents of which I do not know, which you will be receiving shortly, if you have not already. Third, your sister asked me to suggest that you be extremely careful." After another short pause, she added, "The various forms and certifications will arrive in the next day or so, but they should confirm what I have told you."

I just stood there.

"Do you have any questions?"

"Not that I can think of . . . not now."

"I'll be around for several hours yet today, if you do, ser." The image blanked and vanished, and I looked out into the afternoon, at the reddish tinge of the East Mountains, but not for long, because the gatekeeper announced another arrival— the file with the solicitor's return on it.

I called it up immediately, and got the holo image of an ancient chest bound in chains, with a slip of parchment attached to it. The parchment bore a list of question-like phrases.

Rasmussen's friend
The friend I surprised on the veranda
That radical bleeder . . .

I laughed as I read through the short list. For a security code it was pretty good, because some were one word answers, and some were phrases, and no one but Elora and I knew more than one of the phrases.

I answered them in turn, beginning with the phrase "the white weasel." When I entered the last one, which was, "in the wrong corner," an image appeared—Elora's. She was sitting behind a desk, wearing a blue singlesuit, and a light gray jacket, set off with a crimson and gold scarf. Her gray eyes looked at me, almost through me.

"I hope this isn't necessary, and I hope you'll never see this, Daryn. But if you are, you are or could be in great danger. You've already figured out that you're the largest single shareholder in UniComm. What you probably don't know is that despite Father's strong arm, he's not what he once was, and, as we both know, Gerrat's self-opinion is far greater than his ability. If you don't believe me, check UniComm's profit percentages and market share. But don't do it now."

I laughed softly. That was . . . had been . . . Elora.

"I can't tell you all of what is happening, but someone is buying up NEN and OneCys stock, and enough has changed hands over the last five years for it to amount to a working majority. By the way, you also get my NEN stock. It's only five percent, but that won't hurt you. Father has refused to make changes at UniComm, and Gerrat neither wants to, nor would he know how. Before long, there will probably be a de facto consolidation of NEN and OneCys, and together they'll control the market. I've been talking to Father . . . and if you get this, it's a good bet that word has gotten out.

"Gerrat will sell out, so long as he stays as Senior Director, but I'd retire him, and he knows it. No one knows what you'll do, and that's why you have to be careful. You also need to avoid any of those associated with StakeHold and the PST Trust. They're not all raisined grapes, but a number of them are pre-select elitists in the worst sense of the word."

Elora smiled. "Gerrat and Father always guarded the Gates, so that any approach was obvious. I've given you another Gate, and it's up to you to decide how to use it. I won't care if you fail; I will be very angry if you don't try. So . . . do your best to reclaim the family heritage." There was another pause. "I'd suggest you also talk to your old friend Eldyn. He could prove helpful. And don't trust anyone in the family, or in any netsystem."

That was it.

I was now among the powerful and wealthy . . . and my sister was dead because . . . why? Because she'd "betrayed" the NEN and OneCys conspiracy? And the offhand reference to Eldyn was anything but offhand.

My guts churned as I looked through the associated files. Elora had planned this for years. She'd never actually held the thirteen percent of the UniComm stock she'd acquired. Rather a trust, the EDA Trust, held it, with her as the first trustee and me as the beneficiary trustee, and the Federal Union as the tertiary beneficiary. And that meant she had wanted the FU to know something . . . or be forced to look into something . . . if anything happened to both of us.

Forcing a weary and clearly artificial smile, I put in a VR to Gerrat. He took it personally.

"Have you heard?" I asked.

"I was about to call you." He nodded somberly. "It was a shock. We haven't talked that much in years, but still . . ."

"I know. . . ."

He shook his head.

I waited, but he didn't say anything. So I had to. "What's going on, Gerrat?" I had to be careful, playing it smart, but not smart enough.

"What do you mean?" He looked puzzled. He just didn't look puzzled enough.

"I get dropped by OneCys with no real reason, especially right after they've adopted my work and recommendations. Then . . . a wall falls on me for no reason, and an induction tube train explodes around Elora. This isn't exactly normal. And don't tell me it's coincidence. It has something to do with UniComm."

"I don't know." He frowned. "It's no secret we've lost a little market share, but we've lost most of it to NEN, despite all the credits that OneCys has thrown into their new offerings. You know that the senior director who was also killed was the one who supported Elora?"

"No. How would I?" Then, that was Gerrat's way of telling me. "Sorry. I'm not thinking. That almost makes UniComm look guilty."

"Doesn't it, though? There's also been a request entered for a special shareholder meeting. That'll be in forty-five days."

"A special meeting? For what?"

"The request was to discuss and vote on possible management changes. They don't have to be more specific."

"Who filed the request?"

"Something called the EDA Trust. It holds thirteen percent of UniComm. It's a private trust, and no one knows who holds it. Then another trust, the PST Trust, filed in support of the meeting. With more than twenty percent of the shareholders requesting it . . ."

I didn't like that, but I asked the too-obvious question. "Is someone trying to take over UniComm? That's what it sounds like."

"It looks that way. Are you going to be there?"

"Of course." Unless someone dropped another wall on me.

"Good. I know you don't like this sort of thing, but we'll probably need your votes—unless you'd rather give Father or me a proxy."

"I'll be there, and you can explain what you would like."

"Good. Take care of yourself, Daryn."

I intended to . . . if I could figure out how. "You, too."

I broke the connection. There was no point in talking longer, not to Gerrat. There never was, not really.

An attempted takeover didn't seem enough . . . but was that because it wouldn't have mattered that much to me? Or didn't it matter because I'd never thought of myself as part of UniComm? Had someone been after me, trying to get to me *before* Elora . . . or before I knew what was happening?

That was even more disturbing.

The next thing was to try to reach Eldyn. I didn't like that, but I certainly had to try.

The only thing was that, even though I had a netsys address, nothing happened for a long moment. All I got was a blank screen, before a sim appeared. "I am sorry I'm not available. Please leave a message."

The sim didn't quite look like Eldyn, or maybe it did, but that momentary delay bothered me. So I did some research, and came up with the address for his replicator manufacturing concern. Again . . . I got a sim, a different sim, with the same message.

I tried for a physical address, but all I got was a general locator, that of a town in the Central Sinoplex.

I felt cold. Very cold.

The answer was clear. Someone had infiltrated Nyhal's systems, very selectively, selectively enough that my codes, and probably only my codes or a very limited number of codes, were being transferred to a sim. That reinforced Elora's concerns. She had been worried about something, enough that she was willing to try an outside takeover of UniComm—and referred me to Eldyn.

That meant she wanted to do something Father and Gerrat opposed, and it also meant her position with NEN had been about to become impossible.

And the transfers of my calls to Eldyn meant something nasty was going to happen soon, because whoever did it knew that if I kept getting sims, I'd start to get concerned, after a few days anyway.

Again . . . I didn't know why, or at least not what part Eldyn played, although the death of his wife was beginning to make very grim sense.

I looked out at the East Mountains once more, trying to gather myself together for what had to be done, whether I liked it or not.

Chapter 39
Fledgling: Kuritim, 445 N.E.

What with one trip and another, including several back to Epsilon Borealis to deliver more nanites to crush the Ardee Rebellion, the two years which I'd extended passed quickly enough—especially since operations officers were busier than senior pilots.

I'd sent a few VR blocs to the family, as I always had throughout my years in the FS, but didn't get much back except news on how well Elora and Gerrat were doing, rising and conquering in their respective netsystem domains. Father did send one suggesting that I give some thought to a post-FS career, as much of a hint that he expected me to work in something productive, preferably UniComm, as anything. I told him that I certainly expected to work once I left Federal Service, but that I'd probably travel around Earth for several months, since I hadn't seen much of it except Kuritim for more than twenty years.

I was more than ready to start that traveling when the orbiter glided to a halt at the terminal off the Kuritim liftway. Just as I stepped beyond the lock and began to walk toward the terminal, a medtech stepped forward.

"Subcommander, ser?"

"Yes?"

"If you'd come with me?"

I must have looked puzzled, probably more than puzzled.

"You haven't received an augmentation boost, have you?"

"An augmentation boost? No. Not that I know of."

"You'll need one before you can leave Kuritim."

I shrugged. I'd heard something about an augmentation boost, but I'd figured that would come after I'd checked in at personnel. "Lead on."

He even had a small cart, and I did ride in style to the medcenter on the north side of the liftway. From what I could tell, Kuritim looked the same. It also smelled the same, with the salt air and the breeze off the Pacific, just tinged with the faint hint of oil and metal. It had looked and smelled the same every time I'd come down for twenty years. I wondered how places like Yunvil were, though.

A thin, almost gaunt-looking FS commander with the medical insignia on his collar was waiting for me inside the foyer of the west wing.

"Subcommander Alwyn?"

"Yes, ser."

"Good. You're about the last. Please come with me."

I followed him into an open room, more like a laboratory than an examining room.

"You were lucky you were off-planet," commented the doctor.

I frowned. "The pre-select plague?"

"That's not technically correct," offered the doctor. "Anyway, you're getting a special set of augmentation nanites, and you'll be here in the quarantine wing until we're sure they're up to strength. Not more than a day or two, but we wouldn't want you to leave active service and then keel over."

I didn't like that thought at all, and what were a few days, anyway, especially against something like that? "What caused this plague?"

"Evolution, I suspect," the doctor said, as he lifted out a container labeled "AGB-1" and studied it for a moment. "Nanites are biological constructs, artificial constructs, but biological in nature. All the bugs on Earth have been evolving for billions of years, and every time we think we have them beat, nature comes up with another surprise. The pre-Collapse medical types thought they'd destroyed pathogenic bacteria with antibiotics, but in the end, all they did was create nastier pathogens with resistance to antibiotics. Nanites are different, and it took nature longer this time, that's all."

I nodded at that, recalling my history lessons on the incredible death rates during and after the Collapse. But still, I had to wonder. "How come this doesn't hit norms with basic nanite protection? Why only pre-selects and those with full augmentation?"

"It doesn't. It takes a certain concentration of old-style augnites. Why? That, I can't tell you, except I wouldn't be surprised if there will be another bug that hits anyone with nanite support. Nature eventually works that way. We've developed nanitic augmentation, and now there's a pathogen that feeds off the augnites. The only problem is that augnites aren't natural biology, and when this pathogen consumes an augnite, it releases excessive heat. The more augnites, the more heat."

"That's what causes the high fever?"

"Exactly." He lifted the nanite spray. "Stand in the circle there."

I stepped into the circle and felt the cone of positive air pressure rise around me. As the doctor slipped the nozzle into the cone, there was a hiss.

"Just stay there. It will take several minutes for optimal dispersion through your system." He replaced the container and extracted a second, but set it on the table beside him. "The problem with the fever, and that's a natural response, is that nanites resist heat better than most cells in our bodies. To deal with nanites, so do the new pathogens." He shrugged.

"So people, those heavily augmented, tend to get cooked from inside."

I winced.

"You're right. It's not very pretty. I've seen it." He picked up the second spray nozzle and slipped it past the air pressure barrier, releasing it with another hiss. "It'll be another few minutes."

"So . . . what happened . . . who . . . how?"

"I've read the literature. Don't know all the details, but a medical researcher, brilliant norm by the name of Eldyn Nyhal . . ."

"Eldyn Nyhal, from Yunvil?"

"You sound like you know him."

"We went to Blue Oak Academy together." I laughed. Eldyn had always been brilliant, if eccentric with his bright singlesuits, even if he hadn't been a pre-select, and I had to appreciate the irony of a brilliant norm saving the pre-selects.

"Anyway, this Nyhal developed a specialized bug—it's half-pathogen, half-nanite—that takes care of the mutated pathogen."

"Good for Eldyn." I didn't feel any different, although I knew that millions of nanites were already swarming through my body. "What now?"

"In a few minutes, I'll point you toward the quarantine quarters, and you rest. Some people get a mild fever for a day or so. You come back here at thirteen hundred tomorrow and get checked. If your modified augnite levels aren't high enough, you stay another day or until they are."

"And then?"

"You're free to go wherever you were headed. It's for your own protection."

"And this virus doesn't strike norms?"

"It hasn't yet."

"That's strange."

"Why? They don't offer as well-defined a target of opportunity." The doctor nodded. "You can step out of the circle now, Subcommander. Follow me, and I'll point you to your quarters. Your gear should be there by now."

"I suppose it got some decontamination treatment, too."

"Of course."

So I followed him toward the foyer through which I'd entered, still wondering about a plague that targeted only augmented pre-selects, but more than happy that Eldyn and whoever had come up with a preventative measure.

Chapter 40
Raven: Helnya, 459 N.E.

It was almost twilight when I took out the glider to head north once more, and I left the canopy full closed and the remote repeater off. Still . . . if someone had been willing to destroy an entire car of an induction tube train to kill Elora, I doubted that they'd have much trouble with a glider—except I was probably the only one who knew—outside of the plotters—that she was the target, and they might not want to make matters too obvious too soon. I could hope.

Then, no one but the unknown conspirators—and me—seemed to know anything, and what I knew wasn't all that much. Nor did there seem to be much that I could do. What could I do? There was little I could add to what I'd already brought to the CAs. They hadn't exactly been all that much help. They still hadn't come up with anything on the laseflash incident, and that had been three months earlier. They hadn't had much success in following the explosion in Helnya. At least I hadn't gotten any notice from the gatekeeper about anything on the news about it, and no CA had called me back. From all I knew, they still thought the incident with the wall was an accident.

Father and Gerrat hadn't come up with anything—at least nothing they cared to share with me, and Elora had something, but she hadn't spelled it out, perhaps because, like me, she hadn't known enough . . . and now she was dead. But she had been convinced that something was about to happen, or she wouldn't have requested the UniComm stakeholder meeting, or set up the transfer of everything to me.

I tried to come up with other approaches to finding out what was happening and who was behind it all as I guided the glider through the growing twilight to Majora's, where I'd arrive again unannounced, hoping she was home. Not surprisingly, my thinking and speculating still hadn't produced any new and brilliant insights.

Majora was home, and she didn't look particularly surprised at my appearance on her doorstep. She wore a pale blue singlesuit and a darker blue vest, and she looked wonderful. A scent of roses lingered around her.

"Hello . . . again." I offered a rueful smile.

"You look like the ancient version of Hades. . . ."

"Can I come in?"

She stepped back and held the door wider.

"I'm sorry I didn't announce myself. I have to trust someone . . . and I don't know anyone better than you."

She smiled, an expression both warm and sad simultaneously, then closed the door.

"That sounds awful. I don't mean it that way. I told you before . . . I mean that you're the most trustworthy person I've ever met."

"Daryn . . . you don't have to explain." She followed me down the pair of steps into the room overlooking the garden. "Would you like some tea . . . and something to eat?"

But I did need to explain. "My sister was killed. I just found out."

"I know. It was all over the news. I wondered if that was why you were here."

"That . . . and her solicitor contacted me." I shook my head. "I don't know how she did it or why, but she had almost as much UniComm stock as Father. It's all mine, and she'd left a code-keyed message that said if I got it that I was probably in danger as well."

"Maybe people were afraid she would use her stock and her position with NEN to merge NEN and UniComm. From what you've said, she was capable enough." Majora's frown gave her a foreboding expression, and I instantly decided I never wanted to be on her bad side. "Was that why she was killed?"

"It could be, but that sort of thing's usually handled in a bloodless way." I shook my head. "There's something else going on." Except I still didn't know what.

"There usually is. Let me put on some tea." She stepped back up to the up-to-date, yet functionally old-fashioned kitchen, with its modified gas-jet burners and the overlarge oven beneath.

I stood behind her as she put on an old-fashioned kettle for the tea.

"I hope you don't mind. I use the replicator just for emergencies, or when I don't plan well and run out of time."

"Sometimes, I brew my tea. It always tastes exactly the same from the replicator, even with different scans."

"Failsafe units . . . idiot units . . . you have to program it to disable the failsafe."

I could feel myself flushing. I hadn't even considered that. But then, cooking, even with the help of a replicator, wasn't my greatest talent.

"It will be a minute." She guided me toward the lower level, where we looked out on the garden. She linked with the lights, and the room went dark. "Just wait a moment."

I did, and my eyes adjusted, and the spring moonlight poured over the garden. I hadn't thought of moonlight in a long time.

"You can sit down, you know, Daryn."

"You aren't."

"I will be, as soon as I get your tea, and I will have to use the replicator for something for you to eat."

"Anything will be fine." I eased into the same chair where she had fed me breakfast—I hadn't eaten since then, and it felt far longer than ten hours.

Before I knew it, she was easing a mug of Grey tea and a plate in front of me—a moderate omelet with cheese and the hint of chives and mushrooms of a type I didn't recognize. She had the same thing, except for a tall crystal glass of water.

"Just eat," she suggested.

I did, and I was mostly through the omelet, which tasted as good as it smelled, before I spoke. "Thank you. This is good. It must be something you scanned into the replicator."

"It is. Whenever I finish something good, I scan it. Some don't scan, and I just erase them, but after a while you do build up a personalized bank of things." She took a long drink of water. "I've seen more of you today than in the last three years."

I was glad the lights were dim, because I could feel the embarrassment. Finally, I just offered a helpless shrug. "What can I say? I need help."

She laughed, gently.

"First, I need you to make a call to an old friend with your codes. Elora left a request for me to do so. My codes are blocked."

"Blocked?"

"All I get is a phony sim. If I were a net engineer, I could engineer another set of codes to get through. I'm not, but it means that someone doesn't want me to reach him."

"At least this old friend is a man." Majora's tone was warmly humorous.

"We went to Blue Oak Academy together. It's Eldyn Nyhal."

"The scientist? The one whose wife died under mysterious circumstances? Maybe he doesn't want any calls."

"He was more than a little strange then, but . . . well . . . if he doesn't take your calls in the same way he doesn't take mine . . ." I let the words drop away.

"What do you want me to say?"

"Just ask him to give you a call. Say you're calling on behalf of an old friend of his from Blue Oak Academy, and that the friend would have called, but that circumstances surrounding his sister's death apparently make it impossible. Don't give my name."

She raised her thick eyebrows. "Rather mysterious, aren't you?"

"No. If his system is altered the way I think it is, any reference to my name will block the message or shunt it somewhere. There's no one else who meets that description but me; it won't be mysterious to him."

Nodding, Majora keyed in the codes, and I stepped back so that I wouldn't fall into the scanning focus.

A sim appeared immediately on the holo screen before us, that of a stocky man, the thinning but wavy light brown hair just one sign of a norm. The sim wore a green singlesuit, and a dark gray vest trimmed in black, and it wasn't either of the same sim images I'd seen before, not exactly. "As you can see, I'm not available. If you would leave a message, I would appreciate it."

"This is Majora Hyriss. I'm calling on behalf of an old friend. . . ." When she was done, she waited until the connection was broken before she turned to me. "Was that what you wanted?"

"Absolutely."

We both knew that it could be minutes or days before he returned the call.

Finally, after a long silence, I turned to her. "You do a lot of PR work these days, don't you? Think up publicity approaches and the like?"

"It's called conceptual analysis." She smiled. "And it doesn't pay nearly so well as methodizing or high-royalty edartistry, but better than the gruntwork systemic analysis I used to have to rely on. I still do some of that, but as little as I can to make ends meet."

"I could use some conceptual analysis. My own is clearly insufficient." I took another sip of the tea. "And there's no telling if or when Eldyn will get back to you. I don't think I can wait for that."

"I'll need to know more than what you've already told me," Majora pointed out.

"I *think* I've told you all about the attempts on me . . . what else is new? One block of stock Elora controlled through a trust—the EDA Trust. That I found out from the solicitor. I got in touch with Gerrat, and he told me that the EDA Trust and something called the PST Trust had already requested a special meeting of UniComm stakeholders."

"But you're the EDA Trust, now, aren't you? Couldn't you stop the meeting?"

"Elora requested it, and I have to believe she had a good reason. I haven't told anyone except you that I'm the EDA trustee. If I stop it . . ."

"That exposes you."

I nodded. "I also did what checking I could on the PST Trust, and they seem to be wealthy individuals from a range of places."

"All pre-selects?"

"I don't know."

"Most of the wealthiest people are. How did your brother take all this?"

"He didn't know who or what the trust was, and he's worried. He asked me for my proxy, and I told him I'd be at the meeting and to tell me what he and Father wanted."

Majora nodded.

"And the other key person who was killed in the induction tube accident was Elora's boss—he'd backed her all the way, according to Gerrat. Gerrat thought they both might be targets." I paused, holding the mug but not sipping, but inhaling, enjoying the warmth rising from the tea. "Oh . . . from the description of the accident, it sounds like the same method as they tried against me the last time—probably with more than one monoclone."

"Well . . ." Majora observed. "What would happen if the same people controlled all three nets? How much of the world comm systems and nets could they influence?"

I frowned. "They're all mass nets. Maybe fifty-five, sixty percent, but less than ten percent of the pre-selects."

She waited.

"You're suggesting some sort of coup against the Federal Union, and having the nets support it?"

"Nothing that obvious. Say . . . and I have no idea what it would be . . . a regulation, or a change in Federal Union policy . . . wouldn't it be likely to be adopted if popular and media opinion were behind it?"

That thought sent shivers down my spine. "But there are

hundreds of other nets. They'd complain and bring out all the objections."

"There are hundreds . . . but there are the big three, then the next dozen have about twenty percent of the coverage, and the next two hundred squabble over the last fifteen percent." She rose and took my empty mug, moving back toward the antique teapot, from which she refilled the mug.

I could see where she was headed. "The only problem we have is that we don't know what these unknown backers want," I pointed out.

"I'm glad you said we." She handed me the mug refilled with the Grey tea, steaming, then added, "Not in specifics," she agreed, "but what about in general? Don't you have some idea? What do you know about those involved?"

I took a sip of the tea before answering. I let the steam wreathe my face once more for a moment. "We know they have credits, and that they don't want to be too obvious. We also know that, for whatever reason, they feel that they want greater control of the nets and their content. They want to generate support for something, and whatever they want to generate support for is something that UniComm would be opposed to . . . at least it seems that way."

"Who would these people be? Who fits that definition?"

"In general terms, as you pointed out, most of the wealthiest pre-selects." I was the one to frown. "You don't think they're aiming at some indirect way to restructure the Union?"

Majora shrugged, almost impishly, and, again, the gesture seemed so incongruous from a woman that tall. "You don't watch the news that much, do you?"

"No . . . except for project-related things."

"You should. There have been more than a few protests about the growing use of the PIAT as a screening tool."

"That's a stupid issue," I pointed out.

"Is it? Or is it a symbolic one?" Majora studied me, her eyes definitely less welcoming.

I took another sip of the Grey tea. It didn't warm me that much. "Let's say that's it," I said slowly, "that they want to move things toward more PIAT-based testing. I still can't see why they'd target Elora, or Gerrat, and especially Father. He's always been against governing based on popular opinion."

"But would he or Gerrat join a conspiracy?"

"No. They're far too proud, especially Father."

"So . . . none of you would be suitable, right? And you, as a group, control UniComm?"

"It sounds silly . . . imagining conspiracies. . . ." I mused.

"It sounds very silly," Majora agreed. "Almost as silly as your being in the medcenter twice in five months, being attacked by a targeted laser, and by a monoclone with a filament knife and engineered to explode."

My lips twisted into a crooked smile. "It doesn't sound silly that way."

"So you need to track down this mysterious woman—quickly—and see if she can give you any information that will offer a better idea. While you're gone, I'll see what I can find out in my own way—especially about the mysterious PST Trust."

"You don't have to. . . . You've helped a lot already."

"Daryn . . . the last thing I want is mandatory PIAT testing. Or any group requiring it, or anything like it. Despite all the literature, it's exactly the kind of test that's prone to great abuse in the wrong hands. Great abuse."

I nodded. I wasn't so sure about that. What I was sure about was that I didn't want an effective monopoly of comm systems and nets in the hands of a few people. From my own edartistry, I knew where that abuse could go—I knew that all too well.

"I can tell from your words and face that you're worried more about the nets, but they're both dangerous."

"I'm also worried about people with organizations that can plan so well and so far ahead that the CAs are useless."

Majora laughed. "The Federal Union operates almost entirely on consensus and cooperation. CAs are more façade than reality, in anything except tracking down spontaneous crimes of violence. Surveillance systems catch most people, and integrated bookkeeping systems catch most of the rest. If we had things like the widespread riots of the Collapse, or the anarchy of the Chaos Years, the CAs would be almost totally useless, and there aren't enough Federal Union troops to deal with more than a handful of cities. We're just too orderly, Daryn."

I had this feeling that she just might be right.

"What else?" I wondered, trying to stifle a yawn.

Majora yawned as well, then grinned sheepishly. "We're . . . too tired . . . to think well. . . ." She stood.

So did I.

"Thank you." I eased around the table and gave her a hug, and for the moment we were cheek to cheek. For that moment, I felt less alone.

"You need some sleep, and so do I." She smiled as she stepped back. "It would be much better—and safer—if you stayed here tonight. And, if your friend calls back, you'll be here."

"I still need some things from home before I go on this quest."

"In the morning you won't be any more of a target, and you can link with your security systems from the glider, can't you? And you'll be less groggy, won't you?"

I nodded.

"Then that's settled. The guest room is the first one on the left." Her tone was quite clear.

But . . . I did sleep better.

Chapter 41
Fledgling: Yunvil, 445 N.E.

I'd finished a complete FS career, if about the shortest possible one, and was happy to have done so. For one thing, although it was totally personal, no one could ever say that I'd gotten a free ride in life because I was an Alwyn. Second, I'd done it in a field where Father's money and prestige couldn't help or hurt. And third, I had enough credits and income from my Federal Service that I didn't have to bow and scrape to either Gerrat or Father.

That said, I still had to go home . . . and then turn my ideas into real plans for the future—after the welcome home/retirement party my mother had insisted on throwing, and after encountering the several "appropriate" young and not-so-young women who were certain to be there.

So I found myself in a dark green singlesuit, with a silver jacket trimmed in light green, the first time I hadn't been in black and silver for a formal occasion in close to twenty-five years, headed down the stairs to go to a party in my honor that I wasn't entirely certain I even wanted to attend. The heavy Mahdish carpet runner that ran over the polished hardwood floor muffled the sound of the boots I'd grown to like while in the FS and intended to keep wearing.

The carpet didn't muffle my steps enough, apparently, because as I passed the door to the private study, Father cleared his throat. Loudly.

"Daryn." He beckoned for me to enter the study. Usually, the door was closed, and that meant he'd been looking for me, but didn't want to give the appearance of doing so.

I stepped in.

"You might close the door, son. We haven't had a chance to talk." He smiled. "Rather, I think you've been avoiding any serious talk."

With a shrug, I said, "I have been. This is the first time in my life where I've had a chance to think about what I'd like to do. In a realistic sense, that is."

"And what do you want to do? Do you know?"

"No." I grinned. "I promised myself that I'd take six months and travel and think before I made any serious decisions. If I decided the rest of my life on the rebound from Federal Service, I don't think the decision would be as wise as it could be."

Father frowned, then fingered his chin. Finally, he nodded. "You might well be right. I can see the wisdom in that." He straightened up in his chair, then smiled again, more genuinely. "I won't keep you. Your mother wants you to enjoy this." His smile turned to a grin. "She does have some plans."

I laughed. "I know, but those will have to wait, too."

"She is very patient."

We both laughed.

He gestured toward the door. "Go ahead. I'll be down in a bit."

"If you aren't, Mother will send someone after you," I suggested.

"Probably."

I did manage to make it down to the main level and out to the back—and the upper veranda of the house I'd grown up in, where I looked out over the garden in the early evening, to the pool to the west, and then down the grassy swale beyond, while I waited for the innumerable guests to arrive.

There was a hint of grapes in the fall air, mixing with the scent of the late roses, but it was still warm enough for people to circulate outside, and I'd spent enough time inside ships and stations that I didn't care at that moment if I ever went back. I was just enjoying the light and cool breeze.

I walked to the other side of the veranda where I found Rhedya's brother Haywar, sitting on the bench tucked in a boxwood framed nook, the one where I'd first kissed Ertis. He was wearing a long face.

"You look less than scintillating."

His response was almost a glare.

"Sorry . . . I didn't mean to intrude." I stepped back.

"It's not. . . . I suppose you hadn't heard. Frydrik didn't do well on his PIAT." Haywar stood slowly, then shifted his weight from one foot to the other, his eyes going over my shoulder toward the veranda, as if to ensure our conversation would be private. Not that it would be, since Father had a complete net through the grounds.

I frowned. "But . . ."

"We had the best possible pre-select from Denyse and me." He shrugged. "Even today, the process isn't foolproof. Nature still has her say."

"Is it—" I began.

"Not even close. We've worried for the past few years. He seemed . . . well . . . less perceptive than Alyssa . . . but boys . . . sometimes they're later in developing."

"How is Denyse taking it?"

"If we didn't have Alyssa, she'd terminate the contract, I think. She puts on a good front, but I can tell she thinks it's my fault."

I wasn't about to touch that. "Frydrik always seemed bright enough. . . ."

"Intellectual brilliance, and perceptual ability aren't the same." Haywar offered a crooked smile. "Nor stability."

"So . . . what will you do?"

"Send him to one of the good engineering universities, and hope he doesn't get too upset. He's got talent that way."

I nodded slowly. Much as Haywar sometimes had gotten on my nerves, I could tell he was upset. No one liked to realize that his child was unable to achieve on the same level as his parents. It happened, even in families with the best of advantages, but it was hard on the parents, and harder still on the child, no matter what sort of rationale was used.

"Haywar!" called a voice, and then Denyse stepped through the faux French doors and onto the veranda. She stepped forward, looking around until her eyes found us. "Oh . . . Daryn . . . I didn't realize you and Haywar were out here."

"I was enjoying the fresh air," I offered. "It's still a novelty these days."

"I would imagine so." Denyse was a squarish blonde with direct green eyes, and a way of tilting her head to the left whenever she talked. "I couldn't take being closed in like that."

"You get used to it."

"I'm not sure I ever would." She looked at her husband. "I looked around, and you just wandered off. I was talking to Hynman Rykof about engineering schools. He was just behind us coming in, you know, and he had some insights I thought you would appreciate."

"I'll be right there," Haywar affirmed.

Denyse nodded. "I'll tell him. Please don't be too long."

"I won't, but I haven't seen Daryn in years."

The blonde smiled. "I know. I'll tell Hynman you'll be coming."

As Denyse turned, Haywar shrugged, then said, "It's good to see you. I hope I don't have to rescue you from the ladies your mother has lined up—"

"Daryn?" Mother's voice came from between the faultlessly trimmed gap in the hedges that led both to the front of the house and the glider park—or to the hedge maze that Grandfather had created years ago.

"I'm here."

Haywar grinned. "I'll bet she has a young lady with her."

"I'm not about to bet on that."

"I'll see you later," he said, still grinning, stepping back and bowing.

As he walked toward the faux French doors, following Denyse, Mother walked through the hedge followed by a tall brunette.

I smothered a smile.

"Daryn," Mother began as she stepped forward. "This is Majora Hyriss. You know, of the Helnya Hyrisses."

Majora laughed, self-deprecatingly. "I do hope you won't hold that against me."

"I certainly won't, not if you don't hold my being of the Yunvil Alwyns against me."

"Now, Daryn," Mother said. "She's very nice, but remember that there are others inside who would like to see you as well. I'll tell them you'll be in in a few moments."

"If you would . . ." I inclined my head and smiled until Mother left. What else could I do?

Then, for a long moment, Majora and I just studied each other. She was nearly as tall as I was, thin-faced, with dark brown eyes and a wide mouth.

"What was it like, being a pilot? I've never met anyone I knew who was." She put her hand to her mouth. "I'm sorry. I still have this tendency to blurt out things."

"That's all right." I grinned. "People can say what they want about being a pilot, but ninety-nine percent of the time you're a glorified public glider driver. The other one percent, you're a tyrant, fighting terror, and hoping no one else recalls either."

"That scarcely fits the heroic image conveyed by the FS," Majora said.

"It's in everyone's interest not to show that image," I said with a laugh. "And what do you do these days?"

"Me? I'm a systems expediter for GTrans. Very glamorous. You know, analyzing nanite assembly routines and then reverse engineering to determine if systems can be improved or simplified."

"At least it's not in communications," I replied.

"I'd be a disaster there—if I had to appear in public, that is, or in meetings. I have this problem with saying what I feel before I think." A lopsided smile followed the words. "Your mother didn't mention it, but I will. She tried to get your brother interested in me before Rhedya. We went out once, and he brought me home after an hour, saying he wasn't feeling well."

I laughed . . . and kept laughing.

Soon she was laughing almost as loudly as I was.

Finally, I just shook my head. "So . . . she's pairing lost causes, now."

"No . . . your mother is very perceptive. She knows you won't like anyone Gerrat does."

"How do you know?"

"The party's for you, and you're out on the veranda. Your brother's the one inside greeting everyone, as if it were his party."

"I suppose I should go in." I offered her my arm. She took it, and we crossed the stones of the veranda, walking toward the open French door, and the sound of voices that drifted out into the twilight.

I got back to my dwelling early . . . very early, before sunrise. Majora had been right. There were no signs of any tampering with the house, the commsystems, or the security codes and keys—and no trace of intruders.

As Majora had reminded me, before I could leave, there was yet another detail to take care of—making contact with the Director of the EDA Trust, one Lyenne DeVor. I was lucky, and the time differential helped.

The image on the screen was of a square-faced woman with equally square cut brown hair.

"I'm Daryn Alwyn. . . ."

"I was expecting your call. I recognize you from the pictures your sister left. We received all the authentications from Solicitor Bergamo." Her voice carried a faint accent, but not one with which I was familiar.

"I'm assuming that you're the one in charge of day-to-day operations of the trust."

She laughed. "I'm the one who's in charge of everything from opening the office to managing portfolio operations. As trusts go, we are very modest."

"The holdings' list was not modest," I suggested.

"Not for an individual, but for a trust, we are on the small side."

"This is new to me. The only thing I know is that I'll need voting control of . . ." I paused, not really wanting to say more.

"I thought so. You are already listed as the authority to vote all our holdings, but I did not forward that authorization to any of the organizations."

"Is there a deadline for that?"

"It can get rather tight if they don't get authorization at least a week before a meeting."

"I see. How about two weeks?"

"I would suggest timing it to arrive two weeks before. . . . I assume this is the meeting the previous trustee requested."

I nodded. "I'm not trying to change that. That's fine with me. What else should I know?"

"I've taken the liberty of assembling some background materials on the trust and our holdings, and I thought I'd send them out under a code set provided by your sister."

"I'd ask you to wait three or four days, if you would. I'll be traveling."

"I can do that. . . ." She went on to tell me where in Mancha her office was physically located and a few other details, which I committed to memory before I begged off.

After that, I was hurrying so much to pack and take care of the details that I didn't even scan the news . . . which I usually did while I ate in the morning, but there were no alerts on the gatekeeper, and that was good.

Once packed, I debated whether to call a public glider, but decided instead to take my own down to the induction tube station. It was old enough not to be too obvious, and the station parking area was enclosed and covered and monitored.

I supposed there was some risk in making an advance reservation for a private compartment on the TransPac, but there wasn't enough time for someone to bring in another set of the explosive monoclones—and if they were already in place . . . it didn't matter.

I made one last call to Majora, but she still hadn't heard anything from Eldyn.

The tube express to Westi left at ten minutes before the hour and twenty minutes past, for scheduling reasons I never quite understood, and that didn't require anything but showing up, and getting a credlink.

When I left my dwelling at quarter to eight, I carried a small bag that held two singlesuits, coordinated vests, undergarments and toiletries. I did keep the glider canopy closed as I eased down from the lower hill and into the center of the valley. I debated on whether to even take the belt remote, since it didn't work well underground and since I could be tracked if I used it, but in the end, just double-checked to make sure it was off—not on standby, but with the power off.

It could have been my imagination, but Vallura seemed quieter than usual on a threeday morning, and the covered glider parking area was more than two-thirds empty. That could have been because I seldom went anywhere that early. I hope I lasted what would be a very long day.

My boots echoed dully on the hard composite as I walked into the station and down the ramps to the lower level, under the clean unadorned redstone arches, until I stopped by the shimmering barrier and offered my link code. The small sticker appeared on the shoulder tab of my singlesuit, and I walked through the barrier toward the southbound platform. Beyond the barrier, the air was drier, with a hint of metallic acridity.

Unlike some of the older stations, the Vallura station had used local stone, appropriately reinforced and strengthened with binding nanites, with minimalist sculpting, and I'd always enjoyed the simple and uncluttered sweep of the walls and arched ceilings.

Several norms were already waiting on the platform. One of them—a curly-haired young woman in a blue singlesuit with a white vest trimmed in a brighter blue—edged away from me, never quite looking in my direction. An older man with a trimmed white beard nodded and smiled.

A youth—wearing the typical wide-legged red leather singlesuit and a white vest that strobed—stared blankly at me. I stared back until he looked down. The youth in red joined two others clad similarly—wide-legged leather suits with deep vee-necks in single bright monocolors, one green, one blue—the colors accentuated with the strobing white vests.

Another clump of young adults—norms and pre-selects wearing dark green jackets over various colored and patterned singlesuits—milled around at the far end of the platform, students from their matching jackets and probably headed to Westi for something.

A heavyset norm puffed toward the platform as the three cars of the tube train whistled through the pressure barrier at the end of the tube and settled into the shaped platform. No one got off.

I followed the noncon youths into the second car. All three slumped into the bench seats at the end of the car, and I took a seat in the middle at the side, facing away from them.

This train is departing. This train is departing. The words were not only spoken, but echoed through my personal links, and the links of those who had them.

I listened to the noncons, letting my systemics amplify their words.

". . . thinks he's something . . . he does . . ."

". . . all do . . ."

". . . riding the tube . . . can't be that much . . . real ups don't mess with tubes . . ."

I wanted to smile. I'd always spent time on the tubes. So had most of my family.

". . . bigger than most . . . big abs and pecs . . ."

". . . take him . . ."

One of the youths snorted disagreement. "Be the type with defense mods . . ."

He was right about that, although the incident with the monoclone had been the first time I'd used them since I'd been in FS training.

". . . say there's another bug . . . hitting 'em . . ."

". . . sure . . ."

". . . Lynna better be waiting . . ."

". . . with her friends . . ."

A raucous laugh filled the car.

The slight change in car pressure indicated the tube train was gliding to a stop.

Once we were past the pressure barrier, through the armaglass of the car doors came the bright lights of the local receiving platform—filled with men and women, mostly norms, hurrying across the spotless white-gray granite floor.

I let the young men get off first. That way I could watch them.

The one in blue glanced back, once, but they sauntered

toward the ramp leading up to the exit area. I carried the small bag and strode toward the lower ramp, behind a norm couple—wearing large shimmering shoulder-packs.

"Hiseo will be waiting. You'll see," the woman asserted.

". . . be a first, if he is . . ."

I smiled. Hiseo was probably her brother.

At the clearance barrier, I offered the link and reservation code, and received another shimmering sticker on my should-ertab. Then I stepped through the barrier . . . and shivered. The area was considerably colder, but I could sense my system beginning to adjust.

The deep induction tubes were probably the greatest engineering achievement of the post-Collapse world, and were made possible only by the combination of nanitic infrastructure and the mastery of the principles behind the LDD-photon drive. Far faster than anything except a suborbital lifter, the deep induction tube trains linked continents in the ways in which cities had once been linked—and without the adverse impacts of energy and hydrocarbon discharges.

After I used the public comm to make another check with Majora, who still hadn't heard anything, I stood and walked around the waiting platform, thinking.

Nyhal was a norm, a brilliant norm. One Cys had tried to destroy him. Elora had mentioned him. He was being isolated from me, and she was dead. Elora had arranged a stakeholder meeting, presumably to try to take over UniComm. Knowing her, she wouldn't have tried that if she hadn't been very worried.

With all that, I definitely had the feeling that whatever was going on was far larger than a mere netsys battle, but I couldn't quite figure how Elysa and Eldyn fit in—only that they did. And no matter how I arranged the pieces in my mind, something was missing. And that something was still missing a half hour later when the westbound TransPac slid into the loading zone. By then, there were fifty people waiting, perhaps seventy-five, mostly norms. They seemed to be giving me a wider berth than normal, unless I was being more sensitive.

I waited for a moment, until I realized that no one was

disembarking, before I stepped toward the open doors of the middle car, and then inside, into the off-blue shimmering walls and indirect light.

Thank you. Your compartment is four right. Please proceed.

I proceeded, past the chair car section. Even in the coach seating, passages weren't that cheap, and the area was but half filled, and compared to the seating available, there hadn't been more than a few handfuls of people waiting on the platform, far fewer than the few times I'd taken intercontinental or transcontinental before.

I opened the compartment door, gingerly, but the space was vacant, as it should have been. After I stepped inside, I locked the compartment and slipped my bag into the small locker behind the door. Then, I sat down in the chair beside the wall that showed a holo screen scene of the Calfya coast perhaps two hundred klicks north of Westi.

The train is departing. Please be seated. The train is departing. Please be seated.

The motion was smooth, far smoother than with a maglifter or a glider, and as I sat there, hurling westward, I had to wonder at the expense and possible futility of my journey. I couldn't explain it, but I *knew* I'd never learn what I needed through the nets and comsystems. No matter what anyone said, not all communication was carried accurately or completely, even in full VR . . . and I knew I needed every scrap of information.

I could still be on a fool's errand. Or walking into a trap. Or both.

But . . . since people were trying to kill me at home . . . and had killed Elora . . . I had to do . . . to try . . . something.

That scarcely reassured me, as I sat back and tried to relax . . . to rest.

The map said I was nearing Cydonya, with the warning beeper that indicated I was leaving a controlled glider strip and entering an area where no net repeater would operate. Rather than just slip into town, I eased my glider onto the top of a hill on the west side of where the town was supposed to be. Supposed to be, because the area merely showed as a blank on the GPS system—as was the case in any of the enclaves of the faithies or the netless.

I let the glider come to rest on the top of the hill, a surface of small stones, red soil, and boulders. The glider itself, like all those used privately, had the shimmering surface that looked dull from any distance, but glowed with the glitter and energy from thousands of tiny and flexible solar panels coated with polarized polymer when observed closely. Mine shimmered with a green-tinted silver dullness as I slid the canopy wide and then stepped out to survey my destination.

The vegetation around me was mostly creosote bushes, broken by small patches of grass, and, occasionally, by widely scattered clumps of piñon pines. For a time, with the late afternoon sun at my back, I just looked across the town, a town like any other, on first appearance. Then I took out the scancam and slowly panned across the town, bit by bit. After the long pan, I zoomed in on the more eclectic dwellings one by one, like the wooden dome comprised of interlocking alternating hexagons that were composed of either dark sunglass or handmade wooden shingles. And the dwelling-sized cube that appeared to be of highly polished and featureless slate. Then I zoomed in more closely on the town square, or what passed for one, an expanse of winter-tan grass, surrounded by carefully tended trees with pale green leaves, except for a giant fir or pine that stood by itself.

When I had all the background scenes I thought I'd ever need, I packed away the scancam and got back into the glider, easing it downhill and finally into the sole glider park off the town square, a glider park clearly not used that often, since the winter-browned wild grass was knee high in all but the dozen square meters directly across from the adobe building with the antique painted sign that read GENERAL STORE.

The building was finished in a reddish-brown adobe. It might have been constructed entirely of adobe for all I knew. The entrance consisted of a narrow porch supported by a front wall with wide arches in it. Even in the late afternoon, the air was cooler once I was on the foot-polished stones of the portico-like entry. I tapped the hardened finish. The solidity suggested that the building was very solid—and possibly as old as it looked.

Walking inside was like walking back into history. The only concession to modernity seemed to be indirect glowstrips set under the plaster crown moldings that ran around the entire ceiling, a ceiling comprised of tin tiles, each stamped with a pattern.

Long wooden display cases—set parallel to the side walls—filled most of the floor space. At a glance, I could see that most of the "goods" were display items, set there so that would-be purchasers could see what they would get from the store's nanite-scan-and-duplicate system. In most of the world, stores just showed VR images. The air smelled of the faint ozone of replicators, floral scents, and the underlying odors of leather and age.

Along the left wall of the store were rows and rows of shelves, and they held nothing but printed and leatherbound books. I doubt I'd ever seen a third that many in one place, except perhaps in my father's library. I stepped closer and studied the bindings and the titles. The volumes were not dusty antiques, but recently produced with leather bindings, doubtless nanite-formulated, but leather nonetheless.

I scanned the titles, not recognizing many, but finding some most familiar, although I'd never seen some of the work in actual printed form—*The Search for Genetic Perfection, Medical Desk Reference, The Waste Land and Other*

Poems, Drowning Ophelia, The Lost Poems of W. B. Yeats, Dreams of Gravity, Federal Union History Desk Reference, The Suppressed Smith Doctrines, The Brigham Papers, Nano-Pharmaceuticals and How to Use Them, The Collected Plays of W. Shakespeare. The variety was amazing, and I certainly didn't understand the cataloguing or shelving procedure used.

"Looking for something?" asked a heavyset gray-haired man—one of the few I'd ever seen. He smiled politely. Instead of the singlesuit that was the usual garb in most of the FU, he wore old-style black trousers with a white silk blouse, and a black vest hand-embroidered with green and red thread in designs I didn't recognize.

"More like . . . just looking," I confessed. "I've seldom seen so many actual physical books in one place. It's impressive."

"Syd's got a better selection, but she's the only one, and it's a good thirty kilometers out there."

"Out there?" I asked reflexively.

"Cotwood—it's not that far, not for a glider. You are the one who just parked across the way, aren't you?"

"Yes."

"Any particular reason you came to see us netless wonders?" His eyes twinkled, and the corners of his lips turned up.

"Just traveling."

"Must be pretty well off—doing it by glider."

I shrugged. "I saved for twenty years. Interstellar pilot. Retired, and decided I wanted to see some things."

"Sem Thorgel. Pleased to meet you."

From Thorgel's statement and muscularly relaxation, while he might not have a net system, he clearly had nanites and internal augmentation to read my reactions so quickly.

"Daryn . . . Alwyn" My answer was slightly hesitant.

"We're not against technology. We just take the best. No reason to accept the worst."

I nodded, gesturing to the books. "How did you get them printed?"

"Outfit up north, near Cherkrik, called Netless Binders,

they do a good business running off small print runs. Even do a single copy. Course . . . that costs more." He gestured toward the shelves. "These are the ones I sell a few of every year. Some . . . I sell a couple of copies every month."

"I wouldn't have thought . . ."

"They say the netless community in Durngo buys more, but not many, and they're twice our size."

I hadn't been sure what a netless community would be like. Under the privacy laws of the Federal Union, if more than ninety-five percent of the residents of an area petitioned to have the area removed from the universal surveillance provided by the skytors, and the FU determined that all the petitioners had affirmed it from their own free will, then all skytors, net repeaters, GPS, and safety surveillance systems were removed. Biennial secret ballots with a ninety percent majority of adults were required to maintain that status.

Anyone could visit a netless community, but the only VRs permitted were those taken at a distance, or those taken with the permission of all those individuals who appeared in the VR. I understood the penalty for violation involved community service on behalf of those violated, some time in an FU public works project, and up to a twenty percent asset forfeiture. The work requirements kept individuals from violating the requirements and the asset forfeiture kept the nets and system providers like UniComm from intruding.

He smiled. "We're not uneducated, friend. We just prefer to be informed and educated on our terms. About half our kids come back, and that's just fine."

I nodded again, not quite sure of what to say.

He gestured toward the rows of shelves. "You can find all these titles in any net library. Heck . . . you could have any of them printed if you wanted. But most people outside the netless areas don't even read them on the net. Know why?"

"Most people don't read—bound books or off the net." That, I did know.

"How would those who wanted to read even find them?" Thorgel asked. "With millions of volumes at one's beck and call, how do most people decide what to read? Who do you trust to recommend a good book? Have you ever seen a VR or netsys recommending a book?"

I smiled wryly. "I haven't been around any commercial nets for a long time."

"And when you were?"

With a shrug, I admitted, "I never did see a book recommended."

"And if they did find them, how would they find time to do read them? With someone's image appearing in your home every few minutes? With an employer's projects? Or," Thorgel pushed on, "how long would they stick to reading anything? For most folk outside of the netless, reading's work." He paused. "Do you read?"

"I've read a lot, especially in the last few years."

"Any of these?" He gestured toward the shelf.

"Some of them."

"How many?"

"I haven't looked at all of them, but maybe fifty in this section."

Thorgel laughed. "You ought to stay in Cydonya. You won't, but you should."

"I probably won't." I admitted.

"You'll miss it, and you won't ever know why." He shook his head. "You can always come back. You won't, but you could."

He was probably right about that, too, I thought as I walked back outside, and then across the stone lane to the glider park where a youngster, perhaps twelve, was looking at the glider.

He stepped back, looking at me solemnly, before asking, "That's a Tija fifteen, isn't it, ser?"

"Yes."

"With complete solar links?"

I nodded, holding back a grin.

"Told Dad they were the best. I'm going to get one someday."

"I'm sure you will."

"Silvered silver gives the best energy return."

"It probably does," I said, "but I always liked the green tint to the silver."

"Best I be going, ser." He inclined his head and walked back toward the General Store.

As I link-unlocked the glider and slid inside, I wondered if he were related to Sem Thorgel.

Later, after securing a place in the only hotel in Cydonya, I took the glider back to the hill on the west side of town, and in the silvered light of a near full moon, took out the scancam and panned the town below once more.

Then I took out the recording pen and clipped it to the front of my dark green singlesuit and began to speak, hoping the words would come, but knowing I could always edit them later, if I could but capture the feelings that Cydonya raised in me.

When people think of the netless, they think of towns and enclaves like Cydonya, places where there are blank spaces on the netmaps, places where a newsie must obtain written permission to VR any person, individual dwelling, or place of business. Yet, as you can see, in daylight, in moonlight, from just outside the town, Cydonya looks almost like any other town, except for a few more eccentric looking structures.

It is not like other towns. There is a general store, as in many smaller towns. It uses nanite replication equipment, just as in other places. But there is a long shelf of books, almost a small library—and these books are purchased. They are kept and read, and re-read. If the people in Cydonya wish to learn the news, they must have it hard-printed from terminals elsewhere and have the reports physically shipped into the town. . . .

I paused. What else could I say?

After a time, I put away the recording pen, and re-entered the glider to head back to my rented room . . . to think, perhaps to sleep.

Getting to Tyanjin required a transfer to a local at Byjin, and I was glad for the translation nanites. Although the station announcements were in standard, the words swirling around me once I left the transcontinental platform were definitely not. Beyond the outbound barrier, the platform was more crowded than any in Noram, yet no one actually touched anyone, although with the bustle and scurry, I wasn't quite sure how there were no collisions. The arched ceilings were just as high as in Westi, but the arches seemed somehow . . . more Sinoptic.

Since I was well underground, I found a pubcomm, where I could link with my belt gatekeeper and tried Majora. Her sim came on—just my luck—and began to speak. "Since I'm not here . . ."

"Majora . . . this is Daryn." I paused.

The sim's voice damped out. "I'm here," her voice came across clearly. "Your timing is not wonderful. I was in the shower."

"I'd like to see that."

"You had a chance. . . ."

I had, years before, when Mother had first introduced us, but I couldn't change what had been. "I was stupid."

There was a brief silence, before she said quickly. "I haven't heard anything."

"All right. I have to catch a local. Please be careful."

"I will, but you're the one who needs to be careful."

I just stood there in the link booth for a moment after I broke the connection, then hurried to the local platform.

Once in Tyanjin, I did find a glidertaxi, and the driver—or his dashplot—knew the address. I watched carefully as he slid through traffic that was mostly magscooters leavened with a handful of electrobuses. We only passed two or three private gliders before he came to a stop beside an open gate.

"Ser . . . you must walk . . . that way. Eleven credits, if you please." His standard was heavily accented, but clear enough.

"Thank you." I left him with fifteen and got out, still carrying the small bag.

Through the arched and open gate was a semi-restricted community, one where outsiders had to walk from the front gate to the dwellings within, although the residents probably had hidden underground access from the tubes.

The day was cold, and misty rain sifted from the gray clouds overhead. I hadn't even brought an overjacket, but the nanite body screen kept the moisture off me, and helped with the warmth. I walked along the common path, then turned, coming to a stone stoop and a door with the number five and a symbol. The dwelling was a very small cottage, with a second wall extending from the sides, presumably surrounding a courtyard or garden. I couldn't help licking my lips as I walked up to the door. I did remember to check the body-screen once more before I touched the greeting bell stud.

The outer door was clear armaglass. The inner door was black as ebony. It opened, and a woman stood there. Not Elysa, not as I had known her, but the woman whose holo image had appeared at Majora's cottage. She wore a brown-ish smock over dark gray trousers.

Was she Elysa? Or had she been Elysa? Her profile was similar, if not identical, but her skin was several shades darker, and her hair was black and held back in combs, over which flowed curly ringlets. Yet . . . there was something. . . . Elysa had worn combs, if not so elaborate as the silvered ones that this woman wore.

She said something, in Sinese, I guessed, and after a moment, I got the translation. "Yes?" Her voice was closer to what I recalled, if slightly huskier.

I bowed and spoke, hoping I was right—or that at least she either understood standard or had a translation protocol. "My name is Daryn Alwyn. I'm looking for an Elysa Al-Nafir." I smiled faintly. "I think that might be you."

"I am Elysa Al-Nafir." This time the words were in standard, if muffled by the armaglass between us. She frowned, as if puzzled. "Should I know you?"

"You should."

"I cannot say that I do."

"I'm sure you can't." I laughed. "It took a while to find you, and I'd like to know why. That and a few other things."

"You must be mistaken, ser."

I could sense both the unease and the lie, even through the armaglass barrier between us.

"I'm not." I tried to smile gently. "There have been four attempts of some sort on my life, and I still don't know why. You should be able to give me some insight, since yours was the first."

"Do you really wish to continue this fiction?" Her face was impassive, but her emotions were not.

"I almost wish it were a fiction," I admitted. "But you didn't have to leave the hints."

"Hints?" She appeared puzzled. "You must have someone else in mind."

"Mujaz-Kitab . . . the medical references. You could have called yourself Meryl or Meryssa Gonsalves or Casteneda, or any one of a dozen different names. I couldn't possibly have tracked you then. And I'm sure you have another name, the one you work under. So this one is for me."

Another silence ensued before she spoke.

"You might as well come in, Daryn." A slow smile crossed her face, almost regretful.

The armaglass slid open. Elysa stepped back, and I slipped inside, senses and scanners alert for anything. But the foyer and the room beyond contained neither people nor scanners— and only minimal environmental management systems in place. To my right, as I stepped through the foyer, were a set of armaglass sliding doors—closed—looking out over a type of garden I had never seen before. Shimmering ebony rocks, waist-high and polished so that they would have looked like water flowed across their surface even without the mist, rose from a green substance that seemed neither grass nor moss, but holding characteristics of each. Two small cedars—bonzai—grew forward of the rocks.

The double doors clunked shut behind me, and Elysa pointed toward the pair of chairs that flanked an ebony table. "Why don't you sit down? It's been a long trip, I'm sure."

"If you'll join me." I gestured to the other chair as I set down my bag. The room was furnished as sparely as the garden, and like my father's office, was without wall hangings.

She slipped into the other chair gracefully, and the brown eyes, the eyes that seemed to be the only coloration that was not somehow different from the woman I had met at Kharl's, fixed on me. I swallowed as I smelled the scent, not quite like roses, that I also recalled.

"I have some questions for you." She tilted her head sideways, a gesture that somehow belonged to someone older. "Why did you come here? And why did you wait so long?"

"I waited because I didn't have any choice. When I went to the stonesmith to track you down . . ."

That brought a frown, and a look of puzzlement, not counterfeited.

"The combs," I explained. "They were unique. They were the only things that seemed at all factual. I traced down the man who made them, but someone dropped a wall on me, and I spent two months in the medcenter getting rebuilt. Almost as soon as I could move around after getting released, I went back to the search. He only knew your first name, but that confirmed part of it, and then I tried to track down all the women with that name. There are over two thousand Elysas in the world."

"So much for uniqueness," she murmured with a smile.

"Then . . . after I found that out, someone sent a monoclone carrying a monofilament knife and primed with a cellular explosive after me." I stared at her, although it was hard because she was as determined as I was, and didn't even blink. "Why? Why did you dump those nanites on me, and who is trying to kill me? And why? You have to know some of the answers."

"You didn't receive any messages from . . . shall we say . . . old acquaintances?" she asked.

"Old acquaintances?" Was she referring to Eldyn? "Such as?"

She smiled sadly. "I'm not surprised, the way matters have developed."

"What old acquaintances?" I decided to be persistent.

"Such as a schoolmate . . . you saw him at the reception."

"I saw several."

"Eldyn." The name was offered not quite reluctantly.

"Eldyn? I can't reach him. All my codes . . ." I stopped and watched her face.

"That is not surprising. I think I can help there." She paused, but not enough for me to ask how, not without running over her words. "You never answered why you came searching for me, since no one suggested it."

"You're not exactly answering my questions," I pointed out.

"That is true. Answer my last question, and I'll help you find your answers."

I wondered about her wording, but I couldn't exactly force her to come up with answers when I didn't know enough to ask intelligent questions. "To find answers."

She shook her head. "Are you sure?"

I spread my hands. "I'm not sure of anything—except that I'm in the middle of something a great deal larger than I am, without the slightest idea why."

"Without the slightest idea why?" Elysa emphasized the word "slightest" with the gentlest of ironic twists.

I laughed. "I have more than enough speculations. It's becoming clear that I'm an obstacle in someone's efforts to gain power, and possibly control of UniComm or more, but I don't have the faintest idea why all this is happening."

"Why don't you have a drink while I pull on some clothes more suited to a short trip. Would you prefer Grey tea or verdyn?"

I nodded. She had definitely been briefed on my habits. "The Grey tea." My body wasn't even sure what time of day it was.

She slipped out of the chair and headed toward the kitchen-like corner of the single large room. I had the feeling that her quarters were little more than two rooms and a bath/fresher, with the small courtyard garden to my left.

"What matters?" I asked, picking up on her earlier observation. "What matters have developed?"

"Have you watched the news in the last few hours?" she replied without turning.

"No. Between catching one tube train and another, and then trying to find your house . . ."

She slipped the tea and a steaming danish on a blue and white porcelain plate onto the woven blue mat on the table beside me. "The danish is just a standard replicator dish. I doubt you'd like most of what else is programmed there."

"Heziran food?"

"That and Sinese."

I sipped the Grey tea. "Why did you ask about the news?"

"I'll let you watch while I dress. Then we can talk about it while I show you the answers you thought you came for."

"Can't you just tell me?"

"They're not that kind of answers." She flicked something from her pocket, and an image formed on the holoscreen that appeared before me. "I won't be long." She slipped into the adjoining room, and the door closed.

I scanned the room, tried to boost my hearing, but could sense and hear nothing from her room. My attention alternated between the UniComm AllNews and the room around me.

The holo image was that of a low white building with rugged mountains behind it. I recognized neither the building nor the mountains.

. . . mortality is well over thirty percent, according to medical specialists at the Mycauplex Medical Center, although in certain classes of pre-selects it appears to approach ninety . . . where the first cases have appeared. Federal Union health officials have offered no comment on the situation . . . except to stress that only a handful of cases have appeared to date, and none have so far infected norms. . . .

The holo field shifted to a medcradle, with the shimmering

effect of a positive pressure quarantine field blurring the image.

. . . informed medical sources have also indicated that no treatment tried so far has shown any impact on the progress of the infection. . . .

I blinked—another and more virulent pre-select plague?

. . . student disturbances in Ankorplex turned violent today when regional educational commissioners denied petitions to preclude the use of perceptual testing . . . the decision resulted from an earlier determination by the Federal Union secretary director that the so-called PIAT-issue was a matter better determined by regional authorities. . . .

Regional commissioners in Kievplex have not yet announced their decision. . . .

. . . In defending his decision to delegate the issue, the secretary director had stated that a decision had to be made on a regional basis under the Federal Union. He also noted that the petitioners had failed to show defects in the test. The section of his determination that has aroused discontent worldwide was his observation that, while no test is absolutely accurate, perceptual integrative testing represents progress toward more accurate determination of student skills. . . . The secretary director . . .

The screen showed a smiling blond man waving to someone.

. . . has refused to make any further statements on the issue . . .

The next image was that of a heavy-lidded, dark-haired norm woman, and her words accompanied her image.

*   *   *

. . . so-called measures of intelligence which in fact are not the basis of intelligence or ability, but the result of socioeconomic bias should not be even a minor factor in allocating positions in selective institutions of higher learning. . . . Have we learned nothing from the history of the Collapse and the anarchy of the Chaos Years? Can the secretaries of the Federal Union not see that perceptual testing is merely an avenue for the pre-selects to ensure their continued affluence? . . .

I couldn't help but wince. Why wasn't someone addressing the real issue? The whole perceptual testing question was a fool's orbit.

The noted academician, Suel Tomas, speaking on behalf of the Dynae Institute . . .

The image flipped to a dark-skinned man whose voice was deep and resonated.

". . . this issue is not about accuracy in testing. It is not about fairness in education. It is about power. It is about how places are allocated in select academic institutions, and it is based on the assumption that those who graduate from those institutions will have a better chance of attaining affluence and power. The Dynae Institute has opposed the PIAT because we believe it reinforces an effort toward developing an intelligence of a sort too narrow to benefit humanity. But those who argue over its use are not concerned about humanity or its future, but about socioeconomic gain, and in the end those who would use education purely as the basis of economic or political gain will doom the rest of us—once more—to chaos and disaster. Let some regions adopt this misguided testing. Let others abstain, and let the results speak for themselves. . . ."

The image vanished, replaced with the UniComm news symbol, an arc, with a light beam streaking toward the viewer.

And that's the debate on perceptual testing. . . .

The entire screen vanished, and I lurched to my feet, realizing I hadn't been exactly the most alert of would-be investigators. Then, I wasn't an action type. I was an edartist and a methodizer.

Elysa looked at me from the foyer arch. She wore a dark maroon singlesuit with a black jacket trimmed in maroon, and carried a heavier overcoat. "I assume you saw the stories on perceptual testing and the new epidemic?"

"Yes. What's your connection, and what's mine?" I stood slowly, picked up my bag, and walked toward her.

Elysa waited until I stopped less than a meter from her. She studied my face slowly. "Actually, Daryn, your connection is because your sister is dead. Let's leave it at that for the moment. Are you ready to go?"

"Leave it at that? Leave it at that?" I found my voice rising. " 'You're in this because your sister is dead. Please be a good boy and cooperate.' " I snorted. "I'm not going anywhere."

Elysa shrugged. "That's your choice. How do you propose to find out the answers to your questions?"

Again . . . I could sense both the truth and the tension of her response. But I didn't answer the question.

"Let's just say that it wouldn't have to be this way if your sister had survived. She would have come to you and explained it."

"So why don't you?"

She sighed. "That's what I'm about to do, but it's something you have to see as well as hear."

"But I'm the second choice." Again. Second choice behind Gerrat. Second choice behind Elora. Then, if I'd been the first choice, instead of Elora, I'd probably be dead. I still might end up that way.

I stood and waited to see what Elysa would do, but she just looked at me, as if waiting for me to decide. Finally, I shrugged. I knew I was reacting again, but there didn't seem to be that many options.

"Lead on." I stepped forward to help her with her coat, trying to swallow my anger and frustration.

The glider dropped down coming off the last dip before leaving the redwoods, and the mulched bark of the lane crackled under the momentarily higher air pressure. The effect of the standard ground limiters bothered me, and I had an idea that, as time and finances permitted, I would be making more than a few modifications to the glider.

The air around me mixed the scent of firs with that of sun-warmed and dried grass. Then I was bringing the glider to a halt in the tree-shaded glider park that served UniComm. The midsummer sky was hazy as I walked up the polished gray stone steps to the black marble archway set into the hillside, beyond which lay the hidden spaces of UniComm, the largest communications organization anywhere in the human galaxy.

The guard in the green-trimmed gray singlesuit of Uni-Comm security looked up politely. "Might I ask your business, ser?"

"I'm Daryn Alwyn, to see my father."

"Yes, ser. Is your profile on the system?" His voice was slow and even, a sign of a brain-damped norm.

"I would guess so, but I honestly don't know."

He frowned, then touched the console. After a moment, he gestured toward the security gate. I stepped through, and the door beyond opened. After striding along the left-hand corridor, I marched up the inclined ramp past the museum cases displaying the history of communications equipment, beginning with drums and flags, and then models of messengers, first on foot, then on horseback, with dispatch cases. The replica of the ancient telegraph always amused me, as did the small circular CRT screen that had led the way to VR technology.

"You can go in, ser," said the guard by Father's open door. "The director general is expecting you."

Father's office desk was merely a larger version of the antique cherry businessman's desk at home—and neither had changed in all the years I could remember. The office had the same green leather chairs, and even the same setup as his home study with the concealed vyrtor, but the office had three of the large cherry wood bookcases. Of course, there were no window hangings.

The door closed behind me, even before I'd taken two steps into the office that looked out over the inside courtyard.

"Sit down, Daryn. Sit down. You look fit and rested." Father smiled. "We could have talked at home, but . . . I'm old-fashioned. Business should be discussed in the workplace. Otherwise, everything becomes business."

That was one of the few maxims of Father's that I had little trouble accepting. I nodded as I sat down in the green leather armchair directly across the polished cherry desk from him.

"There's a great future for you—almost anywhere you want to go, Daryn." My father smiled broadly. "With the years as an FS officer, and your educational background, you could start in almost any section of UniComm. . . ."

"Did you see the rough cut of the piece on Cydonya?" I asked.

"It's very good. As a stand-alone, it will bring you a few credits, and you can use it to show the talent in UniComm that you understand them."

"I'm not joining UniComm."

"You can't live the way you're accustomed to on occasional net royalties from a few edart pieces." Father's voice was reasonable, as it always was when he was convinced that he was right beyond doubt or question.

"I don't intend to. I've got the FS retirement, plus a fair amount that I saved while I was in the FS. It brings in almost as much as my retirement stipend." I didn't mention the shares in UniComm I'd received in trust from Grandfather's estate. The trust had expired when I'd turned thirty-five, but the only thing I'd done was ensure the dividends were reinvested into a diversified portfolio. "And . . . I've already reached an arrangement with a methodizing firm in Vallura." I shrugged. "I was trained as a methodizer, and they need someone who understands the FS."

"Procurement weasels." Father snorted.

"I have to start somewhere." I smiled. "I guess I'm sort of like Elora. I wouldn't feel comfortable joining UniComm unless I could prove my abilities elsewhere."

Father frowned, but the frown vanished with a rueful smile. "You're more like her than I'd have ever guessed. Well . . . if that's what you want to do. . . . You have to live your own life, son, but I can't see as this freelancing methodizing and edart work will lead anywhere."

"It may not," I admitted. "That's why I also worked out a retainer arrangement as a freelance methodizer for Ec-Long."

"Freelance?"

"I've already gotten my first assignment."

"That won't pay the bills for long."

I smiled. "You may be right, and if you are, I'll have to figure out something else." I knew that my being reasonable would be far more effective than disputing him. "And . . . well . . . if that's the case, we'll probably talk again."

"I'll leave the offer open for now." He fingered his chin. "You understand that I can't promise how long that will be."

"Yes, sir." I understood. At some point, Gerrat would be the one to control UniComm, unless Elora relented, but I had my doubts about that. She'd never forgotten Father's offhand comment about wanting to see his sons continue the family tradition.

"Well." Father smiled again. "I suppose that's it. I'll see you at dinner, won't I?"

"For a few days. I'm getting my own place."

"That would be best, I think."

Since I'd never really had one, it was definitely for the best. I stood, then bowed. "Thank you for understanding."

"I can't say as I do, Daryn, but I understand you well enough to know you'll do things your way and on your schedule."

That was what I hoped, all I could have hoped for.

The light rain that had been falling earlier had become more mist-like, and despite the cool air, with the combination of the swift pace Elysa set, the nanite body shield, and the humidity, I could feel myself heating up after we had walked the first hundred meters past the untended gatehouse—strangely occidental in Sinese Tyanjin.

"Where are we going?" I asked, drawing up beside Elysa.

"To show you your answers and then send you to make a choice."

"Are you always this obscure?"

"When the future is at stake, it's necessary." She didn't look at me, but kept walking. "Look around. Look at the people—those that are out."

Despite the gloomy weather, handfuls of people walked the street, and almost all looked to be norms, fairly well attired, healthy looking people. Unlike in Noram, there were far more wearing multipiece outfits, with trousers and collarless jackets, or even flowing robes in several cases. I didn't see any smiles, but that didn't seem surprising in the rain. I certainly wasn't smiling.

A younger man who was approaching, talking to a dark-haired woman, glanced up, and his eyes met mine, if momentarily, and he abruptly eased his companion into what appeared to be a confectionery shop.

An older woman wearing an elaborate ankle-length robe-gown of some sort, but carrying a rain-parasol, stood by another door, her eyes meeting mine, gray eyes as cold and impassive as the clouds above. Her gaze did not flinch as we passed her and turned the corner onto a fractionally wider street, one with the same low permastone buildings that seemed to dominate Tyanjin, or what of the city that I had seen.

We walked less than eight hundred meters more before Elysa led me down a ramp and onto an induction tube platform, except it wasn't an induction tube, but an older-style subsurface magfield transit system. I hadn't realized that there were any left.

"It shouldn't be long," she said in a low voice.

I nodded, and slowly surveyed the platform. It was filled with people, and we towered above almost all of them . . . standing alone with a circle of space around us. I strained to catch the strange words, but even with the nanites and the translation protocols, my understanding was limited, to say the least, since all I heard was a standard word, often meaningless, in place of whatever the locals were speaking.

". . . outsider . . . his whore . . ."

". . . barbarian boars . . . rut . . ."

I glanced at Elysa and could see the flush beneath her skin, but she said nothing.

". . . time will come . . ."

". . . none too soon . . ."

The train that appeared at one end of the platform rumbled, rather than glided, and it lurched to a halt, a sign of equipment not in the best of repair. Elysa gestured, and we made for the front compartment, stepping inside only moments before the doors hissed shut.

Even in the close confines of the compartment, a compartment where I had to slouch to avoid banging my skull on the overhead, there was a zone of space around us, and the odors were remarkably like an aged space vessel, and totally unlike the scented sanitary air of an induction tube.

Although I felt like a curiosity, the remarkable thing was that no one looked at us—more as though we were an embarrassment to be suffered or endured without being acknowledged.

I leaned toward Elysa and whispered, "Does everyone avoid looking at me because I'm a Noraman? Or because I'm a pre-select?"

"What do you think?"

Another question. "Both."

"You're right."

I stood, hanging onto a polished tubular steel pole, as the old magtrain hissed and lurched through three more stops. At each stop people disembarked, but fewer got on, and those that did tended to be taller, better dressed, although I didn't see any that could have been overtly identified as pre-selects.

As the train slowed for the fourth stop, Elysa glanced at me. "We'll get off here."

I followed her out and onto a platform that was nearly empty, then up another ramp, and back into the open. Elysa took a deep breath, as if of relief, then promptly turned left and began to walk swiftly. Caught off guard, I had to take two quick steps to catch up with her.

The open air felt good—less confining—although the misty rain brought out a pervasive odor of age as we headed along the damp permacrete of the walk that flanked a gentle inclined street. Each step took us past buildings with signs I could not read, and I had to wonder if standard was as universal as I had thought . . . or as the net systems of the world would have had me and others believe.

Only a handful of gliders—mainly taxis—slipped down the street, deftly avoiding the ubiquitous composite magscooters that seemed to comprise most of the vehicular traffic, as well as the silent but awkwardly blocky electrobuses. In Noram, scooters were used seldom, and then by youths, or norms, while in the Sinoplex it seemed as though everyone used them—except for pre-selects.

Elysa caught one of my glances at another unreadable sign. "How does it feel?"

"What? To be illiterate in a culture?" I smiled ruefully. "If I lived here, I'd spend the time and effort to make sure I wouldn't be."

"Most pre-selects wouldn't."

I had never been one of "most" pre-selects, but there wasn't any point in saying that, especially since that wasn't her point. She was trying to tell me that the pre-selects had created a culture foreign to norms, as if most elites in history hadn't. But then, most elites in history had eventually failed. "Where are we headed?"

"To the base of the hill there." She pointed slightly to the left, over a low two-story structure. Over the top of the faded blue stone tiles rose several trees overlooking a red tile roof.

A hundred meters ahead the street ended by running into a larger avenue, running perpendicular to the one we walked. A black wall rose on the far side of the cross street.

The buildings we passed were now newer, with wider display windows, and we passed the first true uniquery I had seen in Tyanjin, with a chrome-trimmed door and mauve window hangings, and a tasteful inscription I could not read within a blue green oval. Under the oval was a smaller standard translation inscribed in silver letters: DINING WITH THE ARTFUL MANDARIN.

As we came to the intersection, I realized just how impressive the wall on the far side of the avenue was, towering as it did over the flow of glider-taxis, electrobuses, and the ubiquitous magscooters. The wall was of black stones, set so closely that I could not discern a joint, stones polished as smooth as glass. It rose a good ten meters straight up from the narrow walk on the far side of the avenue, a structure so even and featureless that it might have been created by a VR artist, rather than being an actual physical construct less than twenty meters from me. To our right, perhaps fifty meters away, was a gate. Although the composite double gates were recessed into the wall, if closed, they would meld with the rest of the wall, and offer a barrier impassible to anything short of heavy military equipment.

My personal scanners also sensed the nanite and electronic fields buried within and designed to protect the wall.

I looked upward, beyond the deep black composite. Immediately beyond the wall were trees, and farther beyond were houses—some more like small ancient palaces with delicate minaret-like steeples, others with red tile roofs that shimmered damply in the gray day.

"This is where most of the pre-selects of Tyanjin live," Elysa said quietly. She did not move.

Standing in the mist that was slowly turning into a steady

light rain, I studied the wall, noting that, if the curvature were as gentle and as uniform as it seemed, it probably enclosed a space almost ten klicks across. The area above and beyond the wall appeared park-like, meticulously maintained in the open spaces between structures. A long black glider slid away from the dwelling with minaret-like steeples, then vanished behind an ancient fir of some sort. The scene beyond the wall was serene, peaceful—different from the scooters and electrobuses and crowds that sifted around and past us.

I could sense the indirect attention from more than a few of the passersby when I finally looked down and at Elysa.

Without a word, she turned and crossed the street we had been following. We walked along the avenue paralleling the black wall—past three other streets, before she turned back eastward once more.

After another two blocks, Elysa stopped and opened a door under a faded marquee of some sort—one in Sinese and without a translation. Behind the door was a small restaurant—something I would have expected to have vanished centuries before, since anyone could get any kind of cuisine by simply lifting replicator parameters off one of the netsys libraries and programming them into a home replicator. At least in Noram, the replicator had greatly reduced the number of traditional restaurants, another factor, the historical economists had claimed, in contributing to the economic disruption that had preceded the chaos. I had never been that sure—restaurants as a major economic factor?

The gray-haired woman standing beside a polished wood table on which rested a blue and white porcelain vase nodded at Elysa and murmured something in Sinese or a local dialect. Elysa replied, but I didn't catch it, and probably wasn't meant to.

"This way . . ." Elysa said quietly.

I bowed to the older woman as I passed. She actually acknowledged my presence with a minute head bow.

Elysa led the way through the main room and past a curtained archway. I tried not to stiffen, but forced myself into greater awareness and alertness. But there was nothing in the second room, more like an overlarge closet containing a circular booth surrounding a table. She slipped to one side, I to the other.

"What did you think about the wall?" Elysa asked.

"It's physically impressive. There are also electronic and nanitic defense systems built into it."

"The defense systems have been upgraded every few years," she replied.

"You're suggesting that we have the same kinds of barriers in Noram. . . ." I paused. "Or barriers, in any case."

"The Sinese lands have been heavily populated for more than six millennia. Land is not inexpensive, and the experiments of holding it as a public trust failed miserably, several times."

"Market economies are the worst form of economic structure, except for any other kind ever tried." I knew I was misquoting a statement about political structures, but it fit, even if I didn't remember the original author.

"You can change a market economy to make it reflect social as well as economic diseconomies. . . ." Elysa broke off as the curtain in the archway to her right was pushed back and the gray-haired Sinese woman appeared with a tray.

The older woman quickly set down two platters, two small cups, and a teapot. She filled both cups, bowed to Elysa, and slipped back past the curtain.

"I need to eat," Elysa said.

As she served herself, I took a sip from the small handleless cup—green tea, and like brewed Grey tea, better than anything from a replicator. Then I followed her example.

I had no idea exactly what the food was, except that it had vegetables I did recognize—such as snow peas and water chestnuts and bamboo slices, with some I didn't, with small chunks of chicken and a totally unfamiliar sauce. I took a bite. It wasn't great, but it was hand-cooked and original, and I was hungry. Then, while it was barely midday for Elysa, it was past dinner for me.

After several bites, I looked up. "What does all of this have to do with me—and with Elora? Except to show me that I haven't looked into the lives and comparative isolation of the pre-selects? That isn't a very good reason for you and others to attack me."

"It is a very good reason," said Elysa after a bite of the spicy mixture she had spread over the rice. "You only know of the attacks against you and your sister. There have been others. Can you deny that someone has a reason?"

"No. But a power grab by other pre-selects doesn't seem to have much to do with the isolation between—"

"You've created a hereditary elite. You deceive yourselves that it's based on ability, and claim that anyone with ability can join you, and with the resources of the nets, and the socialization of UniComm and OneCys . . . and all the others . . . you've conditioned the world to believe it."

"And you're not a part of this?" My eyebrows rose.

"No. I never was." Elysa took a small sip of tea.

The calm certainty and lack of physiological agitation chilled me more than her words.

"You don't want to understand. You look, and still you don't see." She spread her hands, as if helplessly.

I watched, wondering if I could say anything, anything at all. I had to try. "You had me see the barriers here, and you want me to come to the conclusion that pre-selection is just another form of human elite, and . . . pretty clearly, that it's a tyrannical or halfway despotical elite. It may be both tyrannical and despotical in certain ways, but genetics doesn't make that much of a difference in people. There's less than a tenth of a percent difference in DNA between a pre-select and the norm that individual would have been. And even if it did, rebellions don't start with attacks against people who aren't in control of things, unless it's a random uprising, and planned attacks against me don't exactly qualify as random."

"Most honored edartist, I must beg to differ. You don't know what you're talking about. You give numbers. You express reasons. What do you really know about social structures and how they work? How many norms do you work with? How many live where you live?"

"You know the answer," I pointed out. "Almost none."

"What percentage of the population uses pre-selection?"

"Five to seven percent." My answer was wary.

"And how much of the world's wealth and power is controlled by those five to seven percent?" Elysa was acting like a barrister.

"Almost all of the power, by definition, obviously. Sixty or seventy percent of the wealth."

"How does the present situation differ from that in pre-Collapse days?"

"Statistically, it doesn't," I conceded, "but as you were pointing out a minute ago in a different context, numbers aren't everything."

"You're right," she said dryly. "They usually understate problems and overstate happiness and contentment, and they only show what exists now."

"What problem do you see that the numbers don't show?" I asked.

"The same one that's brought down most societies in history—the growing dissatisfaction of most people with the cultural and governmental structure. It hasn't been this bad since pre-Collapse times."

I wanted to ask her how she knew . . . but then, if RennZee were right, she'd seen more than I had, and she was clearly closer to the norms in Tyanjin—or anywhere—than I was.

"It's getting worse."

"Why?" I asked. "Maybe most people aren't pre-selects, but most of the medical and gross hereditary deficiencies are gone. Except for those who choose to be poor—"

"Do the faithies and the netless choose to be poor?" parried Elysa. "Or does their refusal to have the interconnected world intruding into every aspect of their lives doom them to lack of power and comparative poverty?"

". . . everyone is healthy. The average norm tests higher than all but the most gifted of the population would have a millennia ago, and he or she lives better, much better," I pointed out.

"Are you trying to be dense?" she snapped.

I closed my mouth.

"People don't operate on absolute status, but relative status. Even before the Collapse, something like ninety-nine percent of the people in Noram lived better than all but the richest individuals had as little as two centuries before. Yet the sociologists kept classifying the twenty percent of the population with the least control of resources as poor—even when they would have been considered well-off on other continents. And these people truly believed themselves poor and deprived, and they acted that way."

I shook my head.

"It's no different today. Human beings are status animals. We haven't taken that out of the genes, not with all the pre-selection. No matter how much people have, they consider themselves poor if others have a great deal more."

That got a shrug of acceptance from me. "Of course."

"I'd be happier if your calm were based on understanding rather than ignorant complacency." Her voice could have sliced through the empty platters before us.

I refilled my small teacup and waited.

"Go on. . . ." I finally suggested. Even if her observations were correct, and I was beginning to believe that they were, which was disturbing enough, those observations didn't offer much insight into why people were trying to kill me, as opposed to Father and Gerrat, but Elysa had also made it quite clear that she wasn't answering my questions. Not yet, anyway.

"As you pointed out, there's virtually no difference on a genetic level, that is, between the genetic material of a pre-select—before genetic manipulation—and that of a norm."

"And?" I asked the question, even though I had a disturbingly clear picture of where her logic was leading.

"You know what I'm going to say. You just won't admit it."

"You're suggesting that great differences in wealth and control of resources are the result of minute differentiations between human beings, and that the majority of those differentiations are created by pre-selection, because it obviates regression to the mean genetically."

Her eyes were deep and almost sad. "And that means nothing to you?"

"Well . . ." I suggested. "Since any parent can finance pre-selection, it would also seem that those who don't are those who refuse to sacrifice for their offspring, and you're blaming those who are willing to pay for a better chance for their children for the failures of those who won't."

"It's not that simple. *You* come from a family where the cost of pre-selection is a minute fraction of family wealth. You sacrifice nothing, except perhaps a new glider for a year or two or . . . whatever luxury is de trop at the moment. A less wealthy family gives up all but spartan comfort for close to twenty years for each child that they wish to gift with pre-selection. Don't talk to me about sacrifice. You don't even know what it is. You live more modestly than all your family—and less than five percent of the planet could afford what you call an austere life style."

Except . . . I didn't think it was austere, and never would have said that.

"So . . . you're suggesting that the world is about to come apart and that there is a pre-select conspiracy which wants to consolidate its power over the communications nets in order to sway public opinion enough to allow it—or the pre-selects—to maintain power?"

Elysa smiled. "You see. It wasn't that hard to figure out."

"That still doesn't say why people are after me."

"Oh? It doesn't?" She slid out of the booth.

I scrambled after her.

"Where are you going?" I asked.

"I answered your questions, didn't I?" She turned and drew aside the curtain enough to pass.

"No."

She ignored me and kept moving.

I didn't say anything until we were back outside, where the misting rain had stopped, and the clouds were beginning to lift. She had turned back in the general direction of the magtrain station.

"You still haven't told me why you used the spray on me."

"You should be able to figure that out. To warn you. I was the one who set up the laser. Do you remember the old lady who was lost?"

"You?"

She nodded. "That way, it made it difficult for people to

attack you directly. The wall was clumsy, and you had been prepared."

"Prepared?"

"You had the special nanites in your system. You still do." She turned down a side street that was more than an alley.

Outside of a young man in black trousers and a black shirt, lounging against the wall a good hundred meters further on, near where the street dead-ended in a loading dock, the street-like alley was empty.

"But why?"

"To prepare you for what you need to do."

She extended a card. "You asked about Eldyn. He has the other answers."

I took the card, and opened my mouth, then jumped sideways as I saw her pull something shiny from her overcoat pocket.

Light flared around me, and I reacted automatically, using scanners and senses to move. The nanites that protected my eyes helped as well.

When I could see, I was fifty meters away . . . shaking my head.

Elysa was gone, as if she'd never been there.

"Got to be careful with that type . . . man . . . blind you and take what she can." The language wasn't quite standard, but the nanites came up with a rough translation. The young man looked at me, as if suddenly seeing my height. Then he backed away, and a filament knife came out. "Stay away from me. . . ."

I was only too happy to avoid the filament knife . . . and I stepped back, my eyes still on the hard-faced youth, but he didn't move as I eased away, checking the buildings and the muted shadows that suddenly seemed everywhere. There were still crowds on the street that ran between the pre-select wall and who knew where.

I just stood on the corner for a moment, the oblong card in my hand.

There wouldn't be any point in waiting around her dwelling—if it even happened to be her real dwelling. She could avoid me forever, since she knew Tyanjin and I didn't.

I looked at the address on the card, and it made no sense to me.

Just like everything else hadn't. On the surface, none of it made sense. She'd waited around for me to show up—promised me answers, given me a tour of Tyanjin, some philosophy, and an address—and vanished. It all reminded me of the kinds of tests Mertyn used to give, a good thirty years past—bits and pieces, and we were supposed to put them together.

I was a methodizer . . . and having trouble . . . with conflagrations, tours of areas filled with resentful norms . . .

I swallowed—hard, wondering how I could have been so slow. It was like the falling cemetery wall, all over again.

Chapter 47
Fledgling: Cedacy, 450 N.E.

My first dwelling had been scarcely that—five small rooms on the bottom of the lower Hill in Vallura, and a glider hangar that had a manual door barely big enough to accommodate my glider—but I'd been determined to live within my projected means. The first year had been tough, but by the third year, I'd found a vacant hectare up for sale near the top of the lower Hill and purchased it. After that, I'd done the rough design myself before getting Kharl's architect to finish it correctly.

Then, I had to wait to gather funds—none from my inheritance—and find the right builder. Finally, while it was being finished, I took a trip, a very short one compared to what I'd done when I'd mustered out of the Federal Service—and I took the induction tube, far less costly than using the glider.

Along the way, I found myself in Cedacy, the home of Southern University and one of the few places where the effect of the Collapse and the Chaos Years had been minimal. There were even two statuary relics that dated from well before then, untouched—a statuary ring called a Centurium for reasons that the guides couldn't explain and a larger-than-life-sized bronze of a horse plowing through snowdrifts. According to legend, the horse had somehow made the university possible, although how a horse could have done that escaped me. Then, some legends are just that, and better left unquestioned.

Rhedya's brother Haywar and his wife lived there, and they'd asked me to dinner at their place, a low and most modest villa that sat halfway up the hill to the west of the university. Since in two days I'd exhausted both uniqueries in Cedacy, neither that good for all their expense, I was looking forward to dinner. I was sitting on the veranda, sipping a beaker of verdyn, enjoying the breeze that brought the scent of pines, when Frydrik approached. He was in his third or fourth year at HMudd University, but on some sort of holiday break.

"Sit down and join me," I offered.

"Thank you, ser." Frydrik was twenty-one, green-eyed, broad-shouldered, and bright. He'd gone to the engineering school, as I recalled, although Southern University had a perfectly good engineering school, because of troubles with his PIAT scores and because his parents felt that he needed to get away from home. The young man sat on the edge of the cushion chair, his eyes flicking toward the door from the veranda into the great room.

"How are your studies going?" I asked.

"Does it really matter, ser?"

I could sense the tension in his body, even without the augmentation nanites and my internal systems. "That depends on what you want to do. I'm glad I took all the courses that gave me a basis for being a methodizer."

"I'm studying EDI, waveguide, lasers, and other communications technologies. I suppose those will come in useful when I go to work for Uncle Gerrat."

"Do you want to work for UniComm? You don't sound enthused." I straightened in the lounge chair and turned toward him. "You don't have to."

"I don't? Mother and Father just finished paying off my pre-select loan last year. I don't exactly want to spend twenty to thirty years of my life doing that for my children. Especially since I bombed my PIAT. I'm sure you know that."

"If you have talent enough to be studying advanced communications technologies at HMudd, there are all sorts of opportunities out there," I pointed out.

"With which enormous organization?"

"I might point out that I've managed without becoming part of one."

"What did it cost you, ser? Twenty-five years when you scarcely saw Earth?"

"Everything has a price, Frydrik. Independence has a higher one. Do you think you're exempt from the charges life imposes?" I tried to keep the irritation out of my voice.

"You're just one of the tokens, Uncle Daryn," Frydrik said mildly. "My father, and all those who think there are real choices in life, they can point to you and say, 'See. Look at Daryn Alwyn.' But not everyone has the kind of talents you do. Most of us end up working for some organization or another, and I figure I might as well use the family contacts to work for one that pays well."

I held back a wince. "There are other talents besides mine. And . . . anyone can write or compose the sort of thing I do," I pointed out. "It doesn't take special equipment. It doesn't take special access. Almost every school-age child has access to the same equipment I use—or close enough that it makes little difference."

"Little differences aren't that little," Frydrik countered, his voice rising ever so slightly. "Remember, we share something like ninety-eight percent of the DNA of a chimpanzee. And what's the difference in basic writing and communicating ability between you and the average methodizer? A few percentage points? If that? What makes the difference is the viewpoint, the advantages, the training."

He was partly right about that, but whole cultures had fallen because they had adopted partial truths. That distinction wasn't something that did much good to talk about or comm to the entire world. That was something that the First

Age hadn't wanted to understand. And clearly Frydrik didn't, either, but I had to try. "First, Frydrik, every society has leaders and elites. By definition, societies require them. That's not a matter of dispute. The dispute is how those elites are developed or selected and how much power they have. Neither tyranny nor mob rule have proven workable. Too much democracy becomes mob rule; too little leads to tyranny, then oppression, and eventually rebellion and bloodshed." I cleared my throat and risked a glance at my in-law nephew.

He was still listening, I feared, if only to find a point where he could refute me.

"We have developed a system of informally selecting our elites based on perceptual integrative ability, and it works. It's lasted far longer than any other system, and, under it, people have greater freedoms than ever before in history."

"And it all rests on a little test that doesn't even measure everything that a human being is or may do."

"No, it doesn't," I conceded. "And there are many people out there who don't have that high a PIAT score who lead their fields." I took a deep breath. "We all know that observing what is and measuring it correctly are not completely accurate. But to try to do so is not a form of bias. It's a better tool than anything used before."

"That's like saying coercion is an improvement over slavery."

"Inappropriate as the comparison is, there's some truth in it." I agreed, then continued. "Forget about tests for a moment. Some people accomplish various tasks better than other people. That can be demonstrated in a variety of skills and professions. In others, accomplishment is less clearly the result of what might be measured as superior ability. I acknowledge that. So will most discerning individuals." I paused. "Do you think that a choice of occupation should be solely a matter of your choice, regardless of your ability? Do you believe that recognition or rewards should be a matter of chance? Or that the less able should be rewarded, instead of the more able?"

"No." But his frown remained.

"So . . . your objection to the current system is what?"

"You pigeonhole people on the basis of tests and judgments before they can demonstrate anything."

Rather than give an automatic response—that almost everyone pigeonholed people on the basis of fragmentary information—I paused, then almost laughed as I discovered I was fingering my chin, the way my father did. After a moment, I tried to provide a thoughtful answer. "I was an interstellar pilot. Only one in one or two hundred applicants gets picked for training. Less than one in five of those makes it through. The initial selection process is a judgment in advance based on mental and physical tests. The vast majority of those rejected would not make as a good a pilot as those who are chosen. There are doubtless some who are rejected who would make good pilots. Tests and interviews are not infallible. But even the Federal Union does not have the resources to actually try to train those thousands of potential pilots to determine who might be the best. Every few years, the system is reevaluated; it was while I was going through it." I paused. "Isn't your objection really that you dislike systems that depersonalize people, that make them digits and test scores?"

"No . . . it's that only people like you, even like me, have a chance of fully using the system. Everyone else is at a disadvantage, and yet you and Father and your father—they all pretend that the system is absolutely fair, and absolutely just."

"It's not absolutely fair. Nothing is absolutely fair. I agree with you. That isn't the question. The question is what, if anything, can be done about it. And that goes on both a societal level and on a personal level." I smiled raggedly. "One reason why I went into the Federal Service was so that I would have more choices. That's what allowed me to become a freelance methodizer and edartist."

"You had advantages other people didn't. How many people have a retirement stipend and inherited stocks and credits to tide them over while they're trying to establish themselves, to follow their dreams?"

"Frydrik . . . I shouldn't tell you this . . . but you should know. I earned the retirement, and I've never touched one credit of what I inherited."

"But you could," he pointed out.

"I didn't."

"You have all the answers, about how this is the best of all possible worlds." The young man lifted his eyebrows.

"You've cribbed that, Frydrik, but, no, I don't believe it's the best of all possible worlds. I do believe that it's better than any world that's come before."

"Ah, yes. The tyranny of the able, and the tyrants define who is able. You and the ancient racists. I thought better of you. . . . You're just like my parents. You're all already in-humed, even though you're still technically alive."

"That's a bit harsh, nephew."

"It's accurate, ser. You are inured to the pain of people who are intelligent enough to know what they can never have. You're blind to the injustice of a system that categorizes people so early that they can't even have the chance to try for their dreams."

"I'm not blind to it, Frydrik," I said gently. "I just don't have a better system. Anything else that's been tried is worse."

"Words . . . justifications . . ." He rose with a bow.

"Frydrik . . . you have some valid points. You don't like the system." I stood. "Fine. Don't just complain. Figure out how to improve it in a way that doesn't make just your life better, but one that improves it for everyone. Too many revolutions in history made life better for the new elite, and worse for everyone else." I smiled. "And if you bring me a better idea, I'll work it into one or more of my edart pieces—if you'd like that."

"Perhaps I will, ser. Perhaps I will. Thank you for your time." He bowed, then turned away.

I looked out at the sun-flooded cedar and juniper-covered slopes on the east side of town. Frydrik, alas, had just proven the worth of the PIAT with his failure to understand that a society could not be geared to fulfill all dreams of all people.

And yet . . . how many Frydriks were there? Was there a tyranny any more absolute than that of pure ability, and if we did refine the systems and tests to better judge people's potential . . . would that improve matters? Or increase the feeling of tyranny for those who lacked ability—a fraction of the population that was all too big to ignore and not quite adept enough to be trusted to guide society?

I took a sip of the verdyn. The cinnamint tasted bitter.

Chapter 48
Raven: Tyanjin, 459 N.E.

Almost running, I made my way back through the streets, until I managed to find a pubcomm booth in the corner of the lobby of a small hotel—the standard name under the Sinese characters said it was the Hotel Paradise. From what I could tell from the foyer and the lobby, it was clean, if smelling slightly of ginger flowers. I could have turned on my belt repeater, but with the equipment my enemies seemed to possess, that would have lit up my location like a signal beacon. Without a direct access code, it would be almost impossible for them to find me quickly, even if they were accessing Majora's links. I hoped that meant that no one could get to me before I got to Eldyn, even if they could directly backtrack the call to the booth. And I especially hoped Majora happened to be home or awake.

Once again, I got the gatekeeper and Majora's sim.

"Majora, this is me. . . ." I waited a moment.

The sim began to speak. "As you can see, I'm not really—"

"I know. . . ." I mumbled. "You're sleeping. . . ."

"It is the middle of the night, Daryn. . . ." Her voice came in over the sim's before she muted the automatic response. Her tone was half-sleepy, half-humorous.

"I'm sorry."

"How did it go?" she asked.

"She was the one . . . and she left me an address for my old friend."

"He called and left one here." Her voice firmed. "He said that you should meet him as soon as you could, that it was more urgent than you could possibly imagine. Have you watched any news?"

"About the new epidemic? Only once."

"Daryn . . . it's awful. They're suggesting that pre-selects stay to themselves, and that a quarantine for pre-selects might be necessary. More than two thousand have died in Ankorplex already, and almost as many in Macuaplex. They're saying that cases have turned up in Mancha and all over EuroEast, and the medcenters are being flooded in Calfya already."

"That's not good. I hadn't heard that."

"Can you come home after you meet him?"

"What address did he give you?" I asked.

As she read off the numerals and the street—the Way of Seven Steps—I checked them against the card that Elysa had given me. The two were identical. I didn't know whether to feel relieved or even more worried. More worried won out.

"He also said it was within two hundred meters of the Grand Hotel."

"I don't know where that is, but we'll see if we can find it." Then, I didn't know where anything in Tyanjin was.

"Is that the royal we, or is your friend around?"

"She used a flare gadget to blind me for a moment. Have no idea where she is."

"Nice person . . ."

"It's about what I expected."

"I wish you could come back to Noram now. . . ." Her voice had an edge of huskiness to it.

"So do I . . . but . . ."

"I know. . . . You need to go. The sooner you find him, the sooner you can come back."

I also understood that if I didn't find and meet Eldyn quickly I might get stuck in Tyanjin, or somewhere else in the Sinoplex, if the secretary director of the Federal Union decided to impose restrictions on travel. "I'm going."

"Take care."

"I will. You, too." After a moment, I broke the connection.

After I stepped out of the comm both, I glanced toward the hotel's receiving area. No one was there, except for a slender young man wearing, surprisingly, a dark green singlesuit, and a gold vest. I moved toward him.

He looked at me, waiting, his dark eyes blank.

"Do you speak standard?"

"Yes, ser."

"I am supposed to meet a friend at the Grand Hotel. . . ."

"Yes. It is not far. If you turn right when you leave the lobby, walk downhill to the third street. Turn right. Walk one block and turn left. The Grand Hotel is four or five hundred meters east."

"Thank you very much."

His only response was a nod. I had the feeling that he felt I was going to take a room at the competitor, but there wasn't much I could do about that.

Outside, the clouds were beginning to thin, and a few patches of bluish sky were appearing in the west. A few more passersby glanced at me almost surreptitiously, but most followed the example of the passengers on the magtrain—studiously ignoring me.

As I walked eastward, I hoped they all did.

Chapter 49

Social contract . . . a thesis based on an antithesis . . .
brutish and short, because it rests on consent,
never informed, because culture remains
an antique deck of paper cards with five suits,
none of which is a Tarot.

Ser, or sir and lady, salutations of a time . . .
Which time?
The sexless gentility of Tiresias,
the zen birds of Merton,

est-il tempus, in terram?
Time for what? Or for whom which carillon rings?

James, rex angliae, and the version commissioned in his
name,
all the futilities of fame,
codifying the unknowable in stately prose,
gilding an immaterial rose.

Let the music rise; let the sea fall,
seeking an equilibrium dating to the Tethys,
against which fell dates and canal gates.

Gates?
Toroidal . . . or octagonal?
Leading to unchanging stars and a vanished race?
Or mere artifacts from time, buried in space?
Guarded portals in the defenses of systems and cities?
Beyond either are unmeasured distances, dragons,
the equivalent of dragoons . . .
. . . and space.

Personal Notes

LEAVING THE UNKINDNESS

Finding the Way of Seven Steps took a little longer than it would have in, say, Westi or Vallura, or most towns or cities in Noram. I walked past it twice—once walking to the Grand Hotel, and, again, after getting directions, walking back past the narrow lane between what looked to be a boarding house and a shop that seemed to carry antiquities behind grimy armaglass.

There was no sign to mark the way, and I entered the lane cautiously.

Once through the tiled archway I found myself in a cul-de-sac flanked by well-kept, if modest, two-story houses that I would not have guessed existed. All the roofs were of a dark blue tile, and each had a front door set in a recessed alcove under overhanging eaves. The porches formed by the eaves and stone pillars were floored in hexagonal ceramic tiles, with each side of the tiles roughly two decimeters in length.

About half the houses had Arabic numerals. The numbers I wanted weren't on any, but the third house on the right seemed to be in the right order numerically, and I stepped up under the eaves to the door and knocked.

I barely lifted my knuckles from the permafinished wooden door when it opened. A young woman—clearly not Sinese—gestured for me to enter. She was probably of academy age, and I wondered why she was there, rather than in school.

"Doctor Nyhal? Eldyn Nyhal?" I asked.

"He's in his study, ser. If you'd follow me . . ." Her standard was perfect as she closed the door. I could sense no overt electronics, and the dwelling was quiet, almost perfectly silent.

We walked through the tiled foyer and a room floored in dark wooden parquet that held a low sofa set before a fireplace—real, it appeared—and then along another tiled hall. The first door on the left was open, and before we reached it, Eldyn stepped forward. He was stockier, and his wavy brown hair was far thinner than when we had graduated from Blue Oak Academy. Unlike when I had seen him in the past, he was no longer wearing a bright singlesuit, but one in a muted bluish gray. He did wear an ovalish medallion, also a dark gray. Close-up, I realized it was octagonal, not oval.

Eldyn smiled. "Daryn . . . I wasn't sure whether you'd come, but I had hoped you would."

"I'm here." I returned his smile, but my senses were taking in everything in the study, a spare room with little more in it besides a conference table and four chairs.

Eldyn motioned to the young woman. "Mehlysa, you must go now, quickly, as we discussed."

The resemblance between the two was strikingly clear. Both had the light brown wavy hair, and the same small straight nose—and the watery blue eyes.

"But . . ." Her voice had the hesitancy of a teenager.

"Now that my friend is here, it won't be safe for you."

"It won't be safe for you, Father."

"It will be for a time, but I can't do what I need to do and worry about you. Take the hidden way, and I'll join you as soon as I can."

"You promise?"

"I promise."

I could sense that while Eldyn wasn't lying, he was very controlled, and more than slightly worried. That made me more than a little apprehensive. So did the octagonal medallion, although it could have been an affectation to remind us pre-selects of his conquest of the pre-select plague.

With a look over her shoulder, the girl walked toward the rear of the dwelling. She was looking back as Eldyn closed the study door.

"She looks a lot like you," I offered, not knowing exactly what to say.

"She looks more like her mother." The doctor/scientist/

food magnate smiled warmly, if but for a moment before turning to me. "How do you like my retreat? It's so modest that it has escaped unnoticed until now."

"Until now?" I scanned the room. The walls were bare. There was a flat panel holding some energy above the door, and another similar panel over the window that ran nearly from floor to ceiling and overlooked a small walled and formal garden—its trimmed yews and small polished bench looking very damp in the misting rain.

"Before we get started, I need to provide you with several things." He extended a small case, no more than six centimeters on a side and half that in depth.

"You're assuming I'm going to do something."

He shook his head. "I'm certain that there are dozens of tracker nanites around you. You fasten that to your waistband or put it in a pocket, and in a few minutes, all of the trackers will be disabled. I'd strongly suggest you take it, if you don't want the PST types to do you in like your sister." His smile was crooked, but he was almost certainly telling the truth. "It works better if you turn off the body-screen for the first few minutes."

Nyhal wore a nanite body-screen. So did I. Body-screens had some usefulness—they'd stop most projectile weapons, and mitigate or stop a laser—depending on the power output. They were designed to respond to kinetic energy, and that meant I or Nyhal could be wrestled to the ground, and that we were certainly vulnerable to pathogens and nanites—or specialized low energy weapons like filament knives.

I took the box and put my shield on stand-by, but just for three minutes.

My older-looking norm contemporary studied me for a long moment. "Elysa said you didn't get any of my messages."

"No. At least not directly. I got a message from Elora, suggesting I contact you. She'd set it up before she died. I also had several blank incomings. That was why I had Majora call you . . . and why she tried never to mention my name directly."

"That was wise." He sat slowly in one of the ebony chairs

on one side of the table. "Sit down, if you would."

"Eldyn . . . could you please just tell me what exactly is going on. I think I've figured out the general outlines."

He offered another crooked smile. "Despite all the slights and slings of fortune, and the ungratefulness of your peers, I'm trying to hold the Federal Union together—in the way in which it was designed. Your sister was trying to help me. Some wealthy pre-selects, call them the PST group—want to change the Union and have proven that they'll do anything to succeed."

The scent similar to jasmine rose around me. I couldn't help wincing. "Now what? Another set of nanites to send me into shock? Your little helpers?"

"Hardly." He laughed once, harshly. "Mer—you know her as Elysa—she could have done that if I'd wanted that. You're going to need those if you want to function." He paused. "I hate to ask this, but do you care for the woman who called me?"

"Yes." The answer was a lot more complicated than that, but "yes" was more than accurate.

"Have you been sleeping with her recently?"

"What—"

"Or hugged her or held her close?"

"Once or twice."

"Let's hope that's enough." He nodded briskly. "There's a lot to cover."

"Wait—"

"There's a lot to cover," he repeated. "You already had resistant nanites. They tend to spread to others close to you, but this last dosage was to make sure you don't get slowed down immediately. You have much to do. Or you could, if you're interested. Now . . . as you surmised, there is a revolution in progress. The attempts to use the PIAT as a screening tool are just part of that. The other and more dangerous aspect of the PIAT is that you can use those same techniques to assess and, shall we say, assist conformity and loyalty. That's been part of the literature for years, but never really considered. It is one reason why past secretary directors quietly disabused any use of perceptual testing as a requirement for any office or educational assessment."

"If people weren't trying to kill me . . . I still have troubles with this conspiracy theory," I said slowly. "And revolutions. I don't see any wide-scale uprisings."

"Successful revolutions aren't led by the masses." Nyhal snorted. "They're led by the discontented elite who exploit the discontents of others. Every successful revolution has been led and masterminded by those who have been or could have been part of the previous power structure. You don't like your own brother that much, and he's better than most of them." Eldyn's watery eyes seemed to glitter for a moment.

"Most of whom?"

"The pre-select elite."

"You're certainly a part of that elite," I pointed out.

"I'm a half-accepted norm with freak genes." He smiled. "And I'm not a revolutionary. I'm the counter-revolutionary. So are you. You're going to be the true mastermind of the counter-revolution."

"Talking about a counter-revolution . . ." I shook my head. "I've never wanted anything to do with power. Why would I now?" As the body-shield returned to a full active power state, I felt slightly less apprehensive.

"To stay alive. To retain your family's heritage. And as for power, you've never wanted anything to do with power the way your family has handled it. You're going to take over UniComm, and you're quietly going to change the entire world, and because you're almost a martyr . . . because you're perceived as a man who served mankind, and who spoke up and was attacked . . . why . . . no one will dare say a thing. . . ." He laughed, the laugh rising, not quite into shrillness. "That's the way we'd like it. That's not what will happen, but you do have a chance."

"We're missing a few steps here. . . ." More than a few. While watching Eldyn, I was still trying to scan his reactions and be alert for any outside surprises. "Why should I believe anything you say?"

"I need to tell you a story, Daryn. You're an edartist . . .

you should appreciate it." He lifted a blocky weapon from under the table. "This is an ancient flare gun." He gestured with the obsolete weapon. "It's just weak enough to slide under a body shield. I wouldn't bring it up, but you're not going to like everything I'm going to tell you, and you do need to hear it all. Yes, you do."

"Oh." I managed not to swallow. The man with the answers also had a flare gun pointed at me, and he was insisting he was on my side. I was having strong doubts about Eldyn, but I had no doubts that I didn't want to test my systems against the gun, and that meant I was going to hear more—whether I wanted to and whether he would actually answer all my questions. Certainly, no one had yet.

"You remember the scare about the pre-select plague? You remember that almost fifteen thousand pre-selects died?"

"I was off-planet."

"You would have died, too. All of you would have." He peered at me.

"I heard it was bad."

"That's like saying nanites are small." Eldyn snorted again. "I saved every one of you. Every one of you, and what did I get? A letter from the secretary director, and a one-year ten percent salary bonus. Ten percent. Thank you very much, but you're really not one of us, and ten percent is more than you deserve." The smile broadened. "Even after reading my reports, they didn't know. The idiots still didn't get it."

"I guess I'm an idiot, too, Eldyn." I tried to make my tone apologetic. "I'm very grateful to be alive."

"Oh . . . don't condescend to me, Daryn." He offered that not-quite-high laugh again. "But you should know. I was the one who figured it out. It was right in front of them, and they still couldn't see it. You know the forerunner Gates aren't dead. They're just not used often. We're at the end of a transgalactic net, the slums . . . call it what you will." He laughed once more, that same laugh that was cutting across my nerves like a filament knife.

The forerunner Gates? The medallions he wore—they

were probably all octagonal. My eyes flicked toward the dull gray on his chest.

"You see? You're not like the rest." He smiled. "One hint, and you can see. The others, they won't see. They can't see that the forerunners don't want us playing with our genes. . . ."

"How would they know?" There couldn't have been any two way communications.

"They don't . . . or they didn't. The octagonal nanites are just programmed . . . cellular machines designed to analyze structures and react. If the cells aren't integral, or if there's foreign matter there, like augnites . . . they attack."

A long-dead alien race programming nanitic attack machines and spraying them across the Galaxy? Nyhal had definitely lost touch with reality—delusions of evil aliens, and a savior complex as well, and an obsolete weapon.

"I know you have to be upset . . . with the death of your wife. . . ."

"You think I've lost it, don't you, Daryn? Don't patronize me. I haven't lost it. Not at all. You can check the records." He shook his head, and his voice dropped. "The octanites—that's what I call them—they detect what doesn't belong. I told the secretary director that. He didn't believe me."

I didn't either.

"Those little octagonal nanites . . . the ones that Elysa sprayed you with . . . you almost died, but not because of the spray, but because of the treatment. Even for me some of it was a guess . . . that's why I had to have it done again. . . ."

"Again?"

"The laseflash . . . you remember . . . don't you?"

"But that was set up before . . ."

"Of course it was. I know Kharl. He's very bright. Not quite so bright as me . . . but very bright and most thorough. There was a chance, with his access, that he might have decided otherwise and tried to neutralize them. The laseflash was for three purposes. I wanted the PST group to think someone else was after you . . . to make them re-think their strategy. I also wanted your visibility higher. They were thinking you could be removed quietly, and your stock would go to your father or brother. That would have pre-empted Elora's bid for control of UniComm."

A lot of what Eldyn was saying didn't ring quite true, but some did, and I kept listening, trying to sort it all out.

"What does this all have to do with the forerunner Gates? The forerunner Gates are monitoring ports as well. They monitor and send their own nanites to record and monitor all over the Galaxy. Time doesn't matter that much to them, and their nanites are quite sophisticated, quite a marvel, really. I learned much from them."

"No one has seen one of their Gates in operation—except once—maybe—from a distance."

Nyhal just shrugged apologetically. "We don't have time to debate everything. Please listen and save your questions. They dropped nanites on Earth . . . with ice comets, I would judge . . . they might even have been waiting centuries . . . millennia . . . for us to develop augmentation. Those nanites are designed to undo augmentation. Without the effects of pre-selection and augmentation, evolutionary diversity will create a wider range of humanity, and a race slightly less focused on abstractions and conquest. These forerunners, or aliens, well . . . like so many in our own culture, they've underestimated our cleverness. We beat the pre-select plague, and now there are teams of nanitists that have taken apart those little bugs and studied them every way possible."

"We may not understand their Gates," I said, "but we understand their biology techniques, is that it?"

Nyhal plowed on. "After we stopped the first plague, I began to worry. What about the second . . . or the third wave? The secretary director at that time wanted me to design something special—so every pre-select would get nanites that recognize the octagonals." Nyhal lowered the flare weapon, but kept his fingers around it. "That looked like biological warfare on an individual cellular level, and I had doubts about our eventual success. They have been around longer, far longer."

He smiled. "I came up with something better. Octagonal nanites that coopt the invaders. There is a price. You've seen it. The whole world is seeing it now. I'd estimate that the mortality is twenty percent . . . maybe more. Those who survive and their children, if they're not pre-selected to avoid regression to the mean, will be immune almost to anything the forerunner can send through their Gates."

"You just *chose*, on your own, to kill off twenty or thirty percent of the pre-selects? More than twenty percent mortality of the people who run the world . . . who've kept it stable? That's . . . it's insanity."

"Insane? I saved all the pre-selects the first time, and what happened? A ten percent bonus? I unraveled all the codes and offered a way to ensure we'd be safe forever, and they told me to go back to my laboratory and be a good boy?" His voice dropped down again. "I couldn't let that happen, not to Mehlysa and her children. So I left Federal Service, and used all the things they didn't believe. And no one said a thing when I made millions with toys like the variable replicator." Another laugh followed. "They'll believe now. And I'm being generous, far more generous than they are to norms—or to me. I'm ensuring that more than half of those now alive survive when none would have survived before. Besides . . . why not? You pre-selects have chosen genetic traits that allow you to run the world. I'm just trying to reestablish a balance." His smile spread from ear to ear. "I've already taken some steps to ensure it *will* spread."

"Steps . . ."

"I had formal announcements delivered all over the world. Of course, the announcements actually were announcements of a different sort."

"You put your pathogen nanites inside?"

"Nothing simpler. People scan packages. They scan people. But paper? Or expensive parchment? A simple coating to keep them inactive until dissolved by body heat, fingers, you know."

"Why?" I had almost been afraid to ask, afraid I knew that answer.

"Pre-selects should face some risk for their benefits, shouldn't they?" His eyes sparkled. "Isn't that the basis of successful evolution? Now, one could argue logically that we're unsuccessful products of evolution, since successful evolution results in the diversity of a species, not in its homogenization, but the social evolutionists claim that successful evolution is apparent domination of the planet and its resources. That will do for now. Under either definition, genetic improvements come at a cost."

"That's . . . that's ancient social Darwinism." I had trouble coming up with the word.

"No. What you pre-selects have done is *social* Darwinism. Now let me finish before you judge, Daryn. There's a next set lurking in the background, where no one will ever find it . . . until it's too late. The next set is designed to attack on the basis of certain combinations of pre-selected patterns . . . particularly those patterns designed to thwart genetic regression to the mean . . . and, also, every so often, certain configurations of genes that only occur in pre-selects will trigger the same reaction that the nanosprays did on you . . . call it an equalizing factor." Nyhal looked blandly at me.

"What? Just because their genes fit a pattern . . . they'll die?"

"No one should set themselves up as god—or gods. The PST group did. They've been trying to remove you and most of your family. They killed Merhga and tried to destroy me, but they can't stop my science."

"And you don't think someone will take apart your little bugs?" I asked.

Nyhal grinned, and the expression reminded me of a skull. "Mine look just like augnites, and they react in exactly the same way, except when they're in the system of those who are . . . susceptible. No one is likely to discover . . . unless you tell them, and even if you do, they won't find much. They won't believe you. They don't believe me. And the effect will die off, because the special nanites, like those I just sprayed you with . . . well, they're really organic augnites with octagonal properties, and you and your children will be fine. In time, someone will puzzle it out, but not soon. You see, even if they do, it will take a team, and then the techniques will be out there for everyone . . . and the biowars will begin. You don't want those in your lifetime, Daryn."

"You didn't have a team." I was grasping at anything.

"Oh . . . I did. I just had the resources to take those results and adapt them."

I could see exactly what he meant. How many men would ever come along with that combination of intelligence, anger, drive, and expertise, and be in the position to use knowledge the way he had?

"You see, don't you?"

I was afraid I did. "You *are* insane," I repeated. In a way, it didn't matter if he happened to be wrong, and if someone else could repeat his work and find a cure to his plague. The damage already was done. The norms could see that pre-selects were vulnerable, and the pre-selects who survived would attempt to retailor the pseudo-augnites. . . . I winced.

"No, I'm very sane. Too sane. If I were as unbalanced as you think I am, I'd have just tailored a pre-select plague with close to a hundred percent mortality. I'm actually giving you a chance, Daryn . . . and it's because of you and your sister. You're arrogant and self-centered, but you treat people the same. If they're stupid, whether they're pre-selects or norms, you're quietly contemptuous, and if they're intelligent, whether norms or pre-selects . . . you listen.

"I'm giving you the tools . . . or maybe the forerunners did . . . so many pre-selects are dying that no one will take a pre-select conspiracy that seriously, and you can use UniComm to change things. Of course, you'll have to survive an immediate frenzied attempt to track you down and kill you, because the PST group will want to destroy your control of UniComm out of revenge. Or in a last effort to restructure the world into a place even more favorable to inherited position."

That didn't exactly surprise me.

"There's one other thing you should recall."

"What?" I couldn't help the wariness in my voice.

"Human beings are like horses—we're ecological failures."

"If we control the world . . ."

"We don't. The bacteria do. They always have. Remember a couple of things. If you reduced the Earth to the size of an orange it would seem as smooth as a spheroid of polished stone. The Earth has existed for five billion years, give or take a few hundred million. Humans in our present form have existed roughly a million, and we require an ecological niche that is very narrow. The problem with pre-selection is that it artificially narrows that niche further, in an effort to allow those who use the techniques to maximize their control of that ever-narrower niche. It also creates huge social resentments, and an ever-greater arrogance and temptation for those who can show their superiority within that narrow niche to exert greater and greater control over social direction and resources." He laughed. "You don't believe me—yet— but you will. Indeed you will." From somewhere came a folder which he extended.

"Those five names are the people who are behind the death of your sister and the last two attempts on your life. There is background information on each."

"What am I supposed to do? Kill them?" I took the folder, looked at the flat gray cover, then slipped it into the inside pocket of my traveling vest.

Nyhal smiled his dead's head grin. "You may not have to do anything. Then again . . . you may. If you choose to do anything at all. That is your decision."

A dull thud shook the small study. I glanced around.

Nyhal stood. "Go . . . right through the window there! There's a wall gate to a tunnel that opens into the maglift train concourse on the next street."

I moved to the tall window, sliding the casement open, then stopped as I realized Nyhal wasn't following. "What about you?"

"I'll be behind you."

"How about in front of me? No one is ever going to believe me."

I shouldn't have been talking because the door splintered open and a giant of a man, even for a pre-select, rammed his way through. A smaller man, almost my size, followed. Both wore commando-style black singlesuits, with the fabric distorted light, making it difficult to focus on them. Focusing on the black slug-thrower the taller man carried wasn't that hard. It was a model I hadn't seen since FS training—the kind with osmium tipped uranium slugs—the assault weapons supposed to be restricted to Federal Service troops.

A curtain of electric force enveloped the two intruders, shrouding them in an eerie blue-green glow.

The smaller man just pitched forward. The man with the slug-thrower slowly turned it toward Nyhal, moving so slowly that I had a chance for one move. I pivoted and drove a boot through his knee.

A dull cracking and a grimace on the big man's face indicated my success. A nanite shield won't stop that—it's designed to respond to higher levels of kinetic energy. He staggered sideways, somehow catching himself on the door frame, and started to bring the slug-thrower to bear on me.

He never made it, because Eldyn's body slammed into his arm, and across the weapon.

The slug-thrower exploded.

Several moments later, I picked myself up from where I found myself thrown across the table. My entire body felt bruised . . . like ancient armor, the body screen had distributed the impacts, but those had been so great that I was one large contusion.

Both thugs were dead—and so was Nyhal. All three were bloody messes. I had to swallow hard.

I blinked. There wasn't anything else I could do, and there were probably others coming, although I could hear nothing except a ringing in my ears.

My fingers fumbled with the window casement, and I finally slipped out the long window into the late afternoon. My legs felt like lead, but I had been up for almost two days running.

Hssst!

A laser burned into the tree above my head. I didn't know where it was coming from, except it wasn't in front of me. I saw no gate in the stone wall, just what looked to be a tool shed with a rough wooden door, built out of the wall.

Anything was better than standing still and getting fried with an FS-strength laser, the kind that would shred my shield. I sprinted for the shed, reaching for the door lever and yanking the door open.

Inside was a set of steps. I closed the door behind me just quickly enough for it to take another laser bolt. I could smell the wood burning behind me. I bolted down the dozen steps, only to run into another narrow door—this one of smooth steel. I fumbled with the knob, and it turned.

I opened the door to see a passage lit dimly by glow strips—a blue corridor less than a meter wide. Behind me I heard the tool shed door open, and I jumped into the passage and shut the door behind me. I saw the locking lever below the knob and twisted it, glad to hear a dull clunk.

The odor of fresh plastic welled up around me, and I sniffed, but I kept moving. I'd gone about thirty meters along the blue plastic lined way when there was a dull rumble, and the passage shook. Vibrations ran from the plastic underfoot up through my boots.

Although I hesitated for only a moment, there wasn't any doubt that Nyhal's refuge or safe house had exploded. The only question was whose doing it had been. The odor of plastic was even stronger at the far end, where a third door blocked the way. I opened it gingerly, peering into a small cubicle with a sink and mops, dimly lit by a minute glowsquare set in the ceiling. After I stepped through and shut it, the door clicked locked, and I could not turn the knob. The side of the door in the closet looked merely like a gray metal institutional door. I had to chuckle. Who would ever follow a door set in the side wall of a janitorial station?

I eased the janitorial door open just a crack, trying to see what lay beyond.

As Eldyn had said, I was in the maglift train station. I waited until there seemed to be a lull in the foot traffic before stepping out. Still, I almost ran into a young woman carrying a child.

"I am sorry." I bowed deeply.

She smiled, almost as if in mirth.

I flushed, knowing full well what she was thinking—dumb pre-select stranger who can't even find the men's facilities. But I bowed again before walking down the next ramp to the platform.

Chapter 51

Once a poet wrote about the letter C as a comedian, or perhaps it was the letter D as death, or it even could have been the letter P for pilot . . . or pool, and it rhymed with something else, and everyone thought that it was a clever way to begin a poem or a song.

No one but I and perhaps a handful of antiquarian scholars have read those words, just the words by themselves, in centuries, if not in millennia. No one writes poems any longer, not in ink or stone, or even in plain script or typeface upon a screen or a holofield, and the songs people listen to, if they listen at all, are composed with the use of linked arrays based on DNA resonance and the codified mathematical rules of music discovered long before the new era.

Is that why I went from being a pilot to a methodizer to an edartist? Because the only power perceived to be remaining in words is linked to images, music, and resonant voices? In codified rules that no one even examines any longer?

Or is it a deeper reason?

Personal Notes

I found a pubcomm station in the corner of the maglift train station and put in a call to Mother. The last thing I wanted to do was explain things, but she and Father needed to know. She didn't answer. No one did, except the sim. So I blurted out a quick message.

"See if you and Father and Gerrat and Rhedya and their children can get to Kharl. Have him use the treatment he did on me when I got sick at his place. He'll understand."

Then I tried to get Rhedya, but no one answered there. I left a similar message.

I also left one with Majora. She wasn't in, or couldn't answer.

The last call was the direct line to Father's office—with the same result.

I could have waited for hours to reach them, and I didn't have hours. So I fumbled my way from the maglift train to the local induction tube platform to the main Byjin station, where I had to find somewhere to purchase a passage. It seemed to take forever, but it was only about thirty minutes to find the booth in the corner and wait behind three others— just long enough to miss the first departure. And, then, to get on the transcontinental induction tube train in anything other than a single seat, I had to purchase the luxury compartment, the one that cost four times what anything else did. I didn't care about the price.

Taking the transcon was fairly safe, as matters went. Security against energy weapons was good, and there wasn't much of a way the PST group or whoever could get a mono-clone from wherever they kept them to where I was. With the restrictions on clones, they couldn't have an unlimited supply all over the world. Besides, I was safer in Calfya where I could better note things that were strange than in the Sinoplex where everything looked strange.

But I did have to wait. I walked around on the platform under those high Sinoptic arches, and as I walked, I realized that there were only a handful of pre-selects on the platform, and all stayed well away from me—and from each other. In fact, all of the norms on the platform gave us space. I'd never thought that much about pre-selects being different enough to stand out, but we did, not by any one characteristic, but by the cumulative effect, and yet, except for generally greater height, I wasn't sure I could have identified a single specific characteristic.

As I paused beneath one of the Sinoptic arches, my hands touched the box Nyhal had given me. It was warm, but that was all. I could only hope that it functioned as he had designed it. It should, since everything else he had done had worked. That thought, in itself, bothered me. His wife had died under mysterious circumstances, and I'd meant to pursue that as well, but . . . our conversation had been cut short. And within hours of her death, OneCys had news commentaries running against the man.

Kharl had confirmed I did have strange nanites in my system, and calls with my identification codes to Eldyn had been rerouted. Elora's references to Eldyn hadn't been coincidental, nor had her bequests of the UniComm stock. The very epidemic Eldyn had claimed to have begun was occurring. And, also rather convincingly, two rather impressive physical specimens carrying unauthorized weaponry had showed up and attempted, it appeared, to kill us both.

So, insane as Eldyn had sounded, especially with his talk about aliens sending octagonal nanites across the Galaxy, there was a great deal of something there, and I was getting more than a little concerned that he had been right about more than I'd wanted to accept. After all, Kharl had confirmed the octagonal nanites.

I glanced around, but I still had almost thirty minutes before the train was due to arrive. I'd also been debating with myself about whether to try to reach Majora again. In the end, I compromised. I waited until just a few minutes before the train was due, and then went and found the pubcomm booth, trying to convince myself that the positives outweighed the negatives.

Majora answered immediately. She was wearing a deep blue singlesuit with a cream vest. She looked wonderful.

"You look wonderful," I said. "Did you get my message?"

"Yes . . ." She paused. "I can't reach him."

"Keep trying. Otherwise, keep to yourself if you can."

"You look terrible. Are you all right?"

"Besides being exhausted, pursued, and a few other details I'll mention later, I could be better. I met my friend. Things are worse than I thought. What should I know?" I decided against mentioning my travel plans.

"The Federal Union council will decide tonight whether to restrict travel. The analysts say that they won't because the threat is largely to people with the resources to protect themselves by not traveling."

"Somehow, that doesn't surprise me. I take it that preselects are still dying."

"The deaths have dropped off in places like Ankorplex where they started, but people are starting to die in Westi and elsewhere in Noram."

"Majora . . . can you just stay home for a few days? Unless you can reach my cousin?"

Her lips quirked into a crooked smile. "I can manage that—if you're not gone too long. But what about you?"

"According to my friend, when I got sick after the party months ago, I got an early version. So I should be immune."

Her eyes widened, understanding exactly what I meant.

"It's been a long couple of days, and the next few weeks are going to be most interesting."

"You need to be careful."

"So do you. I'll certainly try. That's been difficult lately."

"Try harder," she suggested.

"I will . . . for you."

She smiled, and I wondered how I could have forgotten the warmth that her generous mouth and large eyes showed.

After the call, I headed back to the waiting platform, watching to see if anyone else happened to be following or monitoring me. If they were, I couldn't tell. The only pattern that remained clear was that the norms were staying well clear of the handful of us who were pre-selects.

When the train did glide out of the tunnel and drop into the platform channel for boarding, I forced myself to saunter toward it, rather than run, letting others scurry. Even so, I was among the first to step into the second car. It was probably my imagination, but I could almost feel the scanner run over the shoultertab.

Compartment one is the last compartment to the left. I followed the resonating-nanite instructions, eyes and systems trying to watch everything. Everything felt as it should, and I hoped I wasn't deluding myself.

The first compartment was indeed luxurious, and opened after a scan of my passagetab. It was empty, and I quickly checked the bathroom/fresher to make sure it was as well. Then I locked the compartment door, and sank into the over-stuffed armchair set beside a club table.

A small replicator rested in a recess above the table, and on the far side was a door into a another compartment—just big enough for a triple-width bed, and to turn around.

The faint scent of freesia or something similar disguised the sanitary air that circulated through the other compartments.

The train is departing. Please be seated. The train is departing. Please be seated.

I sat down and tapped in the codes on the replicator for a cup of tea. Nothing happened. I shook my head and extracted a cup from the alcove beside the replicator. The tea was a black tea, mild, and not bad. I still missed my Grey tea, but I sipped slowly as the train accelerated, almost without vibration.

After finishing the tea, I rose and stepped into the bath-fresher. That was one of the luxuries that came with paying multiple times what anyone else did. I looked at myself in the mirror, and I looked surprisingly good—if I discounted a smudge of grease or something on my right cheek forward of the ear. Or the dark stains on the cuff of my jacket, blood, no doubt, but barely visible against the dark gray. Or the dark circles under my hollow eyes.

Somewhere along the line, I'd left my bag—in Nyhal's exploded safe house, I thought, and that left me without toiletries. I did shower. It helped. I didn't feel so grimy when I stepped out onto the thin floor mat—until I dressed in the same old singlesuit.

I slipped back into the main room of my cramped luxury compartments, and, after checking the compartment door to ensure it was still locked, I took out the folder I'd thrust into the inside vest pocket and opened it slowly.

There were five names with, as Nyhal had said, backgrounds and other information. The names were Grant Escher, Mutumbe Dymke, Darwyn TanUy, Anya St. Cyril, and Imayl Deng. All that they had in common, on the surface, was pre-selection, wealth, and membership on the board of the PST Trust.

Escher was from Austrasia, where he was the operating director of his family's engineering firm—EDQ, and apparently very private. There were business addresses, and the locations of three dwellings, and what looked to be a standard business resume.

Dymke and Deng were about the same—different locales, different enterprises, but both carrying on long-established family concerns. Anya St. Cyril was the only woman in the group, and had apparently created her own multinational operation, something dealing with fasteners of all classes.

My eyes started to close, and I started in the chair, but forced myself to keep thinking.

TanUy was another case; he was the descendent of a famous cultural psychologist. I remembered we'd studied some of his work . . . on the PIAT . . . at The College. It came back; the older TanUy had been one of the pioneers in establishing methodologies for accurately quantifying PIAT results—in short, for making the test useful and replicable, so to speak—and more than that, if Eldyn had been right.

I'd have to check, but I began to wonder how many years

ago the PST Trust had been established. I smiled to myself. That history might prove useful . . . if I could survive to use it.

I sat in the compartment, thinking about the whole situation: special nanites in my system, norm resentment, the PIAT issue that had been on the news, some group of pre-selects wanting control over the main information nets and systems. A whole, up-to-now-near-silent, civil war was about to erupt within the Federal Union. Maybe the public would only see scattered riots, but there was definitely a power struggle, and it seemed to revolve around UniComm.

The one thing that nagged at me was the alien connection. Eldyn had been brilliant. He'd been publicly recognized as stopping the pre-select plague. Could he have engineered it? I shook my head. There was little to go on, but what I'd heard, seen, and sensed told me that he hadn't created it from scratch. His resentment at the way he'd been treated had been all too real. But . . . if the octagonal alien nanites/pathogens were real . . . why? Why would an ancient race spread them across the Galaxy?

Were they just pre-programmed and self-replicating nanitic machines designed to act against certain cellular constructions? There had been several "plagues" of unknown origin . . . even before the pre-select plague. Had they been earlier manifestations? And the alien Gates . . . they'd been designed not to be detected from planetary systems. Were the distant or long-gone aliens just trying to keep competitors down? Then why hadn't they just developed really lethal nanites? I shook my head.

I didn't have solid answers, and I was having trouble keeping my eyes open, and the only things I knew were that someone had created octagonal nanites, and that Eldyn had manipulated them into something selectively lethal.

I jerked forward, realizing I'd almost fallen asleep in the chair again.

With that, I put away the folder and went through the narrow slider into the bedchamber, or bed closet, where I lay down. I definitely did not feel like an eagle, but like an exhausted, bedraggled, and bedeviled raven.

I hadn't thought to use the time on the induction tube to sleep, but my body wasn't about to give me that much choice.

Chapter 53

We are but dark shadows wrapped around the thin sticks of others' reputations and powers, physical strength meaningless in a world where all with power have equal strength and nanites to protect them. Being a shadow is not enough. Drifting through the years is not enough. Pretending to be important or powerful or wise is not, either. . . .

As one old poet said, the chronicles of history are filled with cunning passages, winding ways that deceive all but the keenest of those who read them . . . if anyone truly can be said to read in these days. I have seen fearfully ancient Gates beyond the night skies, lost to those who once opened them. Neither fear nor courage saves anyone, nor any species . . . not when the most enduring of creatures vanish in but a fraction of the life of the shortest-lived of stars. Mere survival cannot be enough. Nor is power.

My brother, my father, with their thousand deliberations, large and small, provide the stage on which all the world—actors all, if they wish—can project their images, edit their voices, disguise their beliefs. Through this stage they could control more wealth and power than most rulers in the devious lore of history. Yet what could be their weapons are images projected with energy, merged with song, and sound, and words that do not signify what they say. Hollow men . . . men stuffed with images captured forever, yet departed instantly from the minds and memories of those who watch.

Can I change what is and has been? Can anyone? Will anyone notice? Or listen. Or understand? Or is any effort to do so mere vanity?

Does it matter, given the alternatives?

Personal Notes

Chapter 54
Vallura

From Westi, I purchased an advance tube fare to Vallura, then walked down to the second platform and took a different tube to Nypa. From there I took a public glider to the station at Vallura. The driver probably thought I was crazy, but she didn't say anything, even after she dropped me in the underground parking area next to my glider. I was risking something to get the glider, but I knew I needed it—and its features. So I watched carefully.

The parking area at the Vallura station was strangely empty for an afternoon in mid-week, and I could hear voices echoing through the space—possibly from the square, although it was neither a weekend nor a holiday.

I flicked on the belt repeater, used the distance systems check on the glider, despite the headache it created, because I didn't want to get close to it without some assurance that things were normal. The return readings were reassuring, although I felt like squinting from the inputs, and I quickly turned off the power to the repeater.

A faint sheen of dust covered the glider, dust that had not been recently disturbed. That, and the security system, reassured me somewhat as I looked over the glider.

When I opened the canopy and door, the small box at my waist, the one Eldyn had given me, began to hum, and I could feel the heat building. I forced myself to wait until the humming subsided, using the time to fingerlink directly with the glider and recheck the systems. Maybe Eldyn's system had deactivated the nanite-level trackers someone had dusted over the glider, and maybe they hadn't, but they'd certainly let me know that someone was interested in where my glider might be.

Again, I had only a general idea. It might be one of the five names Eldyn had given me. It might be Gerrat, wondering where I was . . . but Gerrat wouldn't worry about that. He'd just call and ask me to be somewhere. So would Father, and I couldn't see Elysa tracking me, and Eldyn . . . he was dead, and tracking clearly wasn't his style, anyway.

With a wry smile, I eased the glider out of the underground parking, slowly. Even through the closed canopy, I could hear voices—amplified voices as I reached ground level, and, on the square opposite the induction tube station was a crowd. The people gathered there spread from the open area near the monument to Norris, the first secretary director of the Federal Union, and under the trees.

So far as I knew, it certainly wasn't a holiday, and the damp and gray spring weather were not exactly conducive to picnicking.

A few blood-red banners—without any writing—waved up and down in the still air. Mostly, the crowd looked quiet, but even inside the glider I could sense a faint humming that lent an impression of menace to the gathering. Then I heard a high and penetrating voice. I flicked on the external sensors—hoping they worked, since I couldn't think of when I'd last used them—so that I could hear the speaker, a short man, with a brush mustache, probably a norm, who stood on a makeshift platform.

". . . Education and training are restricted to those who get high scores on tests. Pre-selection means high scores on tests. Pre-selection costs creds . . . and who has the creds?

"The pre-selects!

"If you want more creds than a minjob and aren't a pre-select, how can you get creds? You can't . . . unless you steal it somehow. All the snoops set by the pre-selects mean most thieves get caught, and what happens to them? They get brain-damped. Who doesn't get brain-damped?

"The pre-selects!

"You want a house that's more than three closets? You don't get one. Who does?

"The pre-selects!

"You want your kids to have the advantages? You can't afford them, not unless you want to live like a pre-Collapse slave. Who can?

"The pre-selects! . . ."

What he said was true and false, both at the same time, but no one in the small square seemed to notice the false side. Every time he used the phrase "The pre-selects!" the crowd roared, and the red banners went up and down.

Although most of the crowd happened to be watching the agitator on the wooden platform, three broad-shouldered men—two of them with mauls—stood on the edge of the walk that surrounded the square. They wore red armbands and scanned everything but the square.

The balding norm with a maul caught sight of the glider first. His eyes widened, and he murmured something into his collar—or to the minicom probably clipped there. He must have had a link with the agitator speaking because the speaker turned and pointed toward the induction tube station.

"There! You see . . . there's one of them. A pre-select, right there in his glider. Laughing his head off at you."

I wasn't laughing, but trying to turn the glider without making a fuss in order to slip away from the rising sense of anger coming from the small crowd. I suppose if I'd been really courageous, I would have confronted the agitator and his partial truths. Except to turn them . . . I would have had to lie worse than he had. Gerrat could have done that, but I couldn't, and it was far too late for my words to have made any difference in that setting.

Also, I was exhausted, and had a throbbing headache.

The crowd surged in my direction.

"Get him! He thinks he's worth so many of us . . . just how many is he worth?" The agitator's voice boomed over a speaker from somewhere. "He's so sure of himself . . . so filled with himself. He doesn't care what we think. All he wants is another slick way to take our creds, another bunch of unclued norms. . . ."

The logic was abysmal, but the number of norms it appeared to be appealing to was considerable.

As I turned the glider, I could see that, on the far end of the square, several gliders in the small glider pad adjoining the uniquery had been overturned, and the canopy of the most luxurious had been smashed in. The force it had taken to break the armaglass was not inconsiderable. The armaglass of the uniquery facing the square was also cracked, but not shattered, and I had a very good idea of what the men with the mauls had been doing.

"See him run . . . that's what they're afraid of. They don't want us united. They don't want us to learn how strong we really are. . . ."

Mob violence wasn't strength, just unfocused destruction, but that didn't matter to angry and frustrated people, and I was getting a far stronger conviction of just how many norms were both.

As soon as I had the glider headed away from the square, I accelerated, hoping that the violence had been limited to the center of town. I could have turned it into a flitter, effectively, by cutting out the ground limiters, but the glider wasn't licensed as a flitter, and the taxes and penalties for showing it was one would have been horrendous. I had no doubts that the CAs were monitoring the rally, or whatever it was, and I didn't want to break any laws under those circumstances, not unless it became a question of survival, and it wasn't. Not this time, anyway.

Once I was a good klick south, I turned westward and began to make my way back toward the lower Hill and my house.

The gliderways and walks were deserted, and I didn't see a single person outside a dwelling or a structure for the entire three klicks of my roundabout route from the square to the bottom of the lower Hill.

Even before I triggered the hangar door from the glider as I neared the house, I was checking the security systems. The house was untouched, or at least the systems were giving that impression.

A quick physical inspection indicated that no one had been inside, or that they had left no tracks. Nor had anyone tampered with my comm systems and equipment, not in any obvious sense, but those who seemed after me certainly had the credits to hire those who wouldn't leave tracks. From the study windows, I glanced past the empty bird feeder down into the valley toward the center of town, but I couldn't see the crowd.

Then I called Majora.

Her sim flicked on, only to be replaced immediately by Majora herself. She wore a brownish singlesuit, and her eyes were red.

"Are you all right?" I asked.

"I had a little fever last night, but it broke this morning. I never could get to Kharl."

I took a deep breath with her first words, then let it out as she finished. "You didn't get some sort of formal invitation from my friend . . . the one you . . . ?"

"Daryn . . . I haven't gotten a formal invitation in years. . . ." She stopped, and her mouth opened.

"Don't say it. Yes. He said he thought you'd be all right, but he wasn't sure." I looked at her. "I worried about you. Are you sure you're all right? How are things going here? Or there, I mean." The words rushed out.

"It's awful, Daryn. They had a riot near the tube station in Helnya last night. Helnya . . ." She shook her head, and I could see tears.

"Someone in your family . . . the new plague?"

She nodded. "Both Melanyi and her daughter."

"Your sister?" She'd never mentioned Melanyi much, probably because the two weren't that close. Melanyi would have gotten along far better with Gerrat or Rhedya.

"Syrah. She was only ten . . . only ten, Daryn. Just ten . . . and she and Melanyi just burned up. The medcenters . . . they're packed, and no one can do anything, and the norms are rioting, and there aren't enough CAs."

"I'll be there as soon as I can get there."

"You can't . . . you mustn't. I don't want to lose you, too."

"You won't. I'll be there." There didn't seem to be much else I could do. The only person who'd halfway believe what I knew would be Kharl, and telling him wouldn't take that long. But I had to do that. "I will."

"*Please* be careful."

"I will." The fact that she didn't try to dissuade me again told me I should be going there.

Next, even though there were no messages in the gate-keeper from family, I needed to check on my parents, but as soon as I routed the connection, my mother's sim came on.

Hoping that someone was there, I spoke anyway. "This is Daryn. I just got back from a trip. . . . If anyone's there . . ."

Rhedya took the call. Like Majora, she was red-eyed. Unlike Majora, she was shaking, hollow-eyed and flushed. "Daryn . . . it's terrible. . . ."

I was afraid to ask. "What's happened?"

"What hasn't? Gerrat . . . your mother . . . your father . . . I took the children to Kharl . . . like you said . . . but the others . . . it was too late."

"The pre-select . . . plague?" I finally stammered. My father . . . mother . . . Gerrat . . . I had tried to warn then, as I could . . . but if they were already infected, it had been too late even before I called and left messages. "All . . . of them?"

"Your . . . mother . . . she's over the worst. She's weak, but talking. Gerrat . . . your father . . . it . . . was . . . so fast. . . ." She broke off and nodded, and I could see the trace of tears on her cheeks, dried tears, and I wondered if she had cried all she could.

"How are the children?" I blurted.

"They'll be . . . all right, Kharl says."

"And you?"

". . . over the worst, I think. . . ." She swallowed.

"Where's mother?"

"She's at the Yunvil center. It's the closest . . . but you can't go. They're closed to visitors . . . people everywhere . . . dying . . ." She shook her head hopelessly.

"Are you alone? Besides the children?"

"No." I could see a figure in the background. "Haywar and Denyse and Frydrik are here. They'd come to visit . . . you know . . . Frydrik was . . . is working for UniComm. It scarcely bothered . . . them."

"Gerrat had told me they were coming." I suppressed a wince. I shouldn't have mentioned his name.

"Why . . . Gerrat . . . why not me . . . ?"

I didn't answer that right away. How could I? My brother and father were dead. Children were dead and dying, bright intelligent children . . . innocent children. If somehow . . . if somehow I could have learned more sooner. Or been able to get to Nyhal. Had Elora known about his plans? Somehow, I didn't think so, but how would I ever know? How could I ever know?

"I don't know. I didn't even know this was happening until I was leaving to come back . . . and the news I saw in Byjin . . . it didn't show how severe things were." In a way, that was true, but I felt guilty for shading the truth even that much, even though I didn't know what else I could have done.

"What about you . . . ?" she asked.

"They think . . . whatever it was . . . I got an early dose of it several months ago, that time I collapsed at Kharl's." I hoped she didn't ask me who "they" were. I was still exhausted, and stunned by learning of my Father's and Gerrat's deaths—definitely not thinking well.

Rhedya's words washed over me, and I wasn't really grasping all of them.

". . . frightening . . . gone so quickly . . . and . . . afterwards . . . you don't see them . . . cremating them all . . . using monoclones . . . and you're alone . . . and people asking for authentications . . . all over the medcenter . . . doctors quiet . . . people sobbing . . . wonder how . . . how could it happen . . ."

When I finally broke the connection, feeling that I'd failed miserably at trying to console and listen to Rhedya, I tried to get the Yunvil medcenter. All I got was a screen message, not even a sim.

"The Yunvil medcenter is not accepting calls of a personal or business nature. Calls of a medical nature are being taken through the emergency code channels. If this is a medical emergency, and you need transportation, enter red two. If you need advice, enter amber three. . . ."

I broke the connection and sat there. I'd done what I could, and it had been too late when I'd started—except maybe for Gerrat's children.

By keeping my belt repeater off for the trip to the Sinoplex, I'd been trying to minimize direct tracking by those trying to kill me, and that meant I'd missed even a chance to talk to my father. But the way the disease struck, I might not have had that. Then . . . I might have . . . but I'd never know. Not for certain.

I could feel both rage and frustration building. Rage, frustration, and sorrow . . . just trying to find out what was happening and trying to stay alive was costing me more and more.

Slowly, I checked the incomings stacked on the gatekeeper. Besides a long message from Klevyl with all sorts of attachments, finally, one from Elen Jerdyn, and one from the director of the EDA Trust, Lyenne DeVor, with an attachment, there were several from Kharl. I decided those from Kharl needed returning—immediately.

His sim came on, immaculate in a gray singlesuit with a blue vest. "This is Kharl. If you would leave a message . . ."

"Kharl, this is Daryn. I just got back from a quick trip to Byjin. . . ."

The sim vanished. Kharl appeared, gaunt and sitting propped up in a chair, hollow-eyed, a jolting contrast to the picture of health presented by his sim.

"What happened to you?" I blurted.

"Whatever happened to you from your friend Elysa—except different enough—and far more virulent. . . ." He smiled. "I owe you."

"What?"

"I had a culture, if you can call it that, of those replicating nanites in your system. When I heard about the mortality and virulence of this strain, I used some clone tissue to get more of them replicated. I managed to pump enough stuff into Rhedya and her kids and Grete and the kids and me . . . our systems are sort of adjusting . . . I think. Not very scientific, and based on hunches . . ." He coughed, almost doubling over. ". . . if . . . we were going to die . . . we'd be dead. . . ." He fingered a miniature vyrtor control. ". . . wanted to make sure you were there. I'm sending you a report." He gasped, then coughed again. ". . . too tired to talk, not much. It's on what we found in your system."

Even as his words croaked out the gatekeeper clinged.

"Go ahead, read it. I'll stay with you as long as I can. . . ."

"As long as you can?"

"I don't know, Daryn. Grete and the kids seem all right. I'm not sure about me. . . ."

"Get yourself to the medcenter."

"Why? There's nothing there that can help, and damned few pre-selects who'd come near me." He coughed. His face was red. "Read it . . . damn it!"

I opened the file and studied it, noting one thing immediately—the enlarged images beside the test, the images of the nanitic pathogens . . . that's what they were called. I quickly studied those magnified images, but I didn't have to more than look to catch one thing. They were octagonal, elongated octagons, but octagonal.

"Kharl . . . those nanites are octagons." I knew that, in a way, from Eldyn's ravings, except that they definitely weren't seeming like ravings. Not any more. The thought of Nyhal and his alien octagons sent another chill down my spine.

"Exactly . . . saw the reports on the new nanitic pathogens . . . octagonal, too, like the first ones that hit you . . . figured I'd try . . . sent a culture to Union medical center . . . they're culturing, if that's the right word, more . . . but no way to create the hundreds of thousands . . . needed . . . not in time. . . ."

"Are they doing anything?" I *had* to know that.

His face contorted into a caricature of a grin. "Oh, yes . . . someone already discovered the relation of the new bug to the pre-select plague . . . that was octagonal, too . . . they were really happy to get the cultures . . . at least save their skins."

"Are they doing more?"

"What?"

"Can't they do something?"

"What? I forced everything . . . maybe . . . maybe got enough of those eight-sided beasts to save one family . . . this thing moves too fast. . . ." He doubled over, then slowly straightened. "Might help those who can stay isolated long enough . . . feel so hot . . ."

"What do they do, the new bugs, I mean? Attack augnites? That's what they do . . . isn't it?"

". . . pretty much . . . Don't worry. . . . You should be fine. . . . I had a sample of what's in you. . . . They're enough similar that . . ." He doubled over coughing.

I swallowed, deciding I had to ask. "Are you ready to tell me? And explain why?"

"No . . . I can't. Promised . . ."

The connection blanked.

I tried to get back to Kharl, but all that appeared was his sim. When I tried Grete, that was also all I got.

For a moment, all I did was sit there.

Then, almost mechanically, I called up the message from the EDA Trust. Lyenne DeVor had said almost nothing except that she was sending an attachment. So I opened the attachment, coded with another set of personal references, and read through the short list of holdings. The largest single bloc of stock was that of UniComm—roughly thirteen and a half percent. But there were also small blocs of several other multilaterals, including DGen, BGP, and AVida. From the bios I'd gotten from Nyhal I recognized DGen—that was the multilateral holding company headed by the Dengs. AVida was the Dymke vehicle. BGP was an acronym for Best Genetic Productions that had long since been transformed into its less controversial initials, but I had no idea why it was in the EDA portfolio unless Elora had some concerns about clones. The portfolio offered no explanations of any of the holdings, even about the most intriguing of all—the ten thousand shares of something called Octagonal Solutions.

I ran a quick netsearch, and found only a thin sketch, but that was enough, since it listed only two officers—the director general and the managing director. The chairman was Eldyn Nyhal, and the managing director was one Meryssa Elysa D'bou. I had a very good idea who that was.

I hadn't really believed Nyhal, not totally, when he'd insisted that he'd created a tailored bug that would simultaneously kill off about twenty percent of the pre-selects of the world and protect the rest against his mysterious forerunner aliens and their projected bugs. Did the aliens still even exist? The Gates existed, but they were *old*, and there was no proof at all that they still functioned. The one time someone had seen a gas puff . . . that could have been anything.

And Nyhal, brilliant and unstable, might have created octagonal nanites, but he hadn't. He only modified what had been there. But I still didn't understand. If he hated pre-selects so much . . . why hadn't he just let the first plague take its course?

Or hadn't it been strong enough? And what had he done to make the latest one so virulent, and yet so able to spread? Those characteristics shouldn't have gone together, not from what I knew. But it all tied together, just as Octagonal Solutions tied in to everything—again, even if I didn't know how.

More important, what could I do? Could I do anything? Kharl had already contacted those who could. And if I did tell anyone, who would believe that I hadn't had something to do with it? Well . . . whatever I could do, I could do it as well from Majora's as from my empty dwelling, and I needed a friendly face.

I needed a lot more.

I guided the glider northward along the ridge trail—I wanted the least traveled way possible, and I was wondering about everything. I had packed another bag, and hoped I didn't lose it as well.

By the time I'd left Vallura, in the town itself, outside of the norm rally, which seemed to have shouted itself out, nothing seemed that different. There were some people on the walks, but they were all norms, and they looked away from the glider. It was the first time I'd seen that kind of behavior in Noram, but Elysa had led me to believe it was common in the Sinoplex. Then, why hadn't I seen it before? Because it was less obvious? Or because I hadn't wanted to see it?

While it all made sense, it didn't. The pre-selects had been subject to plagues; the norms hadn't, even though many had nanitic health protections. Bright or brilliant norms had every bit as much opportunity as anyone else, as witness the success of Seglend Krindottir and Eldyn Nyhal and others. No one was oppressing or enslaving anyone, not that I could see, and brain-damping only occurred to people who had been caught through physically verified evidence. The Federal Union compact was clear on that. Brain-damping could not be imposed without unassailable physical evidence. More than temporary custody couldn't even be imposed without evidence.

Still, there was no doubt that people were angry at pre-selects, me among them, even as we were dying all over the globe. I still was half-numb over Gerrat's death and my father's death, especially coming on top of Elora's death. Much as I'd disagreed with them . . . dead? So quickly? Erased, so swiftly that they might never have been? Because of Eldyn's resentment and madness? Because he'd been angry and brilliant enough to tweak an alien pathogen into something far more selectively deadly?

And I hadn't even known, partly at least, because I had been trying to minimize the ways in which people could track and find me.

As I watched the guideway, and tried to make sense of the chaos of the world around me, I listened to the snippets of news. Distracted as I was, and with possibly more assassins after me, I wasn't about to use a screen in the glider.

. . . Federal Union forces have restored order in Ankorplex, and authorities have captured several of those thought to have incited the riots. . . .

. . . secretary director has convened an investigatory panel. . . .

. . . the number of deaths has peaked in Eastasia, but deaths continue to rise in Noram, Easteuro, and Sudam. . . .

. . . medical researchers at the High Plains Center in Noram have discovered a complimentary organism that confers immunity to the latest plague strain. . . . unconfirmed reports indicate that it is effective against all versions of the so-called pre-select plagues. . . .

. . . medcenters requesting that no one come to a medcenter except for treatment; visitors will be turned away. . . .

. . . contingents of Federal Union forces have arrived in Westi and Geneva to ensure Union functions continue uninterrupted in the administrative centers. . . .

. . . off-planet travel has been temporarily suspended. . . .

. . . one of the bodies uncovered in the rubble of a house in Tyanjin has been confirmed through DNA testing as that of Doctor Eldyn Nyhal, the noted medical specialist whose work was critical in halting the first pre-select plague . . . apparently a victim of the violence which rocked Tyanjin late yesterday and into the night. . . .

                              *   *   *

I shook my head. Just like that. First accused of complicity
in the death of his wife, then a victim of violence, and now
he was once again noted and respected.

The shadows were long, and the sun was almost ready to
drop behind the trees by the time I reached the glider pad at
Majora's cottage. I'd been ready to use all the special features built into the glider, but the ways were almost empty,
and I'd seen no one.

I decided to take one precaution.

I cut off the ground limiters and lifted the glider over the
trees and set it down on the grass practically next to Majora's
front step.

She was standing by the door when I linklocked the glider
and turned.

"I said I'd be here."

For a moment, her face crinkled into a wry smile. "I
should have guessed you had some tricks under your singlesuit."

"The glider is a little special."

She nodded somberly. "Have you eaten?" After looking
at my face, she shook her head. "Come on in. You need to
eat."

Eating . . . I hadn't thought much about it. I was still
dazed—or half-numbed—by the near annihilation of my
family, and I had to wonder how Kharl was doing, but, again,
there wasn't much I could do personally. There didn't seem
to be much I could do.

Majora closed the door. "I probably should have come to
you, but I only have a magscooter—and the way things are
now . . ."

"That's all right." I just stood there.

"What's the matter?" she asked softly.

I realized I hadn't told her. "The plague . . . whatever it is
. . . my father and Gerrat . . . my mother . . . she'll recover . . .
Rhedya and their children are all right."

"And you still came here?" Her voice was soft.

"Where else would I go? I can't even VR Mother. Rhedya
has her family and the children. You don't have anyone."

Her arms went around me, and we just held each other for a long time.

Finally, she eased away from me. "You didn't have to come."

"Yes, I did." Even if I didn't happen to know whether I needed her warmth more than she needed mine.

"Tell me what happened." She gave my hand another squeeze before she turned and stepped into the kitchen corner.

"I'm still not sure." I stood behind her shoulder as she programmed the replicator.

"I hope you don't mind. I'm not in the mood for cooking."

"Anything is fine. If you scanned it in there, it's better than fine." I could understand that, and I put my hand on her shoulder. After a moment, I went on. "I left messages with my parents, and with Gerrat, just like I did with you. But . . . it was already too late, I think, by then. I hadn't talked to them for several days or so before I'd left. I got Mother's sim, and then Rhedya took over. She had a hard time talking. I don't know the details, except . . . except . . ." I shook my head. The words were hard. "She said that Gerrat and my father had died from the new plague, and that Mother was recovering, but wasn't that strong. She and Delya and Daffyd are all right. So are Haywar and his family. They were visiting." My voice sounded flat in my own ears. "I didn't even know. I had the belt repeater off so that the PST types couldn't use it to track me. I'm looking over my shoulder all the time. I didn't even know. . . ." My eyes were blurry.

She gave me another hug, then turned me. "Daryn . . . you really need to eat. Please sit down."

I let her lead me to the table overlooking the small garden and the golden daffodils. The air was so still they looked like they'd been captured in a single frame VR. I sat down. I watched the daffodils. They didn't move. Neither did I.

"Just eat." Majora set a steaming platter of something—a chicken pasta in a basil sauce, I thought, in front of me with a glass of verdyn and another glass of cold water. She sat across from me with some other kind of pasta, with shellfish, the scampi I didn't much care for, before her. We ate for a time in silence as the shadows lengthened and finally dropped the entire garden into deep shadow.

I couldn't finish the pasta, and I only had a sip or two of the verdyn. It tasted bitter, but that was me, not the verdyn. "Thank you."

"You're welcome. Thank you for coming."

There was a silence, not quite awkward.

"Tell me about what happened in Tyanjin," Majora asked in the dimness of the room.

"You know at least some of it. First, you tell me what's been happening here. With your sister . . . if you want to."

"I've told you about Rob, haven't I, how he just walked out on Melanyi when Syrah was three?"

"Yes." That had been years earlier, but I remembered.

"He called this morning. He was almost grinning. Said I ought to know." Her voice was hard, as if she were trying to keep it from trembling.

I could have tried to read more of how she felt, but that wouldn't have been right, somehow. So I nodded and kept listening.

"Syrah had called him, and he'd taken them both to the medcenter. The doctors couldn't do anything, or not enough. He kept grinning."

"Hysterical reaction," I suggested. "I'm sure he cared for Syrah. You said he spent a lot of time with her."

Majora shook her head, then paused, as if thinking. "You're probably right. I detest him so much, but he was good to Syrah."

"But not to Melanyi."

"No. He was always trying to manipulate her." She shook her head again. "So many . . . they're cremating them all—and the monoclones if they think they're carriers. . . ."

I remembered Rhedya saying something about that. People we'd loved or cared for or both . . . gone in days. Even their bodies. My hands shook as I thought of Eldyn Nyhal, and his words about paying a price. Who was he to decide what prices were to be paid? Or by whom?

"Are you all right?" asked Majora.

"No. I'm upset. I'm angry. I'm angry at myself. I'm angry

at Eldyn. He did this. I guess I'm so mixed up I didn't tell you." I forced a long, deep breath. "I'm angry that I feel so stupid and helpless. People die, people we care for, and by the time I find out enough, it's too late. There's a battle going on. People are fighting, and I don't know why, except in general terms. People are dying, and those dying aren't the ones who are to blame." I wanted to lash out, but lashing out at Majora wouldn't do anything. She was already hurt enough. "And I'm angry at the situation. Eldyn . . . when I talked to him . . . he was stable one minute and almost crazy the next. He kept telling me that the first plague had been caused by alien pathogens from the forerunner Gate builders."

"Is that possible?"

"It could be. Maybe . . . if we look . . . there might be something . . . somewhere. But about that, I could sense he was telling the truth. Then he claimed that he created the current strain to prevent something worse in the future . . . and to make sure all the pre-selects didn't carry augmentation and genetic pre-selection too far." I shook my head. "He said twenty percent of the pre-selects would die. . . ." I forced myself to slow down and to go over the entire conversation with Eldyn. Majora deserved to hear it, and she might catch something I'd missed. ". . . after that, I just ran . . . there was nothing to be gained by staying in Eldyn's retreat. Good thing I did, because once I was in the escape tunnel the house exploded." I shrugged.

"That's . . . horrible."

I nodded slowly, not quite sure what she meant. So many aspects of what I'd discovered were horrible.

"What do you think about the aliens?" I finally asked.

"They are . . . or were real," she said slowly. "From what you've said, and what I know, the original plague was probably their creation. After that . . ."

"Eldyn?"

Majora lifted her shoulders, dropping them as if helplessly. "It's hard to believe, even for me, that anyone could be that angry, angry enough to kill children like Syrah."

"I think he was angry for a long time."

"But . . . children . . . people he didn't even know?"

I didn't have an answer, not a good one. So I stood up and paced to the window, looking out into the garden, dark under dark gray clouds, dark in the growing dusk.

"There's more," I said slowly. "Eldyn gave me the names he thought were behind trying to kill me and Elora. He thought they were after him, too, from the way he acted, but there's no proof, not that would stand up before a justice or even convince an advocate general to investigate. No pre-select would waive privacy. I don't have the resources or the infrastructure to strike back the way they struck at us, and I'm so exposed that if I tried anything direct, the CAs would be at my door in hours."

"Not today, or tomorrow," Majora observed, pausing before adding quickly, "I'm not suggesting you do that. That just lowers you to their level."

"The way I feel, that wouldn't bother me at all."

"The way you feel *now*. You have to live for more than now. You don't want to end up like Eldyn, do you?"

I didn't, but, tired as I was, I was still shaking with rage— and frustration. The only man I knew with any degree of certainty who was responsible for any of the carnage was Eldyn, and he was dead. His wife was dead, and his daughter probably scared and hiding in fear. I could speculate about Eldyn, the aliens, the source of the octagonal pathogens, the names Eldyn had given me, but I had no proof . . . not of anything, except attempts on my life and people dying.

I turned to Majora. "There's another question. Why didn't Eldyn make sure my father had the protective nanites?" I could see why he didn't want to give them to Gerrat, although I wasn't about to voice that thought.

"Did he want your father to be protected?" Majora's dark brown eyes looked shadowed in the dimness of the room. "He had to have considered who would be affected because you said he thought I'd be all right."

"Apparently they're mobile. He actually asked if I'd slept with you." I flushed.

"You obviously thought about it." She was blushing, too, and I could sense that, even if I couldn't see it.

I offered a smile. "I've been thinking about it more often."

"Daryn . . ."

"I know. It's a horrible time to say something like that." I turned back to the window and stared at the grayness of the shadowed garden.

There was a soft sound behind me, not quite a laugh nor a sob.

After a moment, Majora spoke. "Daryn. We can't do anything tonight. You really haven't slept in three days. I didn't sleep last night. Your eyes are red and about to become holes in your head. You're going to stay here and get some sleep and some rest, and then we'll look at things in the morning."

The thought of sleep, I had to admit, even sleeping alone, was welcome. The inadvertent yawn that followed emphasized how exhausted I felt.

Exhausted and numb.

Chapter 56
Helnya

Although the sleep had been welcome, I was up not that much after dawn, worried, and looking out on the garden, where the morning sunlight had already turned the golden daffodils into bright circles of light.

"Would you like some Grey tea?" Majora asked, slipping up behind me and resting her hands gently on my shoulders for just an instant.

I turned. She was wearing the loose gray exercise clothes and a warm smile. Her brown eyes were tired, but warm as well.

"Please."

"How did you sleep?"

"Well enough, until I woke up. What about you?"

"About the same. I kept thinking about Syrah. I have trouble when children or innocents die."

"So do I." That was part of the problem. Most of the time, when someone wanted to control something, everyone else suffered. For all Eldyn's insanity and faults—if he had done what he had said he had—he had placed a price on all of us who were pre-selects. Defining people only as members of groups depersonalized each person, and that meant too many people suffered. And for what? Because we had adopted a social structure that rewarded ability imperfectly? It wasn't as though the pre-selects had gone out to subjugate the norms.

I paused.

Or was it? How far back did it go? Had the ancestor of TanUy actually thought out the implications of the PIAT? I shivered. While it would have been easy to dismiss Eldyn as a grief-stricken and crazed scientist, that felt wrong. Someone had been trying to kill me, Elora, and even Eldyn long before Eldyn's plague had been loosed. And no one had been trying to help Eldyn, except perhaps Elora, and she was dead.

Majora slipped, gracefully for a woman so tall, to the replicator, and I just watched, enjoying looking at her, seeing warmth and solidity in an uncertain time.

"The tea is ready." Majora set it on the table, along with a second steaming mug.

I sat down across the table from her.

"What are you going to do about UniComm?" she asked after I'd taken the first sip.

The question took me with the force of a punch, and, had I been standing, I probably would have staggered. What was I going to do about UniComm? Gerrat and Father were dead, and I was the largest living stakeholder. Now, I not only had to worry about whoever was trying to kill me, and deal with Father's and Gerrat's deaths . . . but UniComm, and Uni-Comm might make me an even bigger target—when I still had but a general idea of what was going on. Eldyn had suggested that I would take over UniComm—and what he had meant hadn't even registered at the time, certainly not in the way he had meant it.

After a moment, I said. "I really hadn't thought about it,

not that way. I should have, I suppose, but . . . with everything that's happened . . . I didn't."

"You mean, after four attempts on your life, the death of
your brother and your father, armed thugs trying to destroy
you, and a fifth of the pre-selects in the world dying or likely
to die . . . you didn't think about what might happen to the
family institution?" Majora's tone was somewhere between
gently ironic and sympathetic. She stood. "We need something to eat before you make any decisions."

"Would you mind if I used your system to access mine?"
Technically, I wouldn't actually be going into hers for that,
but I didn't want to do anything without asking. I'd imposed
far too much already.

The smile that came before the "Not at all" was more than
worth my effort, and while she fiddled with the replicator, I
accessed my gatekeeper using Majora's system, rather than
my belt repeater. Sure enough, there was a message from
Brin Drejcha, the managing director of UniComm. He didn't
say much, but suggested it might be best if I contacted him
at my earliest convenience.

There was also one from my mother. Her eyes were
sunken and hollow, and her hair, usually shining and brown,
looked more like straw. Her face was ashen. But her voice
was firm. "I'm back at home, Daryn. They say I'll recover.
We need to talk, and if you can get here today, it would be
a good idea."

Those were the only messages.

Majora looked at me as she set down a plate that held
some sort of omelet.

I sniffed, catching the scents of cheese and mushrooms
and spices. "Thank you. She's very strong . . . and very
strong-minded."

"Doesn't run in the family, does it?"

"Not at all."

"You ought to eat before you return those calls," Majora
suggested.

I didn't need much urging. I did stop after the first few
mouthfuls. "This is good. Thank you."

"You're welcome."

"How are you feeling?"

Majora looked up from a mouthful of omelet and swallowed. "Better. But I still feel like everything is almost dream-like."

"Nightmare-like." I took a sip of tea. "That's because we live such isolated lives."

"You've wanted it that way, Daryn."

"I know. I know. Then, something like this makes you think. I was off-planet when the last plague hit, and I didn't think it was as bad. No one in my family even got sick."

"Both my parents died in it."

I winced. She'd told me, and I'd forgotten. I shouldn't have.

"It's all right." She reached across the table and touched my hand. "I felt detached then, for a long time. I suppose that's why it hurts so much to lose Melanyi and Syrah."

"There's no one left?"

She nodded.

I felt worse than ever. I still had my mother, and probably would for years. I had—hopefully—Kharl and other people in the family, and Rhedya's and Gerrat's children. Majora had no one.

After standing, I stepped around the table and put my hands on her shoulders. "I'm sorry."

For just a moment, she leaned her head back against me. Then she put on a smile. "Thank you. You need to call some people. I'll clean up the dishes, such as they are."

"I can help."

She was already on her feet. "Just make your calls, and then get yourself cleaned up. You need to deal with things."

So did she, but I didn't argue. I took her hands. "I'm so glad you are who you are."

She squeezed my fingers before disengaging her hands from mine.

I wasn't quite sure what else to say.

She picked up the platters and moved to the kitchen area.

Before talking to Mother, I decided to call my own solicitor—Anna Mayo—she of the fine old Celtic name, if young and ambitious. Her office sim appeared, looking just like her.

Slender, blonde, fine-featured, with eyes like blue agate, and the impression that her entire frame was some form of lithe, but indestructible, composite. "Please leave your coordinates and a brief message. I'll get back to you as soon as I can."

"Anna. This is Daryn Alwyn. I think we need to talk. I hope you're all right. If you are and you can, contact me at my place." I looked at Majora.

She nodded.

"Or at this place." I gave the codes for Majora's system.

I had barely showered and cleaned up when Majora called me.

"It's the solicitor."

Anna's blond hair, cut shorter than that portrayed by the sim, was askew, and there was a smudge of black on her usually immaculate chin. "Daryn, you contacted me. I'm sorry, but it's been a busy time. It's likely to get busier."

"I understand. I may need your services as well. I just discovered that I'm one of the last survivors in the family business, and one of the largest single stakeholders. I have a few concerns about what the management may do. . . ."

"You may be the largest stakeholder, Daryn, but you don't have any official position in UniComm. That means you have no authority, not until you can call a special meeting, and usually, under Federal Union law, you need twenty percent of the outstanding stock, and the company is allowed up to forty-five days to comply."

"What if I can get someone to give me a position—say acting senior director? Then what?"

"Then you can do whatever that position, and Federal Union law, will let you." She glanced past me, as if someone had come into her office. "Is there anything else?"

"There will be, but I need to think, and you have other clients."

She smiled, almost warmly. "Thank you."

After her image faded, I looked out at the sunlit garden, then turned toward the replicator, where I punched the codes for another cup of Grey tea. I probably needed more than that, but the tea was safer.

"How are you going to do that, Daryn?" asked Majora. "Get a position."

"Ask." I smiled.

She nodded. "No one's likely to refuse you, are they?"

"They might. I wouldn't, not in their singlesuits, since I'm the only living Alwyn of majority age besides my mother, and the largest single stockholder, although I'll try not to press that one. I doubt anyone knows that, not with all the chaos."

I wondered. Should I return Drejcha's call . . . or my mother's? I opted for the UniComm director. He was in.

The round-faced and dark-haired director leaned forward as if to study me—or my rather unkempt image. "I appreciate your getting back to me."

"I apologize for my appearance, but I've just returned from a long trip, and . . . well . . . matters have been rather unsettled."

"I can understand that." Drejcha said carefully. "I wish it had not been necessary to contact you under such trying circumstances."

I wondered why he had. Certainly, UniComm could continue for quite some time without an Alwyn in immediate control. "Obviously, there are some urgencies to be considered."

"Not necessarily urgent, but matters that need settling. . . . I would not wish to intrude in this time of grief."

"I understand. Father would have, also." I pursed my lips, tilted my head, as if thinking, although I knew exactly what I needed to do, as far as UniComm happened to be concerned. "Perhaps I should come in and talk with you."

"With the plague, I had thought . . ."

"I've already survived it," I said. "So that's not a concern. I do believe we should talk in person, and despite the unhappy circumstances, sooner is probably better."

"You have not taken an active role in UniComm. . . ." He let the words die away.

"There wasn't much need to, with Gerrat and my father so involved. I have been quite active in the field, though, but

I'm sure we can discuss the details when we meet." I offered a broad and winning smile.

Drejcha actually moistened his lips. "I had hoped that we could continue with a minimum of disruption. . . ."

"I agree, and I think how that's done is something that's best discussed in person . . . don't you?"

"Tomorrow?" he suggested.

"Ten in the morning?" I countered.

"That . . . would be agreeable."

"I'll see you then," I said with a smile.

Once the connection was clear, I turned to Majora, who had stayed out of the pick-up range and watched and listened. "What do you think?"

"He's under pressure. He also wanted your approval to run things."

"But why? He's the managing director."

"He's uneasy. That's clear. He probably wanted to tell people that you'd agreed that he should stay in charge."

"I just wish I knew more."

"That's why you're going to meet him," Majora pointed out in a matter-of-fact tone.

Not for the first time, nor the last, I suspected, I again wished I knew far more about what was going on with UniComm.

I tried my parents' house. Mother's sim appeared, then vanished without speaking. She appeared, propped in an easy chair in her study. Her eyes were red and sunken.

"How are you?" I asked immediately.

"Tired, worn-out, but I'll survive. Lecia's here, and she's rooting around to make sure everything's in shape."

I laughed. Knowing my Aunt Lecia, far more abrupt than Mother, I could understand that. "I just got your message."

"Daryn . . . this is a less than opportune time, but I do think that we should talk over a few things."

"So do I. When would be a good time?"

"If it would not inconvenience you too much, this morning would be better."

"I'll be there shortly."

"Good." Mother broke the connection before I could.

For a moment, I sat there. Mother was usually far less direct. That meant she was tired or worried or both. Weren't we all, though?

I turned to Majora. "How would you like a job as special assistant to the about-to-be-acting senior director of Uni-Comm?"

"You seem rather sure of that."

"I'm trying to be positive. If it doesn't work, and we have to try an outside takeover, then I'll think about all the difficulties that we'll face."

"For someone who wanted nothing to do with the family trade . . ." Majora shook her head.

"Part of it is that I'm one of the few left. Part of it is that using UniComm is about the only way I can see to stop the attacks and find out how everything goes together."

"And part of it is that you don't like to feel helpless," she added with a faint smile.

I shrugged. She was right. Very right. I hated it. "Do you want to come with me? To Mother's?"

She shook her head. "I have work to do, and I'd like to get a little exercise. If I take a position as someone's special assistant, I won't have much time for that. Besides, your mother doesn't want me around. Not now."

Mother would have liked Majora around me a lot more, and I was beginning to see why, and wondering why I hadn't seen that before. Because I automatically had rejected so much planned by my parents?

"You'll be careful?" I asked Majora.

"I'll be careful, but you need to be even more careful." She smiled. "You're ready. Go . . . and let this woman have some time to herself."

I returned the smile, and I made sure to hug her before I headed out to the glider.

The gliderways were far less crowded than normal, but that might also have been because I took a route that kept me away from the centers of both Helnya and Yunvil. I also listened to the audio of AllNews. I didn't want to turn the glider on automatic to watch the glider's small holo display.

... the number of demonstrations and violent incidents has dropped sharply ... analysts ... uncertain as to whether the use of Federal Union troops ... or the realization that the latest pre-select plague appears to have peaked ...

... greatest number of fatalities ... in Eastasia and West Noram ...

... epidemiologists studying the pattern ...

... use of nanite-based antigens developed by the High Plains Research Center ... while too late for full effect ... will reduce future incidences ...

Kharl's effort had borne some fruit—or looked to do so.

... claimed isolation of pre-select populations reduced impact ...

Reduced or merely delayed and strung out the deaths so that the impact didn't seem so great?

I eased the glider practically to the front door of my parents' dwelling, setting it on the grass there, rather than in the lower gliderpark.

Lecia, the broad-shouldered and squarish younger sister of my mother, had the door open before I reached it.

"Come in, Daryn. She's been expecting you. She's fretting

more than a little, and she's not in shape to fret that much."

"I know. I came as soon as I could, but . . ."

"It's not as though you live a klick away, like your brother. She's in her study." Lecia motioned for me to enter.

Mother's study was more like a library, a small room behind the lower front parlor. The armaglass door between the parlor and the study was open, and she still was sitting in the armchair. I eased the door shut behind me.

"I'm sorry . . . about Father. . . . I tried to warn you . . . as soon as I knew," I said quietly.

"I know, and it helped the children, Rhedya said."

"I just wish . . ."

"There wasn't anything else you could have done, dear. He was one of the first here in Calfya—he and Gerrat. The doctors and the medcenter didn't even know what was the matter, just the symptoms."

"I'm still sorry. I leave, and Father and Gerrat are healthy and well, and three days later, they're dead . . . gone."

Mother nodded. "It was . . . a difficult time. It may get more difficult."

"How are you doing?" I turned the desk chair and sat down facing her.

"I'm as well as can be expected, but I'll be fine. Other matters . . . may not."

"With the family? Kharl is having a hard time."

A flat smile crossed her face.

"Then you're referring to UniComm?"

"How much stock do you control?" she asked.

"Twenty-three percent." There was no point in beating around on that.

"The trust your father established has twenty-one percent. Gerrat had nine percent, and Rhedya has voting control of that."

"I thought as much, but I also thought I should talk to you first."

"What do you intend to do?"

"That depends on you. If . . . if you'll support me, I'll take over as director general. Then I'll rebuild UniComm. . . ."

She raised her eyebrows. "And you think Gerrat and your father didn't try?"

"I'm sure they did. I have several advantages."

"Such as the complete programming schedules and strategy of OneCys?"

"And some of the comparative analyses of three of the smaller nets as well, and an understanding of their general approach."

"Gerrat always underestimated you," Mother said slowly. "Your father wanted you in UniComm very much."

"I know. It wouldn't have worked."

"Your father and I talked about that, and he came to understand that, but it was hard for him." She took a small sip from the glass of water on the round cherry side table at her elbow, replacing it on the crystal and silver coaster.

"I had thought so, but Gerrat never listened to me, and my being in UniComm wouldn't have changed that."

She nodded again. "What about . . . Elora was murdered, you know?"

"They all died because of the same people." That was certainly true.

"Do you know who they are?"

"I know who some of them are. One is already dead." I let my words come out flat.

"Can you handle what needs to be done?"

My smile was lopsided. "I don't know. I do know that no one else has a chance, and I do have a plan." I paused. "Don't ask me, and I won't tell you, except that it's totally legal and totally amoral."

"You had a plan to become wealthy and independent. It worked well, Daryn. Let us both hope this one is as successful. I already signed over voting control to you for the next year. You'll have to talk to Rhedya."

"I know."

"I told her that, hard as it was, you would have to talk to her. She wasn't pleased."

"She's here?"

"For now." Mother raised her eyebrows.

"How did you get her to stay here?"

"Let us just say that I played upon her wishes for the best for her children." Mother took a long and slow deep breath. "I told her she could ask you anything, but that you were the only hope she had for some sort of justice."

"You mean revenge."

"Justice is a much more . . . appropriate term, Daryn."

I almost smiled. Mother was definitely on the mend. I stood. "I presume it would be best if I talked to Rhedya before she decides to leave?"

"She won't, but it would be best if you did not make her wait."

"Are you sure you're all right?"

"There's nothing wrong with me that time and sleep won't mend. Now . . . don't you think you should go deal with Rhedya?"

I stood and bowed. "I'll see you before I leave."

"That would be nice, dear."

After another bow, I turned. In leaving the study, I made sure the door was ajar.

Rhedya was waiting in the parlor. She sat on the burgundy sofa, her face blank.

I made a motion for her to stay seated, although she had shown no inclination to stand when I stepped into the room.

"I wish I didn't have to be here, Rhedya," I said slowly.

"Gerrat's hardly dead, and you're ready to take over."

I shook my head. "Less than three hours after I found out about Gerrat's death, Brin Drejcha was after me to suggest that he take over as director general of UniComm. I have to meet with him tomorrow. There are rumors that OneCys has already approached him to suggest a takeover—with him to remain as director general."

"Let them. . . . I don't care. Do what you want. You Alwyns do anyway."

"I need your help, Rhedya." I sat down on the edge of the side chair, leaning forward to meet her eyes directly.

"You want Gerrat's stock, and he's been gone three days."

"No. I don't want the stock. I don't need the stock. I do need your votes to keep control of UniComm, and I need control of UniComm to go after the people whose actions caused Gerrat's and Father's death."

"How could someone cause a plague?"

I decided to be honest, if somewhat careful. "The plague was created by a man named Eldyn Nyhal. He was a brilliant norm, and Gerrat and I knew him growing up. His wife was killed in mysterious circumstances, and he blamed a pre-select conspiracy. He thought the conspiracy was trying to kill off all of us—the wall that fell on me was part of their work, and so was the tunnel train explosion that killed Elora. I don't know all the details, but I got a message from Elora—recorded before she was killed and sent by her solicitor after her death, on her instructions, that told me to contact Eldyn for details in case anything happened to her. That's why I was in the Sinoplex. I was talking to him, trying to get answers when two men in FS camouflage suits burst in with restricted slug-throwers. He threw himself in front of them to save me, and triggered some kind of explosion. I was wearing a body screen, and that saved me. . . ."

"Too bad there aren't body suits against plagues."

I nodded, then continued. "Before we were interrupted, he was telling me that he'd engineered the plague because it was the only thing he could do to stop this conspiracy from taking over the Union—"

"But Gerrat . . . your father?" For the first time, the hardness left her voice.

"According to Eldyn, the people behind it are backing OneCys in an effort to take over UniComm. They wanted to kill Gerrat and Father like they'd tried with Elora and me. Eldyn was afraid, after Elora's death, that no one would stop them. I don't know if he'd tried to talk to Gerrat. . . ." I paused and waited.

Rhedya's fingertips went to her mouth. Then she swallowed. Finally, she began to speak. "It was maybe two months ago. Gerrat said something about an old acquaintance. He never mentioned the name. He said that he was brilliant, but not very stable, imagining conspiracies everywhere. Gerrat said that this . . . norm . . . almost threatened him . . . if he didn't use his influence against these imaginary conspirators."

I took a deep breath. "Eldyn *was* brilliant, and he wasn't very stable. But he was also right. One of the groups that filed the request for the stakeholder meeting is a front for some very wealthy pre-selects who are large stakeholders in OneCys and who are trying to make perceptual intelligence testing a requirement for education and jobs." I hoped I was reading Rhedya right, but she seemed close to her nephew Frydrik.

". . . all this . . . it's monstrous . . . conspiracies and plagues . . . people, children . . . dying . . . and you're playing to it."

"I could do nothing. I could let Brin Drejcha manage UniComm, and watch it be bought by OneCys. I could see your children get a fraction of what their stock is worth. I could stand back and watch as people like Frydrik are pushed away from any real future." I paused. "Is that what you want?"

Rhedya looked at me for a long time. I met her gaze.

"What do you want?" she finally asked.

"All I want is your support for me to become director general of UniComm. With the stock you hold in trust for the children, and with what I can vote, we control fifty-three percent."

"So . . . you have to listen to me?"

I smiled. "I have always listened to you, haven't I?"

She nodded.

"I *might* be able to keep control in the family without your votes. I'd certainly rather not have to try."

"You were the only one who was honest with Frydrik. He told me that, years ago. He was angry with you then, but he still respects you."

"I tried to be as honest as I could, but also to be helpful. I told him that if he had a better idea, I'd listen. I try to listen."

"What are you going to do with UniComm . . . if I support you?"

"Make sure it remains strong and profitable, and ensure

that the people who created this mess that led to Gerrat's and Father's death pay for it."

Rhedya's eyes glittered . . . just for a moment. Then she nodded, and the façade of the sweet loving woman dropped back across her. "It would have taken something like this to bring you back into UniComm, wouldn't it?"

"So long as Gerrat was alive, UniComm was his, Rhedya." That was certainly true.

"I've never quite understood the relationship between you and Gerrat, Daryn, but Gerrat respected and trusted you, and he didn't trust many people."

I wasn't aware that Gerrat had trusted anyone, including me. "Gerrat was very good at making people like him. I'm probably not that good, but I don't want to see what Father and Grandfather and Gerrat built just traded away."

"You'll tell me what you're doing and why?"

"Yes. First, I need to ensure I have control of UniComm. If you support me, I do. The next step is to investigate the names I've discovered. Then, I'll need to take action."

"How long?"

I frowned. "There's the special stakeholders' meeting in about three weeks. That's where your votes come in. After that . . . if I can do what I have in mind . . . less than three months, perhaps much less, but I won't know for a week or so, until I can pin down the legalities."

"Legalities?"

"Rhedya. Everything that was done against Elora, Father, Gerrat, me, and you was totally illegal. But there's not enough evidence to prove it. I know. I've already worked some of this with the CAs. The people who did it have snoops and taps on everything we do. My dwelling has been snooped twice. There have been four attempts on my life, but all set up so cleverly . . ." I went on to explain how both the laseflash and the wall had been set up so that everything under skytors surveillance looked perfectly normal. ". . . and I'll probably get a damage claim from the city of Helnya." I laughed. "So we can add fraud to murder charges—if I can prove it."

Rhedya's face was somber. "Are you going to be con-
strained by legalities?"

"I think I can ensure justice for Father and Gerrat and
Elora, and what I have in mind is totally legal. But it doesn't
rely on the CAs or the Union."

For a second time, I saw the briefest glitter in her eyes.
"Good. I won't ask more."

I also understood that. She wouldn't ask more unless I
failed to deliver.

So I would have to make sure that I did.

"I'll have the papers to you this afternoon." I paused.
"That's for all of our protection. You'll be giving me voting
control for one year, but you can revoke it at any time, and
control will revert to you immediately if anything happens
to me."

Rhedya nodded.

The next step, besides getting ready to take on Drejcha,
would be to beef up the security at Majora's place . . . if she
agreed . . . but that would protect us both, and I didn't like
the idea of moving in with Mother—for lots of reasons.

Chapter 58

Excellence is the manifestation of superiority in some
form of endeavor, and, by definition, there are far fewer
creations or endeavors that are superior than there are
those which are merely competent or less than competent. . . .

Each individual values self more than others, except
perhaps parents who behold their children. Yet in re-
vering their children, they seek another form of self-
affirmation. Even those who adopt nationalistic or
patriotic ideals and offer their lives for the culture are
seeking self-affirmation through a greater "good." . . .

The presence of excellence reminds the majority of

humans that they are not superior. If that demonstration of excellence is great enough, it can be humbling, and humans dislike being humbled. Excellence is therefore established by some form of elite, initially by those who can create it, then hailed by those who can recognize it, and finally used as a tool by those who can do neither.

Excellence is generally ignored by the majority of any society, except when it can be used for other ends. Great poetry is seldom read, because there are few such uses for it, while the excellently simple design of the paper clip dominated paper-pushing cultures for more than a century, its inventor immediately forgotten. Great drama was written or revived only when it could be used to part human beings from a portion of their wealth. Great works of physical art [paintings, sculpture] have been historically the most valuable after the death of their creators, when their excellence could be separated from the superiority of their creators.

Excellence and popularity are seldom manifested in the same work, because popularity derives from the ability of humans to identify with the endeavor or the creator, and few identify comfortably with genius. . . .

The "dead white male" syndrome of the late Noram Commonacracy was highly instrumental in creating the decline of excellence which, in turn, exaggerated the effect of the Collapse. What was conveniently overlooked by the revolutionaries, never accepted by the masses, and never confronted effectively by the declining pre-Collapse establishment was one simple corollary to excellence. It takes training, education, discipline, and intelligence to create and/or recognize excellence. In general, most of the individuals in any society capable in practical terms of creating excellence must come from the privileged or near-privileged strata of society. There are exceptions, often distinguished and notable ones, but statistically, they are insignificant. This has meant that, for most of history, most endeavors of artistic excellence were created, funded, and supported by white males. In those few places and cultures where equal or near equal resources went to others, others also created works of excellence. Resource allocation was the key, but the revolutionaries of the pre-Collapse cleverly established the position that excellence was merely a code for values supporting the white male status quo, rather than a reflection of the allocation of resources necessary for the creation of excellence.

By debunking the entire concept of excellence as status quo propaganda, and by insisting that all artistic values and creations were equal, and that true beauty did not exist, but was only an ephemeral phantom in the mind of each beholder, or a tool of the white male elite, the revolutionaries undermined the very basis of excellence . . . and thus contributed to the Collapse, and, in the end, to their own demise, because once they had destroyed the concept of objective and not theologically-based values and excellence, they also destroyed the social restraints that had shackled the commercial and political elites, to the point that the only value was power. . . .

> "Musings on Excellence"
> Exton Land
> [included in *Personal Notes*]

Chapter 59
Kewood

Majora sat beside me in the glider on the trip from Helnya to the UniComm glider park. The subtle scent of flowers, not too sweet, not overpowering, but somehow appropriate to her—made me realize just how long it had been that anyone I'd cared about had been in the glider.

"It looks and feels like a normal glider," she said as we walked toward the gray stone steps.

"It is a normal glider. It just has a few additions."

"A few? Is that how you brought it over the trees at my house?" Her thick eyebrows lifted.

"It does have additional fuel cells, double the number of solar cells, flitter gyros, and delimiter cutouts."

"So it's really a flitter posing as a glider? Like you're an orca posing as a porpoise? A generally friendly orca, but . . ."

"I think of myself more like a raven, actually, having to deal with eagles."

She laughed. "How about a black eagle?"

"Large raven . . . if I'm lucky."

We moved through the three-meter-high black marble arch to the security station, where the guard in the green-trimmed gray of UniComm Security waited.

"Daryn Alwyn. I have a meeting with Brin Drejcha."

"Yes, ser. He's expecting you." The guard looked at Majora.

"This is Majora Hyriss. She's my special assistant." I smiled pleasantly.

"Director Drejcha did not mention any others."

"You can contact him, but I am most certain my special assistant will be welcome."

"One moment, ser." The guard retreated behind a transparent nanite sound-screen. I watched his lips.

". . . special assistant . . . Hyriss . . . woman . . . ser . . ."

There was a pause.

"Yes, ser."

The screen came down. "If you would both step through the scanner . . . ser, lady."

I let Majora go through first, then followed. Drejcha's office was up the ramp to the left, on the same side of the courtyard garden as Gerrat's was, and past the orchid gardens.

"This is rather impressive, and almost all hidden away," Majora murmured.

"Father never believed in visible ostentation. We weren't

allowed magscooters, and when we learned to play tennis, it was at the local club."

Majora laughed. "Showing you and Gerrat off was a form of ostentation."

I frowned, but only for a moment. She was right, although I'd never thought of it in quite that way. "Maybe he didn't believe in tasteless ostentation." Except that wasn't it, either.

We passed one of the windows overlooking the inner courtyard, and, for a moment, I caught sight of our reflections—two tall muscular figures, me in dark blue with a short gray vest, and Majora in maroon and gray.

A young man in security gray also waited outside Drejcha's office. "Ser . . . he is expecting you." He opened the door for us.

Drejcha's office, nearly as large as Gerrat's, was furnished in the same style as Father's, with a simple cherry desk, a round conference table with cherry armchairs upholstered in green, and one four-shelf cherry bookcase, filled with leatherbound volumes I would have bet that the man had never read.

Drejcha was standing as we entered.

"It's good to see you, Daryn, and good to learn that you are well." Brin Drejcha bowed slightly more than perfunctorily. He was slightly round-faced, perhaps five centimeters shorter than I, and slightly shorter than Majora. For some reason, that gratified me. He had smooth black hair, piercing blue eyes, and a warm professional smile of the type Gerrat had perfected and which I distrusted instantly.

"It's good to see you."

Majora closed the door behind us.

Drejcha gestured to the circular conference table, around which were four chairs. Majora and I took the chairs with the view of the door.

"You suggested that we should talk," I began.

"Ah . . . as you know . . . UniComm finds itself in a rather difficult position . . . losing the director general and the senior director. . . ."

"It certainly was unexpected," I said slowly. "And very upsetting. But UniComm was most important to Father, and he anticipated that it would always be directed by one of the family." I looked directly at the managing director.

Drejcha didn't quite meet my eyes. "I've talked to several of the board members, and they have expressed some concern that anyone not familiar with the existing situation might find matters rather . . . challenging. . . ."

"I would agree wholeheartedly," I replied evenly.

"I had thought . . ." He paused, almost as if realizing that what I had said was somehow not what he had expected. "Perhaps I should ask if you would clarify what you mean."

"It's relatively simple, I should think. UniComm has been losing market share in the neighborhood of one percent per year for the last decade. The decline has been almost unnoticed, except when viewed over a longer perspective. The drop-off is actually greater than that, in practical terms, because AllNews has actually increased marketshare by about five percent, and with the weight behind its exposure . . ." I smiled, coldly. "OneCys has totally revamped its programming, and has analyzed in great detail the weaknesses of every high-revenue UniComm slot. The changes have not had that great an impact . . . yet . . . but UniComm has done very little to address the OneCys changes. Probably more important, the fringe networks have also picked up on those changes, and UniComm is losing share on the edges, with the porndraggies and the high-end dramas." I looked at Drejcha. "Do you want me to go on? If you'd like, I can give you the OneCys analyses of every segment." I smiled. "After all, I'm the one who did them."

Drejcha glanced from me to Majora. Her eyes were colder than mine. He looked back at me. "I see. I appear to have misunderstood. Indeed, you are an Alwyn. But . . . you still have no status within the organization."

I shrugged. "As I see it, there are two ways this can play out. You and I can work together, and you can appoint me acting director general until the special stakeholders' meeting, when a motion will be put forth to install me as director general . . . or you can insist on running UniComm without me . . . until the meeting. I think you understand the implications of either scenario."

A rueful smile crossed Drejcha's face.

I didn't trust it any more than I'd trusted the warm and welcoming one.

"I see a great resemblance to your father. When would you like to begin as acting director general?"

"Now's as good a time as any." I nodded at Majora. "Majora is the only staff person I'll be bringing with me. She'll be acting as my special assistant. She is a *very* good analyst and communicator."

"What sort of announcement did you plan, Director Drejcha?" Majora asked quietly.

"Oh . . . I suppose we should make an announcement."

"Just within UniComm, I would suggest, for now," she said politely. "And offices . . . ?"

"For now, I'll use Father's," I said. "I'd like one for Majora that's close to his, but don't move anyone or talk to them until we discuss the possibilities."

Drejcha nodded politely, his politeness covering anger . . . or apprehension.

"And you'll ensure we're both in the databases with full access." I didn't word that as a question.

"Of course. As soon as we're finished." Drejcha offered his winning smile.

"Why don't we walk over to Father's office?" I suggested.

The managing director nodded, but let me lead the way along the cross corridor.

"We'll need to reset the access and security codes for you, Director Alwyn," Drejcha said as we neared the unmarked closed door. Father hadn't believed in titles on doors. He'd always felt that if you needed to be identified, you didn't belong in UniComm.

Maybe that was why Gerrat had adopted his fancy mist-desk, as a way of identification.

Drejcha touched the access plate, and the security door irised into its recesses. I opened the plain wooden door behind it and stepped inside. Father's office hadn't changed since the last time I'd been in it, and the only difference was a short stack of papers on the corner of the polished cherry wood desk.

"You see . . . just as he left it," offered Drejcha.

I had doubts about that, but merely nodded. "It's very much the way he kept it. Not much clutter."

I picked up the heavy vellum card from the cherry wood desk. Although the card looked like vellum, its surface was slightly sticky, and my fingers left the faintest set of prints. I read the wording.

ELDYN E. NYHAL
IS PLEASED TO ANNOUNCE
THE FORMATION OF
OCTAGONAL SOLUTIONS,
A NEW APPROACH
FOR A NEW FUTURE.

There was an address and a call code below.

I studied the card for a moment, noting several other sets of fingerprints on the surface of the card. Then, the reason for the stickiness hit me, and I swallowed, forcing myself to set the card on the polished wood, as if I had lost interest. Majora's eyes flicked to the card, then to me, then away.

She understood what I was doing—or was refraining from doing—and said nothing.

Drejcha just stood there.

"Brin . . . why don't you get someone to take care of the details of access and security, and all that, and then rejoin us here. While I know the technical side fairly well, I don't know all the people, and I'm sure you know all the key people well enough to brief us on them." I offered a smile at least as false as all those he'd been giving us.

"I can do that, Director Alwyn."

"We'll be waiting for you."

Once Drejcha had left, I walked back to the desk where I noted the codes on Eldyn's traitorous card and tapped them out, using the bypass and my own personal codes and charges, since I was certain it would be a while before Drejcha got around to getting all the authorizations set up.

Instead of a sim appearing the holo image that appeared

in midair before the cherry bookcase nearest the desk, there
was merely a notice, set in red against a beige background.

As a result of recent developments, the programs and
assets of Octagonal Solutions have been transferred to
the EDA Trust.

I swallowed. While I'd known from the EDA portfolio that
Eldyn had operated Octagonal Solutions, I certainly hadn't
anticipated inheriting the operation, even indirectly.

My eyes went to Majora. "I didn't know."

"That's obvious from the stunned look." She touched my
hand. "You're going to be very busy."

I'd never followed up on the EDA Trust as much as I
should have, either, except to ensure I controlled the Trust,
but it appeared, from what little I'd researched about Eldyn,
that the trust was going to play a far bigger role than I had
ever thought.

Then . . . everything was looking bigger than I'd ever
thought.

Chapter 60
Vallura

After I checked the security to my house, Majora and I
walked up the steps from the glider hangar into the front
foyer. So far as I could tell, no one had been inside, but that
only meant that either experts had been there or no one.

Majora studied the empty foyer, then stepped through the
archway into the front sitting room. "Your house is more
like an office, Daryn. Do you ever use this room?"

I had to think. The last time had been when the CAs had
showed up at the front door. I couldn't remember the time
before that. "Not for a while. I didn't entertain much, not in
the last few years, anyway." I followed her.

"This kitchen is big enough for a small hotel, and you even have gas piped in here."

"The architect suggested it." I grinned at her. "It does heat up the kettle quickly."

"I'm glad it gets some use."

We went down to the study.

Majora glanced out at the view of the East Mountains in the late afternoon sun, then at the single finch pecking to dislodge a seed from the base of the empty bird feeder. I missed the juncos, but they were strictly winter birds in Vallura.

Finally, she glanced at me. "You spend most of your time here, don't you?"

"Except when I'm sleeping . . . well . . . it was that way until several months ago."

"I suppose you'll go back to that."

I wasn't quite sure how to read that, but I jumped in with both feet. "I'd much rather not."

"Oh?"

"I'm asking you to give me another chance." I smiled wryly. "Without my mother's prompting."

My words brought a headshake. "You're almost as tactless as I am, dear man."

"You bring out the best—or the most honest—part of me."

Her gesture was not quite a dismissal. "I'll explore, if you'll let me, while you do whatever you have to."

I laughed. "There's not much to explore. Go ahead." That wasn't really true. The dwelling was far larger than I'd ever need by myself, but I'd never accumulated that much in the way of personal items— the result of two decades of traveling light, I supposed, in my formative adult years.

As Majora slipped toward the storeroom that was almost empty, I checked the messages—realizing that I hadn't started work on Klevyl's latest. I put in a call to him . . . and actually found him.

"Daryn . . . are you all right? You don't take this long, normally."

"I was out of touch. It's been a hard week and then some. I'm sorry . . . but this time, I can't do it."

"It must be something," Klevyl said slowly.

"It is. My father and my brother died from this latest plague, and my sister was killed in that tube crash in Westeuro."

The leonine-maned engineer shook his head, then said, "I am sorry. I really am."

"There is one other thing, Klevyl. You might get something out of it in the future, because I respect your work."

"You don't owe me anything, Daryn. Your work has been the best I could get."

"The other thing is that I'm the acting director general of UniComm." I offered a rueful smile. "It only took enough tragedies to wipe out almost all my family."

"I said I was sorry . . . and I am, but UniComm will be better for it."

I appreciated his confidence. I wasn't sure he was right. "Thank you. If we build anything, you'll be on the bid list."

"You don't have to . . ."

"It's not having to; it's getting the best." I took a deep breath. "I'm sorry I didn't let you know sooner, but I hope you can understand."

"I understand. Take care, Daryn."

"Thank you." I'd always liked and respected Klevyl, and I still did.

After clearing my throat, I put in another call to Mertyn. I didn't have to bother. I only got the sim.

There wasn't much else on the gatekeeper, and I went to find Majora. She was in the unfinished bay under the great room.

"You have enough space here for three families." She turned. "You have that thoughtful look."

"I called Mertyn. His sim still answers. Would you mind if we stopped there on the way to take you home?"

"No. I know you've been worried about him."

As we headed for the glider hangar, I reset all the security systems, recoding them, for all the good it might do.

"After you, lady." I beckoned for her to enter the glider, and got a smile for my over-courtly attitude.

Again, I left my belt repeater unpowered, and the canopy

closed as I guided the glider northward once more.

Both Majora and I were uncharacteristically silent, perhaps because we both were considering all that had happened so quickly. I was also trying to figure out how to broach the idea of my staying with her on a much more permanent basis, and not just for security.

When we got to Mertyn's, it was clear that no one was there, and that no one had been, possibly since he had left for his wilderness excursion.

I was appalled. The grass was matted, and the tulips and daffodils were struggling to get out from under the mulch blanket Mertyn had applied. Leaves, dust, and dirt covered the front veranda, enough that I could see bird tracks on the stones.

I rang the bell. Nothing happened. I also pounded on the door. No one answered.

"Something happened to him." That was a stupidly true statement, I realized, immediately after uttering it.

"Wouldn't someone notice?" asked Majora.

"Probably not. He wasn't married long . . . no children. Teaching was his life, but I was probably as close to him as anyone." I shook my head. "We need to notify the CAs that he seems to be missing."

"Let's do it from my place," she suggested.

"Your place?"

"We need to stay together."

"I hoped you'd say that." I couldn't help smiling a little. "Would you mind if I spend some of my funds to improve security?"

She shook her head. "You were waiting for that."

"I was trying to figure out how to say it."

"Separate bedrooms, Daryn. And for now, it's because of the situation. Besides, my garden needs attention. You don't even have one. And fewer people know where I am, and no one has seen us together."

"They could trace. . . ."

"You've used my access codes, remember." She smiled faintly. "Also, I'm closer to Kewood."

I shook my head. "You are persuasive."

"Opportunistic."

"I don't think so." She wasn't opportunistic. I'd never met anyone less so, and in a world where everyone wanted everything, I was coming to value her more and more. "But I will bow to your common sense." And her warmth and support, and everything else that I should have seen years earlier.

Chapter 61

The old Gael wrote about a simpler time, and even then he said that everywhere the ceremony of innocence was drowned. He didn't say in what, but I imagine he meant blood. Today, innocence drowns before it emerges in the oceans that are the comments, linking and displaying, until all values sink in the storms of information.

He also wrote that all the things people esteem endure but a moment or a day. He didn't foresee the time when nothing was esteemed, only valued for its contribution to commercial or social power. More than a handful of social critics have claimed that values or excellence are merely the tools of the elite, used to reinforce the existing structure—or in the case of revolutionaries, to overthrow it.

Is there such a thing as objective excellence?

It's hard for me to believe that there could *not* be such, not when I have seen an endless objective universe, governed by unalterable law. . . .

Personal Notes

Standing at the corner of the cherry wood desk that had been my father's, in the office I'd never even considered holding, I handed Majora the list of five names Nyhal had given me, and the information included with them. "That's the list of people Eldyn said were behind the attacks on Elora and me. If you could see what's available in the UniComm archives and anywhere else on them . . ."

"There's probably something. I assume you want anything that would shed light on their actions and motivations." Majora was in a deep blue singlesuit that somehow enhanced her figure and her color.

"And anything that can be truthfully used to cast some light on their ambitions to rule the world indirectly." I'd meant the words to come out sardonically or ironically, but I could hear more bitterness than irony. Then, they were responsible for all too many deaths, and I had this feeling that Mertyn's might be among them. He should have returned long ago. "Oh . . . when you get a moment, can you check with the CAs and see if they have any information on Mertyn?"

"I did, just a little while ago." Her voice was hesitant.

"You don't sound like you have good news."

"His body was found in the Brys Canyon Wilderness four weeks ago. There was no one to notify, except the Society of Dynae."

"Do they know what happened?"

"They say he fell off a steep trail."

I had no doubts that Mertyn was shoved, and by the agents of those illustrious souls I'd just asked Majora to research.

"You think he was murdered, too, don't you?" she asked.

"I *know* he was murdered. I just don't know why. He

wasn't a stakeholder—or if he had been, he couldn't have had that many shares. He wasn't a public spokesman for the Dynae."

"But he advised you. Maybe they're trying to isolate you."

I laughed, half-bitterly. "Except for you, I'm already isolated, and while it's necessary, even the security services at your place are another form of isolation, in a way, even if most people don't notice them."

"They're necessary, and I'm glad you didn't wait." She offered a faint smile.

"You're worth all the security," I said.

"You're getting more gallant."

"Even as I become more isolated? Most of my previous clients can't hire me now, and wouldn't talk to me, except socially. Half my family is dead, and I've never been that outgoing, anyway."

"That's an advantage, Daryn. Now."

"Because there's nobody left for them to kill or pressure?"

"They should have more difficulty determining what you might do."

"I imagine they will, considering I'm having trouble figuring it out."

"Are you?" she asked softly. "Or are you having trouble accepting what may be necessary?"

"You already know me too well." I didn't have to force the grin. "Maybe because we're alike."

Her deep brown eyes smiled, and for a moment, I just looked at her.

"What do we know about the stakeholders' meeting?" I finally asked.

"The PST Trust has been contacting every institutional holder of UniComm stock, and sending advocates and consultants to visit them." Majora's lips twisted for a moment. "You didn't expect any other approach, did you?"

"No." I nodded. "That doesn't surprise me."

"They're misrepresenting the situation. Are you going to fight? Send out more truthful information?"

I smiled. "Not until after the meeting."

She raised her thick but finely drawn dark eyebrows.

"We'll just keep track ... both of who votes what and how."

Her eyes met mine. Then she looked away.

"One other thing ..."

She looked up.

"The alien connection? Have you found anything that would ..." I let the words drift into silence.

"That would show anything about whether the first plague was alien or contrived?" Her mouth twisted. "There are several FU reports. What I've read so far indicates Eldyn didn't create it. He wasn't even involved with the first teams, and until then he wouldn't have had access to the laboratories and equipment." She shrugged. "There doesn't seem to be much after that, though."

"Somehow, that doesn't surprise you, does it?"

"No."

I winced at the flatness of her tone.

"I'll keep looking, Daryn, but I don't think we'll find more."

Neither did I.

After a long moment of silence, she smiled, a sad smile, but with warmth beneath, and so did I, just because she had.

Chapter 63
Kewood

The stakeholders' meeting had been arranged to be held in the large conference center on the lowest level of the UniComm headquarters structure, just above the induction tube station. Father had thought that was the best location both for the conference center and for most meetings involving outsiders because UniComm retained control. The conference center was not that large, holding perhaps five hundred fixed seats, and the ability to add another two hundred portable chairs. There was a stage, with a covered orchestra pit, that had never been used, to my knowledge, and with wing and fly space—all because Grandmother had insisted that there ought to be some place in Kewood where live theatre and opera could be performed. I wasn't aware that any had been since her death.

The stage was where the advisory board and the directors of UniComm would be seated, with the senior directors in the middle, flanked by the six advisors. In effect, that meant Brin Drejcha was on my left, and Tomas Gallo, the Uni-Comm solicitor general, was on my right, with three members of the advisory board sitting on each end of the long table covered with a gray cloth trimmed in green.

Both Drejcha and Gallo had recommended a closed meeting with stakeholders either being present or represented by a representative physically present. I'd agreed with the requirement for physical presence or representation, as opposed to VR presence, but suggested that the meeting be open. I didn't have anything to hide, and even if I had, closing a meeting was certain to suggest that I did.

From the wing of the stage I glanced out at the audience. There were less than a hundred people present, and I suspected half were media types who held as few shares as they could purchase just to be present. "We might as well go on out," I said, and then walked out.

Drejcha and the tall and slender Gallo followed him. After the two UniComm officers came the six independent advisors, two of whom were actual representatives of the Federal Union. I didn't know any of them personally.

I slipped into the center seat, behind the small authenticator console that was mine. One was issued to each stakeholder as he or she entered, and each was coded to the holder's handprint only. Not foolproof, but fairly close to it.

After we sat, another figure walked to the podium to the right and forward of the table.

"This meeting is called pursuant to Federal Union law one-forty-seven, section C, dealing with stakeholder rights." Feron Nasaki, the UniComm associate general counsel, made the formal opening announcement. He looked very nervous. "Under the multilateral rules of procedure for organizations

established under modified restricted liability, the organization may establish rules for the conduct of such a meeting,
provided they meet the guidelines of Federal Union law.
Therefore, all votes made in this meeting must be cast in
person, either by the stakeholder of record, or by an authorized representative. At any time prior to the announcement
of the results of a vote, however, the actual stakeholder, if
present, may disavow a vote cast by a representative. More-
over, the proceedings of this meeting are being recorded and
made available in realtime upon the auxiliary corporate
UniComm netband. . . ."

I glanced sideways at Brin Drejcha. Although his face bore
a pleasant half-smile, I could sense that he was nervous.

". . . According to the petitions filed by the PST Trust and
the EDA Trust, both have requested a vote on the leadership
of UniComm," Nasaki continued. "As most of the stakeholders should know, the largest plurality interest in Uni-
Comm was held by the former director general, Henson
Gerrat Alwyn. With his untimely death, and that of Senior
Director Gerrat Myrs Alwyn, the shareholder with the remaining largest plurality has been Daryn Henson Alwyn.
Although he has not been directly associated with Uni-
Comm in the immediate past, he has intimate and working
knowledge of the field, and in the interests of maintaining
continuity, he has been the acting director general. This con-
stitutes a change in leadership, since Director Alwyn has not
been previously associated with the company. Therefore, if
any of the petitioners are present, I would like to ask if they
wish to pursue a vote on a further change in leadership."

A slender man rose. "We do, counsel."

"Would you please identify yourself?"

"Simion deBecque, solicitor for the PST Trust."

"What do we know about him?" I murmured across the
link to Majora, who was observing from the office I hoped
would be mine officially after the meeting. "Any ties to anyone specific?"

"He's with deBecque, A'Ahanar, and Simones. There's no
direct tie. They're a firm of public interest advocates, but all
of them are younger advocates, and they usually join one of

the three firms that service the multilaterals of the PST Trust pre-select conspirators. Very legitimate, very legal."

"Is there a question I can ask that will put him ill at ease?" I replied to Majora.

"Not without revealing more than I think you want at this stage."

So I waited.

"Are there any other stakeholders who wish to be heard on this matter?" asked Nasaki, scanning the small crowd.

"Yes, counsel. We object to continuing this proceeding." The speaker was an older, dark-skinned advocate. "Aloys Nyere, counsel of the Society of Dynae. The objective of leadership change has already been effectively handled by the unfortunate deaths of the director general and the senior director of UniComm."

Nyere was telling me and the world that they wanted me in charge of UniComm. A nice, if belated, confirmation of Mertyn's earlier call, and perhaps a reason for his murder, another of those that would never be noted as such.

"We offer a privileged motion to dismiss the petition for a change in leadership," Nyere finished.

That wasn't a bad idea, but privileged motions required a two-thirds absolute majority of outstanding shares, and I doubted I had such.

"A privileged motion has been offered. Is there a second?"

"Second," offered a woman I didn't know.

"Diera D'Ahoud," Majora supplied through the link.

I wondered if she were related to Ibaran, who had attended The College with me so many years before.

"The question is on the motion to dismiss the petition for a vote on the leadership of UniComm. A 'yes' vote is a vote to dismiss and to retain the current leadership. A 'no' vote is a vote to consider the motion for a change in leadership. You have five minutes to record your votes on your consoles." Nasaki took a step back from the podium. Since the motion was privileged, there was no debate. Although individual votes would be recorded, the specific votes cast did not have to be made public until after the meeting.

A Federal Union auditor stepped from the wings to stand by the tally console and beside Nasaki.

I cast my fifty-two point eight percent in favor of dismissal, and waited until the five minutes had passed and Nasaki stepped up to the podium once more.

"Fifty-eight percent of the outstanding shares are in favor of dismissal, forty percent against, and two percent abstain on the question. The motion to dismiss is rejected," Nasaki announced.

I could see the blank expressions on the faces of deBecque and those surrounding him, the blankness substituting for puzzlement. That meant they still thought the EDA Trust was on their side, and that was fine with me.

"The question is on the motion to change the leadership of UniComm," Nasaki continued. "This is a general motion, and debate is permitted. Under the rules of the Federal Union, those speaking in favor of the motion have a minimum of an hour to present their case. They may request an extension of additional time, provided they are supported by twenty percent of those present and voting. The same is true of those opposing the motion."

Simion deBecque was on his feet. "Counsel, we would like to open debate on the motion."

"You may have ten minutes to begin."

"I am certain we all share the same common goal," deBecque began. "We all wish UniComm to be as prosperous and profitable as possible. We all wish that UniComm retain its pre-eminent position among the true world netsystems, and for that we need a proven leader. In the past, that leadership has indeed been provided ably and well by the Alwyn family. We would all like to see that kind of leadership continued.

"Unhappily, that does not appear to be the case. The current acting director general has never held an executive post in any organization. While he has a certain renown as an edartist, his contributions in the field of net management are nonexistent.

"From what we can tell, the only reason for picking him was because he is the heir of the founding family, and because he prevailed upon the operating management. . . ."

I could sense the faint stiffening by Brin Drejcha and almost nodded. We'd been alone in that meeting, and that
meant that he'd either conveyed it directly, told someone
else, or that his office was snooped. I didn't like any of the
possibilities, but I thought the first was most likely. The fact
that deBecque mentioned it meant he hadn't counted the
votes very well.

". . . it might be noted that this meeting was called before
he was selected because of the decline in UniComm market
share, almost ten percent in the last decade, and a continued
decrease in earnings. The current acting director general is
not as qualified as either the former senior director nor the
former director general, and this meeting was called to replace them. . . ."

"Do you want any of our people to speak yet?" asked
Majora over the link.

"Let's see what else they have to offer."

Aloys Nyere stood. "We will be brief and to the point,
Counsel. The honored advocate, and I say honored rather
than honorable advisedly," said Nyere dryly, "has a pleasing
and soothing manner. He speaks well, confidently, and he
acts as though he would have your best interests in mind.
He does not. There are two issues at stake here. One is the
future of UniComm as an independent entity. The second is
the leadership of UniComm. His position is not in the interests of the stakeholders on either issue, although he would
have you believe otherwise.

"First, all stakeholders should be aware that advocate
deBecque represents the PST Trust, as he has noted, and that
the PST Trust is a front for a takeover effort to merge
UniComm with OneCys—under the operating management
of OneCys. For the past two years, OneCys has been attempting to make inroads into UniComm's market share.
They have hired the best consultants available. They have
more than doubled their research budget, and added twenty
percent to their production budget, and they have garnered
about one percent additional broad market share. Since they
failed to gather market share in direct competition, they are

now attempting a back door method to gain greater market-share.

"What we have noted, however, is that in certain areas they have been more successful than in others, and our inquiries determined that in those areas where greater success had been achieved, it was where OneCys followed the recommendations of a particular consultant. Not surprisingly, that consultant was Daryn Alwyn, the current acting director general of UniComm. Obviously, Director Alwyn poses a threat to both the PST takeover and to the operating management of OneCys, and they have joined forces to see if they can remove this threat. Their efforts highlight exactly why Director Alwyn should not be removed, but confirmed as permanent director general of UniComm. The advocate and his clients fear Director Alwyn's abilities. Otherwise, why would they be stampeding to remove someone who has established solid credentials in the field so quickly? Because they do not want Director Alwyn's abilities to become more widely known. If Director Alwyn is removed, the share price will tumble, and OneCys will attempt to pick up UniComm at a bargain price. That is clearly the agenda of the advocate. It is an agenda which should be opposed. All stakeholders with an interest in preserving the value of their investment should oppose any change in leadership." Nyere smiled politely and seated himself.

"The counsel for the Dynae is most persuasive," returned deBecque. "But he, too, has an agenda. The Dynae have always opposed efficiency in multilaterals. . . ."

After deBecque finished, a balding norm stood. "I would like to say that I'd rather see UniComm under OneCys, whatever it takes. . . ."

I wondered who'd bought him, or if he were just misguided.

Diera D'Ahoud stood. "I would like to ask the counsel for the PST Trust to explain why he believes such haste in removing Director Alwyn is necessary."

"You do not have to answer that," Nasaki said from the podium.

"I do not mind answering the inquiry of the gracious lady.

The answer is simple. We have seen a steady decline in the market share and value of UniComm holdings. We do not believe that UniComm can withstand yet another Alwyn."

Another figure—a tall pre-select stood from near the back row. "For what it may be worth, I'd like to support the advocate who wants change in management. There's been enough autocracy in UniComm."

Unfortunately, that was something I couldn't deny, but I didn't have to address it.

People began to pop up here and there.

". . . trying to ruin a perfectly good multilateral . . ."

". . . enough of family dynasties . . ."

". . . ten years of declining market share is enough . . ."

I just sat and smiled, and listened. It was obvious enough to me to see who had been coached by the PST team and who were those speaking their own thoughts. The coached ones were smooth, and each brought up a different point, and all came back and hammered on the declining market share.

As I sensed the debate was winding down, I went back on the link to Majora. "I'd like to meet with Nyere after the meeting, if someone could arrange it."

"I'll see what we can do."

"Thank you."

Nasaki stepped back up to the podium. "Are there any other points of discussion?" He paused and surveyed the audience. "Seeing none, the question is on the motion to remove the existing acting director general. A 'yes' vote is a vote to remove. A 'no' vote is a vote to confirm acting Director General Alwyn as director general until the next general meeting of stakeholders. You have five minutes to record your vote."

The Federal Union auditor joined Nasaki and took possession of the console as the votes began to register.

For a moment or so, I watched everyone. Diera D'Ahoud smiled at me, and I wondered how many shares she was voting.

Then I voted my bloc and waited until the voting was over.

Nasaki looked over the results, and his eyes widened. "The

results are as follows. In favor of the motion to remove present management, forty-four point three percent. Those opposed, fifty-five point seven percent. "The motion is defeated, and Director General Alwyn is confirmed."

"Congratulations, Director General," offered Drejcha quietly.

Nasaki surveyed the hall once more. "The business of the special meeting having been concluded, the meeting is adjourned."

I turned to Tomas Gallo. "Thank you, counsel." Then I addressed Brin. "Thank you, Brin. I have a meeting now, but we should get together later this afternoon."

"Yes, ser."

I couldn't help but overhear some of the comments from the seats below the stage.

". . . how did he do it?"

". . . EDA Trust sold out to him . . ."

I just smiled and nodded to those remaining before making my way back to the office that was mine—at least until the next general meeting in November.

Majora was waiting in the office with Aloys Nyere.

I inclined my head slightly to the dark-skinned counsel of the Society of Dynae. "I appreciate your comments, and your willingness to take the lead in the debate against the PST group."

Nyere studied me for a long time. "They say you were an interstellar pilot, and a good one. I can see why. You had the votes from the beginning, didn't you?"

"Yes, but I needed to see what was out there."

"Did you?"

"I saw enough."

"I'm certain you did. Will you tell me what you plan with UniComm?" His dark eyes twinkled.

"I could tell you that we're a hardworking team, and that we'll reclaim market share." I laughed. "We won't, not immediately, because I have to fix a few things, but I'd be very surprised if we didn't make a sharp turn-around by about a year from now."

The advocate for the Dynae raised his eyebrows.

"If you're asking about our approach to various matters, all I can say is that Mertyn Rosenn was my teacher, and I learned a great deal from him, and I intend to repay that debt."

"You knew?"

"I found out about two weeks ago. I might have discovered it earlier, but it happened while I was in the medcenter. A wall fell on me, instead falling off a cliff. I was luckier." Not wanting to spell it out, knowing that even within UniComm the walls had ears and not all the ears were friendly, I hoped he understood.

Nyere nodded. "I fear interesting times lie ahead for us all."

"They do, but I intend to do what I can."

He bowed. "I won't impose on you more, Director Alwyn, but I do appreciate your taking the time to speak with me. If I can do anything for you or for your assistant, please do not hesitate to let me know." His smile was genuine.

"We will be working on a project where perhaps your knowledge and expertise might be valuable." I returned the smile. "It may be a few days before we'll know."

"As I said, we would be happy to work on efforts of mutual benefit."

I understood the parameters. "I would not ask otherwise."

He bowed, and I bowed again, and then he departed, like a silent shadow.

"You have a friend," Majora said.

"Not exactly. He's a friend because Mertyn was my friend."

"They're not going to be happy," Majora said.

"Deng, TanUy, and the rest of the PST group? No . . . not at all. We'll need to get moving, first thing tomorrow." I needed word to get around UniComm.

Chapter 64

The words of poets distill truth, though their lines may be terse or florid, short or long, and those lines left in dusty tomes, few of which have ever been converted to electrons and bright screen images. For, after all, all they offer is the truth of the past, and the future differs from the past. It must, must it not?

And yet . . .

Is a great disorder an order? One poet claimed such, but few read his words a generation beyond his death.

Another claimed that old violence was not too aged to lead to a new order.

Yet another claimed that men are hollow, and proved he was more so than most, while fretting about the intolerable wrestling of words and meaning.

A soldier poet insisted that death made foreign fields a corner of home . . . forever Anglian . . . forever revered.

Then there were the lines of a ridiculed poet, for he was a militarist, who pointed out all too accurately that our end comes not from staves nor swords, but through the power of small corroding words.

Yet another claimed that time was indifferent to all physical achievements, but worships language. . . .

For all their truths, truths that continue to apply, observations that will outlast dusty tomes, forgotten on archive shelves, why are all the great poets forgotten, unread, unheard?

Because words alone offer truth, a truth betrayed by images flashed upon a million eyes a moment? Because truth takes more than an image and a moment?

I found myself pacing back and forth in front of the cherry wood desk, glancing through the open nanite-screened barrier to the indoor courtyard, brightly lit by a morning sun set in a cloudless sky.

Reacting . . . that was all I was doing . . . reacting to everyone else's moves. Reacting to the situation Elora had set up . . . and to what Eldyn had done . . . even to what my parents had done years before. And to Elysa's efforts at Kharl's party.

I smiled, not at the thought of Elysa, but because I'd finally reached Kharl, and learned he, at least, was on the way to a full recovery. I hoped I'd fare as well, but I needed to start acting and stop reacting. Even my handling of the stakeholders' meeting had been a reaction. Then, was everything?

What did I want? I laughed, softly. Even that was a reaction, because I would be acting based on what I'd been and seen, and the people I'd known and who had influenced me, from my parents to Mertyn, and now because of Majora and Eldyn.

Perhaps a better question might be to ask what I didn't want.

I didn't want a world ruled by a mob, nor one ruled by a handful of people who embodied my father's worst characteristics and none of his best. I half-wondered if Gerrat had been tacitly involved in one of the plots. From what I could see, he certainly fit the mold of those identified by Eldyn, but I supposed I'd never know. The fact that Elora hadn't trusted him wasn't exactly in his favor.

First off, I needed to make sure that what Elora had done

didn't get undone. So . . . there was the obligatory call to Anna Mayo.

She was in.

"Anna . . . I need you to revise some legal papers. . . ."

My solicitor looked slightly less harried, perhaps because the latest pre-select plague had died out relatively quickly, as it should have with such virulence. "What did you have in mind?"

"I want a trust and a trustee, set up in the event of my death. Half my estate—and that's half of everything—to the trustee, the rest split evenly among Gerrat's children and the children of Rhedya's brother Haywar, but voting control of all my stocks to remain with the trustee for the next forty years. If anything happens to the trustee, the secondary trustee will be the general counsel of the Society of Dynae."

"The Society of Dynae?" Her mouth opened.

"You've got it. I want some insurance for me and the trustee."

"I can do it. . . . Are you sure . . . ?"

"I'm very sure." I paused. "The primary trustee will be Majora Hyriss."

Anna nodded, as if that were one of the few points she found agreeable. "She would be a good choice. What took you so long?"

"I'm not sure she knows. That's another thing I need to unscramble, and that's also why the Society of Dynae."

"She's not . . ."

"No, but most people would rather have her than the Society, and probably me more than her." That's what I was hoping, anyway. "How long will it take? This is urgent."

"If it's urgent . . . how about four o'clock?"

"I'll be there."

"I'd better get on it." After a quick and professional smile, she was gone.

Then there were a few more items to take care of, from reviewing personnel in UniComm to checking out market-shares and the offnets I'd need to use before long.

Then I had to get back to outlining the "new" strategy for UniComm.

I didn't want to think about what else I was forgetting.

Even before Majora arrived in my office at three-thirty, I was ready to go.

Her eyebrows lifted as she saw the leather portfolio in my hand.

"I'll be back. Would you mind walking out to the glider with me?"

She smiled. "Since I'm your special assistant, on company time, I walk where you want."

I returned the smile, wishing I could find a way to say what I really wanted to say. "Let's go."

We walked out of the office and down the ramp, without saying a word. I'd been doing that too much, far too much.

Once we were at the end of the stone steps, I stopped and looked at Majora. "I have a favor to ask of you. Another one."

"Ask . . . and you shall receive. Isn't that the way the words go?" That half-impish smile crossed her face, the expression that seemed so at odds with her statuesque appearance.

I shook my head. "It's hard to ask . . . for me." I swallowed. "Bear with me . . . please. I was going to ask you to be the trustee of all that I have, but then I realized that was because I love you and trust you, and that I've never told you that. So . . ." I moistened my lips. "I have to ask another question first. Will you marry me?"

"Yes. I will." Her deep brown eyes met my eyes, and after a long moment I bent forward and kissed her. Then I put my arms around her.

Her arms were around me, almost as quickly.

After a very long embrace, we eased back, still holding each other.

"You're not the type to ask, either, are you?" I said quietly.

Her lips twisted into a lopsided smile. "Why do you say that?"

"It takes one to know one."

She laughed, and then our arms were around each other once more, if briefly.

"Does this mean I can't be your special assistant?"

"You'll always be. . . . No . . . you're more than any assistant, but still very special."

"Sweet words."

"For a very sweet lady with a cynical surface."

"Why now?"

I understood. "Because . . . well . . . you always look for the right moment, and the right words, and life sometimes doesn't provide either. Or, I guess, because I'm not good at creating special moments like that, and I realized that if I waited around, all I'd do would be lose you . . . again, and I wasn't about to gamble on getting a third chance."

"I'm glad you didn't wait."

Reluctantly, we walked, hand in hand, to my glider, its shimmering surface dusty in the afternoon sun of early summer.

"We'll talk about the time when I get back. I didn't tell you, but I need to see Anna about some legal things. I'm trying to set up matters so that people have a certain incentive to keep me around."

"I'd like that very much."

"So would I."

"Be careful. Please be very careful," Majora urged me as I slipped into the glider. She squeezed my hand before releasing it.

"I will be."

The way matters were going, especially after Majora's warning, I made sure all the glider systems checked, and I also made sure the restraint harness was snug and that the canopy was locked closed.

I hoped I didn't have to use the glider to take advantage of the special ways in which I'd rebuilt it, but I liked the thought that I could. Most people didn't realize that a glider was a simplified and limited orbital lifter, linked and heavily limited, for the simple reason that, as I'd discovered in pilot training, most people couldn't handle it. Even for me, it had taken work—as well as some very special microtronic boards and a full gyro system.

As I eased the glider out from between the last of the redwood trees and onto the main guideway, I realized that I'd never asked Majora about being trustee. Somehow I doubted that she'd object.

I'd scarcely gone a klick when a silver-gray glider appeared behind me, moving closer, far too close to be on automatic guideway control.

There was a crackling sound, and I could feel heat on my neck. Another laser?

I glanced back, but could see nothing, except the darkening of the rear of the canopy. I eased the inductors up. Momentarily, the distance between the two gliders widened, and the heat slacked off.

I kept accelerating, but almost immediately the automatic speed overrides cut in and the alert wailed. So did another alarm, the one that signaled I was losing solar cells.

Sometimes, safety precautions were a real danger.

I reached down to the hidden panel on the side of the seat and flipped off all the overrides, and accelerated again, noting I was gaining ground all too quickly on a blue glider up ahead.

Monoclones—even duoclones—didn't have the ability to guide gliders, except perhaps on automated guideways. Nor to carry FS-type lasers. So my pursuers were real people, and there were probably two—one to operate the glider and one to range and discharge the laser. Why a laser? Simple. Tuned to the right frequencies, the skytors would pick up nothing of interest, except the growing temperature of my glider—not until my glider piled into something or exploded in flame.

As the gray glider moved toward me again, and another line of energy focused on the rear of the glider, I checked the opposing guideway, then banked the glider into a reverse turn, one far sharper than a standard glider could manage, hoping that the maneuver would gain me some distance.

It did, but not too much.

I eased the glider farther above the guideway, not all that much but so that I had more ground clearance. Then I clicked the last stud, and forced the wheel, now a stick controller, almost into my lap, concentrating on maintaining heading absolutely.

Looping an orbital lifter is frowned on ... but there weren't any prohibitions against looping a glider, because as delivered they couldn't be looped. I didn't like the idea, but I liked being cooked less, and while I could have lifted my glider like a flitter, and taken off over rougher terrain, the result would have been the escape of those trying to kill me ... or embarrass me ... and a citation for use of an unlicensed flitter.

In less than seconds I was screaming down behind the gray glider.

I slewed my glider-flitter sideways, scrambling both the ground effect and the magfields of my pursuers, and using the magfields and the ground cushion to drive the gray glider sideways, right off the guideway and toward the bordering redwoods.

Then I applied full power and squirted out from under the branches. Something might have scraped, but I was clear.

Behind me, the out-of-control glider careened toward a heavy tree trunk, one that should have crumpled it thoroughly, although most of my attention was on the task of lifting my own glider away, turning to set back down on the opposite guideway, heading in the direction I'd originally chosen. Although I wasn't sure what might happen, I wasn't prepared for the violence of the explosion after the gray glider slammed into the redwood.

My glider was buffeted, but that was all.

I shook my head. Someone certainly didn't want any witnesses left. Again.

And I still needed to get to Kewood proper and Anna.

I kept studying the readouts and the guideway, but no one

appeared, not a CA glider or another pursuer. My breathing was still a bit ragged.

Once more, the pattern was all too clear. Put me in a position where there was no obvious danger, as seen by an outside observer and where I well might have to break some law to survive. While I was licensed to fly or drive anything, the glider wasn't, and in my current position, the news coverage would have been brutal—led by OneCys. And, of course, no one would ever have found the pair with the laser, and there would have been absolutely no evidence to support my story.

I forced myself to take a deep breath, and to look over my shoulder and at oncoming gliders more carefully.

There were no other incidents on the way.

As I eased the glider to a stop on the grass of the park opposite Anna's office, I remembered to reengage all the cutouts, and to arm full security. The glider seemed all right, but I hoped I had a chance to inspect it thoroughly before I tried any other stunts.

Anna's office was on the first floor, and she was waiting.

"For a man in a hurry, you're a little late, Daryn."

"I ran into some delays. There was an accident on the guideway." Both were true enough. "What do I have to sign, authenticate, whatever?"

"There are three sets: your property allocation, establishment of a primary trustee, and establishment of a secondary trustee." She pointed.

I went through the procedure of signing them and affixing a holo print before I turned to her. "These are legal now?"

"They're legal now, but they need to be recorded officially."

"By hand?"

Anna nodded. "That hasn't changed."

"Fine. I'll take you wherever that is, and I'll pay for the time."

She smiled. "I take back my statement about your not being in a hurry. I can't say I'm surprised."

"Well . . . it did occur to me that the family needed to be taken care of."

"Family?"

"Majora and I are going to get married, and, no, we haven't set a date yet."

"Impetuous, aren't you?"

Hardly impetuous, when I'd known her for more than ten years and hadn't seen what she really was until the last few weeks. "You could say that. I don't know as it would be accurate."

I gestured toward the door and the glider that rested in the glider park. "Shall we go?"

Chapter 67

> Can it be said that I saw the sun,
> setting before the day has yet begun?
> Can it be sung that I heard winter's cold,
> howling through green summer's fold. . . .

I'm not a poet, not even a versifier. My lines prove it. I wish that I could put down in verse what I feel . . . the anger and the frustration involved in trying to open others' eyes. I have spent most of my life in the insulated arrogance of privilege. I still do, but unlike the others who share that privilege, I'd like to think that I look beyond it. A brief touch of being outside, not even fully outside, has opened perhaps one eye to the subtleties of control. An earlier generation might have called it oppression. I could be rationalizing, but I don't see it as that kind of oppression. It's more of a transparent ceiling. Most people can do more than any generation previously, and in less fear and greater freedom.

The unseen ceiling bars most of those few norms who are brilliant from entering the upper reaches of the power structure, and even some pre-selects. Frydrik was right, and wrong. Most pre-selects barred from the power structure have no business there. If one cannot penetrate the ceiling with all the advantages of birth and wealth, then there's usually a good reason why.

The norms brilliant and fortunate enough to succeed ... I wonder how many end up like Eldyn, twisted into near insanity by the ravages of the struggle. Or quietly dead like Mertyn, because he raised too many embarrassing questions.

Yet ... for all the questions, I have no answers, not ones that are suitable for a society. Majora would make better choices about who should decide than would I, but no one will select or support a Majora. By accident of birth, by twists of fate, it may be that I can change our world, and I can hope that it will be for the better. But it will be far from perfect, and the resistance to change and the anger of those who dimly perceive that some of what they believe to be their birthright has been denied will ensure that change will not be easy.

Birthright—what a strange word. Do any of us have birthrights ... really? We are born with varying degrees of assorted abilities into families with varying degrees of power and possibilities. If our abilities are great, does that mean our birthright is to achieve great things or amass much wealth? If our abilities are meager, does that mean we are doomed to misery or to be looked down upon? Who decides? And upon what bases?

I am taking power in an attempt to make decisions, knowing that my decisions will be wrong for many, hoping that they will benefit more than they harm, but also knowing that what has seemed to be an inevitable progression toward a tyranny of the self-proclaimed elite is both right and wrong—and a path to destruction. The vast majority of the pre-selects are indeed more gifted and able, and never has there been such great prosperity and freedom of individual action and expression for all of the peoples of the world at all levels. Yet not since the years immediately preceding the Collapse has there been such anger and resentment.

People want to control their own destiny. We never

control that destiny by ourselves, but we must retain the illusion that we have such control, and over time an elite perceived to govern by pure ability shatters that illusion. . . .

Personal Notes

Chapter 68
Yunvil

Although the sky was clouding over heavily, the trip to Yunvil was uneventful. So was the conversation, and so was the procedure of recording the documents in the regional advocate general's office.

We walked out of the recording and transfer office, back toward the underground, multilevel covered permacrete structure for parking magscooters and gliders.

"Are you happier now?" asked Anna.

"Somewhat." I wasn't totally happy with the heavy clouds and the light rain that had begun and threatened to get far heavier. "I'll be happier in a few months." Happier or dead.

"Looking forward to getting married? I never would have bet on that."

"Neither would I, but times can change a man."

I frowned as we started down the ramp to the second level, for I heard voices. Although they were loud, they didn't sound angry.

"People are mad. . . ."

". . . be mad, too . . . friggin' pre-selects . . . think they run everything . . . getting theirs now."

"Bastard . . . bitch . . . right there . . ."

Two pre-selects jumped from behind an abutment, and they hadn't been pre-selected for brains. A third lagged slightly behind.

I saw the glitter of a blade—and blades were the obvious

choice in a covered area—and I swore at myself for not wearing a nanite-screen, uncomfortable and hot and cumbersome as they were. Rather, I began the thought, but my nanite-boosted defense system—and all the routines I'd learned in FS training—kicked in, and I scarcely remembered much of anything that followed.

Several moments later, I was standing in the open space between gliders, panting, with a shallow slash across one arm and a damp feeling on the left side of my skull that I suspected was blood from the stinging of a cut or slash above my ear.

Three bodies lay sprawled on the permacrete.

"Lord . . ." Anna glanced from me to the bodies, and then back to me. "I . . . never saw anything like that."

I kept scanning the area, but couldn't sense anyone else. Another attempt by my dear friends—set up where the skytors couldn't see.

"They're dead. There were three of them."

"They were out to kill us both." My first reaction was to leave the bodies. My second was to avoid committing another crime and to capitalize on it as I could. The problem was unfortunately simple. If I left I was committing a crime; if I remained I'd be charged with murder or something, initially, even if it were later dismissed. As a fictional heroine I'd read somewhere had said, I was faced with two doors, and both of them were labelled "damned."

I glanced toward my stunned solicitor. "If the CAs look into this . . . what's the probability that I'll get off?"

"The garage is monitored, and you waive privacy and let them run truth nanites through you, and you'll be out of the building in a couple of hours." She paused. "I don't know how you feel about waiving privacy."

"Let's do it. But . . . I want you to make sure they ask some questions . . . about why this might be happening . . . and who might be behind it. . . ."

"I can try." She sounded dubious.

I had been looking around, searching for an alarm, and finally located one, on the wall, past a battered glider that was so old that half the solar cells were the dull black that meant they were fused into uselessness. I walked over and pulled the alarm lever.

We didn't have to wait long.

A building guard and a CA appeared within two minutes. They both looked at me, and at the bodies and the filament knives on the permacrete, and then back at me. The way they did almost made me feel guilty for defending Anna and myself.

The CA went into a link even before he addressed me. "Ser . . . what happened?"

"I'm Daryn Alwyn. This is Anna Mayo. She is my solicitor. We were here to register some documents with the regional advocate general. . . ." I described what had happened as factually as I could.

Before I had finished, another CA and a much larger glider had arrived. The second CA was harder looking and more senior, and he gave the bodies, and me, the same kind of look. I wasn't sure why, since all three men were at least my size—or maybe that was the problem, but they should have known what a pre-select with FS training and a nanite-boosted system could do. I wasn't about to explain.

". . . and then I found the alarm and pulled it and waited."

"Ser, do you have a legal representative?" asked the senior CA.

I nodded to Anna. "She's my representative."

He turned to Anna. "You understand, counsel, even in self-defense, with three men dead, your client will have to be held until . . ."

I cleared my throat. Loudly.

Anna and the CA looked at me.

"I'll waive privacy. I'd just as soon get this over."

The two looked at each other. "Are you sure, ser?"

"Absolutely. This lady is my solicitor, and she has advised me of my rights."

Things moved quickly after that, and in less than a half hour I was in the local CA station, my cuts spray-sealed, the blood wiped away, with a senior CA reading a statement at me.

"You understand that under the laws of the Federal Union,

until authorized by judicial authority, you cannot be required to submit to a nanite-based verification of the accuracy of your statements, and that you are under no compulsion and no obligation to testify about the events which occurred?"

"I do."

"And you still wish to waive privacy?"

"I do."

With that, they moved Anna to the side of the room, and a forensic medical tech arrived with his mask, and I inhaled all sorts of sprays, and then we waited until he looked at his screen and nodded.

Then I got baseline tests, from colors and deliberate lies, and everything else.

It was a good half hour later before I got to repeat my story.

No one said anything, not even the medtech, while I talked. Then, the CAs began to question me.

"Could you have avoided killing the attackers?"

"I don't see how. There were three of them, and they had us cornered. I was worried about Anna."

"Why did you kill the attackers?"

"I didn't have any choice, if I wanted to live."

"Could you explain that, ser?"

"I have FS survival training, and I have an implanted augnite defense reaction system. My only choice is whether the situation is dangerous enough to trigger that. I am not someone who uses those systems daily or weekly. The system reacts according to my degree of fear and concern. I was scared blue."

"Why were you scared, ser?"

"All three men were clearly pre-selected for physical attributes. They were larger and more muscular than I, and younger, and all were carrying weapons."

"But you knew you had a nanite system."

"They didn't give me a chance to explain that, and if we tried to run, Anna might have been killed, and I wouldn't have had a real chance to defend myself."

"Are you certain of that?"

"I'm not absolutely certain. I couldn't be in that situation, but I had to decide quickly. They had weapons. We didn't."

The CA must have asked forty minutes of questions about the location, about the attackers, about anything that might have indicated that I had other options. I still didn't see any, and I was trying not to get angry, but that was very hard. Whoever had set up the attack had clearly, I realized in hindsight, expected me to kill the three. It would come out that I was a madman, or at least a dangerous man, and if I'd been foolish enough to leave the site, would have put me under legal attack as a possible felon. Either way I was damned, because no one would believe I'd been set up.

"You seem to be angry, ser. Why are you angry?"

"I was attacked by men I don't know, and I feel like I'm being considered the criminal. I still don't see that I had any choice but to defend myself."

Anna said something, and one of the CAs turned and glared at her.

The other asked, "Have there been other attempts on your life?"

"Yes."

Both CA's eyes widened when the tech nodded that I was telling the truth.

"Would you please describe them?"

"Earlier this afternoon, on my way to Lady Mayo's to authorize the papers we filed this afternoon, two men in a glider van attempted to force me off the guideway. They had a high-powered laser, FS issue." I had to be very careful in phrasing the next sentence. "When they discovered that they couldn't disable my glider with the laser, they tried to get close enough to ram me—or so that the laser would be effective—I'm not sure which—I tried to avoid them. I turned at high speed onto the opposite guideway. They followed me, and when I tried to accelerate they lost control, and their van exploded. I think if you or the Yunvil CAs investigate the accident, you would find traces of explosives in the residue."

"Why weren't they successful in forcing you off the road?"

"I was a pilot, once, and I used that training to take evasive action. Also, my glider has heavier shields and inductors than most passenger gliders." All of that was absolutely true. "There was an earlier attempt that is on the records. Several months ago, someone used a laseflash on me when I was leaving my house. And . . ." I went on to explain that.

"Ser? Is there something else?"

"About two weeks ago, there was a man who looked like a monoclone following me after I visited a stonesmith in Helnya. I was walking to the induction tube station, and he jumped at me. I pushed him away, and ran, and there was an explosion." I shrugged. "I probably should have reported it, but it was under the oaks where the skytors could not have seen anything except the energy, and since the CAs hadn't been able to uncover anything about the laseflash effort, and since there was no evidence there, I didn't. The CAs did contact me, and I did report seeing the man. I didn't report the explosion." That could get me in trouble, but not so much as lying where I was standing—or sitting.

The CA glanced at the medtech, who made a gesture I couldn't see.

"I don't believe that is the entire story, ser. Could you tell us more?"

I hoped not to, but that had always been a risk. "You'll find on the record in the Helnya CA records that I was injured in what was classified as an accident in Helnya. I did not believe it was an accident, but a clever trap set for me. The evidence only proved that the cemetery wall had deteriorated, and that there was ground erosion. I thought I heard and saw a child about to fall, and I ran to help her and the wall fell on me. I realized that the child was a one-dimensional holo projection when my hand went through the image. By then, it was too late." I looked at the two CAs.

They were looking at the screens.

"He's telling the truth. . . ." the medtech murmured.

"While I was in the medcenter, another CA questioned me about the cemetery wall. The skytors showed nothing except the wall falling on me. Then, when I got out of the medcenter, I found a number of snoops in my comm systems. With all that, I didn't see the point in reporting yet another incident where there was absolutely no evidence. There was always the possibility that someone was trying to set things up so that, if I did report the incidents, after a time, it would appear that I was somehow deluded or unbalanced. Either that, or they'd eventually succeed, and I'd be reported dead in some unfortunate accident."

"Do you have any idea why this is happening?"

"Yes." I had hoped to get them to ask for it, and now they had.

"Would you like to explain?"

"I have very mixed feelings about that, officers. Let me explain. As the only surviving Alwyn in two generations, except for my mother, I hold the controlling interests in UniComm. My sister held the largest interest. She was killed in the only induction tube explosion in a generation. There have been a number of attempts on my life, the last two following the death of my brother and father in the latest pre-select plague. I have no proof of anything, but I have no reason to think that anyone has a purely personal motive. I have no spouse. I have no children. So far as I know, I have no one who would wish me enough harm to kill me for personal reasons. That only leaves as a reason my interests in UniComm."

"Green clear, ser," murmured the shorter CA. They clearly weren't used to pre-selects who were augmented waiving privacy, or they would have known about augmented hearing.

The questions about motivation only lasted five minutes, and then they went back over the incident, detail by detail. I was tired and sweating by the time they told me I could go.

". . . the evidence indicates that you behaved strictly in self-defense, ser. The advocate general will review those findings, and you could be called back for additional questions, but the record seems clear enough for us to release you on personal bond. If the advocate general agrees with our findings, you will receive a formal notification that you have been cleared of all charges in this incident. . . ."

I inclined my head. "Thank you, officers."

"Thank you, ser. Wish more people would deal as directly

as you have." The CA paused. "We did have a little trouble with the skytors download, ser. We managed to verify that the accident was pretty much the way you described it, but there was one part that didn't transfer right, just before your attackers crashed. Doesn't happen often, ser, but sometimes the data gets scrambled. I'm sure no one will need that little part, ser."

I inclined my head in thanks. "I wouldn't think so, officer, but I certainly respect your judgment, and thank you."

"Not a problem, ser. We appreciate honesty."

With that, we got an escorted ride back to my glider, accompanied by a pair of CAs.

"What was that about?" Anna asked after I closed and locked the canopy.

"My evasive driving was a . . . little unconventional. They were thanking me for waiving privacy, I think."

She nodded somberly. "They didn't tell you one other thing."

"What?"

"Someone had disabled the viewers in that section of the garage, with enough care that it was planned."

That scarcely surprised me, not so much as a norm covering my illegal loop.

"Daryn . . ." began Anna as I guided the glider through the darkness back toward her office. It was almost midnight.

"Yes?"

"Can you tell me what this is all about?"

"I can tell you what I know, but you already heard that." My smile felt lopsided, perhaps the result of a post-reaction to the truth-nanites. "What I'm guessing is that there is a political move to take over UniComm as the first step in somehow changing the Federal Union system."

There was a silence. "That makes sense." She nodded. "What are you going to do?"

"Fight it."

"Why?"

I grinned, again feeling the expression off-center. "I didn't like the world my father liked, but he was fair. I have the feeling I'd like the world these people want to create even less."

"What do you want from me?"

"A good securities and multilaw specialist I can trust. Plus, I'll probably send Majora to you for a property allocation bequest as well."

"You're not going to fight their way, are you?"

I laughed. "How could I? I don't know anything about fighting that way. I'll have to fight my way." If I could make it work.

I dropped her off at her office.

If what I were doing were scripted into a VR, then I'd be chasing all over the globe, quietly or noisily assassinating or killing one and then another of the evil pre-selects . . . or commandeering a spaceship and traveling to 31 Pavo and Gamma Recluci to blow up alien Gates . . . or something along those lines. Oh . . . and I'd have had it all solved before the first board meeting, and persuaded Majora to have married me by then.

The only problem was that those kinds of actions wouldn't stop or solve anything, however much they might please those who loved bodies and blood . . . and nothing moved quite that fast in the real world.

Then, of course, there was the problem that I didn't know how to stalk people, and the CAs and skytors were probably watching everything I did. I didn't have access to clones, or to thugs who'd been carefully removed from the world database. Nor did I even know those who were after me with enough certainty even to use illegal tactics, and conventional legal remedies were impossible to employ.

I did have some brains, some talent, some friends, and, if I could keep it, the largest comm net in the world.

And Majora.

On the way back from Kewood, I connected myself to the AllNews desk at UniComm and offered a statement. It wasn't perfect, but this was a time when a good statement in a timely fashion was far better than a perfect statement when everyone had forgotten what had happened.

Then I called Mother.

". . . Daryn . . . it's late. Why don't you have an image?"

"I'm in the glider. I just called to tell you that I'm all right. Some thugs came after me this afternoon, and there are going to be news stories, I'm sure."

"You might consider an armored glider and a chauffeur for a time, dear."

"I've thought about it, although my glider is almost that. It was after I left the glider. . . ."

When I'd briefed her, I called Majora.

"Where are you? I saw the stories. Are you all right?"

"On the way back from Kewood. I'm all right."

"I'll be waiting."

And she was, right at the front door. Her full-body hug felt good—warm and reassuring . . . and loving. We hung on to each other for a time before we disengaged and closed the door.

"I saved everything that ran on the news," Majora said as we moved toward her great room. "Your mother also called."

I frowned. "I called her."

"She was calling to reassure me, in case you hadn't."

I laughed. "She likes you." Then I frowned. "But I hadn't had a chance to tell her, about our getting married, or about my staying here."

"She knew you'd called from here before. She's very sharp."

That, I already knew.

"I have tea ready, and a plate for you. I'll run the news clips while you eat."

So I sat and ate a very good goulash with noodles that were perfectly al dente, sipping tea and watching and listening.

The first image was that of a CA office, although not the Kewood one, and then a shot of me presiding over the stakeholders' meeting as the narrative voiced over the image.

> . . . Civil Authorities took the director general of UniComm into custody today in connection with the deaths of three unidentified men. . . . Alwyn, a former FS officer with extensive military training, apparently killed all three men. The Civil Authorities have made no comment, but released Alwyn after perfunctory questioning. Alwyn recently inherited the controlling interests in UniComm, the world's largest communications network after the mysterious bombing death of his sister and the sudden illness-related deaths of his father and brother.

That was the OneCys InstaNews version.

"I'm definitely scum." I laughed, although it was hard. "What did AllNews run?"

"It's better," she said, flicking a control.

This image showed stock footage of the black marble archway into UniComm, and also followed it with footage of me at the stakeholders' meeting.

> . . . Late this afternoon in Kewood, Noram, three men attacked the director general of UniComm. Daryn Alwyn, accompanied by his solicitor, had just left the recording office after registering a property allocation agreement. All three men were killed in the attack, and Alwyn immediately summoned the Civil Authorities. Because Alwyn waived privacy, both the events of the afternoon and the contents of the document were available to Civil Authorities, who immediately released the

director as innocent of any wrong-doing. The legal document Alwyn had filed establishes a trust in the event of his death, the majority to go to members of his family. According to his solicitor, Alwyn felt haste was necessary in setting up the trust because all family members who might survive him are underage and because he was concerned by the number of attempts on his life already.

. . . According to the Civil Authorities, this is the third confirmed attempt on Alwyn's life, and in all cases, the attackers were either never discovered or have no records in the world database. . . . Unconfirmed reports suggest that Alwyn's resolve to oppose perceptual testing may be a factor in motivating his attackers.

Alwyn had this to say. "It is a sorry time when influential pre-selects have to hide behind anonymous hired thugs, and because they don't like what a net organization has to offer. I believe in accuracy and efficiency in operating network systems, and above all honesty in reporting events. So did my brother and my father. So did my sister and her superior. They're all dead. That's the most frightening aspect of it all. Who is it that doesn't want that honesty to continue? And why don't they? UniComm and I intend to get to the bottom of this."

Daryn Alwyn, the director general of UniComm, commenting on the latest attempt on his life.

"Where do the other systems come down?" I asked.

"NEN is halfway between InstaNews and AllNews. Someone there is running scared. Most of the smaller systems are applauding you, and saying things like UniComm is big and they've always used their muscle, but they've never been deceptive, if there has to be a major netsys, then better UniComm than those who would tear it down to replace it with something just as big and far less ethical."

"Oh . . . I think we're definitely going to need to double

the around-the-clock security here." I took a last sip of the Grey tea.

"Ah . . . as your special assistant . . . I already took the liberty. I hope you don't mind."

I laughed.

Majora raised her eyebrows.

"We make a good team."

"We do." She smiled at me, then stood and refilled my cup. After that, she massaged my shoulders.

I closed my eyes and leaned back.

Chapter 70
Kewood

The most interesting thing about the attack was that by the morning two days afterwards, there was nothing in the nets about it, even from InstaNews, and I thought I knew why. OneCys or the PST group had taken a shot, and both my response and the evidence put them in a bad light. Since UniComm had more market share, if they continued to emphasize it, so could UniComm. If they stopped, and Uni-Comm continued, then it would look as though we had trumped up the issue. And I was again particularly grateful to the CA whose name I didn't know for erasing a ten-second record.

Even so, it didn't mean I was anywhere near out of the redwoods.

That was emphasized by a call arriving at almost precisely ten o'clock on fourday morning. The image was that of a perfectly groomed black-haired pre-select, wearing a gray singlesuit with a maroon-trimmed, black short jacket. I began to record as soon as the image appeared.

"Director Alwyn, this is Darius Fynbek. As you may know, I am the regional advocate general. My staff has brought to my attention a statement you made . . . several days ago." He smiled warmly, the same sort of smile that Gerrat had used—the one that I detested.

"You mean, the one I made after three thugs tried to kill me and my solicitor?" My tone was pleasant, not quite humorous. "I think that's the only public statement I've made recently."

"Director Alwyn, much as I understand your frustration, according to the Civil Authorities, there is no physical evidence, nor any financial evidence, to link the attempts on your life to any person or organization. Or to any class of individuals."

"Such as pre-selects?"

"Precisely. I am so glad you understand the situation. I would hate to suggest that a restraining order might be necessary."

"What about my suggesting that an investigation by your office might be in order? Just a suggestion, you understand?"

"As I said, I can certainly appreciate your concerns, Director Alwyn. The Office of the Advocate General cannot dig into the private affairs of individuals willy-nilly, just because another citizen believes they have an interest in something. We cannot question people merely because they *might* have a motive for such an action. In the interest of the civil rights of all people, we must have hard evidence."

"You do," I pointed out. "You have hard evidence of an exploded glider, disabled scanners, thugs who have no record of existence on the Federal Union's database. You also have DNA evidence of an exploded monoclone in Helnya, which is a class-one Federal Union offense, and a documented case of a Federal Service laser being used to attack me. None of those are subject to doubt. They constitute very hard evidence."

"Ah . . . that they do. As you point out, very hard evidence. But there is one substantial difficulty with that evidence."

I waited.

"There is absolutely no evidentiary link between that evidence and any individual or multilateral. It is most regrettable, but we cannot question people, not under the law, if there is nothing to point in their direction. That, as you may recall, is one of the key principles underlying our justiciary system, for very good reasons, given the abuses of the Chaos Years and numerous pre-Collapse legal systems."

"I understand, and I do appreciate your making matters clear to me. I can assure you that I will work to make certain that UniComm will netcast nothing in this matter which is not absolutely factually accurate, and I will make sure that all UniComm managers know this."

"I thought that an informal approach might yield a less ... confrontational result, and I thank you for your understanding."

"I appreciate your guidance, Advocate. I do indeed."

We were both smiling when he broke the connection, and my smile was doubtless as false as his.

My next step was to summon the UniComm general counsel.

While I waited for him to arrive, I linked with Majora. "How's my very special assistant?"

"Hard at work on researching those delightful souls fingered by our departed acquaintance."

"How's it going?"

"About the way we thought. Lots of hints, not much else."

"I just got a warning from the regional advocate general. He didn't like my words of the other night. Apparently, my suggestion that UniComm and I are targets of nasty preselects violates some law or another. Tomas will tell me which one. So we need lots of facts that are absolutely accurate, but the kind that will let people draw the right conclusion."

"You have a devious mind. . . ." I got the sense of that impish smile.

"That's the beginning." Just the beginning. "What about the CA medtech and the privacy waiver thing?"

"They've never heard of it being done. I gave them Nasaki's legal opinion, and they're studying it. I think the local advocate general will agree if she can find a reason to; she'd love to set a precedent, any precedent, that hints that waiving privacy is not an absolute right. Are you sure you want to do this?"

"If I hadn't been through it before, I wouldn't be, but I have to have everyone who will be on the project convinced that I'm absolutely honest about this, and I think all of them are norms. I'm on their side, but they have to believe that it's all up front."

"What if it leaks out?"

I laughed. "Do you think that InstaNews would dare to netcast that the director general of UniComm allowed his news staff to question him under truth nanites? And if they did, how would they react to my charge that they offer the same opportunity to their staff?"

Majora laughed softly. "For someone so direct, you do come up with devious slants."

I looked up to see Tomas Gallo standing in my open door. "Talk to you later. Tomas is here."

"Take care, dear man."

"You, too."

At my gesture, Gallo entered the office, and closed the door.

"You sounded like you needed something fairly quickly. Not that speed is unusual in UniComm." He smiled, ironically, but his expression was far more honest than that of Advocate Fynbek.

"I do. Here's the recording of a communication I just received." After Gallo sat in one of the green leather armchairs, I called up the record and projected it just before the bookcases, where we both could watch Fynbek.

I liked Fynbek even less the second time through, but I just nodded to Tomas after the images faded.

"He's going by the law, Director. He could be more accommodating, but he certainly doesn't have to be. No media outlet, nor any employee or owner, can make or suggest a judgment that would preempt a finding by a regulatory or judicial organ. A private citizen can, but you don't qualify as one. Nor does any member of your family."

"All right." I nodded. "Take this and try to get something

from his superior . . . the secretary advocate general of the Federal Union."

"He'll say the same thing. If he says anything at all."

"Record it. Or get it in writing. Get some documentation. Even if it says nothing. Particularly if it says nothing."

"What good will that do?" Gallo's expression was somewhere between interest and disapproval.

"It'll save us when the time comes. Especially if you can get them to expound on the part about not acting to investigate even when a motive is obvious."

He stood. "I'll see what I can do."

"That's all I ask."

After he left, I just sat there for a time. My choices were limited, and getting more so every day. What else could I do? Then I nodded and placed another call.

I was lucky. Rynold Tondrol was in. He was the director general of TD Reclamation, and he had been at Kharl's party where everything had begun.

"Rynold, this is Daryn Alwyn. . . ." Which was a stupid thing to say because his gatekeeper and system knew who it was already.

"Daryn . . . I was so sorry to hear about your family." His round face was somber.

"Thank you, Rynold. I appreciate it." I did, since he was the first pre-select who'd even mentioned them. "Did you hear that Kharl's going to be fine?"

"I did. I was glad that Grete and the children will be fine, too." He smiled for a moment. "What can I do for you? I assume this isn't just a catch-up call."

"Unfortunately not. Your business depends pretty heavily on monoclones, I understand. Or its profitability does, I suspect."

"It does play a part, Daryn. Everyone knows that." He shrugged. "I wish we could do without them, but the Collapse cultures left such a mess. . . ."

I nodded before continuing. "You know that popular opinion is, shall we say, ambivalent about monoclones. And that benign ambivalence is supported by lack of publicity on their uses?"

"That's also a given." He paused. "You must have a point, Daryn, but it's too subtle for me."

"Lately . . . someone has been using monoclones as walk-ing bombs, targeted at various individuals. It's taken me a little while to come up with documentation, but it appears as though they all come from BGP, and if I'm not mistaken, that's the outfit that supplies you."

Tondrol looked honestly appalled, and although I was watching through a scanned screen, I had the feeling he wasn't acting, or not much.

"It wouldn't take much of an outcry to require far greater restrictions—or perhaps a ban. . . ." I said gently.

"You're not suggesting that UniComm . . ."

"Right now, I'm not planning anything. I don't like things being banned, because then they go underground and no one has any control. I am suggesting that if this misuse of mono-clones continues, life will get a lot harder for both BGP and you, and probably more than a few others. This will lead to more restrictions and more rules and won't solve any prob-lems. Or it won't, and more people will get the idea that the only solution to their problems is to ignore the system and take the law into their own hands. Either way, it's not good."

"And you'd like me to contact Emyl at BGP and see what we can do?" Tondrol's eyebrows lifted.

"Well . . . if something isn't done quickly, I'm not sure you'll have any real options," I pointed out.

The round-faced Tondrol fingered his chin. "I won't prom-ise anything, except that I'll look into it."

"You remember the induction tube explosion in Mancha several weeks ago?"

"Oh . . . that was the one . . . your sister . . . I'm so sorry."

"That was the first public use of explosive monoclones. If BGP doesn't put a stop to it . . . well . . . can you imagine how the secretary director might feel if someone pointed out that a monoclone could be used against anyone, including him, and that body-shields don't provide adequate protec-tion?" I paused. "Or how it might come out that BGP was creating people, not to do dirty jobs, but to blow up other people?"

"Daryn, you do have a way of making a point. I will look into it, and, if matters appear as you say, then I'll talk to Emyl."

"I appreciate it, Rynold. But you'll benefit as much as anyone, if not more."

"I'm afraid you're right." He offered a twisted smile, that faded. "And I am sorry about your family."

"Thank you."

Again, I just looked at the cherry bookcase for a few moments.

Tondrol understood my point, but he was vulnerable. I had my doubts as to whether Deng, Escher, Dymke, St. Cyril, and TanUy had any interest in self-restraint . . . or the public interest.

I was fighting people who had skill and resources and patience and experience. If I tried to retaliate in kind, I'd either be dead or incarcerated, and then released as a brain-damped imbecile.

Sitting behind the cherry wood desk from which my father had enjoyed exercising power so much, I couldn't help but wonder if the average norms felt the way I did at the moment—except I had the feeling that some had felt that way all their lives.

Chapter 71
Kewood

I moistened my lips and stepped into the large UniComm conference room—the one on the lower level just below the office that had been Gerrat's. I looked at the nearly two dozen or so skeptical faces, and then at the three CAs standing just inside the door.

The CA truth team in their off-white and gray uniforms looked very disconcerted and nervous. I probably did as well.

I looked at the presenters and researchers, then toward

Feron Nasaki. I offered a smile. "I'm sure all of you are wondering what on earth you're doing with a CA truth team here, and what awful deeds the new director general suspects you of." I shook my head. "It's nothing like that. You're not suspected of anything. All I'll be asking of you today is to use your brains and your skepticism. As some of you know, there have been several attempts on my life, and my older sister was killed in a mysterious tube train explosion. These have been verified with hard evidence by the CAs."

Several people exchanged glances, ranging from "so what?" to straight confusion.

"I have evidence and a number of leads on what may be the biggest news story of the century. I'm going to assign you to look into this story and to develop stories that flesh it out." I looked around the room once more. "I don't want anyone believing that this is a cynical, management-serving ploy. The issue is too important." I nodded to Feron.

He began to pass out the handouts Majora and I had prepared.

"As you will see, much of the information here rests at least in part on my credibility. Because I'm asking you to undertake a unique project, I believe you have the right to ask any questions of me about this, and to be assured of my knowledge and motivations." I nodded to the truth team. "I am the one who will be subject to truth verification, and you will do the questioning. The reason why the CAs are doing this is that it is known that they are unbiased. We had to get a legal opinion and an approval from the local advocate general." I walked toward the chair at the end of the long table and seated myself, nodding to the medtech.

"You realize you don't have to do this, ser?" asked the taller CA behind the tech.

I did, even if not legally. "I understand."

"Oh," I added. "I am making one stipulation, and I will fire anyone who doesn't honor it."

The faces turned hostile.

"Everything I say here is what I believe, and based on my personal experience. You may not present or broadcast anything that you cannot back up with outside research. That is all." I smiled, lopsidedly. "I'm sure you'll have no trouble with that. Even though I believe that our entire society is under a threat . . . UniComm cannot present that unless we can prove each element factually."

There were a few murmurs, and some of the faces relaxed . . . slightly.

"I'm also making general request of all of you," I said, emphasizing the word "request." "I'd hope that your questions will bear on the UniComm situation in one way or another, and that your questions be devoted to bringing out the truth. That's all."

". . . that one fair enough . . ."

". . . what's the hook?"

I waited for the inhaler mask, then took a deep breath, as the tech studied the portable screen. After several minutes, the tech nodded. First came the baseline questions from the CAs. Finally, one turned to Feron and nodded.

"You may begin to offer your questions," Feron announced, pointing to a gray-haired norm halfway down the table.

"Director Alwyn, why are you doing this, effectively waiving privacy in a public forum?"

I had to think, not about the answer, but about making sure I was being totally honest, because I couldn't afford to convey any doubts. "First, the truth is my best defense against a group of pre-selects who wish to remove me, take over UniComm, and use its power to change the Federal Union. They have already murdered my sister, and I believe that their efforts led to the plague that killed my brother and father. Any other way than what I propose might involve some form of illegality, and I don't wish to stoop to the tactics of my enemies. That's because I've tried to spend my life not being like that or that kind of person, and also, practically speaking, because they're far better at it. Second, if I made a statement like that without your understanding that I am telling the truth as I see it, I doubt that any of you would believe it. Third, I am betting that after hearing me you will at least be motivated to look into the issues we cover here. Fourth, I want you to understand the situation and the stakes, and I hope that I can convince you how important your role is in analyzing and reporting it."

The questioner glanced at the CA tech.

"He's totally in the green," the CA murmured.

"Are you under any form of drugs that would block the monitoring?" asked a balding and stout norm.

"No . . . and I hope there aren't any anywhere. I certainly don't know of any." The question was stupid, yet dangerous, because if there were then the whole thing was a farce, and I was in huge trouble, but I didn't know of anything.

"His physiological reactions are normal," the taller CA replied. "The Union hasn't ever found a blocking drug that works without abnormal physiological reactions."

I almost could have hugged the taller CA for that.

"You claim that this shadow group is attempting to change the Federal Union, and that they are trying to take over UniComm, and that their efforts have killed off most of your family. Do you really expect anyone to believe that?"

"Not unless I did something this drastic. I've felt almost helpless for months. You may recall that someone attempted to kill me with a laser several months ago. I took the incident to the CAs. They found the laser unit—and that's all they found. Someone else arranged for a wall to fall on me. Believe me, I don't go around pulling heavy stone walls down on myself, but the CAs couldn't find any evidence." I paused as a faint whisper of laughter went around the room. "They still have no idea who blew up the tube train that killed my sister. After three months, there have been four attempts on my life, my sister is dead, and so are both my father and my brother. The norm scientist who claimed he was responsible for the plague is dead, and so is his wife. I may not have hard proof of everything, but no one in this room can deny the physical evidence and the dead bodies."

There was a moment of silence.

"How could anyone really change the Federal Union, Director?"

"It's simple, very indirect, and very effective. You all know about perceptual testing. There's been a controversy about it for some time. Unlike other forms of testing, it requires a very controlled situation and elaborate preparations. Also, unlike other forms of testing, pre-selects have an even greater advantage. And, most important, the literature indicates that improper background situations can actually be used to modify the test subjects' attitudes. Even without modification, the test can outline the subjects' predilections and point out ways to manipulate their attitudes. Now ... can you imagine what would happen if all students were perceptually tested and if all the major nets with over seventy percent of population exposure hours were in the control of the pre-selects who already controlled and monitored the attitude of—"

"Wait a minute. . . . Why hasn't anyone mentioned this?"

"They have. I was taught about it in college. It's in the literature. Oh . . . and by the way, you might want to check the connections between a certain Darwyn TanUy and his grandfather . . . or great-grandfather. The younger TanUy has been most active in this movement to take over the media outlets and push for perceptual testing. The elder TanUy was one of those who established the current form of the test."

By now, fingers were inputting notes, and the whispers had died away.

"Did the stakeholders' meeting have anything to do with this alleged conspiracy?"

"I believe it did."

"How?"

"I don't know all of those involved in the effort. Most of the ones I've identified have been associated with the so-called PST group . . . or the PST Trust. The PST Trust organized many of the stakeholders to call the meeting, and the purpose was to replace the leadership of UniComm in order to facilitate a takeover, probably by OneCys."

"So . . . you're using us to stop a takeover?"

"No. I control more than half the stock absolutely. I'm trying to persuade you to look at how control of close to seventy percent of the media market catering to norms could be misused to allow changes in the Federal Union that would not be in your interests. In the short term, I could agree to all of this and probably all attacks on me would stop. That wouldn't be right, but I could do it."

"How can you sit there and expect us to believe this crap?"

"That why I'm under truth nanites," I pointed out. "Most pre-selects wouldn't waive privacy if their lives depended on it—or unless they did."

"Just what is this threat?"

I'd already answered that one, but I guessed I had to again. "If perceptual testing is mandated in all schools, all those students who get the best education will not only be open to attitude manipulation, but the best education will become almost closed to all norms, no matter how brilliant, because perceptual tests can be skewed to get such a result with almost no easy way to determine that such manipulation is taking place. With the media effectively in the hands of the group mandating the tests, and with the majority of advocates general being pre-selects, the chances of any practical challenge to educational changes would be very low."

"Why do you want us to pursue this?"

"Because, except through the media, my hands are tied as effectively as any norm's."

"Do you think you're better than norms?"

"I have more ability than many, but norms like Seglend Krindottir and Eldyn Nyhal are probably more capable than I am."

"Just who are these pre-selects you think are conspiring against norms and you?"

"The names of which I'm fairly certain are Darwin TanUy, Grant Escher, Mutumbe Dymke, Anya St. Cyril, and Imayl Deng. There may be others; there may not be. I don't know."

"You don't have any hesitation naming people?"

"As I noted before, I reserve the right to fire any of you who broadcast those names unless you have documentary backup beyond what I've told you. This meeting is not to give you carte blanche to attack people, but to give you the background and understanding of the situation. You still have to find the story and go through the proper procedures."

This time, there were head nods around the room.

"Aren't you sending us out to do your dirty work?"

"I wouldn't call it dirty work. If I'm right, our system is threatened with an indirect takeover by a handful of pre-selects. That's tyranny. If I'm wrong, then you get paid to prove it, and the advisory board will doubtless meet to discuss my removal, and I chalk up a half-dozen deaths within two months to a series of miraculous coincidences and bad luck."

"Why didn't you just assign a few people?"

"Because time is short, and because all of you would probably get the idea that I was trying to manipulate you." I smiled. "I have to admit that I do want you to look into this, but it's not just because my own family has been hurt so badly. I do believe that our future society is at stake. . . ."

"Don't all people with power rationalize their actions the way you are?"

"It's very possible. That's why I've insisted you be able to prove anything independently. You have a great opportunity. You can either prove that your boss is wrong, with my blessing, or you can save our society." I smiled. "How often do you get a chance like that?"

That did bring a round of laughter, for which I was grateful.

"Director Alwyn . . . you're making serious charges. . . ."

"They're very serious. So are explosions in tube trains that kill dozens of innocent bystanders, and a series of attempted murders."

"But why don't you leave this to the Civil Authorities?"

"I have—for the last three months. In the meantime, we've had more deaths, a pre-select plague, and they have no idea who or what is involved. That's one of the great strengths and weaknesses of our current system. The CA's can't act without hard evidence. That protects our civil rights. But those with great resources have the ability to remove hard evidence without the CAs finding out. The only remaining bulwarks against that abuse of power are the nets. Well . . . if all the nets are controlled by the same men and women . . . what happens to the protection provided by the media?"

"You aren't saying . . ."

"I'll put it a different way. At the stakeholders' meeting,

the PST Trust and several teams of advocates for various pre-selects all opposed my becoming director general. The Society of Dynae, the NeoLudds, and OpenWay all supported me. Can you recall the last time any of those organizations supported a pre-select? Any time *all* of them agreed?"

That also got a few nods.

"Director Alwyn . . . why hasn't anyone brought these issues up before?"

"They have. I haven't seen all the protests and the rallies—but you carried them. So did InstaNews. The Society of Dynae has issued statement after statement, most of them backed with good scholarly research. . . ."

"How could this happen . . . ?"

"An old friend of mine pointed out some time ago that the unsolved crimes today only require resources, skill, and patience. A repairman works on a wall; the skytors note it. Three weeks pass and the loop is recorded over. A week later, the laser unit fires at my glider. Every part in the unit is standard, and they track to equipment that was scrapped, or lost, or theoretically destroyed months earlier. A monoclone's self-destruct unit is enhanced. The clone is recorded as being destroyed for excessive cellular degeneration. Instead it is removed and reprogrammed, and it explodes on a tunnel train. Which of two hundred units being recorded as destroyed last year is it?"

"You are talking as though these incidents actually occurred."

"They did. All the incidents I've mentioned are on the CAs' records. They just can't figure out who masterminded them or why."

"You were released by OneCys. Isn't this just a way to get back at OneCys?"

"No. I have no complaints with the people at OneCys. My own inquiries led me to believe that the managing compositor was ordered to release me from contract. Outside of the time I was in regrowth in the medcenter, I never missed a deadline in ten years and always got high praise for what I did." I offered a crooked smile. "I probably had something to do with UniComm's loss of marketshare."

"So . . . why didn't they keep you?"

"I don't know. I can guess that someone was getting increasingly nervous that I might end up where I now am, and didn't want me to know any more about OneCys operations. Since I was released before the last set of deaths . . . it does make one wonder, but I can't say I know for certain, only that the head compositor insisted it wasn't the quality of my work."

After that the questions tended to be variations on the earlier queries, in one form or another, but I kept answering until they finally stopped asking . . . or actually until the last question.

"Director Alwyn . . . why have you kept answering questions that are clearly repetitive?"

"Because I don't want it said or intimated that management cut off questions because it got uncomfortable or wanted to hide anything."

Most of the room laughed.

Devit Tal, the senior correspondent, stood. "I think we can safely say that, if management hid anything, it's certainly given us every opportunity to find it. The director general's fact sheet and his openness to answering questions have been unparalleled."

With that, I slowly stood. My knees were a little rubbery. "Thank you all very much."

I kept a smile on my face as I left, straining to pick up any comments I could.

". . . got guts . . ."

". . . means we got trouble . . ."

". . . he's right, and we got a real story . . ."

". . . wrong, we still got one . . ."

I continued to smile all the way back to the office where Majora waited.

"You recorded everything?" I asked Majora as I sat down behind the cherry wood desk.

"You were too honest . . . far too honest. What if your words get out?"

"I'm sure that they will. That's why we'll use the monitoring systems to follow everything, including style. With a little luck and your analytical skills, we'll follow those words right into InstaNews . . . and anywhere else."

"Then what?" asked Majora.

"If it gets that far, I'll issue a challenge to those five names to do what I did. . . . I haven't done an illegal act—except cut out the delimiters on the glider to put it next to your door. They can't pass that test, because requesting or ordering an illegal act is an illegal act. Then . . . all of a sudden, the news stories will die out, and I'll be viewed as crazy, but they'll have a hard time in pushing it because they know we'll push back. They'll give more orders, and someone else will try to kill me." I shrugged. "Let's just hope I can survive it. Or we can."

"I think I'm glad you have security patrols around our houses."

"That won't stop everything. I just hope it will delay matters until we can complete our plan. In the meantime, most of my people will begin to realize that they're on to something. The smaller nets will follow—in their own way. . . ." I smiled, evilly. "And then, we deliver the coup de grace."

"What's that?"

"The factual truth."

"And if you can't find it? Or prove it?"

"Then we ask questions, the kinds they can't answer. And we point out the implications—in simple terms."

"You have a very nasty mind, Daryn."

"It's all I've got. I don't have the power to arrange murders with disposable monoclones, or unfindable lasers, or strategically placed walls."

I just hoped I could orchestrate what I had in mind—and complete it before my opponents removed me. And that it would raise the issues enough to bring things into the open. That was about all I could hope for—if that.

The next morning Majora and I were going over the outlines of the assignment areas when my UniComm gatekeeper informed me that one Regional Advocate General Fynbek wished to speak with me. I set it up to record whatever might transpire—on high quality.

Darius Fynbek was leaning forward from behind his wide official replicated mahogany desk. Even in the holo image, his eyes glittered.

"Good morning, Advocate," I said pleasantly.

"Director Alwyn . . . I have just been informed that you . . . employed a CA truth team at a private meeting. . . . I cannot believe that you would . . . undertake such a perversion of duties of the Civil Authorities. . . ."

I frowned. "Let me understand this. You are offended that I asked a CA truth team to ensure that every word I spoke to my employees was factual and truthful? And you are contacting mc about it?"

"I have no objection to your telling the truth. I always favor the truth. I would hope you would not need to use such drastic measures to prove such to your own staff, but obviously, you did, and I'm not sure that speaks at all well of you. Furthermore, the procedure is highly irregular and without precedent."

"I had a legal opinion. I presented it to the local advocate general. She agreed that it was proper. Now . . . you are suggesting that seeking and verifying the truth is something that the advocate general opposes? Or that you are concerned that I set a precedent of suggesting that waiving privacy is not all that unusual for pre-selects?"

"Ah . . . certainly not. But procedures . . . they were established to ensure that the media and legal systems did not coopt each other's integrity."

"Yes . . . I understand that, Advocate. That's why we sought a legal opinion first, and we offered the opinion to the local advocate general."

"She . . . I may have to request that she reconsider her actions."

"That would make a most interesting story, I would think," I mused. "Advocate General opposes use of CA truth team. Considers censure and reversal."

"Director Alwyn . . ." Fynbek's voice hardened. "I am sure I could find a number of interesting legal precedents. . . ."

I grinned. "I'm most certain that you could. However, there is one that I recall, and that is that conversations between Federal Union officials and citizens are privileged only if the citizen requests privilege, and this is one where I certainly don't need privacy. This conversation would be most interesting to many people . . . say, most of the world, and the secretary director of the Federal Union."

Fynbek stiffened. "I see. I trust that you understand the implications of your course, Director Alwyn."

"I fear I do, Advocate. I fear I do. The only problem is that any other course is either unethical or illegal or both."

I found myself looking at my own bookcase.

"You really upset him, Daryn."

"I noticed." I shrugged wearily. "Might as well get on with the assignments." I forced a grin I didn't feel. "After that you might consider how we tie Advocate Fynbek's displeasure to whatever other disaster is likely to befall me."

"After you get the plan rolling. Shall I call Brin?"

"Go ahead."

I looked at the twenty or so stacks of assignments—hard copy. None of the assignments were in the UniComm system. They'd come off Majora's system—a more secured and upgraded system.

Brin stepped into the office, gingerly, almost as if he expected someone to train a laser or something on him. "Ser?"

"Have a seat."

He sat on the front edge of one of the green leather arm-chairs.

I looked at him. "I want a series of commentaries . . . the slant is this. UniComm has revealed the possibility that OneCys programming policies are being directed by a small group of pre-selects. OneCys continues to attack UniComm, including personal attacks on UniComm directors. OneCys is not answering the charges. What—or who—does OneCys have to hide?"

"You do this, and most of the major multilateral sponsors will bail," Brin predicted. "We'll lose massive amounts of revenue."

"Perhaps they won't." I fingered my chin. "Especially if word got out about those multis headed by pre-selects close to the PST Trust group—that they cut sponsorship because they're tacitly supporting what amounts to a political coup. That would make another good news story."

"Then, they'll cut back and give OneCys and the smaller nets more, claiming they're merely diversifying, and we'll still lose revenue."

"Of course we will," I agreed. "Advertisers and sponsors don't like controversy. How's our market share?"

"Ah . . . up about two points."

"And what will happen if we start attacking multis and pre-selects?"

"Market share will climb, probably," he conceded. "For a while."

"What would that translate into if we got back those sponsors?"

Brin swallowed.

"They'll come back," I asserted. All those except the handful owned or controlled by the families behind the PST Trust.

After Brin left, Nasaki and Gallo arrived.

"Feron, Tomas, I need you to find the best solicitors in the world on communications, open speech, and media representations who aren't under contract or tied to any major netsys. Offer what you have to, but we're going to be putting out a series of news and information specials, and I need the entire content of every one reviewed to make sure that we are not liable for damages or misrepresentation. That's after you review them. I want inside and outside review."

The two exchanged glances. Then Gallo spoke. "That could run to the millions."

"It could. Not having that review could run to the hundreds of millions."

"Yes, ser." Gallo nodded.

Nasaki swallowed.

Then the two left, and I looked at Majora.

She shook her head almost imperceptibly. "They're not happy."

"I'm not sure anyone will be." Including me.

"Do you really want to do this, Daryn?" Majora asked while we waited for the senior correspondent.

"I don't have much choice, not that I see. The PST types are using the law as a shield, but trying to deny its use to me and to most norms."

"You didn't feel that way before."

My laugh was rueful. "It's called walking in someone else's boots. The way the law is being used allows them to attack me, and if I do anything to react along the same lines, I'll end up incarcerated and brain-damped."

"Why haven't you gone to Seglend Krindottir?"

"Because I'll need her to put things back together, and because I doubt she can do anything. The last thing I want to do is compromise a truly honest official in the advocates general structure."

"You realize what you're doing?"

I nodded, sadly.

"People are going to get hurt."

"But they'll stay free."

"They don't always want freedom."

I knew that, too.

We both turned as Devit Tal stepped into the office.

"You said you had a project?" At my gesture, he took the chair beside Majora.

"I did, Devit. There's one in particular I'd like you to take. If you feel uncomfortable with it, I can offer you another."

"Let's see what it is, ser."

Majora handed him the outline sheet.

I waited for him to scan it before I began. "Here's what we had in mind—a series of factual articles on brain-damping. The numbers should show, if I recall them, correctly, that a far higher percentage of norms and particularly low-income norms who are convicted of crimes or antisocial acts are brain-damped. We need to show those in human interest terms. Get shots of lifestyles and dwellings for comparative victims. I also want the background on who represents them, and who represents any pre-selects."

"I like it." Tal offered a slow smile. "But we'll lose market slots."

"It could be," I conceded. "But it's part of an overall program. This part is short-term. You and your researcher get the facts together, and work with the presentation folks to provide it with the background emphasis we need."

We talked for a while about possibilities and approaches before he left, assignment in hand.

Next was Mustafa.

"I want a short series on dwellings and residential communities—life-styles—who lives where, and in what style."

Then Recardo . . .

"A series of factual and style pieces on transportation, who has gliders, and their operational and tax costs, magscooters . . . how transport limits or influences lifestyles and residence choice and location . . ."

Cyhal followed Recardo.

"I'd like some pieces on private schools, like Blue Oak Academy . . . what their student composition is, where their graduates go for higher education, where older grads are now, and what they're doing—at least some emphasis on whether pre-select background makes any difference, or whether it's just creds . . ."

Mahmad was next, and I'd checked his background and decided he was the one to handle another special project, except I didn't tell him how special.

". . . need some analytical and mood pieces on the movement to make multilaterals more profitable and accountable to stakeholders . . . is this a fad . . . a symptom of something deeper . . . who's behind it . . . who benefits . . . what does it mean for the people who work for the affected multis . . . does it result in a change in leadership and how does the new leadership compare to the old . . . are there more pre-selects in the new structure, or fewer . . . more centralized decision-making, or less . . ."

In the end, we handed out twenty assignments.

The tough background pieces were mine and Majora's, not so much tougher as more sensitive.

Her deep brown eyes fixed on me. "How are you going to get numbers on perceptual testing? Under privacy, the more elite universities won't let out those figures."

"We ask, and then note that they refused to supply figures. Then we set up some surveys. Students always want credits. Pay them to do the survey. We load the survey results with disclaimers, and note that some inaccuracies may exist, and invite anyone who has better data to provide it."

"Then we do the tie-ins—like reports that the majority of high-paying positions go to perceptually tested pre-selects?" Majora looked at me.

I nodded.

"What if the figures don't match?"

"We try something else, but I'll bet they do. It may be that the key positions go to pre-selects, the decision-making ones."

"You're playing with fire, Daryn. You know that, don't you?" Majora shifted her weight in the green leather chair. I hadn't seen her that tense ever.

"No. I'm trying to light a backfire and clear out the tinder so that our children won't get roasted in the conflagration that's already building."

"Our children . . . ?"

I flushed.

"Why . . . Daryn . . ." Her eyes sparkled. "You actually look embarrassed."

We laughed, and I stepped around the desk and hugged her, awkwardly, because she was still sitting. Then she stood and returned the hug.

It was the best moment of the day.

Majora and I were in my office, reviewing one of the latest InstaNews stories.

Rumors have surfaced that the regional advocate general of West Noram is considering bringing legal action against the director general of UniComm for violations of the laws designed to insulate the Federal Union justiciary from pressure from the media. . . . Alwyn was recently involved in an incident in which three men were killed. . . . While Civil Authorities released Alwyn without charges, questions remain about the way in which the incident was handled. . . .

"That's the same sort of approach they used with Eldyn." I shook my head. "About his wife's death."

"What can you expect?" she said with a smile, reaching out and touching my hand. "You haven't done anything wrong. They want to set it up so that if you do . . ."

"I'm incarcerated and brain-damped. I know."

The gatekeeper informed me that Mother was calling, and I took it.

"How are you doing, dear?" asked Mother.

From what I could see, she was totally recovered from her bout with Eldyn's plague. "It's been rather busy here."

"How is your bride-to-be?"

"She's working hard, too. She's right here." I widened the scope so that Mother could take us both in.

"So I see. I'm sending you a little trifle. It might help with some of your research." She smiled blandly, then more brightly as she asked, "Have you two set a date?"

I looked at Majora.

"We'd thought sometime before the end of the year."

"Well ... don't wait to enjoy being with each other, not that you have, I suspect." Her smile was polite, but her eyes twinkled. Then she was gone.

Majora and I exchanged glances, then laughed.

I checked the attachment that the gatekeeper had announced in the middle of the conversation.

"What is it?" asked Majora.

I swallowed. "It's a manual ... from Sante, Limited. Operating procedures."

"That's St. Cyril's multilateral."

I began to page through it. Most of it was pretty standard boiler-plate although some of the sections offered hints of a more sinister aspect.

... while not required, it is suggested that candidates for upper management positions consider perceptual integrative training of the type provided by Uy Associates. ...

Uy Associates was a subsidiary of TanSen, the TanUy multilateral.

"Hints again," Majora observed over my shoulder.

"Not exactly hard proof, but we can work it in somewhere." I glanced at her. "Could you look through to see what else there might be?"

"I can do that."

The gatekeeper clinged quietly, and I checked the InstaNews holo display that appeared, showing an image of a building I did not recognize.

... another demonstration in Ankorplex ... protesting the planned implementation of perceptual testing as a voluntary additional admission criteria for the elite Sinouk University ...

Proctor General Diem ... "This is not a requirement, in any sense of the word, but merely a means by which students can offer the admissions board another proof of their capabilities. ..."

*   *   *

The image switched to a group of adults brandishing signs and long poles.

Because parents opposing the voluntary criteria have threatened violence against the administration, Proctor General Diem has reluctantly requested Federal Union support to keep the university open. "We will not give in to violence . . . or the threat of violence. . . ."

I shook my head. The locales varied, but the approach was the same—set up the ground rules so that the opposition's only real options appeared unreasonable, illegal, or futile. For years, if not generations, it had worked well. But there were signs that the tactic was getting old, and creating more and more frustration—leading to a social explosion?

Could I put all the pieces together in time?

I wondered.

Chapter 74
Kewood

As I looked at the solid cherry wood desk, I smiled, if faintly. I'd always hated the mist desk Gerrat used, appropriate as it might have been for him. I'd never cared much for smoke and mirrors.

The gatekeeper announced a Lester Liery from MagTron. Even I as accepted, I was on the link, asking Majora to check out who he was.

"Yes?" I said politely to the holo image in front of the bookcase.

"Lester Liery from MagTron, Director Alwyn." Liery was another perfectly featured, straight-nosed, dark-haired pre-select—more like me than my brother had been. Somehow that bothered me.

"What can I do for you?" I asked.

"The word has gotten out that you're rather interested in the use of . . . mobile artificial organics, Director Alwyn."

"That's not quite correct." I forced a smile, waiting for Majora to fill me in.

"Daryn," she reported, "from what I can find out quickly, Liery works for someone at MagTron. MagTron is a subsidiary of DGen, and that's the Deng holding multi."

"Thanks," I linked back, returning my full attention to young Liery.

"I must have been mistaken. . . ." Liery didn't look as though he were ever mistaken about anything.

"Don't MagTron and DGen both use monoclones for specialized testing and other purposes?"

"I wouldn't know about DGen, ser." The "ser" was clearly condescending.

"But you're the one in charge of their use at MagTron?" I pressed.

"I'm a special assistant. I was just following up—"

"That's a rather vague term, special assistant. Whose special assistant are you, Director Deng's?"

"I report directly to Director General Rustau."

"Good. That's very good. I'd like to meet with him the day after tomorrow. That does fall under the duties of special assistant, doesn't it?"

"Director Rustau is rather occupied these days."

"I am certain he is, Liery. I imagine he has a great deal of explaining to do. He may have more if he puts off seeing me." I smiled politely. "That's his choice, of course, but . . . he should be the one to make it. If anything untoward is going on, and I'm certain it's not, but if it were, and it came out that my request were not given to him . . . well, he would have to find someone to blame." I smiled again.

"I'll be sure to convey your request, Director Alwyn."

"Thank you. I'll look forward to hearing from him." I didn't let him respond before breaking the connection.

Then I walked down the ramp to the office where I'd installed Majora. I could have linked, but I wanted to see her face—in person.

She looked up from a small squarish table as I closed the

door behind me. "That call from Lester Liery . . . he works for Tyler Rustau, and he's the head of MagTron. That's the biggest operating subsidiary of Deng's outfit."

I nodded. "I twisted his arm a little, suggested that he set up an appointment with Rustau for me."

"You aren't going out to meet him? After all this . . ."

"It's not that far. MagTron's in Porlan. Deng's in the southern Sinoplex, but Deng will avoid meeting me. I'm sure that's why the follow-up came from MagTron. Someone's worried, or at least concerned about my clone inquiries. If they weren't, they'd ignore me. Liery was set up to feel me out for a deal—same old good old pre-select stuff I heard about but never believed happened. The problem Liery has is that I don't have any special assistants, except you, and they don't know about you yet . . . or they do." I grinned.

"So what will happen? Nothing?"

"Absolutely. Not a thing. Liery will convey my request, and it will be ignored. Then if I press for an appointment, they'll stonewall everything, and then see me and plead total ignorance, and say that, of course, they're happy to meet with the head of UniComm, but they have no idea of the reason for my request."

"What can we do?"

"Can you find out what divisions and sections of MagTron have clone permits? Those have to be public records. And, if he's innocent, I bet Emyl Astol will be more than happy to let us know how many he shipped to each section. If we have trouble there, we know who else is involved. And I'll bet that if we push hard enough, there are going to be some missing clones that can't be explained." I frowned. "Unless they're using Emyl for cover, and are illegally cloning their own, but that would take . . ."

Majora nodded. "I see what you mean. We can check suppliers, and anyone who is shipping stuff will probably tell us."

"If they won't, I might be able to interest the advocate general of Noram."

"Seglend would love something like that."

"Can you check it out?"

Majora nodded. "What are you going to do?"

"Formulate a news series on startling information . . . perhaps beginning with a piece on how widespread monoclones are, and all the big multis who are using them, and for what. I'll have to come up with a better name." I looked into her eyes, and wished I could just look.

Instead, I took a deep breath. "How are we coming? Can we start all those series as planned?"

"We're still scheduled for the third oneday of July—that's gives us ten days." She called up another display and studied it. "Devit Tal has five blocs in, and they're in production for the music and effects you stipulated. He says he can have five more by the end of the week. Recardo just linked in a while ago—he's got six blocs, he says, on transport, and he's in Westeuro to get the right scenes for geographic spread. He claims he'll have three more by the end of the week. Cyhal says he has all the pieces for ten spreads, but he's just started working with production to board them. . . ."

"I need the stuff from Mahmad . . . and Mustafa's would help."

"I'll follow up on those."

With my hand on the door as I opened it, I smiled at Majora, wishing we had more time, just the two of us, but if we didn't get all the special projects on line—and quickly, there might not be any time at all. My guts were tight all the time, far more than when I'd been a pilot.

Back in my office, I walked into the adjoining alcove, where I'd installed my own equipment and called up one of those I'd been working on.

The initial title that filled the image screen was just two words—Hard Choices. The word "Hard" was deep black. "Choices" flashed between white and silver.

My voice rolled over the montage that began with a quick glimpse of Blue Oak Academy, then a shot of The College, the Centurium at Southern University, and various other locales instantly recognizable, if not by name, as educational institutions.

*   *   *

This week Hard Choices looks at perceptual intelligence testing—ability assessment or social structuring? That's the question. . . .

Perceptual integrative testing—there have been demonstrations about it, and claims for it and against it. Is a successful PIAT test an auto-entry to the best schools? To a career with the strongest multis? Or is it a tool for discriminating against norms? Or against pre-selects who don't belong to the right clique?

The next montage was one of building facades that belonged to multis, although no logos or names were displayed.

Does a good PIAT score vault a young man or woman over others of equal or greater intelligence and ability? Or does it show a deeper type of intellectual ability? Do the abilities supposedly measured by a PIAT translate into greater capabilities? Or are they, as some charge, merely a way to screen out those without absolute loyalty to the present power structure? Why do ninety percent of all norms tested fall in the lower sixty percent, when ninety percent of all pre-selects are in the top fifteen percent? The pre-selects get the schools and the top jobs. The norms don't, and much of this choice is based on the PIAT. But how accurate really is this test? Is there a reason based in ability?

Then came a quick flash over testing consoles, old-fashioned written-style tests, and a focus on a figure in a shimmering white singlesuit whose face was obscured by a blaze of light.

Can the psycho-physiologists explain this? All this week, we'll be looking at perceptual testing. . . . What is it, and does it really measure intelligence and intellectual abilities? This series will look into the rumors—and the dark side of the PIAT and other perceptual tests. . . .

*   *   *

I stopped the image. There needed to be another block-buster, slam-to-the-gut fact in the intro . . . maybe two, if I could find them. I began to search through all the raw facts.

I also hoped it wouldn't be too long before the quick and dirty survey data arrived.

Chapter 75
Kewood

From Majora's reports, it appeared as though most of the assignments would be done on schedule. I had also decided against any advance publicity before my massive programming change flooded the UniComm channels. So far I hadn't gotten any rumors through third parties, but those would come. With any luck, they'd come in a few more days.

I frowned. I hadn't heard from Brin Drejcha about the commentaries. I pulsed the link.

All I got was his sim.

"Brin, this is Daryn. Get back to me when you can."

Then I started to review some of the boards that Majora had set up, looking to see what was missing—or more important, what *felt* missing. I didn't get far before the gate-keeper chimed.

"Director Alwyn . . . this is Mustafa. . . ."

Mustafa—what was his assignment? Residential and life-styles—a not-so-subtle way of highlighting the vast gap between pre-selects and even well-off norms.

"Yes, Mustafa?"

"I was getting some footage of the Mancha Polo Club. Let's say we had some trouble. . . ." His dark face beamed. "But we're all right."

"Are you sure?"

"Yes, ser. Got some good footage, too. Already sent it back. Hadn't thought this was going to be that much of a story . . . but, you know, ser . . . really is one."

"I'm glad you're finding it so. Make sure you've got plenty of facts and numbers to go with the footage."

His smile broadened. "We got that, ser. Wier's already boarding it."

"Good!"

"But someone might be calling you. Security here wasn't too happy. They were less happy when I pointed out that we were shooting from a public thoroughfare, and that we weren't shooting people. Buildings aren't protected by privacy."

"Be careful."

"That we will, ser."

From Mustafa's smiles, I had the feeling he'd found something more than I'd thought.

The gatekeeper clinged. It was Brin. I put on a smile as his image appeared.

"You were looking for me, ser?"

"I was. I wanted to look at those commentaries."

"Ser?"

"The ones about pre-select programming being dictated by the pre-select cabal . . ."

"Oh . . . yes, ser, what about them?"

"Why don't you come on up to my office and let's look at them."

"Things are pretty rough."

"That's all right." I broke the link.

Brin appeared within five minutes, and I motioned him to one of the green leather chairs on the other side of the desk.

"What do you have?"

"Just this so far." His words were flat as the projection appeared before the bookcase.

The opening montage showed the word "Commentary" in red in a hard-to-read script, followed by a scan of the marble arch leading into UniComm, then by a glittered stone pyramid before a black building. Someone's voice rolled over the montage. The sonorous voice wasn't Brin's, but the effect was merely dull.

OneCys programming policies are being directed by a small group of pre-selects. OneCys continues to attack

UniComm, including personal attacks on UniComm directors. OneCys is not answering the charges. What—or who—does OneCys have to hide?

I recognized the words. I should have since they were mine, word for word. Unfortunately, they got worse.

Personal attacks are not good. They are scarcely something of which anyone should be proud, let alone a major netsys such as OneCys. . . .

"That's enough." My words were quiet, but Brin cut the images.

My first instinct was to yell—or to throw Brin right through the nanite screen and into the courtyard. I didn't. I smiled. "Tell you what, Brin. Your team's efforts have shown me that perhaps these commentaries weren't such a good idea after all. Just scrap them."

"You mean that, ser?"

"Absolutely. Scrap everything—all of the commentaries I assigned to your team, I mean. We're probably a lot better just staying with a far more factual format." I smiled more broadly. "In fact, I'd like you to spend some time looking at the factual material OneCys is using on their reports on education and multilateral developments. Look into it in some depth, and we'll talk about it, in say, two weeks. Use the same team."

I could feel his confusion. He'd clearly expected me to dress him down. I'd sensed the defiance. "I appreciate your efforts more than you'll know, Brin." And I did, if not precisely in the way in which he would understand.

For one thing, it was clear that the system personnel and I were thinking on a different level than Brin, and possibly some of the other senior managers. And second, it was all too clear where Brin's sympathies lay. For now, it was best to do nothing with him, except try to keep him out of the program development and presentation loop.

"Actually . . . who do you know at NEN?" I asked him.

"Several of the managers . . . Piet DuGroot, Georg Sammis . . ."

"Could you set up some meetings—face-to-face, next week—with them? Feel them out on how they're handling both the OneCys program changes and the personal attack approach that OneCys seems to be adopting. You know these people. I don't, and I think they'd be far more open to you. Maybe you could set it up for me to meet them later, but I'll leave that up to you." I smiled. "Do you think you could do that? We've got to address this continuing attack style, and maybe you could get some insights."

Brin didn't know whether to beam or to be skeptical. "I suppose I could. I don't know how much they'd say. You really want me to go there?"

"People don't say as much on the net, and it's harder to read their body posture, and you're closer than anyone but me to the problem."

That got a smile, if tentative.

"See what you can do. If you have to take a week, then do it, but I'd like you to see everyone you can."

Brin nodded, a bit more enthusiastically.

"When you get back, we'll talk about how to integrate what you discover with the late fall specials I've got people working on."

"Late fall?"

I shrugged. "That's the way it looks. You can't create new products overnight."

"That's good, then. We'll have plenty of time to do it right."

"I want it done right," I affirmed. "I need to get onto to some other things, but keep me posted on the arrangements and who you're going to meet."

"Oh . . . I certainly will." He was already itching to get out of my office, and I thought I knew why.

After he left, I found myself smiling sadly, wondering why Father and Gerrat had let Drejcha stay. Because he was so transparent? Because anyone who replaced him would be more dangerous?

I didn't know, and that bothered me, too, because I hated

to think my father had been losing his sharpness. As for Gerrat, for all his winning personality, he'd had never had that kind of perception.

I looked down at the polished cherry surface. My reflection was murky, like everything at the moment.

Chapter 76
Kewood

I was leafing through the assignment sheets, the ones Majora and I had put together and never inputted to the UniComm system, when there was a rap on the side of my open office door. I looked up. The senior correspondent—Devit Tal—stood there.

"Come on in. Sit down," I offered.

Tal closed the inner door as he entered. He sat in the green leather chair across the corner of the cherry desk from me. His gray eyes fixed on me, cool, penetrating. "Mahmad's missing."

I winced.

"You gave him a tough assignment, didn't you?"

"One of the toughest. He's always been covering the multis, but I asked him to look into the movement to make multilaterals more profitable and accountable to stakeholders and to find out what was behind it."

"The PST Trust stuff?"

I nodded. "I warned him, and I told him to do as much as he could through more distant research."

"Do you have the assignment sheet? It's not in the system."

"None of them are."

He raised his eyebrows.

"None of the pre-selects would ask any of you, or think that anything important wouldn't be there."

"Do you want to tell me what's going on, ser, or do you want me to guess?"

"A war, of sorts," I offered. "It all started when someone tried to kill me, and then someone else tried, and then someone else. . . ." I gave him a quick and dirty summary because he'd heard it, but not where it led, exactly. "Like a lot of people, I went to the CAs. They couldn't find anything. They also insisted that they couldn't investigate people just because they had a motive." My smile was lopsided as I looked at Tal. "Does this sound familiar?"

"I've heard it before."

"So I started looking into it more, and my sister was killed. So was a norm helping her, or maybe she was helping him. That was Eldyn Nyhal."

Tal offered a low whistle.

"You know about the latest events. The CAs can't find anything, and the regional advocate general has contacted me twice already, warning me that he doesn't like my approach to things . . . all very indirect and most legal, but what it amounts to is that he's looking for any legal ground he can to stop us. Then, in the middle of all this, I began to follow the perceptual testing uproar, and I started to look at who controlled what."

"It's a wonder you're still alive." Tal laughed. "Is that why the managing director is in Westeuro?"

"You surely don't believe that I'd send a noted pre-select who wanted to take over UniComm after my father's death to Westeuro?" I snorted. "Anyway, for better or worse, I began to see that what I was facing was just a tiny piece of what gifted norms face their whole lives."

"What about normal norms?"

"I have to admit that I'm an elitist, Devit. People who like porndraggies and shows like *Challenge of the Wild* or *Modern Gladiators* aren't going to change. I just want any children with talent, wherever they come from, to have the opportunities, and I don't want the children of pre-selects to get the guideways tilted even more in their favor. You can inspire people, but you can't force them. So . . . I thought I'd try to stir things up . . . to shine some very bright lights into some very dark corners—all at once, and into lots of corners, so that the insects and parasites can't scuttle from one corner to another."

"I'm about finished with what you gave me. Can I take over Mahmad's assignment?"

"If you'd like, I'd be more than pleased. Here's the outline." I pulled out the assignment sheet and extended it to him. "Do you want some extra help?"

Tal shook his head. "I think what you're doing, ser, is going to create uprisings all over the world. You're dangerous, because you're the first Alwyn who really understands how to use UniComm fully. That's why OneCys and the pre-selects are after you." He offered a cold smile. "I'm not even sure I like you. But you're the only ship on course. If they stop you, they can stop anyone."

"I appreciate your ringing vote of confidence, Devit."

"Like all your folk, ser, you're arrogant. Like none I've seen, you're honest, and you judge on ability."

I wanted to wince, but he was probably right. So I nodded. "I try."

"Director . . . I'm going to do this. I'll do it better than even Mahmad. And your project will work. It's too late to do anything else, now, and I hope we're not too late. But after they count the bodies, I want you to remember that you used people just like every other pre-select before you. The only difference is that you put your life on the line. You chose to. A lot of people are going to die who didn't get a choice."

"I hope there won't be many. If we don't do something like this, I don't think many people, norms or pre-selects, are going to have many good choices."

"That's arrogance, Director." Tal actually sighed. "Maybe truthful arrogance, but arrogance."

Could anyone with ability not have a touch of what others called arrogance? "You could be right. Do you have a better idea?"

His laugh was almost a bark. He lifted the assignment sheet. "If I did, I wouldn't be taking this. You were right about who to trust. We told everyone to keep the assignments among us. I'd suggest you move up your start date to next sixday, before week-end."

"Can we have enough ready?"

"We will. Those that aren't, cover with reruns of the ones we have. You'll need overlap anyway. And don't tell anyone."

"I haven't, and I won't." That was for certain. I hadn't even told Mother, although she definitely knew I was up to something.

I stood and looked out over the inner courtyard for a long time after Tal left.

Once more, I was feeling like a very black raven trying to find sunlight in the cracks and crannies of a tall dark cliff guarded by sharp-eyed eagles with long and grasping claws.

Chapter 77
Kewood

Two days had passed since my disturbing meeting with Devit Tal, and I was still thinking about his charge that I was no different from the other pre-selects in using people. That was bad enough, but his absolute honesty in saying he would do the job—because, in effect, all other alternatives were worse—that was in some ways even more disturbing. From what I could tell, he was telling the truth, and that meant I was either reading people wrong and he was lying, or that he was honestly mistaken about the potential impact of my massive programming shift. I was just hoping that I could get a few key people to look into dark corners and undo the subtle shifts in Federal Union policy—and, of course, get the PST group to back off me and UniComm. Scarcely revolutionary, and I'd figured it would take concentrated information and programming shifts even to accomplish those modest goals, for all my high-flown rhetoric.

From what I'd seen, people didn't change easily, and they

certainly didn't trust the media even as they consumed what we provided.

The gatekeeper clinged. I had to smile, since the ID was that of Klevyl. I took it.

"Klevyl . . . it's good to hear from you."

The leonine-maned engineer smiled in return, but only briefly. "What did you do to Emyl Astol? He's been contacting everyone, looking for anything he could pin on you."

"That's too bad."

"It's like he almost wants you so embarrassed no one will ever talk to you or listen to you again. And you just say it's too bad." Klevyl shook his head. "Sometimes, I don't understand you."

"It's actually fairly simple. After a couple of monoclones blew up, either killing people or nearly killing them, I started looking into it. I haven't heard anything until you called. That suggests to my suspicious mind that he has something to hide."

"I can't believe Emyl would allow the misuse of clones. That would destroy BGP," Klevyl pointed out.

"He doesn't control their use after delivery—or their misuse—but it would still come back to haunt him . . . no matter what."

"It could be. He took a big hit when OS got into the microgene market."

"OS?" I hadn't heard that acronym.

"Octagonal Solutions. Eldyn Nyhal. They say some trust is holding it, letting the management continue."

I hoped my face didn't show too much shock. "I didn't know he was doing that. Eldyn, I mean."

"The man was brilliant, Daryn. You know he stopped the pre-select plague almost single-handedly. Too bad he wasn't around this last time."

"I heard that he was killed in the violence in the Sinoplex."

Klevyl snorted. "Someone used that as cover. Just like they used your accident as cover." He smiled, a smile that lifted only one corner of his mouth. "I don't see much change in UniComm, not so much as I would have expected."

"One-man operations can be more flexible than organizations. I suspect you know that already." I laughed, although
it sounded hollow.

"That's true, but don't wait too long." There was another
quick smile. "I need to go. Bidding conference—VR—on a
new justiciary complex in Sudam."

Once Klevyl's imaged vanished, I linked with Majora.
"Everything's so busy. I forgot to check on the clone business—BGP. Did you have any luck?"

"They referred me to the public records section of the
Genetics Regulation Bureau of the Federal Union Secretariat.
The records break down shipments by industry sector, but
no more, and there's an asterisk that indicates further data
breakdown would result in revealing trade data."

I took a deep breath. "Our friend Emyl Astol is in with
them, I think. He's been checking with everyone he knows
to try to find dirt on me. Can you set up the data we have
to show a rather strange pattern . . . you know . . . only these
sectors use monoclones, and only these firms have permits,
and monoclones have been used illegally . . . therefore . . ."

"Actually . . ." The impish smile crossed Majora's face.
"Yes . . . I was already working on that. The only multis that
have permits are headed by old pre-select families, and most
of them are controlled by those on Eldyn's list."

"Good. We'll have to get that ready for presentation
sooner than I'd thought."

"I've got the data ready. Whenever you're ready to pro-
duce it. . . ."

"Tonight or tomorrow morning. . . . it'll have to be." Too
many things were piling up. "Talk to you later."

Before we broke, she favored me with a warm smile.
Maybe tomorrow morning.

Who else might shed any light on things, who wouldn't
spread it everywhere? I frowned. I hadn't talked to Kharl for
a while.

He answered, or his gatekeeper transferred it, because his
image, still somewhat haggard, but in an oversized medical
singlesuit, appeared almost immediately.

"How are you doing?"

He smiled, wryly. "I'm fine, but I have a bit more sympathy for patients. It's been a long climb."

"What about Grete and the kids?"

"They were fine in days. I told you that."

"I just wondered . . . something like that . . . long-term . . ."

Kharl shook his head. "I think, if you survive, you're probably healthier than you were before."

"Did you ever get any credit for your work on that? I saw some stories . . . but your name was never mentioned." I grinned. "Right then I couldn't do anything. But we could do a follow-up story."

"I'll pass on that." He frowned. "There have been a lot of stories . . . rumors . . . nasty stuff . . . that the plague was created. . . ."

"Like the version I got? How did you ever meet Eldyn? What did he offer?"

Kharl's face went blank. Then, he laughed. "Knowing you, you won't give up. I suppose it's obvious. To you. Technical assistance and insight. You weren't supposed to get hit that hard. He helped with the treatment."

"So you knew Elysa?"

"I'd never met her before the reception. She did want to meet you, and not just for that."

"Did you know about the plague—that Eldyn was developing it?"

"Not as an epidemic. What he told me was that it was targeted at a few individuals. He wanted to make sure that it wasn't widespread. Elora told me the same thing. After what she told me about what was happening, and how UniComm was to be used . . . I'm sure you know."

Repressing a shiver at the implications, I shook my head, then nodded acknowledgment. No one was telling the whole truth. "Then you got taken, too?"

Kharl nodded. "If I hadn't had those samples from you . . . I could have lost Grete and the kids." He offered a wry smile. "No tracks at all. I couldn't say more, obviously. There still aren't really. No evidence, at least."

Had Eldyn hated pre-selects that much?

"Don't look so appalled, Daryn. In his eyes, we're all

guilty, and if he hadn't overdone the virulence on the first strain he tested on you, we'd all be dead."

"I've looked into all of it, but you're right. There's really no evidence for any of this."

"Eldyn followed the pre-select pattern. 'Leave no fingerprints,' " Kharl pointed out. "How about something more cheerful?"

"Cheerful? With all this?" I forced a laugh, then nodded "There is one thing positive. More than positive. I don't think I told you. Majora—"

"Congratulations! I heard from Grete, and she heard from Rhedya. You know how those things go. When Grete and I decided, my cousins knew within minutes of our parents. That's what happens with a worldwide net system."

"You heard anything else interesting . . . about UniComm . . . or your favorite cousin?"

"Not directly. One of my techs is married to a CA in the Yunvil office. The CAs like you. They think someone's trying to bump you off because you're actually human. Words to that effect, anyway."

"Glad to hear it. That I'm actually human, I mean."

Kharl's smile dropped. "Be careful, Daryn. I haven't got a thing to go on, but when people at the club mention your name . . . well . . . it gets very chilly."

"I'm not surprised. I'd appreciate it if you hear anything that's at all definite. Or indefinite. You owe me."

"I do, and I certainly will." He glanced to one side. "I've got to go."

"Talk to you later." Even before my last words were out of my mouth, the projection holo vanished, and I was looking at the cherry bookcase. I missed looking at the East Mountains, and the inner courtyard garden didn't help that much.

I stood and paced around in front of the desk to stretch for a moment, noting that the shadows falling across the courtyard were getting long. I hadn't realized it was that late.

The gatekeeper clinged again, and it was Devit Tal.

"I'm on the move, Director, but there's more here than you ever imagined. Here comes the first package. I know you can put the facts together if I don't get more or get

back." The gatekeeper clinged, indicating an attachment, and
the screen blanked. Tal had sent both as a time delay, somehow.

I copied the attachment into my portable belt gatekeeper
even before I opened it and read it. The first section was an
authenticated copy of the stakeholders of the PST Trust. Not
only did it have the names I knew—Escher, Dimke, St. Cyril,
Deng, and TanUy—but there were another dozen names. The
two I recognized most easily were Emyl Astol and Gerrat
Alwyn.

Unhappily, Gerrat's name explained a few other items,
such as Tal's quick transmission. The correspondent had to
be leery of sending that through. Gerrat's name also went a
good ways toward explaining the Elora-Kharl-Eldyn alliance.
Not totally, but I doubted Kharl knew much more than he
told me, and the other two were dead. It was also clear that
Elora hadn't been exactly lily-white. She couldn't have
called the stakeholders' meeting without either some rather
involuted maneuvering or the cooperation of the PST Trust,
but there was no evidence of either.

I put a call through to Rhedya.

She had an apron on, and I realized it was probably close
to the time she was feeding the children, "How are your
efforts going, Daryn?"

"Full speed ahead, but you won't see anything until they
hit. I think we're getting close. I've already had some warning shots fired. I promise you. I'll make the timetable I gave
you."

"You've never broken your word." Her eyes hardened,
almost glittering, but just for an instant.

"I need to know something, though. Can you look into the
portfolio you're the trustee for, and see if Gerrat had any
holdings in something called PST or the PST Trust?"

"Is this connected?"

"I think so. I don't need to know shares or anything, but
if there are any minutes or things like that . . . they'd be helpful."

She raised her eyebrows.

"Some of those who were after Elora were in that group,

and that's part of what led to Gerrat's death. There are more of them than I'd first thought." All of that was perfectly true.

"Whatever it is, you don't want any escapees?"

"I'd rather not. Would you?"

"No. I don't have many of those I'd call friends left."

"I'm sorry. I hope—"

She waved me off. "Friends like that are worse than enemies, and it's told me, again, how valuable those are who stick by me. I need to get dinner for the children, and knowing you, you need whatever it is yesterday."

"Not yesterday . . ." I demurred.

"Daryn. You don't lie as well as you think. I'll get what there is." With that, the projection screen vanished, even before I could shake my head.

I just sat there for a moment, then flicked to OneCys and InstaNews, listening to the opposition while waiting to see if what Rhedya had would arrive.

. . . regional advocate general denied access to school records on the grounds that the right to know did not outweigh the right to privacy of the individuals . . . since PIAT testing, even in private schools, was a matter of voluntary choice and not a standard mandated by either local education agencies or by the Federal Union. Fynbek also noted in his denial that Parents for Equal Access had no legal standing since . . .

The gatekeeper clinged. There was a scan shot of Rhedya and an enclosure.

"Here's what there was. It seems harmless enough, but I suppose it would if it had to be filed with the Securities Office."

Rhedya was no dummy, and that bothered me too as I copied and then opened what she had sent. She had to have had some inkling of what Gerrat had been up to. Was she merely supporting me into a fall? Or did she think I was the only one who could preserve what Gerrat had left?

I looked over the annual reports. There wasn't much there—except for the ten million creds spent for research on the management on information systems and networks. The description was apparently straightforward.

> . . . funds spend on determining the most profitable information networks, their most profitable aspects, and the most effective managing directors and director generals and their strategies. . . .

Like everything else we'd found, it was highly suggestive, but hardly proof of anything. I took a deep breath and kept reading, but that was it.

I also needed to call Lyenne Devor, the director of the EDA Trust, and I did. With the time differential, I wasn't surprised to get her sim. I just left a message.

Then I went into the alcove off the inside wall of the office and called up the rough outlines of the clone documentaries, scanning what was already there, and listening to the introduction.

> . . . Since even before the Chaos Years, the idea of cloning has been controversial . . . technology and law allow those with credits to clone replacement organs, but that usage has been limited effectively by better medical treatment. . . .
> . . . other use of so-called monoclones has been in locating and repairing leaking toxic and radioactive waste sites . . . questioned often on ethical grounds . . .
> . . . the new question is: where else are clones employed, especially in uses that are either dangerous or controversial—or both. Who—if anyone—regulates those uses, and what about the suggestions that those uses are being kept from Union regulators?

What I had was too wordy, and needed to be pared down and beefed up simultaneously, and more directly aimed at various pre-select multis.

Still . . . after an hour, I closed things down and massaged my forehead. There was still too much to do, far too much, but my head was splitting, and I wasn't thinking all that well.

I picked up the small scanner, recorder—the highest quality type, the same one used by UniComm teams. I'd made sure I knew how to use it, although I hadn't, but I carried it with me now all the time. It fit on a belt loop, even if it happened to be a trace bulky for that. Probably vanity, but if there happened to be something worth scanning for UniComm, and I were there, the last thing I wanted to tell my staff was that I hadn't had any way to capture it.

Definitely vanity. With a laugh, I closed the door and went to find Majora.

Chapter 78
Kewood

I'd already reviewed and asked for changes in Recardo's series on transport. I wanted a harder emphasis on how the glider tax actually didn't fully pay for the guideways, and how the tax was structured effectively to keep it easy for the well-off, but prohibitively high for most others. I also wanted more on the obsolete maglift trains and their cramped and worn confines—and the fact that they didn't exist in areas that served pre-selects, another subtle emphasis on "out of sight, out of mind."

Recardo had just grinned and said, "Those kinds of changes I can make, Director. No problem."

I didn't have to do much with Cyhal's series on education. The visuals and the numbers were striking enough. Ninety-five percent of pre-selects went on to higher education, and ninety percent of those went to institutes and universities that ranked in the top ten in their field on any scale. I'd known that, intuitively, but to have the numbers beat intuition—at least for an information and propaganda barrage.

I had barely finished with Cyhal when the gatekeeper clinged, and the square face of Lyenne DeVor appeared. "You called, Director Alwyn?"

"I did." I used the remote to close the office door, then sat back at the conference table. I still didn't always feel all that comfortable behind the cherry desk that had been Father's. "I'd called about holdings and management. I'd found out from several other sources that EDA is one of the holders of Octagonal Solutions, or perhaps the only holder now."

"We—or perhaps it would be better stated that the sole trustee of EDA holds roughly eighty percent of Octagonal Solutions." A faint smile crossed her lips.

"I see."

"The stipulation requires that EDA Trust make no changes in top management, except with the consent of those involved, for the first year after the transfer."

"Can you tell me who the current director general is?" I asked.

"That position is vacant. The senior director is Meryssa Elysa D'bou."

"So the current trustee really has limited influence for the next eleven months or so."

"That's the way we see it."

"Is there anything else I should know about this arrangement?"

"If anything happens to the current trustee, half goes to his trustee, if he has one, and the other half to the Society of Dynae."

"The Society of Dynae is likely to get quite a bit more power and wealth."

"It has quite a bit already, Director. I'd prefer matters remain as they are."

"So do I."

"Is there anything else?" she asked.

"Are there any communications in the files concerning the request for the UniComm stakeholders' meeting? Besides those you sent?"

"No, ser. Those were all that the Trust has ever had." She smiled. "I can confirm that."

I trusted her smile and words . . . somehow, although the facts were troublesome. "Thank you. I'd appreciate it if you would let me know if there are any other developments of this magnitude—Octagonal Solutions, that is."

Lyenne Devor offered a tight smile, the first indication from her that she wasn't exactly easy with the way things were going, and then broke the connection.

I was back looking at program-script drafts, when Majora slipped into the office. I didn't like the look on her face.

"What is it?"

"Your friend Darius Fynbek requested the results of your privacy waiver before the CAs about the attack on you and your solicitor."

"That's privileged to the case at hand," I said. "That's what Anna told me."

"It may be, but he's appealing it to Supreme Justiciary."

"How long will that take?"

"Three to five weeks."

"I think we need to do a special piece on the honorable Darius Fynbek—his record, his support of his friends, and his threats against me."

"It's already begun." Majora offered the impish smile.

"Oh . . . and if we can find it, his residence, and a good picture of it."

"That's breaking privacy."

"Not if we pose it as a question. Is this the dwelling you expect for an advocate for all the people? Do you expect an advocate to live in posh . . . wherever he does. . . ."

"You could get in real trouble there," she said slowly.

"I already am," I pointed out. "Or . . . we already are."

"This is one you need to run by the legal folk."

"After it's finished. I don't want them suggesting words from the beginning."

Majora nodded slowly.

I could sense the doubt, the kind I was feeling all the time. After a moment, I asked, "Any luck with anything more about the aliens—beyond the first plague?"

"There's not a trace of anything." She frowned. "There's not even a trace of something missing."

"That would seem to mean . . ." I began.

"He did it all himself."

"Or through his Octagonal Solutions," I added. I stood up

and slipped around the coffee table, easing my arms around her and holding her tightly.

We just hugged each other for several minutes.

After she went back to her office, I looked at the sheaf of assignment sheets on the polished cherry surface of the conference table. Paper . . . and words . . . and music . . . and I thought I could change the world with them?

Maybe we'd be more successful than Eldyn . . . hopefully, with far fewer casualties.

Chapter 79
Kewood

With only two days left before I uprooted the entire programming structure of UniComm, both Majora and I were pushing frantically, and yet trying not to seem so, since I'd conveyed to those working directly for Brin Drejcha—who was still in Mancha—that the programming changes would not be implemented, at the very earliest, until the beginning of fall. The production staff—all norms—assured me that the changeover would go smoothly. I had more than a few doubts, since nothing had gone easily in the past six months.

I still only had the first three stories based on Devit Tal's material about the multis, and hoped the rest would come, but we'd run the first ones and hope we could keep ahead. If not, some would get rerun. Some changes would still have to be phased in, and we were still having trouble with all the small "pointer" factoids and cross-leads. And I was trying to create another several dozen, reaching even into the depths of the porndraggies and raw sports challenge games.

The gatekeeper clinged and an image appeared on the screen—one of ours—from AllNews.

. . . powerful explosion rocked the outskirts of Tyanjin, in the Estsino, in the early morning hours this morning.

The site was the research facility of Octagonal Solutions. First reports indicate that the three large structures have been totally demolished. Workers and researchers were sent home early yesterday after reports of difficulties in the power grid. Because of these precautions, it appears that there are no known casualties. . . .

Octagonal Solutions is an applied genetic research multilateral with more than a dozen specialized facilities across the globe. Reputedly, it was originally owned totally by Eldyn Nyhal. Nyhal headed the nanitic research team that stopped the first series of pre-select plague . . . died in an explosion several weeks ago . . . control of Octagonal Solutions passed to a private trust. . . .

The gatekeeper clinged again, and I switched to the InstaNews story, which was essentially the same except for the last few words.

. . . the private trust holding control of Octagonal Solutions is reportedly the same trust that blocked the change in management at UniComm. Some industry analysts speculate that Nyhal's death may yet be linked to Daryn Alwyn. Alwyn is the director general of UniComm and was known to have been seeking Nyhal at the time of Nyhal's death. . . .

Devit Tal was definitely right. I didn't have much time.

I walked out of the office and down the ramp to Majora's office.

"I heard," were her first words. A shock of her thick brown hair, short as it was, drooped onto her forehead, and there were dark smudges on her left cheek. She looked even more frazzled than I felt.

"Can we move things up another day?" The question was stupid, and I wished I hadn't asked it, but that was the way I felt.

"We're pushing as it is, Daryn."

"I thought so, but I hoped."

The belt gatekeeper clinged again. In fact, it was now receiving things all the time, and I'd had to reset it to limit those that got my immediate attention to roughly twenty names.

This one was Devit Tal—but again, merely an enclosure, with a voice-over, not even his image. The enclosure was a OneCys strategy paper for merging OneCys and UniComm. Gerrat would have remained as senior director, and Brin as managing director. Father would have been made an emeritus member of the advisory board.

How much of it I could use was another question—and how.

I gave Majora a quick hug and started back to my office and all the cross-leads and back-promos.

One of the production staffers passed me on the ramp and grinned. "We'll be ready, director."

"Good. We're counting on you."

How much . . . he had no idea.

Chapter 79
Helnya

After a too-late dinner, Majora and I sat sprawled, side by side, on the settee in the great room that faced her garden. Twilight had long since faded into night, yet it had been one of the earlier evenings we had gotten away from UniComm, simply because there wasn't that much more we could do—not that was meaningful. Also, I thought we would need a good night's sleep, since I had a definite feeling we might not in nights to come.

I was sipping verdyn, she a dolcetta-like desert wine.

"Are you worried?" she asked gently, leaning her head against mine.

I laughed softly, ironically. "I don't think there's been an hour since the morning I showed up in your garden where I haven't been worried. I worry that I'm wrong, and I worry more that I'm right. I fret about whether this plan will work, even to get the minor shifts in Federal Union policies and outlooks and to get them to look at the PST group, and I fret that it won't be enough."

"If it's not enough . . . ?"

"Then . . . I suppose that people will get what they deserve."

"That's cynical, Daryn."

"It is . . . very cynical. But people have been trying to kill me, and my family, for the last six months, mostly because, arrogant as everyone claims we are, we've tried to oppose the growth of a hidden tyranny—"

"A greater hidden tyranny." She straightened up and patted my shoulder. "Control of the less able by the more able is still a tyranny."

"I'd agree, but things didn't exactly work out well for anyone when the less able were controlling society. I just want society to be fluid enough so that anyone who is able can rise to the top."

"My husband-to-be, the noble elitist." She smiled.

"You forgot arrogant. The noble arrogant elitist." I shook my head. "That hurts, in a way. Devit Tal said something before he took over Mahmad's assignment—"

"The bit about your being arrogant, and yet the last chance?"

"He's sending me stuff from all over, and it all fits with everything else, but it's always on a delay link. It's as though he doesn't trust me."

"In his boots, would you?"

"No," I had to admit. "He's supposed to supervise the switchover, and I don't even know if he'll be back."

"He will be," Majora predicted.

"What do you think will happen? A few demonstrations? A fizzle? Massive revolts?"

"I don't know. I get angry when I look at what we've produced," she said slowly. "Is that because I was already angry? Are people so apathetic and into themselves that they'll just nod and say it's more of the same, and of course you can't trust those pre-selects?"

"There's anger out there. I'm just trying to get it focused on the real problems."

She shook her head sadly. "No. We can't focus on the real problem. The real problem is the same one that's always been there. Some people have more ability than others, and people with greater ability like to use and often abuse their abilities, and too many of those with less ability refuse to accept their limitations. Nothing we do will change that."

"More targeted violence . . . ? I don't know. I hope that there's at least enough of an outcry that the PST idiots retreat into the background and that the secretary director does something besides attacking UniComm. It doesn't help that we have very little hard evidence, only suggestion after suggestion."

"In this kind of situation, Daryn, really hard evidence doesn't arrive until you lose everything, and until you start seeing norms and pre-selects brain-damped on trumped up charges, and the less-able children of the able taking power that they can't handle, and then it's too late."

In the end, what else could I say? What else could we do? We had little enough that would qualify as hard evidence or proof, not under evidentiary standards.

So I just held Majora and hoped, looking out into a dark garden toward an uncertain morning. Hoped, knowing that we had but a day or perhaps a handful of days before we would find out how right—or how wrong—we had been.

Chapter 81
Kewood

Switchover was set for noon local time, and Majora and I arrived at seven. I kissed her outside her office, and headed for mine. There, Devit Tal was waiting by the door.

"Security said you were on the way up, ser." His eyes

were red and sunken, and he'd clearly lost weight. I hadn't been sure he'd get back, but he was there and had been waiting for a time. "I said I'd be here, ser."

"You did. You're acting managing director for programming, and if anyone gives you trouble, don't argue. Just tell them to see me. I don't want you handling politics right now. I suspect the technical aspects are going to be enough in the way of headaches."

"May be, ser." He handed me a case. "There's the rest of what you need. I'm sorry it's a bit late, but it's worth it." He gave me a crooked smile. "Wanted to do something like this for years. Let's see if it makes any difference."

"It'll make a difference," I suggested. "How much is another question."

"I'd better get on with it." He nodded and was gone, and I took the case into my office.

Once inside, I set the case on the conference table and looked at the documents first. There was actually a budget laid out for the PST group, handwritten, with a signature comparison to that of Grant Escher, which allocated two million credit for "technical support/BGP." Again, not exactly conclusive, but why would the PST Trust need genetic technical support, except for reprogramming monoclones?

I hadn't been in my office more than thirty minutes, and I was still sitting at the conference table going over Devit's work, and with more intriguing suggestions and pointers, yet probably not enough facts to set before an advocate general, when a tall and youngish pre-select appeared at my door. I recognized him—Roberto Paras, Brin Drejcha's deputy. His face was flushed.

"Why don't you come on in and have a seat, Roberto."

Paras looked from one side to the other, then sat on the front edge of the green armchair by the corner of the desk closest to the door. He clearly didn't want to sit across the conference table from me.

"What's the problem?"

"Devit Tal . . . he just appeared . . . said he was acting managing director for programming. He's changing everything. There's nothing on the schedule boards about it.

There's nothing in the technical notes. Director Drejcha didn't say anything about it."

"Have you tried to reach him?"

"Ah . . . no, ser. Tal said I was supposed to see you before I did anything."

"That's right. We're making the program switchover early. There's no point in waiting until everyone knows what you'll do and can counter it."

"But . . . he's pulled everything!"

"Not everything. The suds and porndraggies are pretty much the same as they were, except for some infospots in place of the sponsor spots. So are the sports and outdoor reports."

"But all the news . . . the backdrops . . ." Paras shook his head. "No one told me."

"That was my decision."

"But word's going around that every pre-select in Uni-Comm has been superseded. . . ."

I nodded. "Except me. And I ordered it."

"Ser . . . but . . . why?"

"To save my ass and your future, Roberto, while we still can—if we can."

His mouth opened wordlessly.

"Watch the programming, and watch it closely before you say anything to anyone outside UniComm. Then, if you have any questions, come see me." I smiled. "All right?"

"Ah . . . yes, ser." Still shaking his head on the way down the ramp, Paras looked like a stunned puppy when he left.

Eliasar Bezza was next, not fifteen minutes later. He was the pre-select Gerrat had put in charge of sponsor slots. "Ser . . . what am I going to do? This programming change . . . we have programs without sponsors, and sponsors without programs."

That was the most expensive part of my project, and one that might take years to recover from. I'd tried not to think too much about the financial implications. "Assign them to the closest fit, then wait two or three days, and then contact each sponsor with the viewer data. If their ratings are up or within the past margins, give them the choice of keeping the slot, or selecting what's available. If they're down, readjust the billing, and offer them the same kind of choice."

"Ser . . . why didn't you tell me?"

"Because it wasn't possible. After you see the program changes, you'll see why. And try not to worry too much. A good seventy percent of our program content isn't changing, except for the promos and cross-leads." Those were changing drastically.

After he left, I looked at the small pile of documents and at the small cases that held even more information. It all seemed real enough to me, but most was electronic, mere energy arrangements in magnetic lattices or the like. In a way, life was like that, looked at from the structural level. But after weeks and months of effort, as Majora had pointed out, the only time we got hard evidence, and it was the kind that couldn't be tracked back, was when someone was meant to die—or when some sort of power play or takeover was already in progress.

We had to act on inadequate evidence—or it would be too late to act at all.

And that evidence—or our interpretation of it—could be wrong. Very wrong.

Chapter 82
Kewood

Majora and I sat and watched the noon edition of AllNews, the lead-off program under the "new" regime.

. . . the earthquake that rocked the eastern Sinoplexes on fiveday may be only the precursor to another series of quakes like those of five centuries ago that submerged large portions of old Japan. . . .

. . . information recently disclosed to Civil Authorities in Noram indicates that clones previously registered

as destroyed could have been used as walking bombs.
... BGP multilateral denies the charge, but cannot account for the clone DNA found near the sites of two
explosions. . . .

... more hytripe on the sensiecircuit ... not according to ultrasensie hypster Begas Lazo, who brings in a
flashfire hit on the loway ...

The image of a woman's form barely concealed by flames
gave way to a line of shadowy figures sitting around a conference table, their faces edited into blank ovals.

... Is the hidden cabal of investors who tried to take
over UniComm at it again ... or are they merely after
the man who thwarted them? ... See the comm news at
three.

The openers, buried behind the headline news, seemed in-
nocuous enough to me, beginning with a shimmering image
of the latest Droguet glider.

A new glider ... could it really be in your budget? Not
unless you're up there with the top pre-select multilateral directors. Not at two hundred and fifty thousand
credits. Even on a ten-year lease, you'd pay over two
thousand creds a month, and that doesn't count going
anywhere ... a use fee of two credits a klick on any
guideway ... the taxes add up. According to statistics
compiled by the Economic Bureau of the Federal
Union—the average glider owner pays over twenty
thousand credits a year just in use taxes. So ... if you
want a glider, you need a cool fifty thousand creds a
year—just about what the average mid-level family
makes ... but clearly pocket change to glider owners.
Next time around, we'll show you the really upscale
gliders ... and who uses them. . . .

Then came a slightly disguised image of Blue Oak Academy.

* * *

Thinking about private schools . . . and what they provide to students? Perhaps to your child? Do you have the fortune of a pre-select? It's a good idea, but an expensive one beyond the means of most families. Watch for our series on education, and how the educated make sure their children get all the advantages from a top-level education, almost from birth . . . and how they use the controversial perceptual testing program to make sure their credits remain in the family. Every day at six, morning and night on the eduspur.

I looked at Majora. "Seems tame to me."

"Seems is the right word. The way we've set them up will take time to work."

"Will we have time?"

She shrugged.

We looked at each other, then smiled, and she went back to her office, and I went back to working on the outlines for the last stories from the materials Devit Tal had brought back. I got almost an hour of work done, in surprising quiet, before the first call came in—from Mother.

"Have you hired additional security forces, dear?" There wasn't a sign on her unmarked face of the tiredness that had followed her bout with the second pre-select plague.

"I did that for the houses weeks ago."

"You might consider it an investment for the UniComm offices." Her eyes were amused or coldly ironic. I wasn't sure which. "That is, if this represents a long-term programming outlook."

"You think it will have an effect?"

"It already has, dear, but not necessarily the one you intended. A number of my acquaintances have already contacted me. With their condolences."

The next call was from Klevyl.

"I'd avoid any private clubs for a while, Daryn. Maybe for the rest of your short life." He followed the somber words with a grin and a headshake. "You really don't want many friends, do you?"

"For just offering a few observations on lifestyles?" I
asked.

"Let's see . . . in three hours, you've managed to suggest
on the world's largest net that pre-selects have rigged the
system so that only they can have gliders, arranged the
school system so that only their children have the best
choices, and are using explosive clones as assassins against
those who cross them. Oh . . . and that they want to remove
or kill the man who's out to expose them. Isn't that a little
heavy on the paranoia?"

I laughed. "Could be. Also could be that even if I am
paranoid, they're still out to get me."

"How much of that's true? Be honest, now."

"More than I could possibly put on the nets," I answered.

His image looked at me for a time. "You've never steered
me wrong. I think it's time for a vacation. Talk to you in a
few weeks . . . if there's still a net system."

I was looking at the cherry bookcase again.

Then I looked at the raw infeeds from correspondents.
Nothing. The world beyond UniComm headquarters looked
the same as it always had.

Chapter 83
Kewood

Sixday came . . . and went, and sevenday, and oneday, and
as they did, so did sponsor commitments and revenues. Not
by huge amounts, but by enough that I'd have plenty of
explaining to do at the next stakeholders' meeting. If I survived until then.

Eliasar Bezza had kept coming into my office, with close
to the same set of comments that he was delivering across
the conference table this time. "ComProds . . . they'll keep
the show, but only if we give them a ten percent cut."

"Can you stall them for a week? Our market share is starting to go back up. In some slots, it's higher."

"I can try, ser."

"Point out to them that they're getting a break for greater exposure, and suggest that dumping greater exposure would look very bad at their next stakeholders' meeting."

"Ser?" Bezza looked scandalized. I must have broken some unspoken convention.

"Look. They pay for exposure. In the eight o'clock spot, watchers are up nine percent. Isn't that normally a cause for a three percent rise in charges?"

"Yes, ser."

"If they dump a chance for a nine percent increase at no cost . . . in their target market, that might be construed as against the stakeholders' best interests. It also might be considered collusion with DGen and BGP. Now . . . you've been around a lot longer than I've been, Bezza, but I'm sure you can get the point across . . . if you have to."

"Ah . . . yes, ser."

He understood. He just didn't want to.

I got a bit more worried when Tomas Gallo showed up.

"Director Alwyn, there have been five orders filed with the Federal Union Justiciary. . . ." He inclined his head with a wry smile.

"What do they want us to stop broadcasting? Besides the truth, of course." I motioned to the chair across the conference table from me.

He slipped into it. "Truth is a relative matter, as you know, ser."

How well I knew that.

"The complaints allege that although UniComm has not broadcast any fact that is untrue, the presentation of facts and questions creates an impression that is inaccurate, and that such inaccuracy amounts to libel. . . . They also suggest that the Federal Union evidentiary standard be applied to potentially damaging material. . . .

"So . . . unless we can prove that they've done something wrong, hard enough to stand up before a good old pre-select advocate justicer, we can't say it?"

"That's what they want."

"Can you counterfile, and suggest that their standard is absolutely correct, but that it should be applied to them? That is, a news and information system's job is to question, and that we have every right to raise such questions until they meet the hard evidence standard in rebuttal?"

"I can try."

"In the meantime, we'll write some stories on that."

"It is generally not a good idea to comment on pending judicial issues, ser."

"I am sure you're generally right, Tomas, but in this specific case, I want the whole world to know that the PST types are effectively trying to shut down questioning of their actions and motives. If someone has the resources to suppress or avoid evidence, and you can't even question their motives without the evidence you can't get because it's been suppressed, then, in effect, those who have the resources to suppress the evidence are outside the law, and can do anything they want so long as they can find a way to keep evidence from being found or produced."

The general counsel winced. "I wouldn't put it that way, Director Alwyn."

"You wouldn't, but I would," I said with a laugh that was clearly forced-sounding, even to me. "And much as I hate it, you'd better consult with all those retained advocates we're paying. See if one of them can come up with the kind of argument we want. Also, can you send me copies of the complaints against us? I'm sure those are public."

"Yes, ser."

"Good." I might be able to do something with those complaints. Their very existence would suggest that the PST-related multis had a lot to hide. "I'll be writing some things based on them, and we'll need the outside counsel to vet them quickly."

Gallo nodded, but with the expression of an advocate whose client was losing his mind—or his funds. He got up slowly. "I'll see what we can do, ser."

"Thank you."

In the meantime, I needed to come up with the ideas for more stories. I hadn't seen any public reaction yet, but I trusted the PST group's reaction. If they were going to legal action so quickly, there was something there, and they felt they couldn't wait it out.

"Majora . . ." I pulsed over the link. "Can you come up here? We need to figure out some more stories in each of the target series, and maybe yet another investigative angle."

"I've already started work on some outlines. I'll bring them."

About half the time, if not more, she was ahead of me. We made a good team, and would make a better one, if we could make this plan work.

If . . .

Chapter 84
Kewood

The next fourday rolled around, and I was still watching the news stories, usually on UniComm's AllNews, because NEN and InstaNews were avoiding all the stories and issues we'd broken. One or two of the smaller nets had followed our lead, but only if they had space. It was as though all the comm nets were just waiting to see what would happen.

And not much was.

Majora and I were eating lunch on my conference table, watching the latest stories.

Emyl Astol, the head of BGP, the sole licensed supplier of clones to the toxic and hazardous waste clean-up industry, has thus far refused to comment on the allegations that clones supplied by BGP have been used in a way that violates genetic material use laws. . . .

The video image was that of a sour-faced pre-select, followed by an outside shot of the entrance to BGP headquarters.

* * *

In a related matter, MagTron, DGen, AVida, TanSen, Sante Limited . . . have all filed complaints with the regional Advocate General of West Noram. The multilaterals are contesting material aired by UniComm and demanding that the net system not air any material that could not be used as evidence in a court of law. "That's because they're guilty of suppressing evidence of wrong-doing," retorted Director General Alwyn of UniComm. "They hide evidence. When we suggest they hid it, they say that we can't say that. Not unless we can find the evidence they hid. And they want it so that the Civil Authorities can't even look for evidence without the evidence. What are they hiding and why? Are they behind the exploding clones? Or the murder of the top directors of NEN? Or the death of the brilliant norm biologist Eldyn Nyhal? They say they're not. They ask you to trust them. Just don't trust anyone who questions their benevolence. . . ."

I wondered about my use of the word "benevolence." I'd tried to keep it simple, but the issues were far from simple.

"And why do such notable pre-selects as Darwyn TanUy and Imayl Deng support the use of perceptual intelligence testing? Why do they use a front organization like PST. . . ?" That was UniComm Director General Alwyn. UniComm has received no comment from those mentioned by Director Alwyn."

No comment except legal complaints asking that the issue be buried . . . but I'd asked that AllNews wait a day or so before adding that as another angle. That way I could push the story longer, and that was one story where no one was going to rush to beat AllNews to report. Besides, each legal story took about three times as long, because the legal types were so touchy . . . but that was what UniComm was paying

them for, and hopefully, my audacity and blunt statements
and their expertise would prove effective. Hopefully . . .

"Heavy-handed," I murmured.

"People don't notice the light or subtle touch these days,"
Majora observed from the chair to the left of mine.

I wondered if they ever had.

. . . student and parent demonstrations resumed in Ankorplex over the issue of perceptual testing.

The image shifted to a series of buildings set in a park-
like environment.

Here in Vhat, coalition leader Rysaat urged that his followers never give in.

The next image was that of a dark-skinned norm with silver hair and deep-set piercing eyes that stabbed even from
the holo screen.

". . . can you not see? Only one netsys has the nerve to
show how we are being controlled. The others—they
ignore it. If we give in, then our children will have no
hope. Our children's children will have no hope. Nor
their children . . . we must insist that this evil testing be
stopped now. Stopped forever."

"Someone's listening," offered Majora.

"One fanatic in Sudasia . . ." I leaned forward as the cross-
lead chaser appeared, and the image switched to a shot of
the facades of Blue Oak Academy.

For a related story on how most positions in prestigious
universities and the top entry positions in large multilaterals go to pre-selects, check out The PIAT—Admission
for just the Privileged? on UniComm's Eduspur. . . .

Then another news story followed.

... aftershocks of the earthquake in the Anatolian region ...

"With all those tie-ins, there will be others." she predicted.

Again, I had to wonder. I looked down at the sesame beef salad I hadn't finished, then at the news screen that seemed to have so little effect.

"There will be," Majora insisted.

I took another tasteless mouthful of salad. If something didn't happen soon, I wasn't sure it would matter. The Federal Union wanted UniComm and me to go away, and most people didn't seem to care.

Chapter 85
Kewood

On the next twoday, I was still watching news stories ... and finding my food more and more tasteless, my trousers looser and looser, and my sleep less and less restful. We were getting on to nearly two weeks, and I could see nothing happening—except declining revenues and greater legal bills, and more and more complaints piling up with the regional advocate general.

Tomas Gallo had already informed me that the regional advocate general's staffers happened to be working on a way to come up with a "cease-and-desist" order, but were having trouble finding the legal basis for doing so.

"They'll find a way," he'd said in leaving my office. "It may take a few more days, but they will."

The way things were going, it appeared that the only question was whether the assassins or the advocates got to me first. This was definitely a time when I wished I were the one with access to exploding monoclones or unfindable thugs—except I wouldn't have even known how to use them.

My only talent was using multimedia to get people to think, and I wasn't doing all that well there, either.

Then, I'd only been a hundred-rated edartist, and a hundred rating was like everything else I'd been doing—not quite good enough.

I looked at Majora. "Things could be looking much better."

"They could be worse." From the green leather chair by the conference table, she offered a cheerful smile.

"I could be dead, or incarcerated and on my way to trial and brain-damping, which is where I'm likely to be before long." I paced back and forth in front of the cherry desk, glancing toward the inner courtyard. A misty rain was falling, giving a gloomy cast to both courtyard and office—appropriately symbolic.

I glanced toward the bookcase, then called up AllNews, which displayed an image of lava creating steam as it oozed into a very blue sea.

. . . eruption continues here, less than fifteen klicks from Hylo . . .

Devit Tal appeared at the door. "Did you hear?"

I turned. "Hear what?"

"There have been a series of riots in Ankorplex . . . the mob leveled the regional office of DGen—and in the Kievplex. The CA offices in both places have appealed to the Federal Union for backup. How do you want it handled?"

I didn't even have to think about that. "Straight reporting, except with a little emphasis on the cause of the riots, if we have anything to back it."

"One group issued a manifesto . . . claiming that it was time to end the pre-select cover-ups and half-truths."

"Make it the lead story on the half-hour headlines, and run cross-leads." I shook my head. "You know how to handle that better than I do."

"Probably. Do you want a full push?"

"Not yet. If we jump in with both feet . . . right off . . . it

won't feel right. Can we offer more questions? You know
. . . is this just another indication of the dissatisfaction with
perceptual testing in Ankorplex or a sign of something
deeper?"

Tal nodded. "That's better. We'll do it."

He was gone, and I looked toward Majora.

"You thought nothing would happen."

"Ankorplex is more volatile than anywhere else," I pointed
out. "And Kievplex is almost that unstable."

"That means it happens first there, not that it won't happen
elsewhere."

I still had to wonder about what I had set up. If it worked
. . . if . . . was I any better than Deng and TanUy and the
others? Yet what else could I have done?

The CAs wouldn't look into anything and hadn't been able
to track anything. Eldyn was dead, and so were Elora, Gerrat,
and Father. Was I just supposed to stand and wait until another monoclone finally succeeded in blowing me up? Or go
begging to the PST types?

I shook my head and tightened my lips and waited.

It wasn't until late afternoon that InstaNews even acknowledged the Ankorplex riots, and they downplayed those in the
Kievplex. They didn't mention that the CAs had refused to
protect the AVida operations center or the Sante research
facility.

By then, there were a few other developments coming in—
mostly on AllNews, but one appeared on InstaNews.

. . . Anya St. Cyril denounced the failure of the Loire
region Civil Authorities to protect designers at the multilateral's health template center outside Orleans. . . .

"Talented designers had to run for their lives, and the
Civil Authorities did nothing. These riots were created
by one man, and that man is Daryn Alwyn. Every person who is injured, every credit of property destroyed
should be laid on him. . . ."

The image flicked to one of me, taken at the stakeholders'
meeting.

Daryn Alwyn is the director general of UniComm, and has been charged with using netsys material in an inflammatory and misleading matter. His actions have been brought to the attention of the advocate general. . . .

"Once more, I'm the villain." I snorted. "I can't mention all the deaths in my family. Or the attempts on my life. They don't count."

Majora nodded. I could tell she was worried, and so was I.

That didn't change on the next half-hour's InstaNews headline stories.

. . . Here in Chendu the people are bewildered by the series of explosions that rocked through the TanSen headquarters complex in the middle of the night. Even more surprising is the revelation that Darwyn TanUy, the multilateral's director general, and most of the senior directors, appeared to be among the casualties. Unconfirmed reports indicate that the directors were engaged in a late-night meeting in an attempt to develop a strategy to counter the spate of recent news and netsys stories adverse to TanSen . . . stories maliciously planted by Daryn Alwyn's UniComm net system. . . .

"Once more the evil Daryn Alwyn strikes."

"That really bothers you, doesn't it?"

"These people are trying to install a tyranny—an even greater tyranny. They've used the current system to strangle any opposition. They're responsible for the deaths of half my family, and no one can or will do anything, and I'm a villain for trying to expose them." I laughed, bitterly. "And what's worse is . . . they're right. I'm using people, inciting them to strike where I can't. Manipulating them, and some will die . . . because I couldn't find any other legal or practical way to stop them."

"You admit it."

"Great! I know what a villain I am, and I'm using the power I can muster to try to bring about change, and it's a lousy way to do it. It's just that there aren't any others."

My tirade got interrupted by the next story the gatekeeper flagged—back on AllNews.

Nabul . . . private security guards using banned Federal Service rapid-fire slug throwers killed more than two hundred protesters who marched on the AVida product testing center here in Nabul. The protest leader—Hasad Alami—was among the first killed. Alami had charged that Mutumbe Dymke, the director general of AVida, had refused to promote qualified norms and insisted on perceptual-test-based loyalty screenings for all management positions in AVida. . . .

A stock image of Dymke, doubtless taken from some public archive, appeared on the holo image.

Dymke has refused to comment, and is believed to have fled the Nabul area after the massacre. Civil Authorities have announced that Dymke is wanted for questioning. . . .

Now Dymke was wanted for something. Before it was all over, all of us would probably be ready for incarceration—and worse.

"Daryn . . ." Majora said softly.

"Yes . . . ?"

"There's nothing you can do now. Why don't we go to my place and get something to eat. You need to get out of UniComm for a bit. Devit can always reach you, and there's almost as much security at home."

She was right, as usual.

So I smiled. "That's a better idea than any I've had lately. Shall we go?"

"Please." The smile she offered was far warmer than mine, and I stepped away from the desk and hugged her as she stood, then held on for a time.

Majora and I sat on the opposite sides of the table in her great room, looking out on a darkened garden. I looked down at my plate, and then at Majora's. Her plate was as full of uneaten chicken, portobello mushrooms, and pasta as mine still was.

"Worried?" I asked.

"I'm as worried as you are."

"We have double security tonight, and the glider is right by the door." I pointed out. "I'm the only real danger." I tried to leer.

She offered a wan smile. "That's not why I'm worried, and it's not why you are."

"I know." I took a sip of the lukewarm Grey tea. "I have the feeling that things are getting out of hand."

"What did you think would happen?" Majora asked. "Really?"

"A handful of demonstrations. Some legal scholars looking into things. The Federal Union council backing off the perceptual testing, and OneCys working to destroy me, bit by slow bit while most of the world yawned. I'd thought that the handful of riots and counter-actions would run their course and be forgotten, if there were any demonstrations at all."

She tilted her head. "Then why did you invest all this effort . . . put your entire career, and all that you inherited on the line for this program push . . . if you didn't think it would change things much?"

"Well . . . I could be wrong. But I didn't. . . . I don't know. . . . Eldyn put everything out there, and he put together a plague that killed close to a quarter of a million pre-selects. I was trying to get enough exposure of the problems and the

issues all at once. If I tried educating people slowly, it just
would have been forgotten. Another alarmist story about how
society is deteriorating. Ho . . . hum . . . yes, indeed.

"I thought at least a blitz campaign would pull out enough
issues that the secretary director would have to look at things
and so that the PST types would back off UniComm. I hoped
for more, but I didn't think that much more would happen.
As for why . . . that's simpler. What happens next if things
don't change? Do we build higher and higher walls? Hire
private armies to guard our homes and families? That's
where it's heading. . . ."

Majora caught my eyes with hers. "Daryn . . . don't lecture
me . . . please. I think I knew that before you did."

"I'm sorry. It's just . . . you're the only one who listens. I
even try to tell that to anyone else, and they'd laugh—or try
to find some undetectable way to kill me. Well . . . they tried
that even before I understood." I leaned back in the chair,
not quite meeting her eyes, not really wanting to face the
honesty there, afraid of the judgment I might find. "It's
like . . ." I couldn't find an apt comparison. "Between privacy
rules and hard evidentiary rules, between the PST types' ability to get around the system, and my having the entire system
watching me, between their having all the time in the world
to set me up, to change the entire way the world is run . . ."
My words trailed off.

Majora waited.

"That's not it, either," I finally said. "Everything would
look the same, and appear to work the same, but it wouldn't
be. More and more of the bright pre-selects would be not
only perceptually tested, but the tests would be used to influence and guide them. Then the bright norms would find,
when they were offered upper level jobs, that perceptual testing was required, and the same thing would happen to them."

"Can you be sure of that?"

"The systems and the technology exist, and these people
haven't seemed too bothered about blowing up tube trains
with innocents aboard, pushing people off cliffs, or evading
the laws on monoclones. They've quietly pushed to implement perceptual testing as a requirement—oh, it would be

voluntary at first, but when only those who volunteer get the university slots or the jobs or the promotions, it wouldn't be voluntary at all. . . ."

"You make a convincing case, Daryn." Majora gave me a smile that was slightly lopsided. "Why are you trying to convince yourself?"

"Because what I'm doing—"

The gatekeepers—Majora's and the one on my belt—blared with the alarm signal.

"Security, ser! There's a whole convoy of black gliders—"

There was a harsh crackling sound, and the transmission ended.

I grabbed the portable scanner off the side table, then Majora's arm, and we ran for the door, then down the steps. I was already remote-unlocking the glider, glad that I'd at least had enough foresight to leave it by the door.

I handed the scanner to Majora. "Once you get inside and strapped in, focus it on the house."

"Right."

I flicked off all the cutouts as the glider powered up, and secured the full restraint harness, then eased the glider northway, away from the guideway, and the attackers. We were less than a hundred meters from the cottage when lines of fire converged on it, and a wall of flame skyrocketed into the sky.

"I've got all that," Majora said.

The glider shuddered and shuddered, and I had to work to keep it level and just below the tree tops.

"Can you see if you can use your belt unit to send that back to UniComm?"

"You want me to report that the house was torched?"

"Just say that the place where I was having dinner was attacked and torched by unknown parties."

I finally settled the glider, still holding it just below tree-top level, and began to edge circuitously around and back toward the guideway, if almost a klick eastward of where the flames blazed into the night sky.

". . . is Majora Hyriss reporting. UniComm Director Alwyn was attacked again this evening as he ate dinner with a friend. You can see the destruction created by the attack. The identity of the attackers is unknown . . . more later."

"Good," I murmured. Not perfect, but good and timely was best.

"What are you doing?" hissed Majora.

"Going to look and see."

"After that?"

I was tired of running and scheming, but I didn't say so, just concentrated on following the scanners and my own senses.

There wasn't much left near the cottage—the armed gliders had already slipped back away, and they weren't on the guideway either, but running at close to ten meters above ground over the flatter vineyards to the south of Majora's, and that meant they were really flitters of some sort.

Using enhanced night vision I studied the line, then smiled. "Lock that harness. The little lever on the boss. Push it once . . . down."

Majora clicked the lever, and I fed full power into the magfields. A slight energy nimbus surrounded the glider.

What I had in mind was simple. Tricky to execute but simple in concept.

At the far end of the vineyards was a low berm. I was betting that rather than lift their modified flitter-gliders much higher, and possibly trigger alarm sensors in the skytors, that the four glider-type vehicles would maintain their low altitude, with bare clearance over the berm.

I kicked in long-unused range calculations, personal systems left from piloting years, then maxed my modified glider into a steep climb. At a thousand meters, AGL, we went into a shallow dive—right toward the point where the trailing attack glider would cross the berm.

My flare was perfect, and so was my aim.

The trailing gray glider pancaked into the berm in a shower of sparks, but I was already streaking eastward and behind the low hill from which the berm extended. A single line of flame flashed toward us and sprayed off the rear shield just before we dropped out of the line of sight. I had to hope that they weren't carrying some sort of seeker missiles, but

I had to believe there was some limit on what could be used to evade FU limits.

"I got the laser. . . ." Majora said.

"Good. Don't send it . . . yet." Then I dropped the glider onto the grass.

We waited for almost fifteen minutes before I eased the glider back toward the forced crash site, stopping where I could just barely see the berm.

There were two gliders—the ruined one, and one hovering next to it. Two men were struggling to remove something from the downed glider.

The scanners showed no other gliders nearby—not in direct range.

"Can you get that?" I asked. "With the scanner?"

"I can try . . . hard through the canopy at this angle."

I waited a moment. "Do you have it?"

"Much as I could get."

"Fine. Hang on!" I snapped as I went to full power.

"How—"

Majora's question was lost in the rush of air as we climbed again.

The idea was simple. Use the ground cushion and flare as a concussive.

A single line of flame flashed toward us, deflecting off the front shield as I flared.

One figure went down like a tree snapped at its base.

I wasn't quite as precise, but even with enhanced night vision, low-level stuff in the dark is scary. The rear shields bounced slightly on something, but the system indicators remained solid, and I backed off.

The second glider had nosed into the berm, and no one was moving. There were no EDI or energy traces.

I could see three figures sprawled on the ground.

"Are they unconscious?" asked Majora.

"They should be." They might be dead.

"I'll get one."

"You? That's dangerous."

"I'm almost as strong as you, and I can't operate your glider, and we need some proof."

She was right about that.

I studied the area again— quickly. No sign of anything. While the attackers could be booby-trapped clones, the odds were against it. Even Emyl Astol would have had trouble coming up with that many clones with that kind of training without the Federal Union knowing.

"Be quick . . ." I began, but the canopy was already back, and Majora was moving, swiftly and far more gracefully than I would have. I was ready to use the glider as a ram if anything moved, but nothing did.

In what seemed seconds, she was staggering back toward me, a figure over her shoulder, and something in her other hand.

The figure went into the rear with a dull thump.

"There were three," Majora panted. ". . . other two . . . dead. Grabbed the cases they had." Majora hefted three cases into rear seats of the glider next to the trussed figure in a black camouflage suit. "I took their belts and used them to tie this one up."

She climbed in, and I closed the canopy.

Majora already had the scanner back out, sweeping the crashed gliders, and transmitting.

". . . Majora Hyriss here . . . scanning two of the ruined gliders believed to be part of the group that attacked Uni-Comm Director Alwyn just a few minutes ago. . . . The gliders apparently crashed in going cross-country to escape possible pursuit on the guideways . . . more later."

Now, all we needed to do was get to UniComm.

I decided on straight, high-speed, low-level flight. While I was gambling that no one was going to bother with a lone unlicensed flitter in the midst of chaos, it was a better choice than risking getting attacked on a predictable guideway.

The other problem was that it was night, and without the recharging impact of the solar cells, I was going through power I wasn't coming close to replacing. The glider wouldn't have much of a reserve left when we reached UniComm . . . if we reached UniComm.

I didn't bother with the glider park at UniComm headquarters.
I dropped the glider practically on the stone steps leading up
into the buried building. I half-wondered if Grandfather had
envisioned a siege when he and Father had moved everything
to the headquarters a generation earlier. Once the glider settled, Majora grabbed the cases and the scanner, and I hoisted
the inert commando type over my shoulder, and we struggled
up the steps.

"Director Alwyn." The gray-clad security type behind the
podium actually smiled. "We're glad to see you and the lady
are all right." Her smile was broader as she looked at Majora.
"They've been beaming your reports out on all the spurs."
Her eyes settled on the unconscious man in the black camouflage uniform slung across my shoulder.

"Oh . . . he's one of those who was in the party doing the
attacking. You might want to inform the CAs that he's here,"
I suggested. "We'll keep him in my office."

"They like hard evidence," Majora added wryly.

I paused. "Can you find another security officer to watch
over our friend until the CAs arrive?"

"I'll let them know, if I can get through," the guard said.
She pressed a stud, and two others in the gray of security
appeared and hoisted the limp figure of the commando.

"Thank you."

"Our pleasure, ser." The first security guard smiled. "I'll
see about the CAs."

We walked up the ramp toward my office. There I had the
two security guards—both women—prop the unconscious
commando on the couch.

"Stun him if he looks like he's going to move anywhere."

"We'd be most happy to, ser," replied the taller woman.

The man in black groaned, as if he were about to regain consciousness.

Then Devit Tal hurried through the door. He looked at Majora. "Good reports. Adds a real sense of urgency to all this." His eyes went to me. "They firebombed your house, too."

"I can't say I'm surprised."

Devit looked at the man in black who was moaning softly. "Where did he come from?"

"He was with the crew that attacked Majora's place."

"How did you capture him?"

"I stunned him. Majora captured him and tied him up."

Devit looked at me, at Majora, at the security types, and then at the commando. "I'll be right back." He hurried out.

"Do we have any gloves?" I gestured at the three black cases on the conference table.

"I have a pair in my office," Majora said. "I'll get them."

I watched the captive while Majora hurried out and back, scanning the cases. I couldn't detect anything in them, and the office security system didn't either.

Majora was back in less than a handful of minutes, gloves on, looking at the cases.

"They seem clean. No energy. No emissions," I said.

She flipped open the end case gingerly.

"What's there?" I asked.

"Printed maps, a timetable, photos of you and me and of the cottage. Some credit chips, probably large and untraceable . . . that's it."

"Leave it on the table. Put the other two under my desk."

Majora nodded and did so, barely straightening as Devit Tal hurried back into the office with a large portascanner.

"You want us in it?" I inquired.

Devit shook his head. "Not for this." He leveled the scanner at the figure in the camouflage suit. "We're standing in the office of UniComm Director General Alwyn. You may recall that Alwyn has been attacked a number of times over the last few weeks, and tonight there was another attempt by a force of gliders. Those in the gliders were dressed in Federal Services commando-style uniforms. . . ."

Tal panned the scanner across the groggy prisoner. "This man was captured by the director and his assistant after two of the attacking gliders collided and crashed following the attack."

The eyes of the dark-haired man in the camouflage suit popped open. He'd been pretending to be unconscious. "Bastard crashed us . . ." he mumbled.

"So you admit you attacked the director?" asked Tal smoothly.

"Damned right . . ." Abruptly, the captive shook his head as his eyes took in the scanner and he recognized fully what it was. He shut his mouth.

"There you have it, from the mouth of one of the men hired to attack and kill Director Alwyn." Tal smiled as he cut off the scanner. "You don't mind if we run that, do you, Director?"

"Be my guest."

The captive squirmed as if to lunge at one of us, even with arms, hands, and feet bound.

"I wouldn't try it," suggested Majora. "The last time someone tried to assault the director, they ended up dead, and there were three of them."

". . . bastards . . ."

"Rather unimaginative," I commented.

The gatekeeper clinged. "Security, ser. There are two Civil Authority officers here to speak with you."

"Tell them they can come on up. Tell them that my door is open."

"Yes, ser."

I looked at Majora. She shrugged. We waited.

The two CAs appeared outside the door in less than two minutes. One of them—the taller, hard-faced one—seemed familiar, but I couldn't recall if he had been one of those brought in when Anna and I had been attacked, or if I were just imagining that I'd seen him before. The shorter redhaired woman I knew I'd never seen.

"Director Alwyn?" asked the hard-faced and brown-haired CA. "Officers Krag and Shannd."

"That's me. This is Majora Hyriss, my special assistant." I gestured toward the bound figure on the couch. "This gentleman is a survivor of the team that attacked Majora's house. We were having dinner. I think they killed the security guards, and flamed the house, then fled. The security guards gave us enough warning to get out."

"How did you . . . find this man?" asked the woman.

"There was some sort of explosion or crash, and it looked like one of their glider-flitters had crashed into another one, and this man was the only one left alive. At least, we thought so. We picked him up and came here."

The bound man glared at me, but said nothing.

"At the very least, I think you can find a certain amount of hard evidence, officer. The burned ruins of this lady's dwelling, the evidence of off-guideway travel, a crash site, and possibly even a wrecked vehicle—or the burned remains. . . ."

"Burned remains. Self-destruct charges. We've already looped into the skytors," the taller one said in a strained and clipped tone. "We're stretched too thin . . . wouldn't be here, except . . ."

"You were detailed by the regional advocate general to deal with me?" I suggested.

"Ah . . . not quite that clearly, ser. *We* thought it might be best to ensure that we could verify some hard evidence. If you wouldn't mind allowing us to take this man . . . ?"

"Be our guest." I gestured to the case on the table. "He was carrying that. You probably ought to keep it as well. It might have something interesting in it."

The taller CA slipped out a transparent film bag and slipped it around the case, then tucked it under his arm. "Would you consider waiving privacy on this, Director?"

"I would, but not at this moment. In this case, I'm clearly the victim. My house has been firebombed. So has my assistant's. Oh, she's also my fiancée. Our families know, but it isn't public yet." I smiled politely. "With all the unrest going on around the world, it would be inopportune to go through another truth nanite test. I have a netsystem to run, but once matters settle down, I'll be happy to discuss it."

The two CAs exchanged glances. Then the older and taller one nodded. "Given that you've waived privacy twice, I think your assurance of future cooperation will suffice." He looked at the commando type. "We do like witnesses and hard evidence." He pulled something from the kit on his belt, and slapped it on the back of the prisoner's neck. Then he looked at the dark-haired man. "That's an immobilizer. You move one centimeter out of line, and you'll find yourself falling forward and unable to move a muscle."

The CA nodded to the redhead, who loosened the belt strap around the man's ankles, then stepped back. He glanced at me. "Same sort of belt as he's wearing. Where did you get it?"

"There were two others who were killed," Majora answered. "I took their belts to tie him up. After what they did to my house, I wasn't feeling charitable."

"I wouldn't have been either." The older CA nodded to us. "We'll be in touch."

The redheaded CA looked at the survivor. "On your feet."

The chill in the prisoner's eyes was enough to drop the temperature in the office a good five degrees.

Neither of us said a word until the CAs were out of sight and until the two UniComm security guards had also left my office.

"Do you think they'll discover anything?" asked Majora.

"Well . . . they do have a crash site, two burned-out houses, and a commando type in custody."

"And no evidence to link any of it to the PST group," she pointed out. "I'll bet that there's not one item in the other cases that can be traced." She moved toward the desk, then bent and retrieved the cases.

One of the other cases was identical to the first. The second contained six prepacked Federal Service meals. That bothered me a lot.

"Even if we do a commentary or a factual update on that," Majora pointed out, "it doesn't prove anything."

No . . . it was only highly suggestive of the fact that someone, or a number of someones, in the Federal Service had been corrupted. At the very least, someone was using ex-FS commandos, and equipment most similar. That was chilling in its own way. But like everything else . . . more suggestions, but not hard evidence, and greater pressure on the secretary director or the regional advocate general to shut us down.

I paged Devit Tal through the gatekeeper.

It was several minutes before his image appeared. "I've only got a few minutes, Director."

"I understand, Devit. The way things are going, we may have to seal the structure at any time. Is there anyone or anything that's vital?"

"No, ser. We've got secure landlinks it would take days to get to."

"Fine. Just thought you should know." I paused. "Can we send delay links to the smaller nets . . . the stuff we've already run?"

Tal smiled. "We started doing that this afternoon, ser."

"Good . . . and thank you."

He nodded and was gone.

Then came the calls to the security stations. "Security, this is Director Alwyn. Prepare to seal the structure. Report when ready to seal. You will have one minute when notified. Notification could come at any time in the next twenty-four hours."

Again, I was glad for Father's prescience. Had he foreseen this? Or just worried about a Federal Union takeover?

The security stations began to report back in.

I made a general announcement. "This is the director general. Because of the unsettled nature of the area, as evidenced by attacks on UniComm personnel and their homes, we have prepared to seal the structure at any time. We will remain on system power for now."

I flicked on InstaNews . . . all that was running was a follow-up on the Hylo eruption, and a quick cut on the world korfball championships.

AllNews was better.

*   *   *

. . . the firebombing of Alwyn's home was accomplished
with Federal Service type incendiary rockets and fine-
focus lasers . . . transportation was by heavy-duty rough
terrain flitter-gliders, available only by permit or to Federal Service agencies . . . all this indicates a high degree
of sophistication. . . .

. . . rioting has broken out here in Quecity . . . and the
Sante retail distribution outlets are among those rav-
aged. . . .

. . . Secretary Director Alfonso has mobilized Federal
Service troops in Noram and in Ankorplex . . . consideration is being given to additional mobilizations. . . .

"And you didn't think much would happen?" asked Majora.

"It hasn't yet," I pointed out. "We have no evidence. We
have no links. All we have is violence and riots that we've
generated, and I could be looking at a long incarceration and
maybe even brain-damping." I took a long and deep breath.
"Why don't you lie down on the couch? It's going to be a
long night."

"Why don't you?"

"Because I'm wound up like an overstressed gyro." The
metaphor wasn't correct. My mind was spinning like an
overstressed gyro, and even my words didn't follow.

"So am I."

So we sat behind the conference table, next to each other,
and watched the disaster slowly spread—still without any
evidence appearing that would link the PST group to the
attacks or the subtle coup I knew was being implemented.

By the time dawn arrived, Majora and I had both tried the couch and the floor and dozed some. She was napping on the couch, fitfully, and I was slumped over the cherry wood desk, its surface smudged and far from polished perfection.

The gatekeeper clinged, and, noting the Civil Authority ID, I wearily acknowledged, "Daryn Alwyn."

The image was that of the hard-faced Civil Authority officer. He was smiling, but not particularly maliciously. "This is Officer Krag. I thought you'd like to know, Director. We followed up on those gliders that attacked your assistant's dwelling. They were Federal Service units, and apparently the self-destruct mechanism didn't work fully on one. We've been able to trace that to a commando unit commanded by a Subcommander TanUy. He's the second son of a Darwyn TanUy. We have a discovery order in, but I thought you should know."

Now what could I do? "Thank you, officer. I appreciate that. Given the current situation, unless there is some sort of documentary backup . . ."

Krag nodded. "You should have our report in an hour or so. It could be sooner. It's also been filed with the Noram advocate general and the secretary director's office. While this is not material of an absolute evidentiary standard that would prove any connection, it is a simple and verified fact, and there are some of us who feel it should be public knowledge, since you as the injured party could request it in any case."

I understood. If UniComm didn't broadcast the findings, the CA would be ordered to cover it up, or at least a strong suggestion would be made. "As soon as we have the material, we will be more than happy to act to ensure any and all information in the public interest is revealed to the public."

Krag nodded. "I thought you would like to know, ser."

I thought he appeared relieved as he broke the connection.

Majora looked at me. "They're cracking. TanSen is really worried about you and UniComm."

"It won't be long before the Federal Union weighs in, and it's not likely to be on our side," I said dryly.

"Why? Because Federal Service commandos were used against us?"

"And because we're having an effect, and there's still not much evidence. They'll want to close us down before it turns up." I gestured toward the holo display carrying the latest AllNews stories.

> . . . The pre-select enclave in Tyanjin was destroyed early this morning when mobs commandeered heavy construction equipment. . . .
>
> . . . The secretary director of the Federal Union has appealed for calm and restraint. . . . "The Federal Union is based on the ability of all to achieve their potential and upon self-restraint and discipline. . . . The Council will investigate fully the issues raised. . . ."

"He isn't mentioning what the issues were and who raised them," Majora said.

"You think that the good friend of Darwyn TanUy and Imayl Deng and all the others is going to mention that they're involved in a quiet restructuring of world government? Surely, you jest."

We both laughed, if hollowly.

Majora, sitting on the couch, stretched and then stood. "I'm going down to the cafeteria and see if there's something half-decent programmed into the replicators. Do you want anything?"

"Anything that's half-decent."

"I can do that."

I got a smile before she left.

I began to check the systems, just in case I needed to do something special. Then, I sat back down behind the desk.

Worried wasn't the word for how I felt. I'd researched, designed, implemented, and had broadcast a set of programming developed to make people think and stop subtle but
critical changes in the way the world governed itself. First,
nothing had happened, and then everything had happened.
And while it was clear that I had more than a few enemies,
there still wasn't much, if anything, in the way of hard evidence to link the scheme to change government into more
of a pre-select tyranny to those people who were trying to
accomplish it. Nor was there much more evidence to link
them to all the attacks on me—or to Eldyn Nyhal's death.
There was certainly no way to show that the latest pre-select
plague had been caused by Eldyn's efforts—not that I knew.

That could get even stickier if I opened that VR, because
I'd effectively become the holder of Octagonal Solutions,
without even my own consent. But who would believe that?
In essence, I'd been blackmailed into silence. I could just
imagine telling anyone that story.

I shook my head, then held it in both hands and closed
my eyes.

The gatekeeper clinged.

"Security, ser. We have a package from the Civil Authorities. A CA would like to deliver it personally."

"Ask the officer to come up, or do they want me to come
down?"

"She'll come up, ser."

I stood and walked out to the open door to wait.

The CA was the short redhead who'd been on the team
from the night before. She gave me a crooked smile as she
stepped forward and extended a package. "They're all authenticated and sealed, ser."

"Thank you very much."

"Thank *you*, ser." She inclined her head in a minute bow.
"I need to get back. Things are still a mess."

"Good luck." I felt hypocritical in saying it. I was the one
who'd sparked the mess. I hadn't created the conditions, but
I had certainly put the flame to them, even if I hadn't realized
how explosive the situation had been.

"Thank you, ser." She turned and was gone back down the corridor ramp.

I had barely set the package on the desk when the gate-keeper clinged again. I checked the ID—Federal Union secretariat.

"Daryn Alwyn," I said warily, making sure the return image showed just me and the desk.

The holo image that appeared facing me before the bookcase was that of Secretary Director Alfonso himself.

"Good morning, Secretary Director," I said politely, immediately recording the incoming holo image, and shunting it down toward master control and Devit Tal, hoping he was there.

"It's not the best of mornings, Alwyn, thanks to your irresponsibility." Alfonso's words were like ice.

"Oh? We've been very careful, ser, only to broadcast facts and inquiries based on those facts. I think we've behaved very responsibly under the circumstances. I doubt many directors would be as restrained as I have been after something like five attempts on my life, the last by some sort of Federal Service commandos. . . ."

"You're just trying to cause trouble and raise a rebellion, Alwyn. That's hardly responsible."

"I fail to see how creating VR programming based on the truth is causing trouble . . . unless someone wants the truth suppressed."

"You don't seem to understand, Alwyn, or you don't want to. I'll make it very simple and very clear. You don't stop that programming, Alwyn, and I'll have Federal Service troops in your building in three hours."

I smiled, checking to make sure the incoming was still being fed to master control. "I'm not sure I understand, ser. Everything we're broadcasting is absolutely factually accurate, and it has been reviewed by inside and outside advocates. . . ." I was stretching a point there because Gallo and his consulting advocates hadn't been able to review the material of the last few hours.

"You're inciting rebellion . . . and don't think we don't

know it." Alfonso's face was simultaneously flushed and hard.

"By broadcasting the facts, Secretary Director, we're inciting rebellion? Is there something wrong with the Union? Is that why someone in the Federal Service sent FS commandos against me and my house in the dead of night? Were you aware that the Civil Authorities have hard evidence that the attacks were carried out by your commandos, and that one is already in custody?"

Alfonso was silent for a moment before almost hissing. "You haven't heard the last of this, Alwyn."

"Have you anything else you'd like to tell the people of the world, Secretary Director Alfonso? Everything you said has been recorded for immediate rebroadcast across our entire system."

The connection broke.

I could hear Devit Tal's voiceover through the net. . . .

Now you can hear the secretary director of the Federal Union threatening Director Alwyn with Federal Service troops. . . .

When he realized his words were reaching the world, Secretary Director Alfonso broke off his threats. . . .

I linked to all the security stations. "Close the structure, and close off the tube train station. Seal the structure immediately. All blocks in place."

I could feel the office shiver as the heavily armored shutters covered the courtyard, and the light from the courtyard dimmed. One by one, the stations reported in, and I went through the internal links and cross-checked them all, taking a deep breath when it appeared the structure was sealed.

Last night armed gliders attacked the dwelling where Alwyn was staying . . . and you can hear the secretary director of the Federal Union threatening an independent netsys for broadcasting the facts . . . threatening to use armed force to suppress the news and the truth. . . .

* * *

I sent a message to both Tal and his acting assistant, telling them to cut the delay and feed the secretary director's threat to any smaller net that would take the feed—and anything else. I also left a note for someone to come up and VR the evidence package the CAs had delivered.

I'd just finished that when Majora burst into the office. "I go out for twenty minutes, and everything happens." She looked at me. "Did he really say all that? How could he have been that stupid?"

I shrugged. "Simple. Everything has been handled indirectly and quietly for years. Everyone has been part of the game—everyone with power. Gerrat was even part of it, not that I'll ever tell Mother, although she'll probably find out if she doesn't know already. It was all scripted. That way Gerrat could claim he had no choice, and given his lack of talent, it was probably the only way he could hold Uni-Comm.

"Somehow, Elora found out, and wanted to use the stakeholder meeting to stop it, or at least slow it. I'm guessing, but she didn't have the finances to buy the shares she needed. So she somehow misled the PST group into supporting her. That's also where Eldyn came in. But he saw the even bigger danger, and used his alien bugs to create the last pre-select plague, and he sent special cards to Father and Gerrat, probably impregnated with the octagonal pathogens, or whatever, and he had to use those, I'm guessing, because time was short."

"And the pathogens weren't nearly as virulent as he made them to be?"

"No, they were more virulent—that's why he had to use the cards."

Majora nodded. "Now what do we do?"

"We wait. We keep broadcasting, and we wait, and hope that someone comes to their senses." And I hoped that it wouldn't be too long, because UniComm was the only weapon I—or the norms—had at the moment, and I couldn't afford not to keep pounding away. The headquarters was self-contained, and the multi-satellite feeds from other sites meant it would take the secretary director days to shut us

down—unless he used weapons of mass destruction, and I
doubted he was indebted enough or insane enough to go that
far.

But . . . the way he'd threatened . . . I was far from sure.

Chapter 89
Kewood

It was past midday when the next interesting call came in—
again from the Federal Union secretariat. I didn't recognize
the haggard-looking man's face, but I shifted the signal into
record and fed it to master control once more.

Majora eased from the chair next to me to the couch,
where she wouldn't be caught by the scanner feeding my
image back.

"Director Alwyn? I'm Federico Pynia, the acting secretary
general."

Acting? That was most intriguing. "Yes?"

"The secretariat has just finished a meeting in emergency
session, and Secretary Director Alfonso tendered his resignation. The strain of the position, after the past few years,
and especially the past few days, you understand?"

"That certainly might be possible." Definitely wary, I
waited.

"The secretariat has suspended and incarcerated Subcommander TanUy and his immediate superior, Commander D'sio,
pending an investigation of the attacks against UniComm personnel and dwellings. The commander of the Federal Service
has been suspended, pending that investigation. The secretariat also passed unanimously an emergency resolution sus-
pending any and all use of perceptual integrative ability
testing, except for personal use by individuals or by parents
of underage children. Such test results may not be divulged,
under any circumstances, to anyone except the individual
and/or his immediate family. Further, the Union's chief ad-

vocate general has been charged with investigating the misuse and misrecording of controlled genetic products. The secretariat is also drafting proposed legislation which will require the publication of the statistical construction of all students in all universities and colleges. . . ."

I frowned. "You mean the distribution of norms and pre-selects?"

"Effectively, yes."

I nodded slowly, wondering how best to handle the apparent capitulation of the pre-select power structure, not that it was really giving up anything so much as retreating back to the system that should have been. "I will be happy to disseminate the results of the secretariat meeting, but you understand that UniComm will also continue to monitor the actual implementation of these measures?"

"From you, Director Alwyn, I would expect no less." He nodded gravely.

"And UniComm will remain sealed under current emergency conditions until it is clear that the secretariat has the situation in hand."

"That is certainly reasonable under the circumstances."

Majora came through the link. "Ask him for a detailed study of the underlying political and economic conditions that created the unrest, and ask to be on the commission reviewing the study findings." I could see her beyond Pynia's image, leaning forward intently.

"I do have an additional suggestion," I said.

"Yes, Director?" This time Pynia had the wary tone.

"The current unrest could not have occurred without a great deal of dissatisfaction with current political, economic, and social structures. I would strongly suggest that the secretariat implement immediately a study of those structures, and I would suggest that the study experts include a wide range of norms and pre-selects. The study should be mandated to be completed in three months or less, and once completed, it should be reviewed by a board empowered to make public recommendations to the secretariat and council."

Some of the wariness left Pynia's face. "That is something that has actually been discussed. It should not be difficult to obtain secretariat approval. Although the time . . ."

"Time is of the essence, Secretary Director. If results are not obvious quickly, you cannot defuse decades of resentment."

"Ah . . . there may be something to that."

"And I would like to be on the review and recommendation board. I would also suggest that a representative of the Society of Dynae be on the board."

"You are not suggesting . . ."

"No . . . I think it would be better to have someone viewed as thoroughly dispassionate as the director general of the board. I would certainly not be considered dispassionate. But with all the public outcry, your board would be viewed as more likely to address the problems were I on it."

From over the link came Majora's whispered, "Good."

After a moment, Pynia nodded. "I will bring these matters up with the board. And I would hope that you would feel comfortable in informing those following your news of what has transpired."

"We will report on what has happened, and what the secretariat has promised."

"Thank you, Director. We will be in touch." After a long look at me, the holo imaged winked out.

Devit Tal was on the link immediately. "You were cautious."

"We'll broadcast the part about the resignation of the secretary director, and the emergency steps, and the actions and promises. Nothing about the recommendation board, except that it has been suggested and is under consideration. Then add something to the effect of 'the world is waiting.' "

"I like that," Tal said. "Don't let them slip away."

That was the last thing I wanted.

I put my head in my hands. The days had been long, and they'd be longer.

Majora walked behind me. Her long strong fingers massaged my back and neck. "You're tight."

"Aren't you?" I asked with a laugh.

"Not so tight as you."

We watched the AllNews updates for a good hour, and

the repetition of secretariat's decisions seemed to be having some effect.

. . . with the resignation of Secretary Director Alfonso, and the announcement of emergency action by the Federal Union secretariat, the mob violence appears to be subsiding in most areas, although the Ankorplex is still rocked with demonstrations and devastation . . . violence continues to rage over some areas of Kievplex. . . .

"There's always some place," Majora said.

"The people there started it, and it will take longer—"

The gatekeeper clinged, but the ID was blank. I took it, waiting. I didn't recognize the narrow face, with the dark eyes and smooth olive complexion.

"Imayl Deng. I just wanted to see the man who destroyed four hundred years of progress."

"Then look in a mirror," I suggested. "And don't worry about progress. It's doing fine. If it hadn't have been for a norm by the name of Eldyn Nyhal, you would have died almost twenty years ago. So would your cohorts in conspiracy."

Deng was silent.

Being me, I had to get in the last word.

"If we're all that good, Deng, then we don't need to rig the system. And if we're not, then we won't stay where we are. If I hadn't done this now, then instead of riots and an FU secretariat scared into doing the right thing, in another decade or two, there'd be millions of bodies everywhere, instead of hundreds, and most of them would be ours."

Again . . . I was looking at a blank holo projection, and then the bookcase.

"He didn't like what you said . . . obviously."

"Obviously." I really didn't care what Deng felt. What bothered me was the thought that I'd have to look over my shoulder every day for the rest of my life.

Yet what else could I have done?

I shook my head, and turned to the second projection when

the gatekeeper signaled, indicating a commentary from one of the small netsystems—NetStrait.

Justice should not be imposed by a mob, nor restricted to those with the credits to purchase the best advocates or the best expertise and witnesses. In a sense, the outrages encouraged and perhaps even instigated by the director general of UniComm, Daryn Alwyn, are an example of what can happen when justice is denied.

Alwyn was attacked several times; his death was clearly intended; his sister was killed by a planned explosion; his father and brother died during the second pre-select plague, and more than one commentator has speculated on whether the pathogens involved were deliberately introduced into the Alwyn family. Outsiders attempted to use the deaths and confusion to gain control of UniComm, and evidence Alwyn has made public to the world indicates that this was all part of a pre-select plot to give a small group of pre-select families either undue influence over public policy or out-and-out control of the Federal Union. This plot was in effect confirmed by the confinement of and charges against a number of high-ranking Federal Service officers, some of whom were closely related to the alleged plotters. . . .

Alwyn brought all these matters before the Civil Authorities. He brought the issues to several advocate generals of the Federal Union. No one acted. Were Daryn Alwyn a norm, the matter would have stopped there. Were he less powerful and less talented a pre-select, the matter would have stopped there also. This is what has been occurring more and more to the less affluent people of our world. Most know this all too well.

What happened to Alwyn and his family is scarcely strange or new. Everyone has a story about how multilaterals or wealth have blocked justice. Alwyn merely had the ability to light the match to a tinderbox of frustration.

Alwyn inherited power, but he was a pre-select outside the club, because as events have made clear, Alwyn never wanted to play the old games. The insiders and the rest of the world are paying the price for those games.

It would be easy to condemn this man of power. Many have done so, and more will doubtless so. We will not. Perhaps for personal or selfish reasons, perhaps for nobler motives, the man acted. He acted in a way that showed the entire world the subtle and pervasive corruption that had begun to eat away at the trust that supports and must support every prosperous society.

The question now is . . . what will we do with the chances and choices that have been handed back to us. . . .

I blanked the screen.

For every thoughtful news story or commentary, there were probably twenty that were castigating me—for every reason under the sun.

I laughed, harshly. Here I was, using the protections of the law that had frustrated me to keep myself and UniComm from being destroyed. And was I any better or more noble than Deng or TanUy or the others?

After all, they had used their power to avoid being tied to their transgressions. And so had I. What influence and power I had used was also excessive. I'd killed thousands with the power of the word, a handful with the glider and some with my own hands, and because I was a reluctant champion of sorts, so far, at least, the CAs had covered for me, even destroying evidence.

Could I justify it for the causes I pursued?

Partly, but part of it was simply because I wanted to preserve UniComm, for me, for Majora, and for any children we might have . . . if they had the ability to hold it. I would not follow Father's steps. One example of a Gerrat was enough.

Yet . . . all of that . . . did it really justify my actions?

Half the PST Trust group was either dead, in hiding, or their resources damaged or destroyed, and I still had mainly circumstantial evidence. My brother had been involved, and

I still had no idea exactly what Elora had actually done . . . because she couldn't have gotten the stakeholders' meeting without the cooperation of the PST group. Had she double-crossed them, and been killed when they found out? I didn't know, and I was certainly not likely to find out. The EDA Trust records were silent on that point.

Everything I'd done had been based on incomplete evidence, hints, and no one, not even me, least of all me, was exactly who or what it seemed to be.

How I envied—in a way—the ancients, with their absolute sureties about an uncertain world. With the effort it took to create records, back then there was greater certainty of their existence and accuracy. Anything in any culture could be changed, altered, misrepresented—but the difference was that in our culture there were fewer certainties, fewer footprints left by the misrepresenters, and far less hard evidence.

Or . . . was I merely glorifying an aspect of the past, creating a certainty that did not exist and never did? Was that because, like all beings, whether norms, pre-selects, or octagonal ravens, that I wanted certainty in a world that seemed to promise less with every passing year?

For the moment, I let those thoughts go, although they would never leave me, and enjoyed Majora's massage of my tight shoulders, as we waited—arrogant ravens waiting for the storm to bring down even more arrogant eagles.

More than a week had passed before Kewood, UniComm, and the world returned to a semblance of what once might have been considered normal. There were still demonstrations in Ankorplex; the Civil Authorities had sent me a nominal fine for operating an unlicensed flitter, and I'd paid the fine and the exorbitant licensing fee; and I hadn't quite caught up on sleep. But I no longer looked like a refugee from the riots.

Majora and I were sleeping at Mother's—together. At our ages, and after what we'd been through, nothing else made any sense, and we both needed each other's comfort.

I was sitting behind the cherry desk at UniComm, waiting for her, so that we could stroll down to the UniComm cafeteria together and partake of rather bland replicated fare, when the gatekeeper chimed, indicating that caller was Seglend Krindottir. What other legal trouble was I now involved in?

"Director Alwyn . . . the acting secretary director has requested that I make contact with you." The wide gray eyes were calm, and her voice was level.

"I'm sure he has, Seglend. Which branch of the Federal Union is insisting that I violated something? Or has regional Advocate Fynbek come up with another problem?" I took a deep breath as I saw the irritation on her face. "I'm sorry. I shouldn't have jumped on you. You had nothing to do with all of this."

"You've been under a great strain, I imagine." She was still irritated, but less so.

"You might say that," I admitted. "People have been trying to kill me for months. My house has been destroyed. So has my fiancée's. About half the world thinks I'm the greatest villain since the Chaos Years, and the other half thinks I'm a hero of sorts, but not the kind they'd want to invite to dinner." I laughed, gently.

Her eyebrows lifted. "You expected otherwise?"

I understood why Majora liked her; they were very similar in outlook.

"Not rationally, but one hopes." I paused. "I never let you say why you called."

"I've been appointed review director of the board you recommended. I'm contacting the members."

"I'm sorry." That was a condolence and another apology. "Thank you."

"The acting secretary director is putting before the Federal Union Council a permanent proposed statute to implement the emergency order to outlaw the use of perceptual testing for any use but diagnostics for private individuals and the parents of underage minors. There's no doubt it will pass overwhelmingly. That should address one of the problems."

"One," I conceded. "What about the use of monoclones?"

"Their misuse has always been illegal," she pointed out. "We may need to look into the oversight mechanism, but the law is sound."

"Then there's the underlying question . . . the use of the PIAT was only a symptom. Do we address the issue that most pre-selects actually are superior, at least in terms of the structure of our current culture?"

"How?" Seglend's voice was wryly dry.

I laughed once. "I thought you might have some ideas. I've thought a lot, and I don't, except for self-restraint, and that hasn't worked wonderfully for more than a few generations."

"I've thought about it for years. I don't, either." She nodded. "Except self-restraint, and I agree with your conclusion. There is no workable legal solution, certainly."

I waited.

"By the way, Daryn, Darius Fynbek was killed in the Yunvil riots. He wasn't that bad a man, just a normal pre-select."

I managed not to wince. "I didn't know." I could have guessed—certainly hoped—that Darius might have suffered from my edited broadcast of his several threats against me.

"You were pretty brutal to him."

I offered a crooked smile. "Corruption has its own reward."

"Are you that pure, Daryn?"

"No. I know what I've done. Fynbek, TanUy, Deng, St. Cyril, Dymke, Escher—I doubt that a one of them understands what they were doing. Deng called me. He still doesn't understand. What I did was legal. It was wrong, but I didn't see any alternative, and I still don't. That may be my weakness, but doing something before it's too late is better than doing nothing because it's not perfectly pure." My smile got more lopsided. "And I've just given you the rationale used by tyrants and reformers through the centuries. But I understand that."

Seglend nodded slowly. "Best I inform the other board members. You will receive monthly progress reports, and we will meet, probably in VR session to begin with, after each report. Our last meetings, to develop recommendations, should be in person."

"I agree."

Then her image was gone.

"Who was that?"

I looked up to see Majora standing in the office doorway.

"Seglend Krindottir. Secretary Director Pynia appointed her as the chief of the survey review board, and she was calling to confirm my appointment."

"She's perfect for that."

"A brilliant norm with a reputation for fairness and hard work."

"The secretary director seems to be keeping his word."

"So far," I said.

The gatekeeper blipped, and again, there was no ID.

"Don't take it. We'll never eat. Everyone's calling you." Majora's voice was filled with humor, and I saw the impish grin. "Oh . . . go ahead."

Still, I hesitated, then accepted.

The image was that of Elysa—the Elysa I'd met in Tyanjin.

"Hello." My voice was more than wary. I looked at the holo image closely. For the first time, I could see the age in the eyes set in a youthful face. "Eldyn made you young, didn't he?"

"I was always vain, Daryn. He appealed to my vanity. I didn't know how long it would take, or how painful it would be."

"You're going back to Hezira, aren't you?"

She nodded. "As my own granddaughter. He arranged that, too."

"Is his daughter going with you?"

"Yes. Hezira doesn't have pre-select technology. She'll be happier there."

"I imagine so." I paused. "I have a few questions. That laboratory building of Eldyn's that exploded. You wouldn't know anything about that, would you?"

"It was where he did his most important research."

"All his records were there?"

"Daryn . . . any answer on my part would be a guess."

Not that much of a guess, since she had to have engineered the explosion. "So . . . no one will ever be able to prove just how much of the last plague was alien and how much was created by Eldyn?" I emphasized the word "prove" just a bit.

"Proof is very elusive, Daryn, as you have discovered." After a brief pause, she added, "Brilliant as he was, Daryn, I doubt that Eldyn could have created octagonal pathogens. Not from scratch."

"But why you?"

"Me?" she asked softly.

"I don't understand where you come in."

"I left Hezira when Amad died. I came back to Earth. Check out the name Meryssa Elysa D'bou." Her fingers touched her lips, and she blew a kiss. "I like you, Daryn. I would have liked you even more sixty years ago. Try to hold on to the goodness." She was gone, as suddenly as she had entered my life, changing it in ways I never would have expected.

"The mystery lady," Majora said.

"I'm grateful for her. Without her, I never would have discovered you."

She offered her incongruously impish smile, then laughed. "That kind of other woman I can deal with. Let's get something to eat."

So we did.

Look for

ARCHFORM: BEAUTY

by
L. E. Modesitt

Now available in paperback
from Tor books

I stepped into the Department foyer off the underground garage. Like everything in DPS, the foyer was done in muted gray and forest-green. Smelled like pine, roses, with an overtone of oil. I released the hold on the gatekeeper, could feel the rush of data pouring into me, then the priority override.

Lieutenant Chiang! Captain Cannizaro wants you soon as you're on duty.

Even on link, I recognized Sarao's voice and back-linked. *On my way.*

I took the ramps briskly, didn't run. Stopped running through the Department years ago. Didn't seem to matter. Street's the only place to run, and only there if you've frigged up bad.

Never open your links to your work until you're there. You do, and you work all the time. Learned that one the hard way a long time back. One day, linked into main ops, and caught an allpers alert. That was the beginning of the Tularo Trouble. Before I could unlink, Cannizaro caught me on-net, called me in. When I got back home a week later, Catalya was gone with the twins. Might have been better if I'd been like Ahmed. He spent a month in rehab. Family clustered all around, worrying. Me, I came home tired to empty rooms.

Catalya had gone back to Porlan, left a note. Said when I wanted to give up the Department she'd be there.

VRed her, and we had talked. She wouldn't budge. I don't like ultimatums. Never did. Figured that if I gave in on that, I'd be giving in on anything. VRed the twins every night till they grew up and went off on their own. Estafen's still in Porlan, but Erek moved back to the east coast. Still VR them, more like once a week, now. Think they're beginning to understand, but you never know.

After that, Cannizaro insisted I go trendside. She'd just made lieutenant, then, insisted she needed someone like me. Guess she was right. I made sergeant along the way, then lieutenant four years ago, when she took over the Department, and I got her old job.

Someone had to put the trends together, study all the facets, try to figure out what was going to happen before it became too big. That lesson, we learned from Tularo. In Denv, that was me. Lieutenant Eugene Tang Chiang. Official title was Trends Analysis Coordinator. Had just six people under me, but the job was a lieutenant's because the trends head has to have had street time and credibility. Need that to brief the District Coordinator and his staff, work with the SocServ types, and hold the right kind of chill in dealing with the media netsies.

Didn't take me long to get to the captain's office. It was on the third level, overlooking the square, with the old state capitol to the east and the dozen remaining dinosaur towers to the west, all set in the middle of the Park. Lots of trees and green grass. Grass was green, even in winter.

I stepped into the office. Captain had done it in light blue, with darker blue trim. Very restful. She'd paid for it from her own pocket. Most of the other offices, mine included, were off-white.

"Close the door." Those were Cannizaro's first words.

I dropped into the ergochair at the corner of her desk console. Captains and lieutenants were the only ones who rated desks. Couldn't have been more than a half dozen in the building. Then, outside of the dispatchers, there weren't much more than a dozen bodies there at most times. Patrollers and dets don't do much good if they're not out on the street. The netops people were all in the annex, on the other side of the garage. I couldn't take that, patrolling the net for scams, larceny, and general misreps. Did it in training, long years back. Understood the need, but hated the job. Even hated analyzing their weekly reports. Didn't miss a word, though. Couldn't afford to.

I looked at the captain.

She didn't look like a Cannizaro. Except in her eyes, a

penetrating black. Thin long face, squarish body, short blond hair, worry lines running from the eyes that had seen too much. "Chiang . . ."

When she used my name like that, it wasn't good. Meant trouble in Denv. I waited.

"Your weekly report . . ." That was all she needed to say.

"Something's going to happen." I shrugged. "Can't say what. Start getting upticks in the little stuff . . . ODs, car delinks,

TIDs . . . always happens before something breaks. Lot of upticks, too many for coincidence."

"District Coordinator Dewey is up for reelection. He's got an opponent with creds. Unlimited creds." Cannizaro's voice was flat.

Dewey had always supported the Department, even when no one else had, even as far back as Tularo.

"He's being opposed by Jared Alredd. Son of Aylwin Alredd. The younger Alredd claims the Department lets matters get out of hand before acting. Old broken windows school."

"Can't tell you what's coming down, Captain. Only that it is."

"As soon as you know . . . ?"

"You'll know." I'd always let her know. First.

I got a nod and a faint smile, as much as I ever got, before I stood.

"Even when I'm off," she added. "Use TP code."

"Stct, Captain." Then I headed down to my second-floor corner office.

Stopped outside in front of the consoles. Duty coordinator was Sarao—brunette, intense. Her name sounded like "sorrow." It fit. Sometimes gave me grief. Practiced antique combat with sword and board. Married old-style to a body-sculptor, but refused to let him sculpt her. Good choice, I thought.

"Resheed's report is in your linkfile." She looked at me, but she was still monitoring the inlinks.

"Thanks." It always was. Resheed was dependable. Then, all of trendside was. "Thoughts?"

"Like you said yesterday, something's coming down."

"Captain's worried."

Sarao nodded, her attention really on the feeds she was getting. Then she blinked and looked at me. "Happy faces all over the place—at the Pavilion, on the shuttles. Face scans show a good ten percent increase in soop use—or something like it."

More soop use meant that people weren't happy, turned to the designer exhilarant. But they couldn't stay sooped forever. Lot of jobs required a nanite cleanjob before taking over a console or a system. Then, most folks on soop were either students or servies, sometimes permies. Wondered at times if soop could make life better for a permie. Then, should it be? People didn't get permanent nanite behavior mods unless they'd been convicted of two violent offenses or three significant offenses.

"Any localization?"

"Everywhere but southside and the towers." Sarao's voice was dry.

We both laughed. Hard laughs. Southside and the towers were gate-private. Nothing happened there in public. Rumors about the filch orgies came up, but private was private so long as no one got hurt. Wondered about that, too, after the Halburt clone scandal. How many others had been offed silently and replaced with more tractable clones? Had any? Who could tell?

Trendside you learn early that you don't guess. Not about the filch. Hard evidence, that's fine. But you don't fish there. Not without the captain's backing and full milspec nanite armor.

"I'll read it."

I walked through the door. It opened to my aura, then closed. My office was small, a third the size of the captain's. Just enough room for the desk and the console and two ergochairs in front of the desk. Leaning forward, I could see sunlight glittering the gold-leaf dome of the antique state capitol—back when a state meant something. Now it was a museum. Couldn't see the Continental Complex, down south beyond southside. Could almost feel it, though, at times.

Called up Resheed's daily update, direct-link to my implant. Didn't tell me that much. ODs up, nothing to flag any group. Except age—all were under twenty-five. Then, more than eighty percent always were. A handful of vehicle delinks, including one electrolorry. The netops reported a new scam targeted at the netless, offering them "free" access. Wasn't, of course. Area comm section had taken over on that.

Data and more data. There's more to public safety than data. Data doesn't feel. Crime happens because people feel. You feel what they do, the data makes sense.

I tried NetPrime News—the local reports. Best of the worst. Again, direct-feed. Just closed my eyes and let the words and images appear. Didn't care much for holo projections off the net. Crap blown larger remained crap.

Most newsworthy item was a bit about the west-coast wygs were modifying scanner glasses. Mods let the perps see who had nanite body shields, make it easier to pick victims. Just what we needed. Another gadget to make public safety tougher. Wish someone had told the Department. If the street hadn't been quiet, probably wouldn't have been on news at all. I flashed a memo to the captain, suggested it be disseminated Department-wide.

After that, checked all the incomings. Mostly routine. Only things new were a rash of phony soop sprays that were only glucose with a boost and the theft of lorries for house smashins. Mass overwhelmed most house shields. Also, a notice of higher DPS deductions for health care. That was because of improved internal nanite diagnostics. Took more equipment to read and repair.

Higher health care, water surcharges—not one thing it was another.

Almost two hours later before I stretched and walked back out to the consoles.

"Going to run the towers? Or westside?" asked Sarao.

"Westside. Can't get into anything in the towers. Not without appointments or a cause warrant. See me going to the regional advocate asking for one just to prowl because I feel something's coming down?"

"Too bad they don't let us do more of that."

"Never have. Never will."

"How long?" Sarao looked at me.

"Long as it takes. I'll be on link if you need me." Didn't need to say that, but it made people happier to hear it. Even Sarao, and she knew better.

Ask why I go out? Why I don't link? People don't talk. They don't talk in person sometimes, either. But the way they don't talk tells stories, too.

Went back down to the garage. To transport. Entered my codes through GIL link. Linking ID to gene codes—genetic identity link—made a lot of the old-style crimes almost impossible. Almost. Next came the code for recon. System paused, like always. Recon was a special code. Only trendside could use it. I got a white electral. Nothing special except a beefed-up comm unit and military-level defscreens.

Electral was recoded just for me by the time I crossed the garage. Door still squeaked. Always would. Smelled like plastics inside. That wouldn't change. Touched my hands to the stickwheel.

Cleared for recon. Estimate return.

"*Fourteen hundred.*" I always spoke, but linked when I said it.

The gates irised wide. Took the west tube and came out beyond the Park and towers. Westside's on the other side of the river, if you can call the Platte a river. The metroplex quarters fan out from the Park. Northside's production; eastside's transport and sariman housing; southside is filch, wishfilch, and upper sariman. Then, there's westside—trades, servies on the way up, servies on the way down, and a scattering of netless blocks—the downs. DPS links worked there, but not much else.

Could have taken the express tube, but you don't learn much underground. Instead, I went over the Elletch Bridge. Saw all the servies in their old scooters or on the shuttle glideway headed to southside or northside. Off the bridge, I turned north on the Bryant Guideway, then west past the Westside Fields.

First stop was Morss's Galleria. Fancy name for an old-style pool joint with a couple of formulators that served food at four times the cost of home units. Mornings were slow. Only a side table was used. Two old ex-servies. They leaned on their cues as much as used them. Both watched when I walked in. Was wearing a dark blue singlesuit—sariman business style. They still watched.

Morss moved to me quickly, then stopped. "It was looking to be a beautiful day. Been a while, Lieutenant."

Morss always said that. Could have been talking to him the day before. Still tell me it had been a while.

"Little stuff. Lots of it." Didn't look at him, exactly. Not with the scar running from the corner of his mouth to his ear. Just waited, my eyes mostly on the street.

"You always had a sense 'bout that. Remember the time you walked to Gian's, then walked away? You couldn't a been ten. Chou and his boys goin' over Gian."

"Gian didn't forget."

"Sure didn't." Morss shook his head. "Today . . . this week . . . nothin' I know about." He frowned. "Was Luke's kid Al. Disconnected the overrides and safeties on his dad's lorry. Ran it off the guideways and into Clear Creek."

Didn't sound like what I needed. "Know why?"

"No one does. He didn't tell no one. Not even his girl. She been crying nonstop, they say. Young Al, he was a quiet kid, mostly. Been to FlameTop concert last night. Found him early this morning. Luke was real broke up. His boy was a good kid."

"Sorry for them both. And the girl."

"You might know her, Lieutenant. Tasha Lei."

"Zhou Lei's daughter?"

"His youngest. Zhou wasn't too happy about the two of them. Never said much, but I could tell."

"You think it was a screen?"

Morss shook his head. "Naw. Zhou figured it wouldn't last. Al never stayed with a girl more than a few months."

Made a mental note to my linkfile to check out the accident. "Anything else?"

"Remember old Arturo Kemal?"

"Went with his daughter once."

"Say he's about to die. Hanging on for now. Only ninety.

Drank too much. Nanites can't beat that. And last week, maybe the week before, his grandniece Antonia died. Rock climbing up north somewhere. Old Arturo was all broke up."

"He does love his family." That was about all I could say for him. "Hasn't Chris been running the outfit, anyway?"

"Has for years. You're not his favorite, Lieutenant."

I laughed. "Never was. Not after his sister. He still got Grayser on the heavy equipment?"

"Far as I know." Morss stopped. "Boys tell me Chris is working to make it all legit. Put stuff in place once he takes over official-like. He claims he owes it to his kids. Got a lot of creds from someplace—all legal Bulsor says. Chris has some idea about spinning the heavy stuff off to someone no one heard of. Guy's an ex-wyg that came out of the Ellay desert."

I laughed. Kemal going legit? Even with their big company, and all their credits, the family couldn't walk straight with a laser guide. Been true of Kryn, too.

We talked for another half hour. Didn't offer me any more insights.

When I left, the ex-servies stopped their game and watched. So did Morss. He was still watching when I eased the electral back toward Bryant.

Second stop was Westside Physical Systems, only about a klick southwest of Morss's place. Small office building with a formulation shop behind it. No other electrals around. So I parked right in front of the door. Like all DPS electrals, the white one self-locked the moment I stepped away.

Inside, there was a foyer, a counter, and a permie at a console behind the counter. Walls, floor tiles, countertop—all were maroon, all spotless.

The permie looked up from the console. "Yes, ser?"

"Lieutenant Chiang, Department of Public Safety. Here to see Kama." His full name was Kamehameha O'Doull. I'd never used it. Hadn't asked how the Hawaiian in his past met the Irish in NorAm, either. Kama was more than two meters tall and well over 120 kilos.

"I'll tell him, ser." The servie went link, his eyes blank. Then he said, "He'll be right here, ser."

Kama slipped out of the back room. Hard to believe he was so big. No fat, and he moved like a dancer. He wore a spotless white coverall. The shiny boots were black.

"Trouble, I see." Kama grinned.

I grinned back, then shrugged helplessly. "How's business?"

"Fine. People still need plumbing and pipes along with their nanite-based house systems. You're lucky you caught me in." The grin vanished. "You still owe me a game of chess."

Owed him that game of chess for more than twenty years. "I know. You'd beat me. You always did."

"That's not the point. It's a game of beauty."

"If you say so." I wasn't sure that was the point. If we both linked, usually got a draw, based on old grandmaster games. If not, Kama won in twenty moves, maybe thirty. That was beauty? "Just asking. Got a feeling something might be happening."

The contractor's eyes narrowed. "I've never liked your feelings, Eugene. Is it anything I should worry about?"

I shrugged. "Couldn't say. That's why it's a feeling. Minor offenses up. Pols worried. No one says much."

"You could be wrong."

"Been wrong before. Be happy if I am. Anyone building a fortress?"

"I wish someone would. Business is a little slow, except repairs here in westside." He laughed. "Something always goes wrong here. You have to make dozens of little service calls to make ends meet."

"Too bad you can't do service southside."

"Most of the filch mansions have self-repair systems. Here, who can afford them? Only business I get there is either new systems, total disasters, or upgrading whole systems."

"Getting any of that?"

"Maybe one every other week, about the same as always."

"Each one more elaborate?"

"Why else would they upgrade?" Kama smiled more broadly.

"So it would take a cargo lorry loaded with lead at full

velocity to break into one of those filch palaces?"

"For most. Some would take more. One place has a fuel cell power room that would run half of westside."

"That has to be Alembart."

"You can guess all you want, Eugene."

"What about the McCall thing? That your system? Pretty horrible."

Kama shook his head. "Brazelton's. He's a hundred times our size. He's got system techs. They do it by the link manual. I do all that myself. I couldn't afford a tech."

"Bet your system designs are better."

Kama smiled. "Probably, but from what I can tell, it wouldn't matter. McCall reengineered it. That's what your DPS techies claim."

"What do you think?"

Kama frowned.

I waited.

"McCall is a solicitor. What solicitor knows nanite systems that well?"

I nodded. "He used to work for O'Bannon and Reyes. O'Bannon was pretty close to Chris Kemal."

"Do you know something?" Kama raised his eyebrows.

"With privacy laws, who *could* know?" I offered a grin. "Chris Kemal . . . heard anything?"

"We're not exactly friends. His circle is higher than mine, Eugene. It's much higher. You've been closer to him than I have."

I waited.

"I haven't heard anything. They say Kemal's hurting. Dewey doesn't like him, and neither does Senator Cannon. Kemal's been seen with Heber Smith lately."

"Heber Smith?" I hadn't heard that name.

"He's the campaign manager for Alredd. They don't call him that. He says he's a business consultant, but it's no secret that Alredd's going to take on Dewey in the summer election. Alredd's also backing Hansen against Cannon in the fall."

"Because Cannon mandated the guideway study and the changes in the maintenance requirements?"

"Something like that," Kama said.

"Kemal wants the guideway repair business back?"

"He never had it. Brazelton did."

I snorted. "Brazelton had the business, before it went to GSY. Creds behind it were Kemal's. He wants a return on those creds."

"I'd guess so. Wouldn't you?"

I'd have guessed a lot more. So would Kama. "Heard Arturo's hanging on. Might die."

"He already died where it counts a long time ago."

I sighed. Loudly. "I may be back."

"You're worried."

"Goes with the job."

"Remember . . . you owe me that chess game."

"How could I forget?" How could I? Owed him since before I'd gone to the DPS Academy. Kama never forgot anything. Never would. Might not tell, but wouldn't forget.

I walked out to the electral, standing by itself out front. Kama watched me from the door. Sometimes felt that everyone watched me.

Had barely pulled away when Sarao linked me. *Lieutenant . . . Captain wants to know if you've found anything.*

Nothing. Might help if I knew what I was looking for.

She asked to be linked if you came up with anything.

I'll do it.

That was the way it went all day. Knew I was on the edge of something. Just didn't know what. Couldn't even figure out where to ask. Or what.

Got back to the garage at fourteen-forty. Took a few minutes to satisfy the transport system. Needed a statement if I was back more than fifteen minutes past the estimate.

Stopped by the captain's office before going to mine. She looked worried. Worried and tired.

"You didn't find anything, did you?"

"Nope," I admitted. "Something's coming. Street's too quiet. Too . . . normal."

"Not all the problems are on the street." Cannizaro leaned back in her ergochair and smiled faintly. "They never have been."

"No. But the slick problems cause street problems, and big slick problems cause big street problems."

"You think it's a slick problem or a filch one?"

"I don't know. Let me work on it."

"You're the last of the street cops, Chiang. After you, things will change."

Shook my head. "Always be street cops, Captain. Just fewer. Two kinds of perps—the sariman and filch slicks, and the twisted servies. Need people who know both." I knew servies and permies and the netless. Didn't know the slicks. They were for the netops types. Even as I thought that, knew I'd have to look deeper into the netops reports.

"Let me know." That was all the captain said.

"Soon as I do." I walked out of her office and down the ramp to mine.

Sarao raised both eyebrows as I neared the consoles.

"Just more feelings. Need to look into some things."

"Anything I can check on? Screens are slow now."

"Not yet. Don't know where to point you."

"Whenever."

I smiled.

Back in my corner office, I called up lorry accidents. Three flashed into my mental screen. Second one was in Clear Creek. Medical had added info since the morning. Young Al had been drinking. Alkie levels just below impairment. No other drugs. Baseline nanite body protectors way down. No infection, and no sign of past injury before the crash. Probably Luke had been short of creds, put off his son's annual medcheck. Bad idea, but hadn't killed Al. Crash had.

Still bothered me. Couldn't say why. But had more incomings to check on, and my own report to the captain. No hurry to get home. Nothing to get home for.

Linked to the system again. Could always check on Heber Smith, and some of Kemal's other associates. Maybe . . . some tie with McCall . . . maybe there was something . . . somewhere . . . that would tell me my feelings were right.